I0740114

SIC TRANSIT TERRA 4

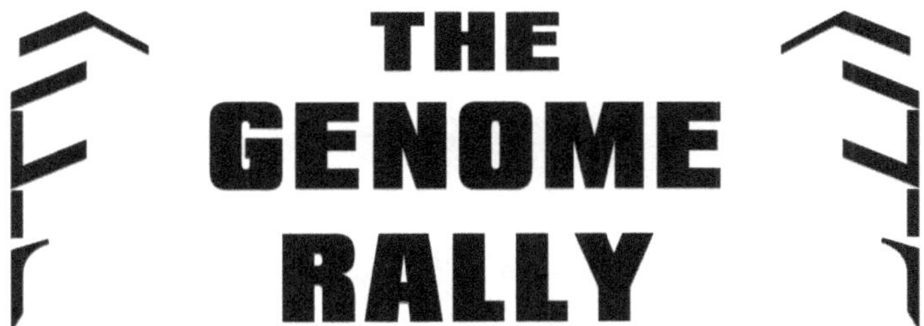

THE GENOME RALLY

ARLENE F. MARKS

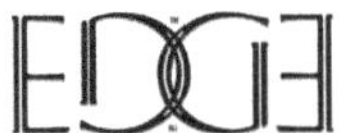

EDGE SCIENCE FICTION AND FANTASY PUBLISHING
An Imprint of HADES PUBLICATIONS, INC.
CALGARY

The Genome Rally
Sic Transit Terra Book 4

Copyright © 2018 by Arlene F. Marks

This is a work of fiction. Names, characters, places, and incidents are the products of the author's imagination or are used fictitiously and are not to be construed as real. Any resemblance to actual events, locales, organizations, or persons, living or dead, is entirely coincidental.

EDGE SCIENCE FICTION AND FANTASY PUBLISHING
An Imprint of HADES PUBLICATIONS, INC.
P.O. Box 1714, Calgary, Alberta, T2P 2L7, Canada

The EDGE Team:
Producer: Brian Hades
Acquisitions Editor: Michelle Heumann
Cover Design: Brian Hades
Cover Art: Lynn Perkins
Book Design: Mark Steele
Publicist: Janice Shoults

ISBN: 978-1-77053-184-0

EDGE Science Fiction and Fantasy Publishing and Hades Publications, Inc. acknowledges the ongoing support of the Alberta Foundation for the Arts and the Canada Council for the Arts for our publishing programme.

Library and Archives Canada Cataloguing in Publication
CIP Data on file with the National Library of Canada
ISBN: 978-1-77053-184-0
(e-Book ISBN: 978-1-77053-183-3)

FIRST EDITION
(20180724)
Printed in USA
www.edgewebsite.com

The Sic Transit Terra Universe:

Novellas:

Lydia's Royal Ace
Candles

Novels:

The Genius Asylum (Book 1)
The Otherness Factor (Book 2)
The Relativity Bomb (Book 3)
The Genome Rally (Book 4)
The Cockroach Crusade (Book 5)
The Identity Shift (Book 6)

Dedication

As always, for my family.

PART I

THE FINAL BEQUEST OF DENNIS FORRAND
Earth space 2400 C.E.

Riviera Hub, Vegas Hub, and **Ginza Hub** were designed and built to provide Earth's Eligible citizens with a choice of exclusive vacation spots in space. Riviera Hub was the preferred destination for families with children and for those who loved to relax in gentle climes; Vegas Hub featured gambling and stage shows; and Ginza Hub offered every pleasure of the flesh. Not surprisingly, all three resorts did a brisk business, right up until their decommissioning as stipulated by the Reunification Treaty of 2420 C.E. Modeled after their namesake tourist areas on pre-Reorganization Earth, these orbiting stations were distinctively furnished and decorated, and were outfitted with every convenience available at the time, creating a luxurious holiday experience. Riviera Hub was the first to be brought online, in 2302 C.E. Privately financed, it set the hospitality standard for the other two. Vegas Hub came next, funded by a consortium of corporate interests and brought online in 2318 C.E. Last to be commissioned was Ginza Hub in 2330 C.E. Although it was rumored to be backed by a criminal organization expanding its drug trafficking market, the allegation could never be proven.

— *Sic Transit Terra, An Unauthorized Planetary History*
(2673 C.E.)

Chapter One

Transfer Point Charlie sat roughly equidistant from four separate Gates, each leading to a different sector of Earth space. Like all such installations, it was kept secure by a resident detachment of Rangers who took their job quite seriously. As he stepped through the portal from the screening area, Watch Commander Gael Dedrick paused to readjust his clothing. It had been a long time since he'd been so thoroughly examined by someone without a medical degree.

The waiting area was designed to resemble an airfield lounge. Clusters of falsahyde chairs and sofas randomly populated a huge open space monitored by securecams. Everything was either low or transparent, to avoid interrupting the surveillance eyes' line of sight. At the center of each furniture grouping was a plastiplex service module offering a variety of snacks and beverages, all packaged in colorful, edible containers.

Dedrick scanned the room, not really surprised to find that nothing had changed in the past nine standard years. There was still no hope of privacy here, except perhaps in the unobtrusively marked washrooms (and even that wasn't an odds-on bet). There was no escape from reality, either — InfoComm light screens had been mounted on every wall, putting nonstop news programming at seated eye level.

At least the sound was muted. It was a small mercy, he thought as he dropped onto a dark green armchair. Another bit of luck was that he had apparently arrived between dockings on a very slow day. The lounge was empty, and the next transport going to Riviera Hub wasn't scheduled to stop here for another standard hour. He eyed the chocolate brown sofa to his immediate right. It appeared long enough to accommodate his nearly two meters of height, and sixty-four minutes gave him plenty of time for a nap.

"Commander Dedrick!" a voice called behind him. Curious, Gael turned in his seat. A stocky man with familiar-looking features was striding across the room toward him. The hopeful smile on the newcomer's lips was belied by a hardness behind his eyes, and it was the hardness that twigged Dedrick's memory, flashing into his mind the image of an advocate in a dark blue business suit, seated behind a desk.

"You may not remember me," said the man, settling himself with a grunt onto the cushion at the near end of the sofa. "It's been about thirteen years."

"Actually, I do. Mister ... Chase, isn't it?" The man nodded, visibly impressed. "You're the one who read my uncle's will, back in '87. So it's 2400 C.E. on Earth now?"

"It is. We turned the century seven and a half months ago."

"Quite a coincidence, our running into each other like this," Dedrick remarked.

Before replying, Chase drew himself up, squaring his shoulders and pushing out his chest. "It's not a coincidence at all, Commander. I asked to be notified when you next took leave, so that I could arrange to meet you here. As the executor of Dennis Forrand's estate, I have one more duty to perform. His final bequest, to be given to his last surviving relative."

Dedrick frowned. "I'm not the last."

"It's a matter of semantics, isn't it?" said Chase with a shrug. "You're his last legitimate relative. Dennis Forrand was quite the ladies' man in his youth. If I tried to track down every errant twig on his family tree, I'd have no time for anything else, and I do have other pressing matters to attend to. So, since he is not in a position to contradict me, here we are. And here *you* are."

The advocate extended his hand. Dedrick paused, staring at the datawafer resting on the other man's palm.

"Please, take it," said Chase. "It's a shame your uncle died before he could see what a fine officer you've become. I think he would have been exceptionally proud of you. And if

I may say so, I also think he would have agreed with me that you more than anyone ought to have this."

Reluctantly, Dedrick picked up the wafer with a thumb and forefinger. As the rest of his hand closed around it, he was startled to feel a curious tingling sensation.

"What the—?"

Chase's bland expression matched his tone of voice as he said, "Don't be alarmed, Commander. Your DNA has just decrypted the contents of the file. Anyone else's will re-encrypt it. All they'll hear if they try to read it will be a poorly-recorded compilation of music."

Scowling, Dedrick warned, "If this is some kind of joke—!"

"I assure you, Commander, there's nothing remotely amusing about it. The protection that's been placed around this information is entirely warranted, as you'll understand once you've read it."

"What the devil is in this file?"

Chase leaned in, prompting Dedrick to do the same, and lowered his voice. "I'm under strict instructions not to discuss it with you. However, I must caution you that the contents of this wafer are a closely guarded family secret, to be viewed in privacy and only on an offline playback device, what members of your generation refer to as 'rogue technology'. Such a device will shortly be falling into your hands. Do not activate it anywhere near an InfoComm unit. Disable the vox and use the keypad only. And tell absolutely no one what you now have or where it came from."

This man was delusional, Dedrick decided. Tell no one about an exchange that had just taken place in an area bristling with monitored recording devices? Then he noticed the light screen on the opposite wall. There was nothing on it but static. Swiveling his gaze, Dedrick saw the same thing on every screen in the room.

A jamming field had been activated. Alarms should have gone off immediately. Why hadn't they?

"When did you—?"

"As I said, Commander, there was nothing coincidental about this meeting. And now I must leave you."

"What if I have questions? How can I reach you?"

"I'm afraid you can't. I've closed my office on Earth and am on my way home to deal with some rather urgent problems, so I won't be available for the foreseeable future."

"You're from a colony?"

Chase grinned mirthlessly and got to his feet. "You might say that. Good luck, Commander. Enjoy your stay on Riviera Hub."

Without another word, the advocate headed for one of the embarkation portals. As soon as he passed through the door, all the light screens in the room switched back to displaying the continuous approved news feed.

Dedrick returned his attention to the datawafer cupped in his hand. It looked so innocent, so utterly ordinary. And yet…

A closely guarded family secret, Chase had said. The Forrand fortune had been made in pharmaceuticals, almost literally a cutthroat industry since the pandemic of 2172. This could well be some sort of proprietary chemical formula that a competing firm would love to get its mitts on. Or it could be something much darker and more dangerous. It could even be worth killing for.

With that thought, a floodgate opened in his mind, releasing a torrent of unpleasant realizations. If Chase had known where to find him, others might know as well. Dedrick was tall and strong, but he could still be surprised and overpowered. With a growing sense of unease, he slipped the wafer into his jacket pocket and sealed the lip shut. There could be no napping or even dropping his guard now, not until he learned exactly what sort of "hot potato" dear Uncle Dennis had handed off to him.

——— 《》 ———

WELCOME TO RIVIERA HUB!
WELCOME!
WELCOME!

With suitcase in hand, Dedrick exited the docking ramp, negotiated a more crowded version of the waiting lounge at the transfer point, and stepped through the arching portal beneath that effusively flashing sign. He was now in a hallway tarted up to look like a boardwalk on the beach. He measured its length in long, purposeful strides, nominally registering the brightly colored façades of the snack shops and souvenir stands that lined one side of the corridor, and no more than glancing at the holographic mural of a tropical lagoon that occupied the other.

Gael Dedrick hadn't come here to relax and have fun in the simulated sun. That was just a cover story. He was meeting an old family friend with connections, someone he hoped could help him make a problem go away. It was a risky enough undertaking without the added worry of what might be on that damned datawafer.

The micro-circuited slip of plastiplex had been front of his mind for days now, unsettling his thoughts and abrading his mood. By the time he'd debarked from the transport vessel, he was cursing himself for letting curiosity overrule his common sense and accepting a gift — *any* gift — from Dennis Forrand, alive or dead.

Growing up as the nephew of a largely disliked Supreme Adjudicator had made Dedrick more sensitive than most to the power wielded by those in control of the truth. Power and secrets seemed to go together. Every influential family on Earth had something lurking in its past, some blot or taint or evil deed that waited, like a land mine in a meadow, for an innocent to stumble onto it and blow himself sky-high. Before Angel of Death had broken out, the Forrands had been one of the five most powerful families on Earth. Gael had always suspected that it also meant they had more than their share of ugly secrets. Now the power was gone, along with the Forrand name, and it all came down to him — Dennis Forrand's last surviving legitimate heir — and whatever unspeakable truth Forrand had decided to entrust to him.

For what purpose? he wondered. As leverage, so he could rebuild the Forrand empire? Not a chance. Gael was a spacer and always would be.

Spacers tended to spend as little time on Earth as possible. So, it had come as no surprise to anyone that he'd chosen to take his R and R on one of the resort hubs.

Fleet personnel on leave liked to party. They generally requested billeting located as close as possible to the action. However, Dedrick had reserved quarters for one in Beachfront Ring, the one farthest from the social sector in the station's core. It also tended to be the most sparsely occupied, a situation that suited his current mission, not to mention his current mood, to perfection.

The tube car let him off in a hallway that had seen better days. If there had been a worn carpet on the deck or fraying curtains on the viewports, he would have described it as shabby. Instead, the word "weary" sprang to mind. Someone had apparently spared considerable effort while this last part of the hub was being built. The interior bulkheads, uniformly plaincoated a nondescript bluish gray, were visibly patched in places, and numerous dings and scrapes had simply been painted over. At least the deck under his feet was even, saving Dedrick from having to constantly watch his step.

He located the correctly numbered door and pressed his thumb to the lock.

With a low hum, the metal slab slid aside, admitting him into a room about the same size and shape as his suite aboard the *Marco Polo*. The décor was a pleasant surprise. Mainly burnt orange and shades of gold, the colors reminded him of a painting he'd once seen of an Earth forest in autumn. Dedrick didn't need much beyond the creature comforts. Fortunately, they all appeared to be present. From the entrance, he was able to identify a more-than-ample bed, a bright green table and two matching chairs, and a partly-closed wall panel that suggested the location of the personal hygiene closet.

Before he could explore any further, a crackling sound made him turn to his left, where a hologram had materialized.

"Welcome to Riviera Hub, Watch Commander Gael Dedrick," said the hologram in a cheerful, if staticky, voice. "I am Jeeves, your concierge. My purpose is to ensure that your vacation is as relaxing and enjoyable as possible. If you need anything, tell me and I will have it brought to you. If anything displeases you, tell me and I will have it corrected or repaired at once. If there is anything I can do to enhance or improve your holiday experience, request it and I will comply. To summon me, simply call my name and I will appear."

The image was sketchy at best. It pixilated in random bursts, as though it were absorbing small caliber weapons fire, and the sound quality left a lot to be desired. Nonetheless, this was clearly meant to be a version of the manically grinning bellboy depicted beside the hub's logo in the InfoComm ad. The figure in the ad wore a sharply pressed, burgundy-colored uniform with dark blue stripes on the cuffs and down the sleeves of the jacket, and a large, ornately scripted golden 'R' embossed over the left breast pocket.

The figure Dedrick was staring at now looked dingy and rumpled, as though he'd just been pulled out of a gutter somewhere after an interval-long drinking binge while wearing that same uniform. Somehow it seemed appropriate. This Jeeves was old technology, relegated to the least desirable part of the station. Eventually he would be replaced by an upgraded version of himself. Or maybe he would just be scrapped and not replaced at all.

It was rather sad, actually. The hologram looked more like a ghost. Dedrick could probably have walked through it to get to the sleeping area, but he'd been Fleet-trained to protect the weak and helpless and chose to step around it instead.

"I need information, Jeeves," he said, swinging his suitcase onto the bedcovers and flipping it open.

"I have full access to the hub's intranet. What is your question, sir?"

"Are there any messages for me?"

"You have one message."

Gael waited for more, realizing after a long moment of silence that Jeeves was even older than he'd thought. The concierge had little or no intuitiveness.

"Please repeat the message to me."

"Of course, sir! 'Meet me in the Luau Lounge at eighteen hundred hours station time.'"

"Did the sender provide a name?"

"No, sir."

Dedrick paused thoughtfully. His contact was exercising caution. He should probably do the same and assume that whatever he said in the presence of this hologram was being recorded somewhere. "And what time is it now, Jeeves?"

"The current station time is seventeen hundred forty-two hours."

He did a quick mental calculation. Twenty-two standard minutes gave him just enough time to wash up and change his clothes before heading out to the rendezvous point. "Thank you, Jeeves. You can go now."

"Very good, sir. Have an enjoyable evening." And with that, the concierge seemed to implode before his eyes.

Chapter Two

The Luau Lounge was decorated to make patrons feel as though they were in a palm-fringed clearing at dusk. Soft jazz drifted through the air, piped through unseen speakers, while a piano and a microphone stand loitered together on the tiny, darkened stage. Everything about this place was intimate and vaguely depressing: the dim lighting, the cloistered booths scattered around the small open dance floor, and the looks Dedrick received from the three female servers on duty as he wandered from table to occupied table, occasionally brushing a drooping frond out of his way. A knot of dread had taken up residence in his stomach, growing tighter and colder by the second. He was only five minutes late. Where was his contact? Had the meeting been blown?

"Are you looking for someone, sir?" said a melodious female voice at his left elbow.

He turned to reply and saw a face he recognized. It belonged to the grinning man seated with his arm around a server — obviously the one who had just spoken — in a booth nearly hidden by foliage.

"Not anymore," Dedrick told her.

The man murmured something into the server's ear that made her giggle. Then she slid off the end of the bench and onto her feet as he moved over to make room for the new arrival to sit down beside him.

"Can I take your order, sir?" she asked.

"He'll have one of your fabulous Singapore slings," the man cut in. "And I'll have another one of these," he added, tapping his glass with a forefinger. As she spun and headed for the bar, he turned to Dedrick and said expansively, "I'm glad you could make it. We've got a lot to discuss, my friend."

"Are you drunk, Novak?" Gael demanded in a harsh whisper.

The grin evaporated. "On root beer and club soda? What do you think?" came the equally intense reply. The other man pulled something resembling a gem-studded pillbox out of his pocket and set it on the table beside his glass. "This will jam any surveillance mics that happen to be pointed in our direction," he explained. "I've been posing as your late uncle's investment manager from Ares for the past two days, waiting for you to show up. If questioned by Security, I'm going to say we met here to discuss the future disposition of your inheritance. That should be your story as well. Now, what's this favor you need that couldn't be communicated to me over the usual channels?" The sharpness of his voice was matched by the look in his eyes, an expression that not even the subdued lighting of the lounge could soften.

Barry Novak hadn't changed much since their last face-to-face meeting (thirteen Earth years earlier, according to Chase). Novak was several years older than Dedrick and just as prickly as he remembered, perhaps even more so. It was a timely reminder, Gael reflected, never to underestimate the hazards of dealing with anyone Dennis Forrand had called "friend".

The server swung past their table then, to deliver their drinks. Dedrick waited for her to leave before answering, "It's two favors, actually. Were you aware that my late cousin Abner had a daughter?"

Novak scowled and shook his head.

"Abner was genetically altered by the Thryggians, against his will," Dedrick continued. "When he escaped, about sixteen Earth years ago, he took a girl with him, one of the other test subjects. A year later they had a baby together. Long story short, in spite of this child's strong resemblance to Abner, her DNA does not register as Human. The Thryggians tried to claim her by force, but we stopped them, using alien technology. They've since been convicted of scientific crimes against other races and have been imprisoned indefinitely by the Galactic Great Council. So, we no longer have to worry about a threat coming from that direction. The Earth Relocation Authority, however, is another matter altogether."

Novak exhaled noisily and relaxed against the booth's padded backrest. "If they know about her, I can see how that would pose a problem."

"They know, and so does Fleet Control. She was discovered on a plague-dead world by a ship conducting a census, so there was a flurry of official memos to and from Fleet HQ, all on the record. And our Supervisor of Medical Services was given a direct order to add her to the civilian database. Doctor Deneuve delayed as long as she could, but it wasn't long enough. She was forced to file her report just after my request for leave was granted."

"And that report said...?"

"What I just told you: Abner's child, alien DNA, and a theory that it was the alienness of her genes that protected her from Angel of Death. My guardianship is conditional on her being confirmed to be a member of my family. So, if some bureaucrat on Earth decides to classify her, sight unseen, as non-Human, I lose my only living relative. Fleet Control could order Captain Takamura to surrender her for deportation. Worse, the Disease Control Department could take custody of her for research purposes."

"If that bureaucrat finds her to be Human, she becomes just one more pawn for the Relocation Authority to slap a label on and move around the board. Ineligible, she goes to Earth and stays there. Eligible, she's posted to a colony or hub at the age of sixteen to live among strangers. I made her a promise, Novak. I told her we would stay together as a family from now on, no matter what, and I refuse to break my word."

"Your uncle would say it was a foolish promise to make."

"His idea of family was a lot different from mine. Will you help me?"

"You don't need my help. You already know what needs to be done and so does your SMS. Get your captain onside, then file a bogus death certificate. No more child, no more problem."

"Until Earth Data Management catches up to us, as they inevitably will. I'm prepared to lose my commission over this, but I can't ask Doctor Deneuve to risk sullying her professional reputation, and only a Council-certified doctor can file a death certificate."

"That's true. From where I sit, you seem to have an impressive grasp of the situation, Gael. Now I just need you to tell me what exactly you think I can do to fix it."

Dedrick let out an exasperated breath. "I don't *know* what you can do. That's why I'm asking for your help. I know that you're a lot more than you appear to be. I know that you have influence and that you've assisted my uncle with problems like this in the past. I'm not sure I want to know how you get things done, but I'm at the end of my rope right now and I don't really care."

"So, you believe I can just reach into my bag of tricks and pull up a way to make everything all right without implicating you or your SMS?" Novak paused, his lips pressed tightly together. "I appreciate your faith in me," he said at last, "but the best that I can promise you at the moment is that I'll look into the matter and see what I can do."

Dedrick repressed a sigh. He'd been hoping for something more definite. Still, Novak hadn't refused him outright, and the older man had always come through for him before. "Understood."

"Now, I believe you mentioned a second favor?" Novak picked up his glass and took a long swallow of the amber liquid inside it. This was root beer? Somehow Gael didn't think so.

"Yes. I need you to find out information on two men, Ian McCormack and Paul Travanti. They were the so-called friends who talked Abner into going to Thrygg in the first place. Their betrayal set things in motion that effectively destroyed my family, and I want to know who put them up to it and why."

Novak gave him a narrow look. "What makes you so sure they weren't acting on their own?"

"Because I'm a strategist, and I recognize a planned attack when I see it. Whoever orchestrated this knew precisely where and how to drive the wedge that would break the Forrand family apart. In his voice log, Abner expressed a desire for justice. That's what I want too. Trust me when I say that I will not stop until the person responsible for this has been exposed and made to pay, with interest."

"Is it justice you're after, or is it revenge?"

"In this case, they're the same."

"Well! It appears there's some Forrand steel in you after all. For years, I was convinced you were a Dedrick through and through. I'm not sure whether to be happy or disappointed that you're not. Dennis Forrand could be a ruthless, calculating bastard at times, but he changed a lot of lives for the better, including my own. So I'll do this for you, in his memory.

"I brought you something, but it's not assembled yet. Let's meet again tomorrow — mid-morning, on the beach. It'll be good for your cover. If you didn't bring a swimsuit, you can buy one on the boardwalk. Oh, and by the way," he added before downing the last mouthful of his beverage and replacing his glass on the table, "I told the server all our drinks would be on you tonight. Enjoy your cocktail, Commander. It contains real alcohol."

Wait a second. Real alcohol? That meant it would cost—!

Before Dedrick could utter more than a squeak of protest, Novak had palmed the jamming device and was on his way to the exit.

—— «» ——

There were children in the water, splashing one another and screaming with delight. Watching them from his chaise tucked up against the bole of an artificial palm tree, Dedrick drew a mental line between the youngsters in the turquoise lagoon and their parents lounging on blankets on the clean white sand. He felt a momentary pang. But it wasn't the parents he envied — it was the kids. They were genuinely enjoying themselves.

As a young boy on Earth, Gael had forced himself to take swimming lessons. The Forrand-Dedricks had spent a lot of their leisure time in and on the water, and being able to swim had been the price of admission to those family activities. He'd never liked getting wet, but he hated even worse the way it felt being the only one left on the dock while everyone else went off and had fun.

It was ironic how things had played out, he mused. Grown-up Gael had turned the tables, setting out on a ship, abandoning the rest of his family ashore. And now they were dead, and he was what young Gael had most feared becoming — the one left behind. He and Lania, he amended, nearly smiling at the further irony of her being Abner's child.

For that was where the Forrand steel had truly settled, not in Gael but in Abner; and from Abner it had passed to Lania. In fact, if Doctor Deneuve's suspicions regarding Abner's death were correct, Gael's troubled teenaged cousin was more Forrand than he could ever be. Steel recognized steel. It could explain why Uncle Dennis had kept bailing Abner out of trouble, and why Abner had changed his mind about killing Lania at birth as he'd threatened to do in his voice log.

That decision might have led to Abner's downfall, but to Gael it had proven a blessing. If Abner could see how much Lania now meant to the cousin he'd barely tolerated while alive, he would probably be spinning in his grave.

"Can't say I think much of your holiday attire," said Novak, breaking into Dedrick's thoughts.

Gael tore his eyes away from the domestic scene to his left and watched the other man open a green folding armchair and level it by pressing its legs into the sand.

"Didn't they have a swimsuit in your size?" Novak remarked, easing himself into the chair with a syllable of contentment.

Dedrick returned his gaze frontward and said frostily, "This is how spacers dress on the beach."

"Covered head to toe. Uh-huh." He shook his head indulgently. "I give you two more days and you'll be out of those trousers and walking barefoot along the shore."

Running out of patience, Dedrick leaned toward him and hissed, "This meeting was your idea. It's the only reason I'm sitting here. Now, you said you have something for me?"

Novak reached into the thigh pocket on his shorts and pulled out a brightly colored object that might have been a child's version of a compupad, stamped on the back with a large golden 'R'.

"That looks like one of those cheap replicas they sell on the boardwalk."

"That's where I got it. If anyone inquires, you can tell them you asked me to buy it for you at a souvenir shop to give to a young friend. I've replaced its inner workings with something better suited to our purposes — an offline playback device with a decryption key built in. I've permanently disabled the vox, so it's keypad only. Keep it away from InfoComm units and surveillance vidcams, because I'll be sending you encrypted updates embedded in routine messages. Download them onto wafers, find somewhere private, and use this device to read them."

As Novak passed it to him, Dedrick felt a sudden chill.

"Such a device will shortly be falling into your hands."

Advocate Chase had known about this meeting.

Gael pinned a smile on his face. "Thank you. I appreciate this."

"Save your gratitude for when I'm able to give you answers. And do yourself a favor — stick around for a few days and relax. You are wound much too tightly, my friend."

Without another word, Novak heaved himself to his feet and yanked his chair closed. Dedrick forced himself to wait until the other man had strolled out of sight down the beach. Then he got up and headed toward his quarters, his hand going reflexively to his side to confirm the presence of Forrand's dirty secret in his jacket pocket.

———— ‹‹›› ————

If you are reading this, then you are the last surviving member of the Forrand family. You have my condolences, not only for your losses, but also for drawing the short straw and ending up with the information on this datawafer. It's been my burden for much of my adult life, and now it's yours.

In the 2370s I created an organization called the Earth Intelligence Service, partly because of what you are about to read. Its mission was to discover the truth and make it public knowledge, but only as long as it was in Humankind's best interests to do so. If it wasn't, the EIS was to safeguard said truth until such time as the Humans of Earth were prepared to hear it, accept it, and do the right thing with it. Sounds simple? It isn't.

The EIS is pretty much running itself these days, with operatives all over the planet and moving out into Earth space; but there are some truths that not even Earth Intelligence is equipped to handle yet. Hence, the datawafer currently in your possession. Every powerful family on Earth has one just like it. I know, because I checked. The Harrises in Americas, the Greenoughs and Vargases in Pacifica, the Mkabes and Tonotulas in the League of African Nations, the Cassinis and Theodakises in Greater Europe, and the Khadris and Yungs in Indo-Asia have all been sitting on information that could blow up like bombshells if it came out prematurely.

If you're standing, you may want to find a comfortable chair right about now, because what you're going to learn will shock you. It certainly shocked the hell out of me.

Let's begin with the Forrand family tree. Our bloodline did not originate on Earth. This is not hearsay. I spent years verifying it at the source. Gervais Forrand was a member of Adam Vargas's team when it arrived from Stragon in Earth year 2178 to pick up the pieces after the second pandemic. Four entire nations had been wiped out, along with all the attendees at upward of thirty-five scientific and technological conferences and institutions worldwide. The final death toll was more than a billion Humans, including most of the finest minds on the planet. Not surprisingly, this left a lack of leadership on Earth, a power vacuum that the Stragori immediately stepped up to fill…

Ignoring the sudden pounding of his pulse in his ears, Dedrick continued reading, his attention gripped as firmly as though each word on the screen had grown claws and sunk them into his mind. Half an hour later he was done. Emerging from the personal hygiene closet in his quarters — the only place that he'd felt confident would afford him the necessary privacy — Gael set his "souvenir" down carefully on the bed. Then he fell backward into one of the chairs, his brain and gut both reeling.

Explosive didn't begin to describe the information on this datawafer. For one thing, it meant there was alien blood flowing through the veins of not only every one of Gervais

Forrand's descendants, acknowledged or otherwise, but also every living member of the other powerful families as well. If their combined number was large enough, it could even rewrite the definition of Humanity.

Dedrick had to stifle the urge to laugh. Once he began, he wasn't sure he would be able to stop. Uncle Dennis hadn't handed him just one hot potato — it was a whole barrowful. No, he amended, it was a truckload. A truckload of secrets had just been dumped on top of him, suffocating him in truths that would probably haunt him for the rest of his life. There could be no unlearning what he had read today. His only consolation was that there were apparently enough Forrand cousins running around out there, unbeknownst, to populate a small colony, and he would someday be able to pass the datawafer along to one of them.

Not to Lania, hopefully — she'd already endured enough pain to fill a lifetime — although, if Dedrick died before the others could be identified and the wafer became *his* last bequest, he might not have a choice in the matter. Like Uncle Dennis, whose advocate felt it would be a waste of his precious time to track down "every errant twig on the Forrand family tree".

Dedrick snapped erect in his chair. Chase had been on his way "home" — not to Earth and not to one of its colonies — when he and Gael had met at the transfer point.

Just how close were the Forrand family's current connections with Stragon?

Something told Dedrick he would soon be finding out.

——— «» ———

The minimum turnaround time on Riviera Hub was three standard days. According to the experts, that was how long it took for a Human to decompress after the stress of the space journey required to get there. Clearly, that hypothetical Human was traveling from Earth. Just as clearly, none of those so-called experts had ever served aboard a Fleet star cruiser like the *Marco Polo*. Dedrick's ship wouldn't be swinging back to pick him up from the transfer point for another six days. No matter how he did the math, he now had about three days to kill.

This was only the second leave that Gael Dedrick had requested since joining the spacegoing Fleet some sixteen Earth years earlier. Since he was the nephew of a former Supreme Adjudicator, Fleet Control had gone to some trouble to accommodate him. Vice-Admiral Nelligan had personally arranged his itinerary, rerouting other ships of the line to enable the *Marco Polo* to pick him up on schedule at Transfer Point Charlie. Official eyes were on him now. There would be a lot of unwanted questions if he cut his leave short or changed his travel plans on the fly. If anyone suspected what his actual purpose had been for visiting Riviera Hub, there could even be a judicial inquiry. So, like it or not, he was stuck there.

Dedrick had never been the sort of man who enjoyed doing nothing. Quite the opposite, in fact. And now he had that damned datawafer to worry about, along with a piece of rogue technology, the mere possession of which was a violation of his duty oath as a Fleet officer. He could practically feel the tension tying his muscles in knots, minute by minute. The last thing he wanted to be doing right now was sitting around somewhere, mulling over his situation. Strolling on the beach or going clubbing in hopes of making a brief, possibly sexual connection with a fellow guest or a friendly staffer was definitely out. That sort of thing had never been his style, even before Leslie Eberhart had become an important part of his life.

In the top drawer of his nightstand, Dedrick found a compupad offering a menu of daily planned activities that he could register for online. He scanned the list. It included low grav sports, martial arts classes, and a couple of crafts he'd never heard of. All right, he mused, he'd originally been skeptical, but this could be interesting...

...to a twelve-year-old, he amended five frustrating minutes later. He'd forgotten that Riviera Hub was a family resort, and families traveled with children. Clearly, these sessions were designed to keep the youngsters occupied while their parents pursued their own neglected interests. Unfortunately, the adult activities were all for couples or involved sitting in chairs, and none of them appeared likely to bring Dedrick's blood pressure down.

One menu item looked as though it could be fun. It was a sandcastle building competition on the beach, open to entrants of all ages. However, it wasn't scheduled to begin until the day of his departure.

He keyed "gym" into the search window, followed by "workout room", "weight room", and "exercise room", and got the same apologetic message each time: *Sorry, can't help*.

"Then what the hell good are you?" he growled, and tossed the compupad back into its drawer.

There was one more thing he could try. "Jeeves!" he bawled.

"At your service, sir." The concierge's voice arrived a half-second before his holographic image did. "What can I do to make your stay more enjoyable?"

"You can find me a gym."

"I can check our current registration records for individuals named Jim. Please specify parameters to narrow the search."

Dedrick reminded himself yet again that he was talking to a kludge with one foot on the scrap heap and the other on a virtual banana peel.

"A gym*nasium*, Jeeves. A place for adults to work up a sweat by engaging in strenuous and prolonged physical activity." Gael's body knew exactly what it needed. Just saying those last words aloud seemed to release endorphins into his system.

"There is a fitness salon at the north end of the core," the hologram replied brightly. "It is currently being used for giving classes in yoga, modern dance, and martial arts for beginners."

"Beginners" was code for "children", Dedrick had discovered from the compupad. He swallowed his next question, already knowing what the answer would be. If he wanted a rowing machine or anything like it, he would have to build the equipment himself. This "fitness salon" was certain to be a large mirrored room containing mats and music and very little else.

All right, then. Time to switch to plan B.

"Jeeves, is Beachfront Ring blocked by a wall at any point?"

"No, sir. Barring an emergency that would necessitate sealing off a section of it, the interior of Beachfront Ring is quite open."

"And what is the distance around the Hub at this ring level?"

"The station perimeter at Beachfront Ring is four kilometers, sir."

"Thank you, Jeeves. You can go now."

And I can run.

As his mind articulated the thought, an image popped out of his memory: Ixbeth Minegar.

It had been a standard year since the alien had left the *Marco Polo* in order to present evidence at the Galactic Tribunal, and nearly two years since she had joined the Human crew. Her legs were designed for running, something she hadn't been able to do the whole time she was aboard ship.

Looking forward to his first lap around the circumference of Riviera Hub gave Dedrick a glimmering of how she must have felt on the day she departed for Kula'as.

Chapter Three

Two days later, Dedrick dressed in shorts — Novak had been right about that part, at least — and stepped into the corridor to begin his morning run. The twice-daily exercise was already having a salutary effect. For up to three hours at a time, his entire consciousness was focused on the sensations (both pleasant and painful) of his physical body, giving his thoughts no chance to dwell or even settle on Dennis Forrand or Barry Novak. And — a bonus — Gael could feel his muscles burn as he worked them in a way the Shared Programmable Activities room on the ship couldn't possibly match.

Novak had been right as well about Dedrick's need to unwind. The more he ran, the clearer his perspective became. The exercise was like a broom, sweeping away all the doubt and worry that had built up inside him over the past year. Last night he had fallen into bed exhausted. This morning, for the first time since Lania had entered his life, he had awakened refreshed, with no memory of any of his dreams. This had to be what peace of mind felt like.

Jogging in place, Dedrick locked the door to his quarters. Then he turned and began his clockwise run. He'd completed three laps yesterday morning, and another three in the afternoon. Today he would aim for four. Sixteen kilometers before lunch. After lunch he would do it again, going counterclockwise.

Fifty meters along the corridor, he stopped, gripped by the certainty that something was — not wrong, really, but different. A doorway sat open on his right, a doorway that he hadn't noticed sitting open the last ten times he'd passed it. There had been stenciled words plaincoated onto the door, but he had been too preoccupied with the physical sensations of running to pay them any attention before. Now the gray metal slab was tucked inside the bulkhead and he could just make out the rightmost letters on the top and bottom lines: 'D' and 'L'. Authorized personnel? Decorated admiral? Renovated concert hall?

Enchanted waterfall?

Staring at the long, dimly lit corridor on the other side of the doorway, he thought he could hear music drifting toward him from somewhere deep inside the gloom.

Anticipation tugged at the corners of Dedrick's mouth. Tomorrow morning he would be returning to the transfer point with only a datawafer of secrets and a piece of rogue technology to remind him of what was supposed to have been a relaxing vacation. Was that how he wanted to remember his stay on Riviera Hub?

No, it wasn't, he decided. Temporary peace of mind wasn't enough, and lasting memories seldom came about as the result of playing it safe. Doctor Marchenko, the ship's psychologist, was always going on about the needs of the inner child. Right now, the one inside Gael Dedrick was clamoring to find the source of that music.

And so, feeling very much like a character from a classic children's story, Dedrick stepped through the doorway. He found himself standing at one end of a narrow passage with apparently unbroken walls. It stretched before him, with no other end in sight. The light bars stuck to the ceiling grazed his hair — his inner child being the same height as grown-up Dedrick — and a chorus line of shadows danced on the deck and walls around him as he made his way cautiously along what he guessed was an emergency route of some sort.

Just as it was dawning on him that he had no idea where he was going and could no longer see where he'd been, he noticed a wall-mounted light screen on his right, emitting a faint glow. He halted in front of it, pleased to see a map appear. *Motion sensor activation*, he thought approvingly as he scanned the display on the screen.

The map showed him how far he was from the station's main core — or rather, how close he was to it. He was in a north-south maintenance conduit tucked between two of the Hub's outer hulls, quite literally crawling around under its skin.

Dedrick had been walking for about thirty-five standard minutes at this point, in a tunnel with a decidedly ominous feel to it, made even more unsettling by the repeating melody that beckoned, siren-like, from directly ahead of him. It was a good thing he wasn't actually a child right now. Or claustrophobic. In fact, if he weren't a seasoned spacer, accustomed to creeping along dark, tight-fitting access tubes, he would probably not even have made it this far. But he *was* a spacer, and the music was getting louder. He decided to push on.

According to the map, this passage ended in a 'T' intersection at the entrance to a room with a second door that opened onto the boardwalk. Was that what he was hearing? A sound track from one of the stalls? He sifted his memory. Had there been music playing when he'd arrived on the hub? Had he seen a service door near the ramp? He couldn't recall. More to the point, would the door to the little room be unlocked, or would he have to pick a direction and search for another exit?

Dedrick stepped up his pace, determined to find out.

Fifteen minutes later, he did.

"Well, look who it is! Miss Abigail, in the flesh!"

Dedrick stared at the imposing figure that had just emerged from the shadows and now stood blocking the door at the end of the passageway. "Rosie Posey?" he ventured, his voice rising in disbelief.

"Yep. Get your caboose in here, boy. Let me take a look at you."

Boy? They were the same age, or at least they had been, that first year at the Fleet Academy.

"You can turn off the music, Sykes," Posey shouted to someone behind him. "Our guest has arrived." He stood aside, letting light spill into the corridor, and waved Dedrick into an office containing three desks and two other men, both wearing scarlet jackets and dark blue trousers. Turning, Gael saw the same Ranger uniform on his old friend. It looked ill-fitting.

"Rosie Posey?" repeated one of the men, grinning broadly.

"Watch your mouth, Caruso," Posey warned him. "Only one man in the universe gets to call me that, and I'm the only one who can call him Miss Abigail."

"Sounds like the beginning of a great story, boss," the third Ranger chimed in. This was Sykes, Gael guessed.

Posey shrugged. "We met when he was transferred into my platoon, about a month into our first year at the Fleet Academy. I gave him his nickname, he immediately gave me mine, and we baptized each other that night behind the barracks. It had to be the quietest brawl in the history of the Academy. Neither of us wanted to wake up Captain Ironpants."

Caruso spun in his chair to face them. "He was tough, this Ironpants guy?"

"*She* was our martial arts instructor," Dedrick told him.

"There were tales about how she'd gotten that moniker," said Posey, "all colorful but none of them substantiated. All we knew for sure — because she'd made a point of telling us earlier that day — was that the wrath of God was nothing compared to what would descend upon anyone who interrupted her beauty rest. Her words.

"Anyway, the next morning we both turned up in the infirmary with identical stories about falling down the stairs while sleepwalking, and we were practically inseparable after that. Until graduation, anyway. That was — what? Sixteen Earth years ago?"

"Sounds about right," Dedrick replied.

"Seems like an age. Now he's *Commander* Gael Dedrick, on leave from the good ship *Marco Polo*," Posey announced to the room, adding with a significant look at Dedrick, "and I'm Ranger *Captain* Posey. All right, you slackers, it's time for your patrol. Go show off your uniforms. Impress the tourists."

Gael waited until he and Posey were alone in the office, then commented quietly, "You were near the top of our class, and I know you were aiming for a berth on an exploration vessel. So what happened, Ross?"

"The Relocation Authority happened. They didn't need me out in space, so they sent me back to Atlantica. Attached me to a Security precinct to mark time until a posting came available. I had a lot of anger to work off, so I didn't just sit around. The next five years were very educational. Mainly, I learned that the best way to survive in Atlantica is to be a damn good cop and an even better fighter. When I heard that there was a shortage of Security personnel on the hubs, I put in my application to join the Rangers. I'd still be a cop, but at least I'd get to go out into space occasionally, right? Uh-uh. Spent the next seven years on Ginza Hub, running down traffickers in assorted illegal commodities.

"I'd just about decided to quit the force and take my chances with an independent ship owner when the captaincy came open on Riviera Hub. I jumped at it and have been here ever since. Compared to my previous two postings, this is like being on permanent R and R. Want some java?" He gestured toward the dispenser installed in a corner of the office.

Dedrick shook his head in response and watched Posey pour himself a cup. "You're just three men? Seems like a small detachment for such a heavily used hub."

"We manage. First of all, it's not just three men. This office is one of several distributed throughout the core of the station. Second, there's hardly any criminal activity here." Posey rolled a guest chair over beside his desk and signaled to Dedrick to sit down. "The detachments at the various transfer points do a pretty thorough job of screening passengers before they board any of the interhub liners or long-range transports, and the vast majority of our guests are family groups looking for a G-rated good time. Of course, we do get the occasional individual who has something else in mind. So, we check all inbound passenger manifests and monitor guest movement aboard the hub pretty closely. When I spotted your name on one of the lists, I knew we would have to talk."

Posey drained his cup, dropped it down the recycling chute, then strolled over and sank onto his desk chair.

Meanwhile, it was becoming uncomfortably clear to Dedrick that this was never intended to be just an informal reunion of two old friends. "So, you used music to lure me into following that passageway? It never occurred to you to simply walk up to me and say hello?"

Posey shrugged. "Now, where would the fun be in that? Especially since I knew you never could resist a mystery." He paused, then trained his gaze on Dedrick's face and continued in a weary voice, "R and R is great when you need a break, Gael. Not so much when it's your whole life. There's still work to do here, but nothing that seems to make a difference. You know what I mean?"

He certainly did. Dedrick was all too familiar with this sort of talk. Nine times out of ten it was a preamble to asking him for a favor. "Yeah," he replied softly. "I imagine babysitting tourists can wear on you after a while."

"Oh, we don't babysit. That's what the holo-concierges are for. Mainly we track. We track and we monitor. It helps us locate lost articles and reunite wandering kids with their parents. And in the process, we sometimes overhear things. Snatches of conversation, you know? Not enough to make any sense of, but just enough to tickle our curiosity."

No, thought Dedrick, his skin prickling a warning, Ross was too tough to ask for favors. This would be a demand. He'd caught part of Dedrick's meeting with Novak on the beach and would agree to keep silent about it in exchange for some benefit from the influence he thought his old friend could wield. And the worst part was that it was unnecessary. Gael already owed him the favor, and Posey didn't even realize it.

"Before you arrived I heard something," the Ranger went on. "Someone who'd had a drink or two was apparently disapproving of some of the decisions being made by the Council of Americas. He used the word 'puppet' in reference to the current Supreme Adjudicator. Said it was as if Dennis Forrand was still running things."

As a wave of relief rolled through him, Dedrick managed an "Oh?"

"Gael, nothing that's said or done in this office is recorded, you have my word. So you can tell me the truth. You're his nephew. Is he?"

"Is he what?"

"Is Forrand still pulling strings in Americas?"

"Absolutely not. The man has been dead for the past thirteen Earth years." *And I received his final bequest just days ago,* he added mentally, *and it was something he wouldn't have parted with while he was alive—*

For a moment, Dedrick felt light-headed.

It explained so much. The Security blanket that had been thrown over Transfer Point Charlie during their meeting. The sense of familiarity he'd experienced when Advocate Chase had smiled. The fact that Chase had apparently known Gael was meeting with Novak on Riviera Hub.

"You're sure about that?" said Posey, breaking into his thoughts.

Dedrick swallowed hard. "As sure as I can be. Don't forget that I've been out in deep space. We don't get the latest breaking news unless it affects Fleet Control somehow."

"Well, I'm a little closer to the 'pulse of Humanity'." Posey frowned, visibly weighing his next words. "I'm getting a sense that things on Earth are moving, and not in a good direction. I want you to do me a favor. When everything blows up, I want to be on the front lines. Can you arrange that?"

"Ross, I'll do my level best to make it happen."

And he would. Gael owed him at least that much, since it was Dennis Forrand's determination to send his nephew into space that had robbed Posey of his career.

Chapter Four

"Gael! You'll never guess where we're going!"

Stepping out of the short-hopper onto the *Marco Polo's* landing deck, Dedrick looked up and saw Lania running to meet him. She wasn't slowing down. He dropped his suitcase and braced for impact, a split-second before she launched herself into his arms. He gave her a long hug, swinging her around a couple of times before gently putting her back on her feet.

"Guess!" she commanded him, her dark eyes sparkling as she swept her fall of brown hair off her shoulders.

Only one destination could have made her this excited. He pretended to think really hard. "Hmm. Does it have anything to do with a certain furry alien we both know?"

Doctor Deneuve appeared beside them, laughing. "Ixbeth has invited the *Marco Polo* to come visit Kula'as. She actually submitted the request almost a year ago. Getting approval from the various government levels at her end has apparently been like pulling teeth. However, the Great Council has finally agreed, promising us safe passage through alien space, and Fleet Control just green-lighted the voyage as well. Now that you're back aboard, Captain Takamura can give the order to proceed."

Lania was grinning so hard it made Dedrick's cheeks hurt just to look at her. He tacked an answering smile onto his face. "That's wonderful, ladies. Great news."

The doctor's expression shifted to one of concern. He'd almost forgotten how intuitive she was. "You didn't sleep much on that transport ship, did you? Lania," she decided, "let's give your cousin some room. He just got back from a long trip. He needs to report to the captain and then he needs to unpack. And then I want to see him in Med Services for a quick checkup before he goes back on duty. No arguments, Commander," she added, her voice carrying the full weight of her authority as the ship's Supervisor of Medical Services.

Dedrick had been carrying a heavy load of his own. It didn't leave him a lot of energy to object to the order. "Yes, ma'am," he replied, reaching for his suitcase with one hand and reflexively patting his jacket pocket with the other. The datawafer was still there.

The tube car let him off on the officers' deck of the ship's community sector, where he found his and Lania's quarters, exactly as he'd left them. He paused briefly inside the door and looked around the suite, noting with a twinge of disappointment that his were the only belongings visible in its shared living and dining spaces. Lania had made great strides in the past year, but she still didn't feel at home here. Everything she owned was crammed into her between-bulkheads sleeping module, as though she were a mouse living inside his wall. She'd even removed her computer from the top of his desk.

The day he found a half-finished homework assignment sitting on the table, or her sweater carelessly draped over the arm of the sofa, they were going to celebrate, he decided.

Dedrick went to his own sleeping area and opened his suitcase on the bed. His attention was snagged immediately by the playback device. No one could know that he had this. Casting about for a safe hiding place, he finally settled on a small compartment in the bulkhead at the head of his bed. If he stacked his two pillows and tilted the top one, they almost concealed the finger recesses of the little sliding door. A casual glance would miss them entirely.

Perfect.

Once the datawafer and playback device were stored out of sight, Dedrick finished unpacking and slid the empty suitcase into its vertical nook at the foot of the bed. Then he headed toward the door, bracing himself to undergo Doctor Deneuve's intuitive, and no doubt extremely thorough, examination.

Med Services occupied the entire first deck of the ship's science sector, making it easily accessible by tube car from the community sector as well. As he entered the triage area, he found Deneuve waiting to usher him into a cubicle. It didn't take long for her to perform the battery of routine tests and, with a gradually deepening frown, record the results. Finally she stood back, leveling determined green eyes at his face.

"I don't know how you're going to convince anyone that you've just come back from R and R," she scolded him. "The numbers say you're medically fit for duty, but you look worse off now than you did before you left. Talk to me, Gael. Doctor-patient privilege will apply. Something must have happened on Riviera Hub. What was it?"

Seated on the edge of a diagnostic bed, Dedrick gazed wearily around the room. Deneuve could be relentless when she sensed information was being withheld. So, he scanned his memory and picked something relatively harmless to share.

"I ran into an old friend from the Fleet Academy. His scores were higher than mine when we graduated, but I got the *Marco Polo* and he ended up in Security, first on Earth and then on the resort hubs. He's had a rough career, if you could even call it that. It's not what he was planning to do with his life."

"And your friend's situation has made you sad." This was not a question. "Why?"

"Because I know who to blame, even if he doesn't. During my final year at the Academy, Abner was making a splash in the tabs — again — and Uncle Dennis went into damage control mode. Abner was beyond his help this time, so the Supreme Adjudicator pulled some strings and got me sent into space, far away from the scandal."

She gave him a long look. "He did you a huge favor, Gael, and yet you sound bitter. Do you need a referral to Doctor Marchenko to help you sort out your emotions?"

"No. It's just— I'd never thought about it before. About my good luck being at the expense of someone else's future. But seeing Ross like that, his dream of exploring the galaxy shattered because of Uncle Dennis reacting to something Abner had done—!"

"You're feeling guilty," she remarked evenly. "I can understand that. But things are seldom as simple as we think they are. You don't know for sure that your assignments were switched at graduation. Without your uncle's intervention, it's possible that you could *both* have ended up in Security. I guess the important question is, how was your friend when you saw him? Was he glad to meet up with you again after so many years?"

Dedrick thought for a moment. "I'm not sure whether he was happy to see me, exactly, but if he's been nursing a grudge, he never let on. Mainly, he's worried about his current post being too far away from the action. He doesn't feel that he's making a difference anymore. And that got me thinking about whether *I'm* making a difference."

"What?" Deneuve exclaimed. "I take back what I said earlier. You don't need Doctor Marchenko. You need Lania to come in here and give you another hug. A year ago she wouldn't even let you touch her. Most people in your situation would have turned her over to a team of professionals and gotten on with their own lives. But not you. You worked patiently to win her trust. You gave her a family again. Thanks to you, she's happy for the first time in her life. If that's not making a difference, then I don't know what is. And what about Leslie Eberhart's brother?"

"Sam Eberhart? That was nothing."

"I don't think Leslie would agree." Raising both eyebrows, she asked, "How are things between you two, by the way? I couldn't help noticing that she wasn't on the landing deck to welcome you back earlier."

He shrugged. He'd noticed too, but after their heated discussion the morning of his departure, he hadn't really been surprised by her absence.

"She may have been busy. We'll find each other later."

He could tell by the expression on her face that Deneuve wasn't buying that for one standard second. She muttered something in French under her breath, then added, "Well, regardless, I stand by what I said before. What you did for Sam made a huge difference."

"All I did was pull a couple of strings that Dennis Forrand had left dangling."

"You're making my point. You were in a position to pull them. Leslie wasn't. To her and Sam, this was not nothing. It was life-altering. How can you say— How can you even *think* that you're not making a difference, Gael?" she chided.

"I don't want to be a string-puller, Doctor."

"You don't want to be your uncle. All right, then. Be Gael Dedrick. Be true to who you are and everything else will fall into place."

It was good advice. Posey had seen rough times coming and had begged to be put into the front lines to meet them. Right now that was looking to Dedrick like a good place for him to be as well.

PART II

THE FATE OF THE SUHORE
Alien space 2400 C.E.

The Galactic Central Archives was established on the planet Reyi'it in Year 2755 of the Galactic Common Era (approximately 2530 B.C.E. on Earth) by order of the Great Council. The Reyota, among the earliest spacegoing races in our arm of the Milky Way Galaxy, had already amassed a vast library of information. Now they were mandated to gather data from all fourteen member worlds on the Council, curate the amalgamated database, and make it freely available to any citizens of those worlds on demand, both electronically and in person.

When first contact was made with the Stragori on Mars in 2230 C.E., the Earth High Council was granted permission to access the Central Archives through one of the member worlds on the Great Council. In practice, this multi-step process for obtaining information proved unwieldy. Therefore, in an informal vote taken in approximately 2335 C.E., the Great Council granted Earth's government — and anyone acting on its behalf — the right to request information directly from the docents at the Archives. Following the Interplanetary Conference of 2417 C.E. on Reyi'it, all restrictions were dropped, giving Humans the same full and free access to the database as any other citizens in our arm of the galaxy.

— Sic Transit Terra, An Unauthorized Planetary History
(2673 C.E.)

Chapter Five

Anxiety. "*Doshaya medhane*, you have a visitor."

At this tremulous statement, Ixbeth Minegar turned away from her office window and saw her student, Ellisan Rugh, standing in the doorway. The young one was new to her duties, having only recently been appointed to the position of docent's assistant. Her constant fear of making a mistake hovered over her like a tethered cloud. Now she leaned into the room as though expecting something to be thrown at her, and she seemed not to know what to do with her hands.

"And you've come to announce this individual's name?" Ixbeth prompted gently.

Guilt. Ellisan started as though stung. "It's Prime Docent Enne from the Central Archives." Her voice was little more than a whisper.

Ixbeth smiled. Yorell Enne, the revered scholar and intrepid High Councilor from the neighboring planet Reyi'it, had been a force of nature even before the Kularian deity Avo'or had selected her to be his agent, ensuring the successful completion of the recent Quest. Now she was a living legend. Her passage left lesser beings gasping for breath. Her presence apparently stole it completely.

Except from Ixbeth Minegar, the pure-blooded Child of Kula'as whom Avo'or had also summoned and trained to carry out his will. One standard year earlier, she had used an ancient psi-driven machine to fold and stitch the fabric of space, enclosing the Thryggian system in a pocket universe and thus imprisoning the Thryggians forever as punishment for their crimes. Maybe that was why the young one was so nervous around her. In Ellisan's first language, *doshaya medhane* was a term of address signifying the highest possible respect, with shadings of abject terror.

"Show her in, Ellisan. And then bring us some spiced *caranth*, please. Make it the way I taught you."

Ixbeth pulled her chair around to the side of her work table, directly facing the one her guest would be occupying.

Yorell Enne's visits were unplanned and sporadic, but always welcome. Whenever her responsibilities brought her to the Kularian Archives, she made a point of dropping into Ixbeth's office for some conversation, however brief, and a warm drink. Sometimes she carried news. More often, she provided praise and encouragement. Over the past year, a special bond had formed between these two females, and every being at the Archives was aware of it.

Today, the Prime Docent swept into the room, her unadorned dark blue robes billowing behind her. There were ceremonial badges and sashes of office that she had earned the right to wear, but she didn't need such things in order to be recognized. Yorell's facial coloring was distinctive, the fur shading from silver to black, darkest at the edges of her uniformly white mane. And her aura radiated enough authority to serve five ordinary beings.

Satisfaction. "Docent Minegar," she said, giving each syllable equal weight. "The title suits you, my dear. You have a great deal to teach others, and not just about the Humans."

Ixbeth bowed from the shoulders. "We are all docents, and we are all students."

"As I have told so many of them over the years," supplied Yorell with a nod of approval.

"And as the Human healer Deneuve said to me when I first boarded the Earth ship," Ixbeth added. "The Humans on the *Marco Polo* have accepted my invitation to visit Kula'as and will be arriving here very soon. I would be honored to introduce them to you. In many ways, Humans are no different than we are. On an instinctual level, they even understand the principles of resonance."

Delight. The Reyot's eyes widened with exaggerated surprise. "Really! You see, Ixbeth? Less than a minute in your presence has taught me something new and given me an exciting opportunity to look forward to. I've said this many times, and not only to you: once the Kularian Archives is fully re-established, you will be an excellent Docent of Human Studies."

"Thank you, Councilor Enne. And please," she said, gesturing toward the work table, "have a seat and share some refreshment with me."

Yorell spread her robes and sank gracefully onto the provided chair. In that moment, Ellisan appeared with a tray holding two mugs filled to the brim with steaming dark liquid. Her head lowered in respect, she offered it first to the honored guest. Ixbeth tasted amusement — a salty sweetness at the back of her throat — as Yorell carefully removed her beverage from the tray and took an experimental sip.

"I am developing a liking for this *caranth* of yours, Docent Minegar," she remarked. "It's especially flavorful today. What's the name of that Earth spice that you use?"

"Nutmeg," Ixbeth replied, concentrating on keeping her own mug level as she moved it with both hands from the tray to her lips. Two sips later, she could safely hold her drink with one hand. She used the other to dismiss her assistant, tasting the young one's relief as she scurried from the room.

Yorell took another mouthful and savored it for a moment before swallowing. "We use *bokhara* root in many dishes on Reyi'it but have always discarded the leaves. Once the Kularian database has been added to our Central Archives, I suspect that practice will change. Your data package on Dimmla does include the recipe, I trust?"

Ixbeth paused, picking her next words. "Yes, but — about the data package: The Council of Docents refuses to accept any input relating to a separate race called the Dimmlesi."

A faint sadness. "And you're wondering why?"

"Shouldn't I be? There's a gap in the records. I have first-hand information that will fill it, and yet I'm being prevented."

Yorell let out a sigh and placed her drink with deliberate care on the table. Then she reached into one of her voluminous sleeves, produced a datacube, and set it down beside the half-full mug. "I had a special reason for coming here today. When we received the first inquiry from Earth regarding the Dimmlesi, a race I had never heard of, I became curious. I assigned every docent and sub-docent I could spare to search the database for information. There was none to be found. Then I thought of the forbidden files."

Regret, and something else. Relief? Ixbeth stared a question at her.

"Thousands of years ago, there was an interplanetary war. When it was over, two home worlds had been destroyed. The Great Council was reconstituted, a tribunal was held, punishments were meted out, and a treaty was drawn up and signed. One of the agreed-upon terms of the treaty was that in exchange for complying with all of its conditions, every member world on the Great Council would receive amnesty — complete forgiveness for anything done during the war. To that end, it was also decreed that all official records pertaining to the Great War were to be expunged, to prevent any race from holding anything over any other race in the future.

"The Reyot Prime Docent at the time argued against this order, on the grounds that purposely destroying information about the past would only set the stage for history to repeat itself. Finally, the Great Council accepted a compromise. The record of past events was not eradicated. Instead, it was encrypted and sealed off in a section of what soon afterward became the Central Archives. Each incoming Prime Docent since then has been entrusted with the access codes and decryption key, in case there is a need to unseal the data.

"I haven't told you anything you're not allowed to know, by the way," Yorell added. "You're a docent now, and every docent is aware of the existence and general content of these files." Lowering her voice to a taut murmur, she went on, "However, what I'm now about to tell you is for your ears only and must not leave this room."

Ixbeth raised a silencing hand and called over her shoulder, "Ellisan?"

The young one leaned through the doorway. "Yes, *doshaya medhane?*"

"Just 'Docent Minegar', please. Go down to the market and find me some of those small yellow fruits that I like for firstmeal. Get enough to last several days. Docent Omassi can give you a credit voucher."

"And if there aren't any available, Docent Minegar?"

"Then find a substitute. Sample the taste to make sure it won't be too sweet."

Gleeful anticipation. "Right away, Docent Minegar!"

As Ellisan's footfalls receded down the stairs, Ixbeth remarked, "Now we're alone. It will take her at least half an hour to complete the errand and return."

"Excellent." Yorell continued, "I searched the forbidden files, and this is what I found: the two destroyed home worlds belonged to the Mitrades and the Suhore. Everyone knows what the Mitrades look like because any vessel registered to a member of the Great Council is required to use a Mitradean pilot for interstellar travel. But no one has seen a Suhore since the war ended. The race was reported by the Mitrades to be completely wiped out. So, when you mentioned the piloting contract between the Mitrades and the Dimmlesi, I realized—"

Yorell hesitated briefly. Then she plugged the datacube into a port on the work table and pressed the recessed button beside it.

A holograph sprang from the top of the cube. The being it showed was long-necked, with a hairless head, a muscular torso, and sturdy legs. Feathers marched in iridescent rows down its back and along its arms, which ended in skeletal, double-thumbed hands.

A wave of recognition broke over Ixbeth, raising her sense hairs and sending a shiver through her body. "That's a Dimmlesi."

"In fact, it's a Suhore," Yorell corrected her. "I copied the image from one of the encrypted files. From what you've described of your situation on Dimmla, I'm guessing that a colony of them must have survived the war, and the Mitrades decided to keep everyone else from discovering them. It would have been easy enough for all the Mitradean pilots to steer ships away from that system. And if the Mitrades kept a presence on or near Dimmla, they could have entered into a piloting agreement with the Suhore, without recording it in the Archives."

"But why?"

"I don't know. Unfortunately, the decision was made so long ago that it's doubtful whether anyone now living can state with certainty what motivated it. That is why I instructed the Council of Docents to reject parts of your data package. Until more information surfaces to explain why the remaining Suhore went into hiding in the first place, you and the other pure-blooded Kularians on Dimmla must officially be known as the only Dimmlesi in existence. I don't suppose your hosts kept an Archives...?"

Ixbeth tilted her head from side to side. "If they did, it would probably not be in any form we would recognize. The Dimmlesi shun all but the most basic technologies. In their language, *dimmla* means 'garden'. They even insisted that our Archives be set up on a neighboring planet in the system, in order not to spoil the natural harmony of the garden world they'd established. That was why we needed the piloting contract — to shuttle students back and forth between Dimmla and Altera."

Puzzlement. "Interesting. According to the files, Suha was a heavily industrialized world before the Great War broke out. In any case, the way of life you're describing makes me wonder even more why the Mitrades would choose to conceal the colony's existence. There is no possible way your Dimmlesi gardeners could pose a threat to any other race in the galaxy."

Something clicked into place in Ixbeth's mind. "That would have been the Great Council's main concern, wouldn't it? Identifying and eliminating potential threats to peace?"

Curiosity. "Of course. The war had been devastating. They would have done anything to avoid the start of another one. What are you thinking, Ixbeth?"

Until that moment she hadn't been sure. Now, with growing conviction she replied, "That the Mitrades might have lied to the Great Council about all the Suhore being dead in order to keep the survivors alive. You said that all the member worlds of the Great Council received amnesty."

"Yes, because they signed the treaty."

"Did the Suhore sign it?"

"They couldn't. They had all been—" Sudden comprehension. Dawning horror. "They'd been slaughtered." Her voice sank to a choked whisper. "A genocide. Oh, Ixbeth, you're a better teacher than you know. How could I have missed this?"

Tasting her deep sadness and regret, Ixbeth silently completed Yorell's thought: *...and whoever ordered the genocide evidently made the Mitrades responsible for carrying it out.*

That explained Dimmla, at least. All it took was one Mitradean ship's war-weary crew, sickened by all the killing, seeing a harmless pastoral community and deciding instead to protect.

To conceal.

For several heartbeats, Ixbeth and Yorell could do nothing but stare helplessly into each other's eyes. No wonder the Great Council had wanted the files erased!

Dread. "Do you think any of the Dimmlesi are aware—?"

"I don't know. Survivors are witnesses, so it's possible a record exists somewhere on Dimmla. But after thousands of years, there may not be anyone left who understands its significance. And even if there were—"

Words failed her.

With unsteady hands, Yorell extracted the datacube and replaced it in the pocket of her sleeve. "You realize that neither one of us can ever reveal what we learned today?" she said stiffly.

Unfortunately, she was right. Although the reason for it was long forgotten, the descendants of those disobedient Mitrades were still protecting the last remnants of the Suhore. Bringing the ancient past to light would be a betrayal of both races. It could even polarize the current Great Council, leading to a second interplanetary war.

Ixbeth reached for her *caranth*, by now a cold and bitter drink, and watched Yorell do the same. The two females proceeded to empty their mugs in silence, as though returning to this calming activity could somehow overwrite their memories of the past twenty minutes. Then Yorell got to her feet. Shaking off the awkwardness of the moment, she said a firm and formulaic goodbye, then left.

Ellisan appeared again, immediately after the Prime Docent had departed. Evidently tasting the mood in the room, the young one said not a word, just plucked the two mugs off the corner of the work table and hurried out the door, leaving the Docent of Human Studies alone with her darkening thoughts.

PART III

THE REYOT QUEST OF THE *MARCO POLO*
Alien space 2400 C.E.

Hiromasu Takamura (b. 2333 — d. 2437 C.E.) was an avid sailor and Earth's most renowned post-Reorganization space explorer. Born in Sydney, Pacifica, he had already won more than a dozen cups and ribbons in worldwide sailing races before his acceptance to the Fleet Academy at the age of 17. He continued competing on the water until 2370 C.E., when he was given command of the Earth star cruiser *Marco Polo*.

Takamura is credited with the discovery of at least twenty habitable worlds for colonization, as well as the diplomatic breakthrough that eventually led to Earth being recognized by the Galactic Great Council. Wounded while helping to quell civil unrest on Stragon in 2409, he retired from the Fleet and accepted a professorship at the University of Brisbane, which he held until shortly before his death. An annual sailing regatta, the Takamura Cup, is held in Pacifica in his memory.

— *Sic Transit Terra, An Unauthorized Planetary History (2673 C.E.)*

Chapter Six

The *Marco Polo* was met by an alien ship at the edge of Earth space. Slightly smaller than a short-hopper, the wedge-shaped craft nonetheless communicated in a very loud, very deep voice.

"You are the Earth ship. Your destination is Kula'as. I am your assigned Mitradean pilot. Prepare to receive me aboard your vessel."

On the *Marco Polo*'s bridge, all eyes turned to the man in the captain's chair. Hiromasu Takamura stared at the image on the forward viewscreen for a moment, then remarked with practiced composure, "Well! It appears we are about to make a first contact on our landing deck. What do we know about the Mitrades, Commander Dedrick?"

"Almost nothing, sir. When the *Vasco da Gama* made this same voyage a year ago, it was escorted through alien space by three heavily armed ships, none of them identified as Mitradean. It was most likely a protection detail, ensuring the safe arrival of the witness and her evidence at the Galactic Tribunal."

"Fleet Control must have assumed that we would be dealt with in like manner," Takamura concluded. "Well, it's a little late for us to be requesting background and cultural information, since the alien will be aboard in a matter of minutes."

"There is Fleet protocol in place to cover an unexpected first contact situation," Dedrick pointed out.

"The same protocol we followed with the Nandrians?"

Dedrick flinched, remembering. That encounter had not ended well. "Do you want me to assemble a reception party, sir?"

"No," Takamura decided. "This alien is clearly here to do a job. Treating a Mitradean as an honored guest might be considered inappropriate. You and I will greet him on the landing deck, Commander Dedrick. Ask Doctor Deneuve to be there as well. If he should require medical attention during his stay with us, she will be the one providing it."

"You're assuming the Mitradeans are gendered, sir?" Dedrick ventured.

A shadow crossed the captain's face. "I'm recalling what happened when Lieutenant Franconi referred to one of the Nandrians as 'it', and basing my decision on the voice we just heard on the comm. Until we are corrected, either by research or by the alien personally, I want everyone using the masculine pronoun when speaking aloud about him."

"Yes, sir. I'll let the crew know."

"Good." Raising his voice, Takamura added, "Open the landing deck door to space, Mister Tsieng. Let's not keep our pilot waiting."

———— «》 ————

Standing upright, the alien was about a meter tall not including its eyestalks, and it was clad in a segmented brown carapace with gold and bronze tortoiseshell markings. As he watched it emerge from the hatch of its ship, Dedrick couldn't help thinking, *I've eaten Earth creatures that looked like that.*

The Mitradean halted, its rearmost legs and bifurcated tail keeping it balanced and erect, and rotated its eyes to take in the three Humans lined up in front of it.

Captain Takamura stepped forward, introduced himself and the other two officers, and bowed from the shoulders. "Welcome aboard," he said.

Moving in tiny, click-shuffling steps, the alien turned its back on them. Then, as Dedrick and the others gazed in fascination, the markings on the Mitradean's shell seemed to come alive. Slowly, then faster, then slowly again, the colors flowed across its surface, merging and separating, trickling and swirling in a mesmerizing ballet. A minute later the dance was over, and the alien angled itself around to face the Humans once more.

This had evidently been a form of communication. Just as Dedrick was wondering how they could possibly understand it, let alone respond to it, the Mitradean reached a clawed hand beneath the edge of its carapace and pulled out a thin metal box on a wire.

In the same stentorian voice that they had heard before, the box began to speak. "The rules are these. I will take control of the helm of your ship and will remain in control until you have reached your destination. Do not interfere with me in any way while I am controlling the helm of your ship. Do not speak to me or attempt to distract me. Do not offer me nourishment or lodging. My vessel contains everything I need for the duration of this space voyage. Take me to your control room now."

Dedrick was tempted to ask whether the pilot would need to be carried there. Fortunately, he decided to keep quiet. Any doubts he might have had about the alien's mobility were laid to rest when he saw the creature drop to the ground and use all eight of its legs.

A hush fell over the bridge when the Mitradean scuttled out of the tube car, followed by Captain Takamura and his senior watch commander.

"Helmsman, stand away from your post," Takamura ordered. "From this point on, our pilot will be steering the ship."

Wide-eyed, the officer obeyed.

The alien had no need of chairs. It swarmed onto the console, its body arching over the controls as its many slender limbs worked them, apparently independently of one another. Meanwhile, the rivers and lakes of color on its carapace had resumed their liquid motion, against a perceptibly darker background than before. No metal box was produced this time to provide a translation, however, and almost immediately Dedrick realized why. The Mitradean was talking to itself. It was probably just as well that they couldn't overhear what it was muttering about them and their Human technology.

Gael's duty watch had already begun. Deneuve was in Med Services, having gone there directly from the landing deck. Takamura's gaze swept the bridge twice. Then he dipped his head in Dedrick's direction and stepped back into the tube car, leaving his watch commander in charge.

Gael braced himself for a flurry of whispered questions. But the bridge crew were all silent, watching the hypnotic display on the alien's back.

Nearly an hour later the metal box announced, "The pilot has control. The course is set for Kula'as. Estimated travel time is two standard intervals."

Dedrick smiled and leaned into the cushioned back of the captain's chair. At last they were on their way.

———— «» ————

The Mitradean craft parked on the landing deck was the same shape as a wedge of layer cake. A candle was all it needed to resemble the generous slice Gael had put in front of Lania at her birthday party three intervals earlier, the day she'd turned fifteen. She paused to savor the memory, licking her lips as though hoping to capture a sweet, lingering taste of it.

On that day, Lania had sensed nothing but joy and excitement. Now there was something else hanging in the air. Anger. It settled like a sooty film on her skin, making her want to scrub herself all over until she burned. She'd spent too many years around Abner not to recognize this particular emotion. And she'd quickly realized where it must be emanating from, since she had first become aware of it shortly after the Mitradean pilot had boarded the ship.

Anger in general made the air harder for her to breathe, but this alien's anger was different. It had somehow managed to pass through the ship's thick metal decks and bulkheads and burrow deep inside her, creating an itch she couldn't scratch. Worse, it was blocking her from escaping to the safe, quiet place in her mind. Lania had no choice. Since she couldn't avoid the itching, she had to try to stop the emotion that was causing it.

The Mitradean vessel looked locked up tight. Cautiously she circled it, keeping her distance to avoid setting off any proximity alarms, and staying alert for the sound of the landing deck door sliding open. She would have to take cover if anyone came through it. The short-hopper bay was restricted to authorized personnel only. Lania was breaking several rules by coming here alone. However, as she had learned from one of the bridge officers, it was easier to ask forgiveness for a thoughtless action than it was to get permission for a forbidden one.

"What are you doing?" demanded a deep voice behind her. It nearly launched her out of her skin.

Lania spun, half-expecting to see Commander Dedrick, and froze when her gaze alighted instead on the alien. Doctor Deneuve had shown her a snap of the pilot, so his outward appearance came as no surprise; however, he was much larger than Lania had anticipated. His eyestalks stood rigidly upright as well, bringing his height nearly up to her shoulders.

She'd guessed correctly about the Mitradean being the source of her discomfort. Anger was spreading away from him in waves, each one briefly worsening the itching inside her.

She struggled for a moment to find her voice, and then to think of something to say that wouldn't intensify his emotion. "I — I was just admiring your ship. I guess you were inside it."

As she watched, the alien reached across his body and produced a metal box connected by a wire to the inside of his carapace.

"And what do you find so interesting about my ship?" said the box. This was the same loud voice that had startled her before.

The landing deck was surrounded by reinforced bulkheads. No one should have been able to overhear him from out in the corridor. Nonetheless, Lania glanced around nervously. She'd been wrong about such things before.

Several heartbeats later, she let out the breath she'd been holding, looked the alien straight in one of his eyes, and replied, "Your species is new to us, and I was curious."

A pause. Then the box said, "You are a child," sounding as though it were accusing her of a crime.

"And you're angry all the time," she accused it back.

"I cannot be angry," said the box. "It is not permitted."

"Then you're breaking the rules, because you *are* angry. I can feel it."

The alien's carapace had been growing progressively darker. By the time the box finished informing her, "This discussion is pointless. You are a child. You notice nothing of consequence, and you cannot understand enslavement," it was nearly black.

"You're wrong. If enslavement means you have no freedom and aren't allowed to live a normal life, then I know a lot more about it than you think," she retorted.

There was a longer pause than before while the alien digested this. Then the box demanded, "You are a slave?"

"Not anymore. But I was."

"How did you free yourself?"

She hesitated, selecting the safest version of the truth to tell him. "The people on this ship are my family. They fought a battle and won me my freedom."

"The Mitrades do not have families," said the box, and once again it sounded as though the alien thought Lania was to blame.

Was this the reason for his anger? Was he feeling trapped and bitter because he believed no one cared enough to help him break his bonds?

"It doesn't matter," she assured him. "Humans will fight to help anyone who wants to be free."

"Anyone?"

The alien subsided into silence just as a familiar voice erupted from an overhead speaker. "Lania Dedrick, please contact the bridge. *Now!*"

The commander was upset. His final word made her flinch.

"You are Lania Dedrick?" asked the box, in a much softer voice this time. The Mitradean's shell was lighter in color now as well.

"Yes. I have to leave. I'm not supposed to be on the landing deck by myself," she told him, backing away in the direction of the corridor.

"And you weren't," the box said. Its words were followed by a series of buzzing sounds. She had no idea what they meant.

———— «» ————

"What were you thinking, Lania?"

"She *wasn't* thinking. That's the problem," growled Dedrick.

Deneuve threw him a frown. "Commander, please, I—"

He batted her concern aside. "I expected more from you, young lady! Entering the landing deck without authorization — all right, you were curious, that I can understand. But you broke a personal promise to me by leaving your wristcomm in our quarters so that no one could track your location. What if there had been a shipwide emergency? If Ensign Petersen hadn't spotted you from the control room and alerted me to what you were doing—"

"What exactly *were* you doing, *chérie*?" cut in Deneuve.

Lania stood in the strategy room, sensing curiosity from her doctor and annoyance from her guardian and darting anxious looks at both of them. Captain Takamura had almost certainly been made aware of this meeting. Right now she was counting herself lucky that he had chosen not to attend.

"I was trying to find out why the pilot is so angry."

Deneuve inhaled sharply.

"On the landing deck?" Dedrick prodded.

"No one is allowed to talk to him while he's on the bridge," Lania explained, "and he doesn't have quarters assigned to him. So I decided to wait for him near his ship."

"She's right, Gael," Deneuve told him. "I felt it too, the moment he arrived. Anger, and plenty of it."

Returning his attention to Lania, Dedrick asked, "And did you speak to him?"

"I did," she replied uncertainly. The mood of the room had changed. Was she in trouble or not?

"What did you find out, *chérie*?"

"I think he's a slave. Or he believes he is. The conversation ended before I could find out any details." The rest came out in a rush. "But I wanted him to know that Humans are good people, and whatever else might be making him angry, he shouldn't be taking it out on *us*, so I told him how you fought to free me a year ago and—"

Dedrick and Deneuve exchanged worried glances.

"And...?" When she didn't answer right away, Dedrick continued in a low voice, putting an edge on each word, "What exactly did you say to him, Lania?"

He was displeased with her. The itching inside her was getting worse, but she didn't dare lie to her guardian. "I wanted him to understand that we sympathize with him, so I — I may have suggested that we would help him win his freedom as well."

Dedrick clapped a hand to his forehead and uttered a brief, mirthless laugh. "We're traveling through alien space on the sufferance of the Galactic Great Council, tiptoeing on eggshells the whole way, and she wants to free the slaves. Unbelievable."

"I'm proud of you, *chérie*," declared Deneuve.

"Doctor, this isn't something—"

"Her talents are blossoming, Commander. Given her past history, it shouldn't surprise us to learn that she is especially sensitive to anger. However, instead of escaping from it into a coma, as she would have done a year ago, she went to confront the alien about his emotion. This was an act of courage, Gael. Your cousin has made great strides. We should be celebrating her progress, not scolding her for speaking out of turn."

His shoulders dropped. "I know," he said, "and I'm happy for her too. But I'm a senior ship's officer as well as her guardian. The captain has made me responsible for her conduct aboard the *Marco Polo*, and I doubt whether he will want to celebrate what she's done."

Lania felt a pinch of conscience. She wasn't really as brave as Deneuve had painted her. And it had never been her intention to get the commander in trouble with his superior.

"I don't think the alien likes children. Maybe, if one of you came with me next time—" she began hopefully.

"There won't be a next time," Dedrick cut her off, his features settling into an expression that matched the hardness of his voice. "Our pilot made the rules quite clear when he arrived, and we won't be doing Humanity any favors if we break them the first time a Mitradean is aboard an Earth ship. He has a job to do. We'll let him do it. Meanwhile, young lady, this is your fair warning. Remove that wristcomm once more and you will be on galley duty for the duration of this voyage."

The comm unit on the wall chose that moment to buzz.

"Commander Dedrick," said Takamura through the speaker. "Is Lania still with you?"

"Yes, sir."

"Please escort her to the bridge." The captain sounded bemused as he added, "Our pilot has requested her presence."

Dedrick's jaw had fallen open. He closed it again and replied, "On our way, sir."

Lania followed her cousin out of the room and onto a tube car, in silence. The itch inside her had become almost unbearable. Gael Dedrick wasn't angry the way Abner had been — all the time and at everything in general, like the Mitradean — but he was definitely upset with her right now. The safest thing to say was nothing. The most calming expression to wear was an emotionless mask.

When the tube car door slid open and Dedrick didn't step out behind her onto the bridge, Lania was relieved. Then she noticed the stern look on Captain Takamura's face.

"Approach me, child," commanded the pilot's metal box.

In the time that it took her to cross to the navigation console and stand beside him, the alien must have turned the volume control way down, for the next words to come out of the box were clearly meant for her ears alone.

"Tell me more about these fighters-for-freedom Humans you travel with."

Chapter Seven

It had taken a year and thousands of pairs of hands, but Capital City on Kula'as had been completely extricated from the dense tangle of roots and branches that had enveloped it during the Kularians' centuries-long absence. Many of the buildings inside the city walls were made of the same material as the walls themselves — a seamless, stone-like substance that (according to legend, at least) could be programmed to absorb or repel any energy that collided with it. These structures had emerged from their cocoon of vegetation intact, and nearly all of them were now occupied.

It was Ixbeth's daily practice to go for a run after first-meal, seeking out the company of others to fill what was rapidly becoming a void in her life. Some mornings, she passed through the gate and followed a road to one of the settlements where she knew other chosen ones lived. On market days, when the roads were busy with travelers carrying goods to and from the city, she tended to stay within its walls, hoping to bump into an old acquaintance or make a new one.

Today, Ixbeth trotted along the perimeter of the central marketplace, inhaling the comforting fragrance of fresh-baked bread from the communal ovens and watching a motley collection of beings go about their business. A female with red markings on her fur and a matching red mane was filling a basket with produce at one of the foodgrowers' stalls. Meanwhile, a dark-skinned female from Murrala 5 was looking over a display of colorful robes and capes in front of a clothworker's shop. And two furless males, one wearing a shiny apron, stood at the entrance to a small-machines factorium, negotiating a barter price.

Kularians came in a variety of shapes and colors now, with and without fur, manes, and tails. They had traveled back home from every part of the galaxy, bringing their trades and technologies with them, and they knew whom to thank for this new beginning for their peoples. Everyone turned to smile and wave at Ixbeth as she passed by.

It would be hard for them *not* to recognize the only pure-blooded Kularian on the planet, she reflected sadly. Not a single other being on Kula'as had a face that looked like hers.

It was ironic, really. On Dimmla, she had felt alone because of all her failures. Here on her ancestral home world, she not only felt alone, she truly *was* alone. If it weren't for the periodic visits from Prime Docent Enne—

"Doshaya medhane!"

Tasting a strange mixture of excitement and trepidation, Ixbeth spun and saw her assistant rushing breathlessly toward her.

"Ellisan, what have I told you about muting your feelings—?"

"But the Humans have arrived! Their shuttle just landed! And Councilor Enne's as well! She is with them!"

The young one could hardly stand still.

"The Humans? I need to meet them," Ixbeth said, gulping a breath as she realized, "and bring them back here. It's ten kilopaces to the airfield and the beings on that ship aren't accustomed to running such distances. Find Gorse Pirrit. Tell him I require one of his—"

"With your indulgence, *doshaya medhane*, I informed him as soon as we knew your guests were on their way to Kula'as. He's been working in secret for the past moontide."

"Working on what?"

"Your ceremonial *trada*. It should already be waiting for you just outside the gate."

Ixbeth kept her first reaction to herself. A broad, wheeled cart generally used for carrying heavy loads was not exactly the mode of transportation she had had in mind for this occasion. However, Ellisan's confidence was still fragile, and she was looking so pleased with herself just then that it would have been cruel (not to mention unteacherly) not to at least acknowledge her initiative.

"That's a good choice for a dramatic entrance," said Docent Minegar, pinning on a smile. "I'm sure Councilor Enne will approve." She turned and headed toward the city gate.

"Shall I make some spiced *caranth*?" Ellisan called after her.

"No," she replied over her shoulder, "Humans don't like the taste. Find the metal container of java in the chest in my office. It's prepared the same way." Struck by a sudden thought, she added, "But leave out the nutmeg!"

On market day, the main gate of Capital City was thrown wide open from dawn to dusk, welcoming any being with goods to trade or a need to fill. In an hour or two, the roads would be streaming with shoppers and vendors arriving from the nearby settlements. The central marketplace would soon be bursting with activity, forcing Ixbeth to walk as she negotiated a path through the crowd.

Soon, but not yet, thank the stars. Ixbeth ran at full speed, past empty stalls and sparsely scattered city folk to the tall, arching frame of the gate. Beyond it, the world was a patchwork of forest and meadow, dotted with dwellings and outlined by a network of roads and paths, some cleared and flat, others not. The main road was kept wide enough for two vehicles to pass each other. Once the planet was fully repopulated, this one thoroughfare would link all the major cities together. For now, it provided access to just a few, but primarily to Capital City, where the Archives was.

Ixbeth halted just beyond the gate and stood gazing left and right, her ears twitching impatiently, her tail rigid beneath her light blue robe. Then she saw something that looked like a wagon, tucked up against the massive trunk of a *plaxa* tree on the other side of the road. As she hurried toward it, curiosity and disappointment began jostling each other in her mind.

This was her ceremonial *trada*?

It was out of the ordinary, that could not be denied. Painted in a rainbow of colors and outfitted with backless bench seating for up to a dozen passengers, it had a type of engine Ixbeth had never seen before and no obvious way to start, stop, or steer its wheels.

"It's my own creation, Docent Minegar," came Pirrit's proud voice from behind her as he approached. "It's psi-powered, requiring only a single focused Kularian mind to operate it. There is no other conveyance like it on the planet, and I offer it to you as a gift. I hope you are pleased." He bowed deeply, holding something out to her that resembled a nest of wires.

For a moment Ixbeth was speechless. "I am honored, Gorse, truly," she finally managed to get out. "But I don't have time to practice with this right now. I need to go to the airfield right away."

"Understood, Docent." He flipped the nest of wires over and placed it on his own head. The device reached downward, clasping the underside of his jaw on either side and revealing itself to be a sort of helmet. Gorse turned and stared fixedly at the side of the *trada*. Ixbeth watched in fascination as a section of it swung wide. A small, square platform slid through the opening and dropped halfway to the ground, forming a step. "May I assist you into the vehicle?" he asked, extending his hand.

His emotions were muted, but Ixbeth recognized the expression on his face. Evin Lurrlo had worn that same look on Altera as he attempted more than once (without success) to inspire the condition that Doctor Deneuve had once referred to as "heat", and that Kularians called *disvan*. Lurrlo had been a cloistered computer technician with a tendency to slouch. Gorse, on the other hand, stood tall and was broad in the chest. Furless and short-nosed, with skin the color of steeped *caranth*, he was also a talented inventor and engineer who had crisscrossed the galaxy as one of the chosen ones during the recent Reyot Quest. A docent with a wanderlust could do worse—

No. It was with such thoughts that *disvan* began. Ixbeth instantly banished this one.

"Are you offering to be my driver, Gorse?" she asked stiffly.

He smiled. "Only this once, so that I can demonstrate the use of the headnet."

"Good idea," she told him, lifting the front of her robe with both hands and mounting unaided into the bed of the wagon. "And next time, I'll be the one to drive."

The smile migrated to his eyes. They were almost as dark as Commander Dedrick's. "As you wish, Docent Minegar."

He stepped up and sat down beside her. Then — all by itself, it seemed — the vehicle executed a tight right turn and headed along the road in the direction of the airfield.

They rode in silence for several minutes, his growing impatience a sharpness at the back of her throat. She had been down this path before and knew what was probably going through his mind. He wanted her to be more than pleased at receiving his gift — he wanted her to be curious. He wanted her to ask questions so that he could instruct her, thus establishing a closer relationship.

It was Evin Lurrlo all over again. But she'd known from the start that Lurrlo could never win her, and that had made him easy to resist. With Gorse, she couldn't be certain. Ixbeth still had vivid memories of her *disvan* aboard the *Marco Polo*, without any female friends nearby who could bleed off its effects and help her keep a clear head. Feeling just as alone now on Kula'as, and in a position of great responsibility as well, she couldn't risk going through that again.

She let the silence stretch on.

At last Gorse said, in the conversational tones of one who was simply responding to a query, "The headnet is a resonance amplifier. It collects your ambient psi energy, intensifies it, then feeds it back to you for focusing and direction. Because it's your own resonance pattern, there's no integration required. You imagine it and the vehicle does it. The engine mounted under the frame of the *trada* is programmed to translate psi impulses into a limited range of maneuvers by the wheels of the wagon. Forward motion, backward motion, turn right, turn left, stop," he recited. "And I added the gate and retractable step so that passengers could embark and disembark with ease."

He paused, and Ixbeth tasted his hopeful anticipation. He was expecting a compliment.

"I like the paint job," she remarked, suppressing a smile.

"I wasn't sure what your favorite color was, so I decided to use them all. I can repaint it if you like."

"No," she told him, "it's perfect this way. Don't change a thing."

Silence fell again. This time it rested much more lightly on both their shoulders.

——— «» ———

The airfield near Capital City had been a busy place before the cycle of concealment. It was at least as busy now, with entire communities of Kularians arriving from distant parts of the galaxy, bringing with them the furnishings and technologies that had come to define their various lifestyles after the past three and a half centuries. The population of Kula'as currently stood at half a million, and that number was expected to double in the next year.

Ships and shuttles of every size and description were strewn over the broad apron. Wheeled and unwheeled freight vehicles sped back and forth across the pavement, carrying newcomers and their belongings to the main terminal to be officially welcomed home.

One vessel sat apart, an island in the midst of all the traffic. As the *trada* drew nearer, Ixbeth was able to discern the distinctive shape of the *Marco Polo*'s short-hopper. She counted six beings standing on the ground beside it. One of them pointed in her direction, and the others turned and waved at her.

Ixbeth!

The urgency that suddenly flooded Ixbeth's mind made her gasp and stiffen in her seat. *Tal? What's wrong?*

We're stranded and under siege. We need your help, my sister.

The vehicle had slowed to a crawl. "Docent Minegar, are you all right?" Gorse was demanding. She shook her head and motioned to him to stop.

Who is attacking you and what can I do to help?

A ship entered our system four days ago and came directly to Altera. He shared its image with her. Her heart dropped. A flying egg. It was Thryggian. But the Thryggians were all confined to a pocket universe. She had sealed them into it herself, with the entire Galactic Tribunal as witnesses. How could this be?

Did your Mitradean pilot fly out to meet it?

He told us his obligation was to protect Dimmla, not Altera, and that we were on our own. We couldn't agree on what to do. A few of us joined our psi powers and tried to send the ship back out into space. Unfortunately, we lost control of it. It crashed in the middle of a Dimmlesi field. Now the Dimmlesi are enraged and insisting that all the Kularians leave their system immediately. And if the Mitradean decides that we're a threat to Dimmla and comes after us with weapons, we'll have no choice but to bring him down as well.

The Dimmlesi are right, she decided. *You need to leave as soon as possible. How long will your food supply last?*

Mother planted a large garden last year, so we can hold out for several moontides. Can you get a ship to come pick us up?

Gorse had brought the *trada* to a halt and now sat staring at her. His concern was tinged with sadness and jealousy, creating a smoky taste at the back of her throat. "You're bonded with someone, aren't you?" he said softly. "And he's in trouble."

Ixbeth stood up at her seat, her gaze riveted on the curved shape of the Human shuttle as possibilities tumbled together inside her mind.

I think I may already have your transportation. Tell everyone to start packing.

"It's my litter-twin," she replied at last, sensing relief from Gorse as she sank back onto the bench beside him. "And my whole family is in trouble. But I have a plan to rescue them."

The *trada* began rolling again. "You're going to rescue them in that?" Gorse said, pointing at the short-hopper directly ahead of them.

He wanted to come with her. Ixbeth had tasted the same strong desire emanating from Tal after the Oracle had chosen her for the Quest. That time, she had responded reflexively. This time, she would think things through.

"Of course not," she told him. "I'll be doing it with the Earth star ship it came from."

Surprise. Curiosity. *Yes*, she thought, a silent reply to his unasked question, *they're that far away*. Sensing no further reaction from him, she continued, "The *Marco Polo* is no ordinary Earth vessel."

"Oh?"

"It's retrofitted with Kularian-style shields."

His aura brightened. "Then you'll need a Kularian-style engineer aboard to inspect and maintain them."

"Stars! You're right!" she said with exaggerated emphasis. "Do you happen to know where I can find one?"

He let out a growl of reproof. "I know of several. But the best one on the planet is sitting right beside you, Docent."

"Yes, and he's so modest," she teased, grinning as the *trada* pulled up in front of the half-dozen beings waiting beside the small craft.

Belatedly, Ixbeth remembered that Humans were *pritvanu*. In the second that it took her to throw up her mental shield, her scalp muscles were already spasming from the strength of the emotions being spewed into the air. A sideways glance at Gorse's face showed that he'd been affected by them as well.

"I'm sorry," she murmured. "I should have warned you."

He said nothing, but his annoyance was a faint sourness at the back of her throat.

Ixbeth stepped down to the ground, thinning her shield just enough to let her sample the auras of her guests. Commander Dedrick, Doctor Deneuve, and Captain Takamura were all radiating admiration. Gorse's gift was apparently being well received. Then Ixbeth's eyes met Lania's, and a wave of pure happiness broke over her. The young one's emotions were as powerful as ever, but much lighter than they had been a year earlier. Pleasure began vibrating in Ixbeth's chest.

"Docent Minegar," said Yorell, breaking into the sharing, "on the occasion of this first visit by Humans to your world, we bring you greetings from the Reyot High Council. I present to you my son, Councilor Arfan D'Ull. You may recall him from the Galactic Tribunal a year ago."

"Prime Tribune," said Ixbeth as the second Reyot stepped forward and the memory clicked in. D'Ull's facial fur was blue-gray, and he wore his dark mane flat and close to his head, in the current style of his social caste. "I'm honored that you would make time in your busy schedule to attend our little reunion."

Amusement. "Docent Minegar, I'm honored that you invited me here."

Invited him? Ixbeth shot a questioning look at Yorell. When the older female avoided meeting her gaze, she finally understood. This was what happened when an unmated female confessed a moment of loneliness to the mother of an unmated male. Had Yorell been Kularian instead of Reyot, she would have understood that this was not the way *disvan* worked.

Meanwhile, D'Ull appeared to be enjoying the awkwardness of the situation. It was probably not Yorell's first attempt to pair him up.

Valuable time was being wasted. Certain that the Humans and Reyota had already introduced themselves to one another, Ixbeth pressed on. "And I present to you Gorse Pirrit, a Kularian witness at the same Tribunal."

She turned and found him still sitting in the *trada*, facing stolidly frontward as though he were no more than a hired driver. *Oh, no, you don't*, she thought. Aloud, she continued to the group, "He is also the gifted Kularian engineer who designed and built our transportation to the Archives in Capital City."

As if on cue, the vehicle lurched forward, pulling a syllable of surprise from Gorse's lips and nearly tossing him off his bench.

He sprang to his feet and swept accusing eyes over the seven beings on the ground. "Who did that?" he demanded.

"Did what?" said Ixbeth, tasting nothing but confusion around her. "That wasn't you?"

"This wagon is psi-powered," he explained, "but it takes a very strong and focused signal to activate the engine. That's why I built the headnet, to boost the average Kularian's psi output to the required strength. I didn't move the *trada* just now, and I'm wearing the only headnet. So someone in this group must have extraordinary mental abilities."

As one, Ixbeth and all the Humans looked at Lania.

The young one was broadcasting fear. Projecting trust, Ixbeth stepped forward and took her hand. "Lania," she said softly, "you're not in any trouble. We just want to know. Did you think about the vehicle? Did you imagine it rolling forward?"

"I was wondering what made it move," she replied in a small voice.

Gorse leaped down to the ground and took off the headnet. "Do it again," he urged her. "Backward this time."

The vehicle rolled several paces in reverse, then stopped.

"This is amazing," Gorse declared.

Apprehension. Agitation. "Actually, it's extremely dangerous," said Yorell tightly. "And so are you, Gorse Pirrit. We all need to go somewhere private so I can speak freely."

Chapter Eight

Captain Takamura had offered the interior of the Human shuttle, but Yorell had refused, insisting that the only place she trusted to give them complete privacy was Ixbeth's office on the top floor of the Kularian Archives. To Lania's delight, Gorse let her drive part of the way to Capital City. The young one was a quick study. After less than a minute, she had the *trada* completely under control, rolling it smoothly along the road and turning it left and right with ease.

Ixbeth couldn't help noticing that the more Lania demonstrated her Kularian mental powers, the darker the emotional auras of the two Reyota became. When Gorse stopped to let his passengers disembark outside the city gate, Yorell put a hand on his arm and advised him, "Conceal this vehicle from curious eyes, and then come up and join us. You need to hear what I have to say."

His misgiving was a salty taste at the back of Ixbeth's throat.

Ellisan had borrowed chairs from several offices on the floor below and had arranged them in a semicircle around Ixbeth's desk. In the center of the desk sat a thick, stone-like tile beneath a large transparent pot of steaming hot dark brown liquid. Beside it, ten mismatched cups had been crowded onto a tray.

Anxiety. Ellisan stood just inside the door as the docent and her visitors entered the room. When Ixbeth turned to look at her, she bowed low and murmured, *"Doshaya medhane,* is everything to your satisfaction?"

"Not quite, Ellisan. Please run down to the kitchen and tell Suska Lorn I wish her to make a dozen of her special biscuits for my very special guests. Stay there and make sure the task is completed before she begins preparing the midday meal."

"I will, *doshaya medhane.*"

Over the sound of Ellisan's receding footfalls on the stairs, Ixbeth explained, "We have a very talkative cook, and I have an exceedingly polite assistant. I have already timed this particular errand. It will take her at least an hour to return. Until then we are alone. Everyone, please sit."

Yorell gestured toward the pot on the desktop. "Is that *caranth*, Docent Minegar?" she asked hopefully.

"No. It's a Human beverage that I learned to make aboard the *Marco Polo*," she replied. "It's called java."

With that, Ixbeth began filling the cups and handing them out. She was pretty sure the Reyota wouldn't like the flavor of this drink, but she didn't much care. It had been brewed to welcome her invited guests. If the uninvited ones found it bitter enough, perhaps they would take the hint and leave a little sooner. Then she could ask the Humans for their help.

To her surprise, she was tasting enjoyment from Arfan D'Ull. His aura contained a streak of cruelty that was causing her sense hairs to rise. Apparently, Yorell's son found his mother's disappointment entertaining. It began to explain why a being in his position of power was not yet mated. With an inward shiver, Ixbeth returned her attention to Captain Takamura and his party.

For Humans, java was a symbol of hospitality. Commander Dedrick smiled and raised his cup in a silent salute to Ixbeth before taking a sip. She did the same and smiled back.

Sensing a tentative presence in the doorway, she glanced up and extended her smile to include Gorse as well, then waved at him to enter.

When everyone had been served, Yorell got to her feet. She placed her java untouched on the desktop, stared sadly at Lania for a couple of heartbeats, then turned to Ixbeth and said, "This is going to sound like a docent's lecture, but it can't be helped. Spurred by our earlier conversation, I've been researching some ancient history."

"Mother...?" D'Ull warned.

She silenced him with a look. "Kula'as is being reborn. Like a kit fresh from the womb, it has no memory of events that took place in the distant past. And it needs to remember. We all need to remember. The Great Council may not care if entire races are left stumbling in the dark, but I do. You should care too, Arfan, because this visit by the Humans has opened a door that will never close tightly again."

Takamura shifted in his seat. "Forgive me for interrupting, Madame Councilor, but is this a discussion you would rather we Humans didn't overhear?"

"No," she replied firmly. "What I'm about to reveal concerns both your races. I would ask, however, that you not repeat any of it outside this room."

The Humans exchanged sober looks for a moment. Then all three adults faced forward and nodded assent. So did Gorse, although his eyes held a speculative gleam.

Ixbeth stole a glance at Lania and tasted a mixture of dread and anticipation. The young one sat attentively, holding her cup with both hands.

Satisfied, Yorell resumed speaking. "Thousands of years ago, there was an interstellar war. The Great War. When it was over, two home worlds were gone. One had been rendered uninhabitable by conventional weaponry, and the other had been completely destroyed — by Kularians using psi-powered ships."

Ixbeth felt a sudden chill. "Like the one we used to isolate the Thryggians?"

"Exactly like it. The power these vessels demonstrated was out of all proportion to their size. It shocked and horrified every race in the galaxy. It also brought the war to a rapid conclusion. Because no one wanted such a terrible force ever to be unleashed again, the peace treaty included a promise by every signing race never to develop psi-powered technology, and never to allow their natural mental talents to become strong enough to pose a threat to any other race."

"And the Kularians, who already had psi-powered technology...?" Gorse cut in.

"...were stripped of it," D'Ull supplied. "Their psi-driven ships were dismantled and scrapped and they were forced to surrender every psi-powered device on their world. And for the next ten or fifteen generations, until alternative energy sources became the norm, Kula'as was carefully monitored."

"Are we being watched now?" Ixbeth inquired.

"The Council has adopted a wait-and-see policy for the time being," Yorell replied. "However, Kularian hybrids are returning from all over the galaxy, bringing with them technologies that they've been using on other planets. If word should ever get back to the Great Council that a brilliant inventor from one of those planets has developed a psi-driven vehicle *and* a way of amplifying psi energy to power it — or, worse, if his entire community has brought psi technology back to Kula'as..."

...or if a group is actually working to increase its psi powers, like the brotherhood on Altera...

Ixbeth swallowed, but could not banish the taste of her own dawning horror from the back of her throat.

"That's not fair," declared Gorse, nearly spilling his java as he sprang to his feet. "First of all, it's not my whole community, it's just me. And second, it's a wagon, not a planet killer."

"The treaty your ancestors signed does not distinguish greater or lesser degrees of transgression," D'Ull informed him sternly. "It is binding on the Kularian race in perpetuity, and penalties will apply if any member of that race does not adhere to its terms."

"Provided the Great Council finds out about it," Yorell pointed out loudly, with a single hand gesture commanding D'Ull to be quiet and Gorse to sit back down. Looking straight at Ixbeth, she added, "At this point, there is no reason that it *should* find out. So, Gorse Pirrit is going to convert his wonderful *trada* to run on a more conventional power source and put his — headnet? — into storage, saving it for more important tasks."

Intense curiosity. Opening his mouth to speak, Gorse was silenced by stared warnings issued simultaneously by Yorell, Ixbeth, and D'Ull.

The Humans had been sitting wide-eyed meanwhile, hardly daring to raise their cups to their mouths as they absorbed the scene unfolding before them. Ixbeth had been tasting their uncertainty and confusion since Yorell's opening words. Now, the force of nature turned as though noticing them for the first time and said:

"Lania may look like a Human, but she has the mental abilities of a Kularian, and that is how the Great Council will see her — as a returning hybrid Kularian. When Docent Minegar told me of her plan to invite Lania to join her here at the Archives, I was intrigued. After hearing about her and seeing what she can do, I have no doubt that she would have found a peer group and flourished on this world. However, under the terms of the treaty, I'm afraid it cannot be allowed. As soon as the Great Council learned of the strength of her psi talents—"

"She would have to leave," said Ixbeth sadly. "I understand."

"No, my dear, it's much worse than that. She would have to die. And if she fled, she would be hunted down and killed." Speaking to the Humans, Yorell added, "If you value this young one's life, you must never let the Great Council find out that she exists. Nor can they learn about any other Humans with the same mutation. Not having signed the treaty, Humanity is uncontrolled and already disquieting to the rest of us. Humans with psi powers would be considered the most dangerous race in the galaxy."

Fear! Lania's body went rigid. *No, no, no, not a healing sleep, not now!* As the girl's empty cup rolled off her fingers to bounce on the floor, Ixbeth gathered every scrap of trust she possessed and began projecting for all she was worth.

An eruption of anger. "Gorse is right. This isn't fair," declared Deneuve, throwing a protective arm around Lania's shoulders. "Captain, I'm sorry, but I can't sit still and listen to this any longer and she shouldn't have to either." To Yorell she continued, "This child is no more a threat to the galaxy than his rainbow-colored wagon is. She isn't even a natural mutation of our species. She's a victim of the Thryggians, just as her parents were."

That got both Reyota's full attention. "A victim how, exactly?" demanded D'Ull.

Still hugging Lania, Deneuve made herself taller in her chair and stared a challenge at him. "She's the last generation of a Thryggian genetics experiment performed on unwilling test subjects."

Curiosity. "A genetics experiment?" Yorell echoed. "To produce what? What else can you tell us about her?"

After a moment's hesitation, Deneuve replied, "When I analyzed her DNA, I found anomalies, some of which were also present in Ixbeth's nucleic material."

"So, the Thryggians have been purposely attempting to create beings with Kularian psi powers?" said Yorell, throwing a triumphant look in D'Ull's direction.

"Purposely? That would be hard to say," Deneuve remarked, visibly choosing her words. "But considering how determined those Thryggian pirates were to reclaim Lania's parents and then Lania herself, I would strongly suspect that they had anticipated she would be special. They clearly wanted to keep her for themselves. It does suggest that someone with her extraordinary talents might have been the intended product of their experiment."

A sudden cocktail of dark emotions flooded the room, taxing Ixbeth's shield. The java was sweet, compared to the acrid taste that now invaded the back of her throat.

D'Ull was on his feet, confronting the Human healer. "Might have been?" he spat. "You strongly suspect? It suggests? But you don't know anything for certain, do you? You're guessing!"

Enough!

Ixbeth let out a growl, loud enough to command everyone's attention. This was her office and these were her guests. They hadn't come all the way from Earth space to be abused. Rising from her seat, she glared at D'Ull until he backed away from both her and Deneuve.

"She may not know, but I do," Yorell informed him stiffly. "This isn't a tribunal, Arfan. Just because a thing cannot be proven, that does not mean it isn't true." Picking up her cup, she settled onto a vacant seat. "I've been telling you for some time that there had to be another ship. Why else would the Thryggians have accepted their punishment so meekly? They didn't even try to appeal their sentence. It was because we were giving them exactly what they wanted — complete privacy in which to continue their work undisturbed. After what we've just heard, perhaps now you'll admit that I was right."

D'Ull remained standing, his attention now riveted on his mother. "*If* you're right, then they're one year closer to achieving their objective. It may already be too late to stop them."

"Not if we target the ship. And once again Avo'or has brought us together with everything we need to accomplish the task," she told him, indicating with a wave of her hand all the beings sitting around her.

Ixbeth glanced at Lania and was pleased to see the young one sitting erect in her chair, guardedly observing the proceedings.

Wariness. "Forgive me, Madame Councilor," Takamura broke in, "but before we are included in any sort of — activity? — especially if it involves the Thryggians, we Humans would appreciate some clarification as to its purpose."

He was asking to be enlightened. Her gaze filled with teacherly indulgence. "It's quite simple, Captain. The information your healer has just provided confirms a long-held suspicion of mine that the Thryggians may be in possession of a piece of Kularian psi-powered technology — in all probability a heavy ship capable of working the fabric of space. Recreating the Kularian genome in their laboratory would enable them to grow beings with the mental powers necessary to activate the device. Once they'd done that, the Thryggians would be impossible to keep imprisoned. They could make a space gate and leave their pocket universe anytime they wanted."

"But if, as you say, all the psi-powered ships were confiscated and scrapped—" Dedrick began.

"Several had been reportedly destroyed in battle," D'Ull explained. "However, the actual number was never verified. There was always a possibility — never proven — that one or two might have been hidden away as insurance just before the signing of the treaty. And it's a matter of record that Kula'as and Thrygg were allies during the Great War."

"We learned of the existence of one such concealed ship a number of years ago," said Yorell. "Now, thanks to you, there is reason to believe that a second lies secretly stored somewhere in the Thryggian system. In the interests of averting interstellar conflict, it is of paramount importance that this device be removed and destroyed as soon as possible.

"We could share our knowledge with the Great Council, but then there would be a Tribunal, which would not be in the best interests of anyone in this room — or outside it, for that matter. The Kularians would be retroactively penalized for falsifying the tally of their ships after the Great War, and Lania's existence would become known. If we notified the Reyot High Council, they would have no choice but to inform the Great Council. That leaves us with only one possible course of action."

"Are you suggesting what I think you're suggesting, Madame Councilor?"

Yorell drew herself up in a show of indignation. "Madame Councilor is suggesting no such thing, Captain. It would be highly inappropriate. However, private citizen Enne is proposing a clandestine visit to the Thryggian system, aboard your star ship."

Swelling anticipation. Apparently, mystery wasn't the only thing Humans enjoyed. Danger was exciting to them as well. "It sounds like an adventure. Normally, we would be glad to help. However, we have a Mitradean pilot aboard," he pointed out, "and a Council-approved itinerary that does not permit side trips. I suspect that could present an insurmountable problem."

"It won't be a problem," piped up Lania, instantly attracting startled looks from all the adults around her. "Odysseus is my friend. If I ask him for a favor, I'm pretty sure he'll say yes."

Bemusement. "Odysseus?" echoed Dedrick. "That's the pilot's name?"

"Well, no. His actual name isn't even a word, but we need to call him *some*thing. I thought Odysseus would be a good name for him. After I told him the story of Odysseus, he agreed with me."

"And what is this Odysseus's story, Lania?" Yorell inquired, smiling.

"Odysseus was a warrior in ancient times on Earth, who sailed far from home to fight in a war. He won a great battle, but he offended the gods. So they decided to punish him by not letting him go home. After the war was over, they ordered the winds and the currents to work together to keep his ship traveling all over the sea for a very long time."

Sadness. Yorell said, softly enough that she might have been talking to herself, "Yes, that is a very fitting name for a Mitradean."

———— «» ————

Half an hour later, the sound and aroma of Ellisan bringing a plate of freshly baked biscuits forced a temporary stay of their discussion. However, the eight beings in Ixbeth's office — including Lania, now feeling much braver and eager to "stick it to the Thryggians", as Commander Dedrick had so colorfully put it — had already struck a groundbreaking agreement to work together on the Reyot mission. It hadn't been an easy arrangement to hammer out. Listening to them bicker over details, Ixbeth realized that there was far too much disharmony for this ever to be more than an ill-fitting, short-lived collaboration. Then again, she consoled herself, it didn't have to be. It just had to hold together long enough to get the job done.

And she had to figure out a way to piggyback onto it the rescue of fifteen treaty-violating Kularians. It wouldn't be an easy task, but it could have been much harder. Thank the stars the entire Kularian community hadn't chosen to stay on Dimmla!

When the biscuits were gone, Ixbeth sent Ellisan back to the kitchen to return the plate, thus purchasing the mission team another half hour of privacy in which to continue planning.

"We don't need the original twelve senders," Yorell insisted. "With a bit of practice and Gorse's headnet, Lania should be able to direct enough psi energy at Ixbeth to run a Kularian ship and make and reseal a space gate. It's a stealth mission, after all, and the fewer beings who know about it the safer we'll all be."

"*Should* be able? We had better be a lot more certain than that before we commit to this undertaking," D'Ull declared.

"With your permission, Councilors," Takamura broke in. "We installed alien shields and weapons aboard the *Marco Polo* on the strength of a 'should be able' and Lania's AI used them to defeat nearly a dozen attacking Thryggian vessels. If Mr. Pirrit can confirm that what we're carrying is in fact Kularian technology...?"

"...then I might be able to enhance it, enabling the *Marco Polo* to create its own gate into Thryggian space. That would remove the need for the first psi-driven ship," Gorse offered. "No guarantees, but if it will simplify our plan and reduce our risk, I think it's worth a try."

Impatience. "And then what?" D'Ull sputtered. "Are you suggesting that we ride the Earth ship through the gate? Without knowing what will be waiting for us on the other side? Provided the Thryggians don't detect the incursion immediately and send a heavily-armed fleet out to intercept us, we still have to shuttle Ixbeth and Lania to wherever the Kularian ship is hidden, exposing them to danger all the way down. And even if we managed *that* without losing anyone, the *Marco Polo* would be left without a strong psi talent aboard to maintain the shields. The Earth ship would be completely open to attack, no matter which side of the gate it was on. And Ixbeth is smiling," he added, his exasperation a sharpness at the back of her throat. "Why are you smiling, Docent Minegar?"

She recomposed her features, then quietly announced, "Because I happen to know where there is a Thryggian vessel we might use to enter Thryggian space undetected."

"Impossible!" snapped D'Ull. "We found and destroyed all their ships before the Tribunal's sentence was carried out."

"Like the Great Council found all the Kularian psi-driven ships?" Yorell countered. Even his mother was tiring of him at this point. Ixbeth could taste her irritation, as well as his resentment. And his fear. He doubted that the mission could succeed and was probably wishing he'd gone back to Reyi'it when he'd had the chance.

Too bad. Ixbeth fixed her gaze on his glowering face and told him in her sweetest voice, "If Avo'or wills it, Arfan, nothing is impossible." Addressing the whole team, she added, "I also know where we can find a group of Kularians with strong psi talents who would be more than happy to help us on this mission and never speak a word about it later. But there's a condition."

Suspicion. "What's the condition?" growled D'Ull.

Picking her words carefully, Ixbeth explained, "These Kularians are pure-blooded, like me. They've decided not to return to Kula'as. However, their current situation is no longer tenable, so they must find another place to live. They'll need assistance in relocating. And our word that the Great Council will never learn about them. They'll keep our secret, but we'll have to keep theirs as well."

"Pure-blooded with strong psi powers," Yorell murmured. "They're scholars, aren't they? From Dimmla. That's how you know about them. Is it safe to ask what they've been studying?"

It wasn't, but pretending ignorance or refusing to answer would only raise other, more dangerous questions. So, Ixbeth replied, "They're just trying to make sense out of some ancient writings. My parents and litter-brother are with them."

Alarm, quickly muted. She turned in time to see Gorse consciously relax his shoulders.

Yorell traded looks with D'Ull, who then said, "All right. If they will help us to successfully complete this mission, then I promise that we'll find them a sanctuary and keep their existence a secret."

And if the mission failed?

It couldn't fail, Ixbeth decided. In fact, she refused even to entertain the possibility.

Chapter Nine

"Are we really going to do this, Captain?"

Takamura and Dedrick were sitting alone in the *Marco Polo*'s strategy room, several minutes before Dedrick's next duty watch began on the bridge.

Leaning back in his chair, the captain gazed benignly at his senior officer. "Are you having doubts about the mission, Commander?"

Dedrick thought for a moment before responding. In truth, he'd had reservations about it right from the start, when Yorell had so blithely co-opted everyone in the room, claiming that a deity had placed them there expressly for her to use. (She was like Abner in that respect. Anything that sat within his reach he'd felt he owned.) But Dedrick hadn't begun having serious doubts until Yorell verbally put the headnet on Lania and placed her inside the Kularian ship, in Thryggian space. What that might do to the child didn't matter. In fact, none of their lives seemed to matter to this alien, including the nearly two hundred Humans who made up the crew of the *Marco Polo*. All she cared about was completing her mission.

"I've been counting up all the ifs in the equation, sir. There are a lot of them."

"Agreed. The risk is great. But the reward — preventing interstellar war? That is enormous. And even if the *Marco Polo*'s contribution can never be revealed, it could only prove advantageous to have someone like Yorell Enne in our debt."

The captain was evidently looking forward to an adventure. Dedrick bore that in mind as he chose his next words.

"I've also been thinking about Councilor Enne," said Dedrick. "Mainly, I'm wondering whether this ship will be large enough to hold her."

Takamura chuckled. "It could be a tight fit. She certainly filled up Ixbeth's office today." After a beat, he went on, "The Prime Docent is a powerful woman on her own world, accustomed to taking charge, and she's made it quite clear that she considers herself to be the mission leader and the rest of us to be her subordinates. But it's just as clear to me that when one of us speaks up, she listens. She appears willing to compromise. And she strikes me as a realist. She calculates the risks, and she knows how high the stakes are for all of us. So, with or without Fleet Control's blessing, we are going to take part in this mission if we can, not just to help the Reyota but to keep Earth safe."

"Captain?"

There was a steely glint in Takamura's eyes. "The Reyota aren't the only ones who consider the bigger picture, Mister Dedrick. The psi-driven ship that we're planning to steal does more than establish shortcuts through space. If I heard correctly this morning, it's identical or nearly so to the one that was used to create the Thryggians' prison — a pocket universe containing a single star system, sealed off from the rest of the galaxy. The Thryggians are sociopathic spacegoing scientists. What does that suggest to you, Commander?"

Dedrick paused, turning over possibilities in his mind. "Scientists creating pocket universes for purposes of experimentation?" As the truth sank in, he turned widened eyes to his captain's face. "They could turn the whole galaxy into a laboratory. Planetary systems would become their petri dishes."

"And in the process, they could permanently separate the races from one another, making it impossible for an alliance to form against them. I believe Earth space would be a prime target, perhaps even the first target. Yorell said it herself: Humanity isn't controlled by the treaty and that makes us dangerous. We always thought the alien races avoided us because they considered us too inferior to associate with. In fact, it appears we make them nervous. I must confess," he added with a faint smile, "I find that idea rather appealing. We're like the barbarians on the outskirts of the ancient Roman Empire, our very existence a threat to those who wield great power because it's in our nature to resist domination."

"To free the slaves," Dedrick muttered to himself.

"What was that, Commander?"

"Nothing, sir. I was just thinking about Lania. It's one thing for her to ask Odysseus for a favor or psi-power her AI to operate our shields, but—"

"—but quite another to put her on a shuttle and drop her into Thryggian space. I understand, Commander."

Dedrick pulled himself to attention in his seat. "With respect, sir, I don't think you do," he said with quiet determination. "At fifteen, Lania is still too young to give informed consent. I am her legal guardian. If I feel that she is being pressured to take on more than she can handle, I have an obligation to protect her, mission or no mission."

As the words left his mouth, he knew what Takamura's response had to be. Dedrick was a command-level officer on a star ship. That put the lives of every being aboard her in his hands. He also had a professional responsibility to respect the chain of command, and to carry out the orders of his captain. What Dedrick had just done was threaten sabotage. It wasn't a wise thing for a career officer to say in any company, let alone to the one person aboard ship who outranked him. Dedrick braced himself for official consequences.

Takamura surprised him. Leaning confidentially across the corner of the table, he said, "Commander, this plan of Yorell's is in such a state of flux right now — all those ifs in the equation that you pointed out — that we could very well end up with something that doesn't include your cousin at all. As well, everything we've discussed could be moot if Odysseus refuses to cooperate. So why don't we wait and see what happens when Lania asks him for that favor?"

Immensely relieved, Gael responded, "Thank you, Captain."

"I haven't heard him speak more than a couple of words on the bridge," Takamura remarked. "Lania says they're friends. What do you think her chances are of getting him onside?"

"If the alien is answering to a name that she's given him, then they've certainly got a relationship. Don't know whether I'd characterize it as friendship, though — not until we see how he reacts when she asks him to break the rules for us."

"And we still know next to nothing about him?"

"I've questioned Lania a number of times about their conversations. He hasn't been exactly forthcoming with information about himself. In fact, it appears he's more interested in learning about *us*. However, from what he's told her so far, I gather that the piloting contract between the Mitrades and the Great Council is some kind of penance or debt repayment. The Mitrades make excellent pilots because they have a perfect sense of direction and they're able to share navigation data telepathically with one another whenever two of them get close enough together in space. Eventually, every Mitradean will be able to travel unerringly to every place that any one of them has visited."

"So, even if Odysseus has never personally been to Dimmla, he can still take us there as long as he's crossed paths with a Mitradean who has," Takamura said. "That's good."

"Maybe not, sir. It's possible that more than space coordinates might be exchanged in one of these data transfers. If so, other Mitrades and maybe even the Great Council could be alerted to the fact that a pilot has deviated from the terms of his assignment. A friend's request might not be enough to persuade him to take that risk and help us."

"You think we need to dangle a carrot to secure his cooperation?"

"I think it would have to be extremely large and very sweet before he'd take a nibble."

"Of course. Meanwhile, Commander Eberhart is waiting for you to relieve her on the bridge," Takamura informed him. As he stood up to signal the end of the meeting, he added, "Listen carefully to everything Odysseus says in your presence, Mister Dedrick, and keep me posted. Perhaps he'll drop a hint as to what kind of carrot might sway him."

"Aye, sir."

———— «» ————

"That is impossible," declared the little metal box. Its voice sounded upset. "It is forbidden for any ship to approach Dimmla."

"Forbidden? Why?" Lania asked.

Now the alien was looking agitated as well. His carapace was perceptibly darker, and his eyestalks were manically looping and swaying. "The Mitrades have sworn an oath. To bring a ship into that system would be a betrayal. I would be cast out," stammered the box.

"But there's already a ship there," Lania told him.

"Yes. A Mitradean ship. Only Mitradean ships enter that system," insisted the box.

"I'm sorry, but you're wrong," she said. "It's a Thryggian ship."

The eyestalks froze in place. "Thryggian? What is a Thryggian ship doing in Dimmlesi space?"

"We don't know. But we do know that it doesn't belong there, and we want to do the Dimmlesi a favor by getting rid of it for them. That's what friends do, Odysseus. They help each other out. We're asking you to do us a favor by piloting us to Dimmla."

"Do friends ask each other to die? Any Mitradean who brings outsiders to Dimmla will be cast out."

"Friends don't ask each other to die. But good friends are willing to take risks for each other. Sometimes they even choose to do it without being asked, so they can help someone they care about."

"Mitrades have no choices. All Mitrades are slaves. In perpetuity," declared the box.

Observing this exchange from the captain's chair, Commander Dedrick perked up at the last two words. "In perpetuity? And where have we heard *that* phrase before?" he muttered to himself. Whatever their penance, whatever the debt, it obviously had something to do with that damned treaty, which meant it had something to do with the war.

Lania straightened her spine and squared her shoulders before responding. "I've learned something important from the people on this ship. There are always choices, even when you don't think you have any. You told me you wanted to be free. Well, freedom isn't something that you're given. It's something that you choose. And it's like a muscle. It gets stronger each time you exercise it by making another choice. There's a choice in front of you right now, Odysseus. Free yourself or be a slave. What are you going to do?"

"You are a child. Everything is simple to a child. Black or white. Good or bad," the box complained. "You believe that one unlawful act can restore what has been denied to my entire race for thousands of years."

Smelling a possible carrot, Dedrick couldn't sit by any longer. "I'm not a child, Odysseus," he said, joining them at the navigation console. "Talk to me. What was taken from you after the war?"

The alien's carapace darkened by several more shades. "A home," replied the box. "Our world is gone. Now the Mitrades are few. We are not allowed to settle or gather in groups. We must remain in space, working as pilots aboard interstellar ships. When one assignment ends, another begins. Sometimes they are half a galaxy apart."

"You said you would be an outcast. It sounds to me as though you already are," Dedrick commented.

A pause, then, "Not outcast. Cast out."

Something clicked into place in Dedrick's mind. "Cast out. As in, kicked out the door and not allowed back in? Who would do that to you, Odysseus? The other Mitrades? The Great Council?"

The eyestalks drooped, and for a long couple of minutes the alien was completely inert. Feeling Lania's anxious gaze on his face, Dedrick kept his expression neutral. "All right, if you don't like that question, here's another," he said. "If we had a way to prevent the Great Council from learning that we had ever visited Dimmla, would you help us get there?"

They waited. Still no answer from the box.

"Well, this is useless," Dedrick remarked. "Maybe we'd better—"

"You have no way," blurted the box. "All Mitradean ships are given by the Great Council. If contracts are broken, if assignments are changed, the ships are taken back."

"And without a ship, you can't travel from one assignment to the next," said Dedrick, his skin prickling as the remaining pieces finally came together. "And you aren't allowed to make planetfall, so without the assignments to keep you moving around in space..."

"Space is all that is left to us. Space and death. Helping a friend is not a simple choice to make," repeated the box.

Lania's features puckered thoughtfully. "But how would they know that you've broken the rules? They can't be watching all the Mitrades all the time."

"No need to watch. They listen. They know where we go."

Of course, Dedrick realized. It was probably done remotely, using signal-emitting tracking devices. One planted somewhere inside each Mitradean ship would give the Great Council the ability to follow the movements of all of them as they traveled between assignments. As a bonus, once those ships were parked aboard the vessels being piloted, the Council could map *their* itineraries as well. And space the Mitradean pilot of any ship that had wandered off course.

Well, he thought grimly, as Takamura had said earlier, it was written right into the Human genome to resist domination. If being kept on an electronic leash and killed for tugging it the wrong way wasn't domination, he didn't know what was. However, the presence of tracking devices also suggested a way for the Earth ship to sneak out of orbit undetected.

"Lania," said Dedrick, "we need to leave Odysseus alone to work now. Go to our quarters and find something to keep you busy until my duty shift is over. We'll talk then."

"But—"

"No arguments, young lady. Just do it."

———— «» ————

Tension hung in the air of the strategy room like drifting smoke after an explosion. Dedrick sat to Takamura's right, across the table from Doctor Deneuve. Despite the fact that no one could overhear them, all three of them had leaned forward and lowered their voices.

"Commander Dedrick, are you absolutely certain about this?"

"I am, Captain. Odysseus practically told us straight out that the Great Council had bugged his ship, and that they've been tracking the *Marco Polo*'s movements as well since the moment we let him aboard. And if it were me, I wouldn't stop there. I'd put a tracking device on the pilot as well in case someone got the same bright idea as I just did."

Takamura paused reflectively. "It certainly makes sense. Assuming that our pilot is not overstating his situation for dramatic effect—?"

"I don't think he is, sir."

"Such a device could be anywhere on or inside him," Deneuve supplied. "It could even be organic technology, making it impossible to detect by noninvasive methods."

A speculative expression slid across Takamura's normally inscrutable features. Dedrick could practically hear wheels turning inside his captain's head. "Why don't we find out? You know, Doctor, as long as we're parked in orbit and the Mitradean has nothing better to do, wouldn't this be the ideal opportunity for you to expand your knowledge of alien physiology? We Humans are, after all, such an inquisitive race. You could take some samples, run some scans..."

"...check for foreign bodies inside the alien one?" She gave him a mischievous smile. "I agree, Captain. It would be a most enlightening way to spend my time."

"Indeed. And I don't see how the Great Council could possibly suspect us of having ulterior motives, since we already have information on two alien races in our ship's medical databank. However, detecting the device isn't going to help us much if we have no way to neutralize it. Commander, how certain are you of the Mitradean's cooperation?"

"Provided the carrot is tempting enough," said Dedrick, "and we can find a way to free him from the technology that's being used to control him, I'm pretty sure he'll join the mission."

Takamura leaned back in his chair. "Very well, then. If Doctor Deneuve can identify our pilot's 'foreign body', as she put it, then our next step will be to see whether one of our non-Human passengers is familiar with it and can supply the means to either detach the bug or clone it and turn it off."

"*If* she can find it. What if she can't? We're finished before we begin."

"If it doesn't show up in noninvasive scans then I'll switch to more aggressive diagnostic techniques, but I'll keep looking until I find it," Deneuve promised.

"Commander, we haven't come this far just to drink java and give a couple of Reyot dignitaries a tour of the ship. To help expand Human knowledge about Kula'as, the Great Council has authorized extended on-planet visits for several of our scientists. But I suspect that Ixbeth had something else in mind when she issued our invitation. She fought her way through a jungle of red tape to bring us here, so there must be something important at stake, something that matters to her personally. In any case, part of this mission to Thrygg is the rescue of her family's study group. We owe her too much to even think about giving up on that. So, in answer to your question, if Doctor Deneuve fails to detect Odysseus's tracking device, then someone else in our little cadre will have to try. We have no other choice."

Chapter Ten

The short-hopper was eight standard hours late returning from Kula'as with its four alien passengers. When it finally touched down on the *Marco Polo*'s landing deck, a committee of Humans was waiting to welcome it. Ixbeth could taste their trepidation right through the hull of the little craft. It mingled with the similarly uncertain emotions of Gorse Pirrit, who had sprung to his feet and loaded himself down with sacks of tools and technical gear in preparation for debarkation.

"You can stop projecting now," he growled at her. "I'm not one of your students, meeting Humans for the first time."

"But I'm tasting anxiety."

"Yes, about the mission. From what I've seen so far, the beings aboard this ship are going to be the least of our worries."

Ixbeth chose not to respond. It was easy to underestimate Humans. She'd once done it herself. But after living among them for a year, she had come to respect and appreciate how complex they were, and how well they hid their many strengths. Gorse would learn this too, in his own time.

Hearing the hiss of the hatch unsealing, she gathered her belongings and fell into line to disembark. The Humans' relief tasted faintly bittersweet as they saw that everyone they'd been expecting had arrived safely.

Dedrick was the last to leave the short-hopper.

Takamura greeted him. "Did you encounter a problem, Commander? Your transmission was a little cryptic and we were becoming concerned."

"No problem, sir. Our scientists were met at the landing field by a delegation from the Kularian Archives and transported away immediately. The return trip was delayed because a passenger had to go back to the Central Archives and fetch something," he explained, casting a significant glance at Yorell Enne.

"And you'll be glad that I did," she declared, holding out a small sack and giving it a shake. It made muffled clicking sounds. "When Commander Dedrick told us about your plan to clone the squawker that your healer found inside the Mitradean's translation device, I knew exactly what you would need."

"And what is that, Madame Councilor?"

"Please!" she exclaimed with only half-feigned horror. "No titles! As I said earlier, we are acting as private citizens in this matter. What would be a polite Human form of address to use in such a situation?"

"Human politeness actually dictates that we use your title. However, as you've rightly observed, familiarity might be more appropriate under the current circumstances," he replied. "How do you feel about being called simply Yorell and Arfan?"

She didn't like it. Ixbeth sensed the darkening of the Prime Docent's aura and was unsurprised to hear her bristle, "If there is no middle ground, then I suppose that will have to do. And I presume we're to continue addressing you as Captain?"

Takamura's expression remained benign. "That would be fitting, since the *Marco Polo* is my ship," he pointed out evenly.

Ixbeth braced for an explosion, but none came. The force of nature had evidently decided to behave herself for the sake of the mission. "Of course it is," she returned, her buried resentment a sourness at the back of the Kularian's throat.

Before any further barbs could be exchanged, Takamura ordered the meeting moved to the strategy room. "You were right, Docent Minegar," Gorse whispered into her ear as they took their places around the conference table. "Humans *are* more than they appear."

Yorell spilled the contents of her little sack onto the table in front of her. There were about a dozen items in total, none larger than a finger pad. Ixbeth saw some that shone like polished metal and others that gleamed like crystal. Most sprouted wires that reminded her of tiny legs. At least one resembled a capsule from the pharmacy in Medical Services.

"One of the things we collect at the Central Archives is invention prototypes," Yorell explained. "These are the first working models of every type of squawker the Great Council has commissioned. There is a good chance that one of them will match the device in the pilot's translator. If so, it gives Gorse a starting point from which to solve your problem."

"*Whose* problem, Yorell?" Takamura said, his voice ominously quiet. "Surely you'll agree that any problem that affects the mission belongs to us all."

Rising anger, savagely repressed. "You're right, Captain. I misspoke and I apologize."

He nodded a silent acknowledgement.

At this, Ixbeth breathed a little easier. Forces of nature could be ill-mannered guests, but the captain was evidently quite capable of asserting his own authority when necessary. They might come through this adventure unscathed after all.

"Doctor?" said Takamura. "You've studied the images. Is there a match on the table to the device you detected inside the translator?"

"That one comes closest." Deneuve pointed to something that looked more like a piece of jewelry than a signal transmitter. It was a pale yellow stone set in a piece of molded metal with six pinpoint-sized holes evenly distributed around its outer edges.

"Mr. Pirrit, are you familiar with this technology?" Takamura asked.

"Not yet, Captain, but I soon will be." Gorse scooped up the device and dropped it into the pouch at his waist. "If someone will show me to my workbench?"

"It will be my pleasure," said Dedrick. Ixbeth tasted their ebbing discomfort as they escaped out the strategy room door together.

Gathering the remaining squawkers back into their sack, Yorell produced a second, larger bag and laid it in the middle of the table. "These are the translation devices I promised earlier," she said, reaching inside and pulling out several metal disks, each the thickness of a finger and wide enough to cover the palm of a Kularian hand. "And this one is the reason I was invited to join the Reyot High Council." She plucked a smaller version of the Mitradean's metal box out of the sack and held it up to show them. "It's an improved version of the device currently attached to your Mitradean pilot. I revised and tested the programming myself. It can be used for communicating with a number of different telepathic races, not just the Mitrades. We shouldn't be needing it on this mission. However, Ixbeth has told me about your Human deity Murphy and his various laws, so I brought it along as an offering, to prevent anything from going wrong."

Amusement. To his credit and Ixbeth's relief, Captain Takamura managed to keep a straight face as he replied, "Thank you, Yorell. We'll treat this with special care."

"That would be wise, Captain," D'Ull warned. "Earth is not bound by the treaty as we are. Yorell and I are taking a huge risk traveling with you."

Irritation. "We aren't the only ones taking a risk, Arfan," Yorell corrected him, slicing off each word as though with a blade. "Captain Takamura answers to his planetary government for whatever happens to this ship and its crew. And make no mistake, we are leading more than two hundred sentient beings into danger."

D'Ull said nothing but had the grace to look sheepish.

Meanwhile, Deneuve had been inspecting the items on the table. "Tell us about these other devices, Yorell," she cut in.

The mood in the room shifted abruptly as the Prime Docent was cast once more in the role she most enjoyed.

"I have brought enough for every member of the team, plus a few extra. Not everyone speaks Galactic Standard, so these are personal translation devices, programmed with several vocalized languages that we might encounter during the mission. Thryggian, Dimmlesi, and ancient Kularian." Fixing her gaze on Ixbeth, she added, "Shortly after the Tribunal was concluded, I had a sudden urge to study them."

Ixbeth felt a shiver burrow under her fur. Yorell's sudden urge could only have been an instruction from Avo'or. The Kularian deity had foreseen what they were about to attempt and knew that they had to succeed. The Quest might have ended the cycle of concealment and brought the Children of Kula'as back home, but it had not yet achieved peace in the galaxy. There was still work to accomplish. And Yorell was correct — from this point onward, everything they did had the potential to go tragically wrong.

"You certainly are a being of many and varied talents, Yorell," Takamura was saying.

Smiling, she nodded acceptance of the compliment. "We are all students, and we are all docents. Life is a learning experience. And one doesn't get to be the Prime Docent of the Central Archives by limiting the scope of that learning."

⟨⟩

It took a lot of fast talking and at least one veiled threat to persuade Odysseus to return to Med Services for a follow-up examination. Deneuve had already seen how quickly he could scuttle on those eight legs of his and how devilishly hard he was to catch. She sealed the Trauma room door as soon as he'd crossed the threshold.

Yorell and Gorse were already there, waiting for him. When he saw them, his carapace seemed to explode in flashes of crimson, orange, and bright yellow. Mitradean profanity, Deneuve guessed, best left untranslated.

"There's nothing to be afraid of, Odysseus," she assured him. "Mister Pirrit just needs to make some adjustments."

"No more scans!" declared the box.

"No more scans," she repeated.

"No more needles!"

"And no more needles. I have all the information I need for our database."

"What adjustments then?" the box demanded.

It was a reasonable request. "You'd better tell him what to expect, Gorse," Deneuve advised. "Do it *before* you start pulling out tools from your kit."

"That sounds like the voice of experience," he remarked with a smile.

"It is. Believe me, you do not want to spook this little fellow."

"All right," said Gorse. "Odysseus, Doctor Deneuve found a tracking device inside your translator."

"They listen twice?"

"Yes. They don't want you to abandon your ship and go running off somewhere," he explained patiently. "We need to free you so you can help us to complete our mission. Yorell and I have cloned the tracking signal using another device. Now we're ready to activate it and turn off the one you've been carrying around in that little box. In order to do that, we'll need to open up the translator."

Another silent nova splashed reds and oranges all over the alien's carapace. He reminded Deneuve of a Human child fearing his first haircut because he was convinced it was going to hurt. It wouldn't, because Human hair contained no nerves. But the translator was grafted into Odysseus's neural network, transmitting signals back and forth. What if some of them went to sensory receptors? If the box had literally become part of the pilot's body, Gorse was talking about performing surgery without an anesthetic. That would make anyone curse a blue streak.

"I will be cast out," wailed the box.

"Only if you don't let us shut down that tracking device," Yorell pointed out sternly.

Deneuve winced. This was no way to talk to a frightened patient.

"Odysseus, look at me," she said, purposely positioning herself so the Reyot would be out of his view. "Has this box ever been opened before?"

"Once only, when it was attached," came the reply. "I was young. It was painful."

Behind him, Gorse and Yorell exchanged a look. "To install and activate the squawker," Gorse confirmed in an undertone.

"How long did the pain last?" Deneuve asked.

"Two years. They were very bad years."

"And have you had any pain since then?"

A pause, then, "No."

"That makes sense." Deneuve turned to the others and explained, "The graft sites would have been tender for as long as it took the translator to fully integrate itself into his body." Addressing Odysseus again, she said, "I do not believe that opening this box will cause you any further discomfort. Will you let us try?"

When the Mitradean hesitated, Gorse stooped down, putting himself at Odysseus's eye level, and assured him, "We'll go slowly, and if it hurts you, we'll stop."

"You're not a child, Odysseus. This is your choice to make, not ours," said Deneuve.

"I have a choice?"

It was the moment she had been waiting for. Before Yorell could say anything to spoil it, Deneuve told him firmly, "No one will force you. We are only asking for the chance to try."

"Lania Dedrick says that freedom is a choice. If I choose freedom?"

"Then you are also choosing to help us carry out our mission," said Yorell. At least the tone of her voice had softened.

Odysseus paused, all movement on his carapace stilled for a moment. At last the box spoke again. "And after the mission is completed?"

"Then you will be free to make other choices," said Deneuve, throwing a defiant glance in Yorell's direction. The Reyot gave no sign of noticing.

"In that case, I choose to let you try."

—— «» ——

At this late hour, the ship's mess was almost empty. Ixbeth was glad. She was in no mood to engage in casual conversation right now.

She had come to bring the cook a supply of Kularian foodstuffs, and he had very kindly set aside his chores and put together a lastmeal just for her. Sitting alone at a table near the galley door, she let her hands take over the business of getting the food to her mouth while she turned her thoughts inward.

Tal?

There was no answer. This was not the first time she had tried to reach him since leaving Kula'as, and his continuing silence was worrisome. She reviewed everything that she had done and said that day, searching for the misstep or poorly chosen word that could have caused him to cut off contact with her. That had to be the reason for his lack of response. She refused even to consider any other.

A hand appeared in front of her, holding a cup of steaming hot *caranth*. It was freshly brewed and fragrant with nutmeg. She gave the cook a grateful smile as he set the beverage down beside her empty plate.

"You can take this with you if you like," he said, and produced an airtight lid for the cup as well.

Good idea. Gorse had been hard at work since the briefing meeting and could probably use a sip of something right about now.

The corridors were deserted. She was able to run all the way to the landing deck.

Ixbeth found the engineer lying on his back with his head and hands inside the control console of the Mitradean ship. Still holding her cup, she surveyed the outside of the little craft. Its angle was slightly wider than on the wedges Krodus used when splitting wood into planks to build furniture. The memory made her restless. She hadn't seen or spoken to her parents in two years. Everything could have changed. Or perhaps nothing had changed. She wasn't sure which would feel worse.

Shaking off the rest of that unsettling thought, Ixbeth deliberately scuffed her foot in case Gorse hadn't yet sensed her presence. He was handling technology. She didn't want to startle him.

"How is it coming?" she asked. "I've brought some *caranth* if you want to take a break."

His voice sounded as though it originated from the far end of a narrow tunnel. "I've isolated the control components. Captain Takamura wants me to modify this ship to run on psi energy so it can be flown remotely. I thought it would be more complicated, but it isn't really so different from the *trada*. Is there something you need, Docent?"

She sighed inwardly. He was so formal around her. Anyone would think he was her servant.

"While we're on this mission, you can call me Ixbeth. And you can answer a couple of questions for me."

"I'll try," he said, making her wonder briefly to which of her requests he was responding.

"When you were chosen by the Oracle, you must have had nightmares."

Curiosity. Gorse slithered free of the console and sat up to look at her. "Yes, all the chosen ones did, every night leading up to the prophecy. I'm a defender, so mine were about a conflict. I was on a battlefield, surrounded by the dead bodies of warriors from a dozen different worlds and unable to lay my hands on a single weapon. It infuriated me."

"*Yours* were? You're saying there were different recurring dreams?"

"Yes. When it was time to choose companions, we gathered in groups and compared notes. The details were different in each case, but since the defenders in our group had all dreamed about battle and the scholars had all dreamed about an archives, we figured our nightmares had probably been influenced by the various domains we served. It wasn't the same in your community?"

For a moment Ixbeth couldn't speak. "It probably was," she said at last, venturing a smile, "but our guardians must have put a stricter meaning on the cycle of concealment than yours did. We never discussed our dreams with others, and we never chose companions."

Sympathy. "You were forced to travel alone," he murmured. "That's why you bonded with your twin."

She stiffened her spine. All the pure-blooded chosen ones had traveled alone. Besides, sympathy wasn't what she wanted right now. "I'm a defender too," she told him, setting the cup of *caranth* down carefully beside him, "and I've been trying to make some sense of all this."

"And by 'all this', you refer to...?"

"Ever since the Earth ship arrived, I've been wondering. Did you find any hidden meaning in your dreams?"

"Meaning? Certainly. But the Oracle's message seemed pretty transparent to us. 'Go on this Quest or the past will repeat itself, Great War and all.' What?" he added after watching her for a moment.

"Were there Humans in your nightmares?"

He frowned. "No. Why would there be? The Great War was fought thousands of years ago and—" Puzzlement. "You saw Humans in your dreams?"

"Before I'd ever met one. Humans fighting like warriors alongside Mitrades and Kularians and Nandrians. I didn't think much of it while I was on the Quest, but now— Gorse, it's giving me a bad feeling about this mission. What if Avo'or was sending me foreknowledge of times to come? What if he was warning me that we will fail? That there will be another war?"

"So you're a defender *and* a Believer? All right, then, Ixbeth, what if he was? Do you believe the future is engraved in stone and nothing we do can ever change it?"

"What I believe," she told him, picking her way through her thoughts as though negotiating a minefield, "is that the Quest isn't over for me. I think it's just begun."

"To be honest, I think we're all on a never-ending quest. I think it begins the day we're birthed and doesn't stop until we die. Most of the time, we don't even know we're on a quest until something happens to make us aware that who we are and what we do matters in the grand scheme of things."

"My brother once told me something similar to that. It came from the ancient book he's been helping to decode, the *Dr'rava Kula'as*. When I made reference to him earlier, you tensed up and your aura darkened. Why?"

"It wasn't him. It was—" He looked away, expelling an audible breath. "You mustn't repeat any of this within hearing of the Reyota," he said, turning back to gaze into her face.

"I won't," she promised.

Satisfied, he continued, "When I was a kit, my eldest-father died and my elderfather had the chore of redistributing his belongings among the family. He asked me to help. Eldestfather had been a clothworker. Buried deep in a bin of woven materials we found a cloth sack, and inside the sack we found a well-used copy of the *Dr'rava Kula'as*. I sensed fear and surprise from my elderfather and asked him what was wrong. He instructed me never to reveal to anyone that Eldestfather had kept this book, because it had been forbidden to own it back on Kula'as. Tell me, how long has there been a brotherhood of scholars on your birth world?"

"Always. My father is our Guardian of Time. He once told us that the brotherhood had arrived on Dimmla at the very beginning of the cycle of concealment."

"They probably split up and went on a number of different ships to ensure that some of them would be able to continue the work. According to my elderfather, also a Guardian of Time, the brotherhood was a secret society on Kula'as. It had to be, because studying the book was a direct violation of the treaty. The *Dr'rava Kula'as* teaches us how to purify and master our innate mental abilities. When the war was over and the Great Council ordered every copy of this book to be found and destroyed, the original brotherhood was formed. The members worked quickly to make and conceal encrypted versions of the text so that the wisdom contained in the *Dr'rava Kula'as* would not be lost. Different scholars worked on different parts, using different encryption keys, and some chapters were doubly or even triply encoded, to ensure that none but the most dedicated Kularian scholars could unlock their contents."

There had been no secrets on Dimmla or Altera, other than those contained within the book itself. As Ixbeth's mind replayed the discussion in her office, dread welled up and began gnawing like acid at the very heart of her being. "I never spoke its name. I never even said what it was."

"You didn't have to. Yorell is an authority on the past. She knew what you were talking about and told D'Ull telepathically. It showed on both their faces. She probably suspected your Dimmlesi scholars were the brotherhood even before she asked what they were studying. That's why she worded her question so carefully."

"D'Ull made me a promise," she persisted.

Gorse's expression became fierce. Meeting his gaze made her feel as though strong hands had clamped onto her head and shoulders, preventing her from turning away. "Also carefully worded. Ixbeth, listen to me. When this mission is over, they'll leave me alone because my skills may continue to prove useful to them, and they'll leave you alone because you're famous and there would be repercussions if you simply disappeared. But my eldestfather's eldestfather was part of the brotherhood on Kula'as before the Oracle ordered us all into hiding, and I grew up with a different recounting of history than you did. Trust me when I tell you that the Reyota have no intention of rescuing your family. I saw the look that passed between Yorell and Arfan just before he agreed to meet your condition. Once the mission is completed, the 'sanctuary' he offers will probably turn out to be a scattering of cells on some deserted moon."

The air was suddenly thick with urgency. "I have to warn my brother," she said. "I've been thinking to him but—"

"He won't answer? It's best if he doesn't. The Reyota are telepaths, and your bond with your brother is telepathic as well."

"They can listen in?" she whispered, horrified.

"Yorell's range will be shorter than D'Ull's because of the difference in their ages, but yes, the Reyota can eavesdrop on any telepathic conversation taking place close by. As a social courtesy, they generally refrain, but—"

Without warning, Ixbeth's leg joints dissolved beneath her. Gorse leaped from the ship and caught her. He lowered her gently to the deck, his aura brimming with sympathy and concern. Then he leaned his back against the vessel's outer hull and slid down to sit beside her.

Staring numbly into his face, Ixbeth said, "After the Tribunal handed down its sentence to the Thryggians, Yorell supervised our training with the psi-driven ship. She was around us constantly for nearly a moontide, and I was in contact with Tal the whole time."

"Then she's known for a year that you and Tal are bonded, and that someone on Dimmla had to be studying the book. There's no other way your telepathic link could have reached that far."

"If I can't warn them, then what *can* I do?"

"Right now, nothing. We have a mission to complete. Yorell and D'Ull won't move on the brotherhood until they're no longer useful. When that happens, we'll need to have a plan in place."

"But won't the Reyota—?"

"No. Yorell can't read your casual thoughts, or mine. They can only connect with other telepaths. Kularians aren't telepathic. We're tel*em*pathic. And the brotherhood are a lot more than that."

Suddenly suspicious, she ventured, "Gorse, by any chance are *you*…?"

He smiled. "We'll be a good team, Ixbeth."

Chapter Eleven

This was the go-or-no-go meeting, and the air in the strategy room was heavy with tension as the mission team went through their prelaunch checklist.

"Your pilot is onside?" demanded D'Ull, one elbow pinning the table top as though to prevent it from escaping.

"Our pilot is ready, willing, and able to navigate to Dimmla," Deneuve replied. "His carapace is currently a festival of colors, and the translator is buzzing and beeping nonstop."

Concern. "Is the device not working properly?"

She grinned. "I think that's just what happiness sounds like in Galactic Standard."

"What about the Mitradean ship?" Yorell cut in.

Gorse reported, "It has been modified to the captain's specifications and tests out perfectly. By my calculations, it has enough fuel to maintain a high orbit for almost four full moontides. The Human scientists visiting the surface of Kula'as are sufficient reason for the *Marco Polo* to remain parked here for that length of time. Odysseus is going to synchronize our orbit with the planet's rotation, keeping us beyond the range of the scanners at the airfield so we can depart undetected. As long as no one tries to contact the ship while we're gone, our secret should be safe. When do you expect we'll be returning?"

The Reyota exchanged a meaningful look. Another telepathic conversation, Ixbeth guessed. "Barring complications, we should be back well before anyone becomes curious enough to investigate," Yorell assured him. "Arfan and I have taken a travel leave from the High Council. It's something we do periodically, so it shouldn't arouse any suspicions. Ixbeth—"

"—is spending time with the Humans aboard this vessel for research purposes, in preparation for writing a textbook," Ixbeth interrupted her. "During that period, Ellisan will be assisting the other docents at the Archives. I've told the Council of Docents that I'll be unavailable for as long as the Earth ship remains in orbit around Kula'as."

All eyes turned next to Gorse, whose expression was a mask of indifference.

"No one is going to miss me if I'm absent for a while," he said.

"No one? But what about your family on Kula'as?" demanded Ixbeth. "What about Salven, your superior at the transportation factorium?"

"Salven *is* my family on Kula'as. We're sibs, and she's accustomed to seeing me come and go without explanation. I'm often away for moontides at a time. As I said, I won't be missed," he concluded, giving each of his final words equal emphasis.

Dissatisfaction. Nonetheless, Yorell did not challenge his answer. "And your crew, Captain? We know that this is an exploration craft, and that you're accustomed to granting them opportunities to visit the worlds you discover. Are you planning to do that when we arrive at Dimmla?"

"No. Not all crew members get to explore every new planet we come across. In any case, my people understand how diplomatically significant this voyage is, so shore leave of any duration is being regarded as a special privilege, extended only to the authorized few. The scientists currently visiting the Archives have been fed a suitable cover story and are under strict orders to maintain the fiction that we are still in orbit. The rest of the crew have been told that we're ferrying Ixbeth back to her birth world for a reunion with her family, whom she has not seen in two years. Any additional officers required for the mission will be briefed and sworn to secrecy on an as-needed basis. Any necessary revisions to our 'official explanation' will be made as we go. And now it's my turn to ask questions," Takamura announced, getting to his feet. "Mr. Pirrit, what can you tell us about the alien technology already installed on this ship?"

"I've had a look at your modified shield generator, Captain," he replied, "and I've inspected the workings of Lania's computer." He paused, appearing to savor the taste of the expectancy his words had created.

"And?" prompted Dedrick, clearly in no mood for suspense.

"The technology is not Kularian, but you definitely have Kularian shields."

Unease. Takamura shifted his weight from one leg to the other. "What does that mean, exactly?"

Gorse paused again, visibly searching his mind for the right words. Finally, he said, "Are there Humans who need no instruction because they understand instinctively how to do complex things?"

"Yes," Deneuve told him. "We call them naturals. If they're children, we call them prodigies."

"Then Lania is an engineering prodigy," declared Gorse. "In her computer I found wires made from different metals fused together in very specific ways and wrapped in a variety of manufactured materials. Each metal has its own characteristics and limitations, but when alloyed and carrying psi energy through a synthetic conduit— It's as though she knew intuitively how to assemble Earth-made substances to duplicate the properties of alien components. Quite remarkable, actually."

Impatience. "Can you alter this hybridized technology to enable the *Marco Polo* to open a Gate into the pocket universe?" Takamura wanted to know.

"You mean a space gate? No, but I can supplement it with a compatible form of Kularian technology, and that should do what we need. First, however, we'll have to segregate the Human and non-Human technologies from each other aboard the ship. Ideally, whenever one of them is operating, the other should be completely shut down."

Alarm. "Completely? Including life support?" demanded Dedrick.

"I did say 'ideally'," Gorse replied. "What you have to understand, Commander, is that we're talking about a greedy technology. It's like a living creature with a gluttonous appetite for energy. We Kularians can provide it with a generous supply of psi power, but if the beast becomes aware of the ship as another source of nourishment, it will feed on that as well."

"As it's done once before," remarked Takamura, "destabilizing almost every system. All right, then. Order some emergency drills once we're under way, Mister Dedrick. Let's see how low we can dial everything down without endangering the passengers and crew." Addressing Gorse once more, he asked, "And how does the computer fit into this?"

"The last time the shields were activated, Lania was the sender and her computer was the controller," Gorse explained. "Together with all the energy that the shields drained from the ship, that was sufficient to activate and maintain them. Creating space gates requires much more power, and that in turn demands an organic lens to handle it. On a Kularian ship there were usually twelve senders, plus one very strong talent to focus and direct the psi energy. We don't have twelve senders. Instead, we have two naturally strong talents, one of which has served as a focusing lens before. That's why I brought the headnet with me. It will increase Lania's psi output to the equivalent of a dozen Kularian senders, and the only resonance patterns Ixbeth will have to integrate will be Lania's and the ship's."

Dedrick opened his mouth as though to speak, then closed it again, his aura darkening.

"So, you can make this work?" said the captain.

"I believe I can," Gorse confirmed.

Satisfaction. "Then we're a go," Takamura announced to the room. "In four standard hours we'll plant Odysseus's vessel in orbit and depart for the Dimmlesi system."

"You seem to know a great deal about psi-driven technology, Pirrit," commented D'Ull, scowling, as the meeting broke up.

Unexpectedly, Gorse grinned at him. "That's because I'm a natural, Arfan."

———— «·» ————

The *Marco Polo* had been in space for nine days, an uneventful journey that had given most of her crew little more to do than find ways to pass the time. The Shared Programmable Activities room had been a busy part of the ship. So had the learning center in the community sector. A new Earth History course was proving to be quite popular. And Dedrick had reread Forrand's datawafer three times, vowing each time never to look at it again because it gave the lie to everything Humans thought they knew about the past — doing to him, in essence, what Yorell had done to Gorse and Ixbeth back on Kula'as.

Dedrick had always believed that knowledge conferred power, but even that assumption was turning out to be wrong. It was raw information that translated into power. Knowledge — in particular, secret knowledge — simply sat on the mind like a scab, itching and tugging, begging to be picked at. He'd thought once or twice about sharing some of it with Leslie Eberhart, then dismissed that as a bad idea. There was enough tension between them already.

"Commander? I think we're here."

Pulled from his thoughts by the voice of the communications officer sitting behind him, Dedrick lifted his gaze to the forward viewscreen.

The *Marco Polo* had just emerged from a Gate on the margins of a system with four planets and eleven moons, seven of them circling the blue-gray gas giant farthest from an orange dwarf star. The first planet was an airless rock, burned brown by stellar energy and pocked and dimpled with craters. The second and third were medium-sized and too many shades of green to count. One of these two worlds had to be Dimmla.

"We are here," Odysseus confirmed through his translator box.

His gaze fixed on the screen, Dedrick instructed the comm officer, "Summon the captain to the bridge, Mister Brandt."

Moments later, Takamura stepped out of the tube car. He paused to take in the display on the viewscreen, then came alongside the captain's chair. Dedrick had vacated it in deference to his rank, but Takamura remained standing. "Now what?" he asked.

"Now we wait," said the box.

As they watched, two gray dots emerged from behind one of the seven nearest moons and sped to meet the new arrival, acquiring a familiar wedge shape as they drew closer. These Mitradean ships were much larger than Odysseus's vessel, however, and they were armed.

"Weapons are locked onto us, Captain," reported Harding from his console.

"Odysseus?" Takamura murmured.

"They will challenge before firing," the box assured him.

"Open comm channels, Mister Brandt."

"Aye, sir."

Immediately they heard the stentorian voice of the craft sitting almost nose to nose with the *Marco Polo*. "Alien ship! You are in a forbidden sector of space! Withdraw at once or we will destroy you!"

Dedrick glanced at the tactical display and felt his skin begin to crawl. As he'd suspected, the second ship had taken a position below them, its weapons targeting the *Marco Polo* amidships. The community sector. More than half the crew were there, engaged in off duty activities. Blissfully unaware of the mortal danger they were in.

"Mitradean vessel, I am Captain Hiromasu Takamura, commanding the Earth ship *Marco Polo*. We have come on a mission of mercy and ask that you let us land shuttles on Dimmla and Altera."

There was a long pause. At last, "You come from Kula'as," the other pilot declared, his translator sounding like the voice of doom. "You come for the Kularians."

Dedrick and Takamura traded looks. Evidently, the prolonged silence had been a telepathic exchange of information.

"And for the Thryggian ship that crashed on Dimmla," Takamura added.

"No. We protect Dimmla. That one is ours," came the reply.

"That one?" Dedrick repeated.

"Mitrades hate Thryggians," Odysseus told them. "This pilot believes you intend to rescue the crew."

Takamura frowned. "How do we convince him to let us have the ship?"

"You cannot," said the box. "I can. Be quiet, please."

Dedrick's jaw nearly dropped. *Please?* Politeness was a first for this alien. Perhaps their Humanity was rubbing off on him.

"Captain, they're standing down their weapons," Harding reported.

"Earth ship, you have clearance to land on both planets."

"What did you tell him, Odysseus?" demanded Takamura.

"Everything Lania Dedrick told me," the box replied. And that was apparently all the answer they were going to get.

《》

They went to Altera first, parking the ship in orbit and sending a short-hopper down to the planet's surface. At Gorse and Ixbeth's request — and over the objections of the Reyota — Takamura had assigned Dedrick, Lania and the two Kularians to make the initial contact and recruit the brotherhood for their mission.

"Set us down there," said Ixbeth, pointing through the viewport to the large swath of green adjacent to the Archives building. It wasn't a smooth or easy landing, but Dedrick kept everything right side up. As soon as he'd cut power to the thrusters, she reached out telepathically.

Tal, we're here. Two Humans and two Kularians. We have a proposal for the brotherhood.

Bring your group to the docents' main meeting room. We have a proposal for you as well.

How are Mother and Father?

Waiting, with the others. Do not delay. There is much business to discuss.

Curiosity. Added to her own, it created a strong, smoky-sweet taste at the back of her throat. "What now?" said Dedrick.

"Now we go inside. Follow me."

The moment Ixbeth's feet touched the ground outside the shuttle, her sense hairs stiffened in warning, and her fingerclaws tried to extend. This place was not her Altera.

Everything about it felt wrong. The air was too cold and the breeze much too strong. It swept in gusts across the commons, whipping the tall grass into a punishing frenzy. Even the light was harsher than she remembered. Forced to squint, Ixbeth peered around her at student habitats and outbuildings that seemed to hunker down against the weather like stolid sentries. The Archives building stood apart, pale and resolute and somehow reproachful. Reflexively, she felt a pang of guilt for having left it to suffer this fate.

"Are you all right, Ixbeth?" Gorse asked, raising his voice to be heard over the wailing of the wind.

Tasting his concern, she forced her lips to curve in a smile. "Yes," she shouted back. "They want to meet with us. It's over there."

The little group began making its way toward the front doors of the central building. Gorse trekked beside Ixbeth, matching her pace, as the others struggled along behind them. Dedrick gathered Lania to his side and kept a steadying arm around her shoulders. They had to pick their steps carefully across the footpaths that serpentined outward from the Archives. Burgeoning vegetation had heaved and angled the stone tiles, turning once-level ground into a series of obstacles.

As the landing party neared the entrance, one of the doors swung inward, admitting them into the reception area. Ixbeth remembered it as a bright and bustling hub of learning, bubbling with laughter and ideas. Now it was a cold and empty cave with passages leading away from it into a seemingly endless gloom.

"Is this the right place? It looks dead," Dedrick remarked.

Deep sadness. "It isn't," said Lania, speaking up for the first time since they'd boarded the short-hopper. "It's just lonely. It knows it's being left behind."

Ixbeth gave her a sharp look. "They're waiting for us in the docents' meeting room," she said, adding as an incentive, "It's warmer there."

With that, she picked a direction from memory and set off at a trot, trusting the rest of the group to follow.

The meeting room was hard to miss, especially in the dark. The door had been left ajar, releasing a shaft of light into the hallway to serve as a beacon. Ixbeth quickened her pace when she saw it. The others broke into a run to avoid falling too far behind her, and all four of them dashed across the threshold as though finishing a foot race.

The light in the room was unnaturally bright. It took a moment for her eyes to adjust, but eventually Ixbeth was able to see the beings whose auras she had sensed out in the corridor. They were sitting on benches around a polished wooden table that occupied most of the room. It was one of her father's pieces — Krodus's work was distinctive.

For a moment, all those expectant stares seemed to pin the newcomers in place.

Then, "Perfect timing," declared Dallia. Ixbeth's mother leaped to her feet and gestured to them to approach. "You must be chilled to your bones. Come have some hot *caranth* with us."

In no time, space was made, seats were filled, and cups of steaming beverage appeared. Ixbeth sipped slowly and let her gaze wander around the table, noting the presence of her father and brother, as well as almost every docent she'd been assigned during her five years as a student at the Archives. Only a handful of these Kularians were unfamiliar to her — the four wearing purple robes who sat together at the head of the table, emanating austerity.

The brotherhood, Tal confirmed.

Instinctively, Ixbeth turned her eyes away from their faces as Ellisan's title for her came to mind. *Doshaya medhane.* In this case, it more fittingly applied. And it explained a lot. The social imperative to mute one's emotions in the presence of other empaths was bound to intensify around such august and intimidating beings. Her parents were probably waiting for a private moment in which to express their happiness at seeing her again. At least, she hoped so.

"Welcome back to Altera, Ixbeth Minegar," said Docent Ribara, breaking into her thoughts. "Tal tells us that you've been awarded the title of docent. Our congratulations! In what discipline, if I may ask?"

"It's a new discipline," she replied. "I'm the Docent of Human Studies at the re-established Archives on Kula'as."

"A new discipline for the new era," commented Docent Quibbo, adding with amusement, "And you've brought along a pair of visual aids, I see."

Chuckles rolled up and down the table, but Ixbeth — and the brotherhood, she noticed — didn't share in the merriment.

Of course not. They had business to discuss. Filing away her doubts and speculations, she got down to it.

"This is Watch Commander Gael Dedrick, a senior officer on the Earth ship *Marco Polo*. It will be your transportation away from this system," she announced, with emphasis on the second sentence.

"We've come to help," Dedrick added earnestly.

"And we are grateful for that help, Watch Commander," said one of the brothers. This was the leader, Ixbeth realized. His voice, like his aura, was deep and warm.

Sensing a telepathic prompt, Ixbeth continued the introductions. "Lania Dedrick is the commander's defendee, and Gorse Pirrit is a returning Kularian and former chosen one. According to the Reyot Prime Docent, they are the two most dangerous beings in this arm of the galaxy."

There was a snort of laughter, too quickly stilled for Ixbeth to identify its source.

Another of the brothers spoke up in measured tones. "The Earth ship carries Reyota." It wasn't a question.

"It does complicate the process," a third observed, "but it may open further possibilities."

"It may," the first brother agreed. "Watch Commander, I believe you have a proposal for us?"

"I do, sir. The Reyota are convinced that the Thryggians have one of the psi-driven ships your ancestors used during the Great War, and that they're manipulating Human DNA to produce beings with Kularian psi powers to operate it for them. Lania is a product of that experiment, and she has already demonstrated her Kularian abilities. To thwart the Thryggians, we are on a mission to retrieve the ship from its place of concealment in the Thryggian system, and we are asking for your help to ensure that we succeed. In exchange, Prime Docent Enne and her son, Reyot High Councilor Arfan D'Ull, promise to find your entire group a safe and private place where you can continue your studies. They also swear to keep your existence a secret, especially from the Great Council."

Tal, don't trust the Reyota. They know what the brotherhood have been working on and have no intention of letting them finish. Warn the others once we've left. Gorse and I are formulating a plan to save you.

Tal's amber eyes widened briefly, but he did not respond. Meanwhile, the brothers were passing looks back and forth. Ixbeth stole a glance at Gorse. He was nodding. To himself? Or was he—?

"Indeed," said the fourth brother with evident distaste. "The Reyota are well known for their secrecy. And for giving themselves preferential treatment at every opportunity. But truth has a habit of seeking the light. Soon everyone will know."

"I don't understand. Are you turning us down?" Dedrick asked.

"No," the first brother replied. "We are making a counterproposal for you to take back to your ship. Look around this table, Watch Commander. What do you see?"

"Besides the four of us, I see fifteen Kularians wearing robes, one red and the rest blue or purple."

"In our society, red is the color of a defender and blue is the color worn by a scholar," the brother explained. "Those are inherited domains, not necessarily each being's day-to-day work. Dallia is a defender, but also a midwife, and for the past year she has been growing and preparing our food. Krodus is a scholar, but also a furniture maker. He has been maintaining our living quarters. It is the same with all of them. They wear blue because they are the descendants of scholars, and to honor that heritage they agreed to stay behind and make it possible for the four of us in purple to focus exclusively on studying the ancient writings.

"We four are the brotherhood. We are all you'll need to accomplish your mission, and we will happily join you in that endeavor if, and only if, those who have helped and served us during the past year will be permitted to return to their ancestral home world afterward. We chose seclusion long ago, and being isolated from society for an indefinite period of time is acceptable to us. To these others, however, it would be an undeserved hardship. They should be allowed to resume living their lives."

"You want us to transport them to Kula'as once the mission is over?" said Dedrick. "I don't see a problem with that. But what about you? Won't you still need the kind of support they've been providing?"

"Perhaps," the third brother replied. "In any case, we're certain the Reyota will make appropriate arrangements for us."

Carefully worded. Carefully omitting all mention of Tal, who had been studying under the brotherhood for years, and of the docents, all full-time scholars whose wearing of blue was anything but symbolic. Ixbeth had even heard Docent Ribara quote from the *Dr'rava Kula'as* between lectures. A shiver of excitement mingled with trepidation rippling through her, she darted a glance around the table. Every face was smiling. Every aura was serene and confident. Evidently, the brotherhood had devised their own plan, and all was well in hand.

Still, the pure-blooded Kularians on Dimmla had decided a year earlier not to return to Kula'as. They'd been convinced that their presence on the home world could only lead to bloody conflict. Had something changed?

Tal? What has happened here?

Don't worry, Ixbeth. The brothers know what they're doing. It will all come clear very soon.

The first brother took a deliberate sip from his cup and added, "There is just one more thing."

———— «» ————

"What is this?" demanded D'Ull, thrusting the compupad back into Commander Dedrick's hand.

Returning from Altera, the contact party had found Captain Takamura and the Reyota waiting for them on the landing deck. Ixbeth sampled the auras of the two Councilors from Reyi'it and was glad they'd yielded to Takamura's authority and stayed behind on the *Marco Polo*. D'Ull's temper and Yorell's high-handedness — not to mention their telepathic eavesdropping ability — would only have prevented meaningful communication, making it all but impossible to get the brotherhood onside.

"It's a written agreement," Dedrick explained. "The scholars that Ixbeth told us about call themselves the brotherhood. They understand that we're asking them to undertake a dangerous mission, one from which they may not return. While they're perfectly willing to risk their own lives on the strength of a verbal contract with the two of you, they want to ensure that their household staff arrive safely home on Kula'as once the mission is over, regardless of how it turns out."

Curiosity. "These scholars have household staff?" Takamura echoed.

"Yes, sir. There are eleven Kularian helpers in all, including Ixbeth's family. They've been making sure the brotherhood are well cared for over the past year, so now the favor is being returned." Looking directly at D'Ull, Dedrick continued, "The four scholars in the brotherhood are trusting that the Reyota will keep their promise and make appropriate arrangements for them if they survive the mission."

"This is ridiculous," D'Ull fumed. "It's a secret mission, unsanctioned by any government. How can they expect us to sign a written agreement when, by definition, there can be no documentation of any kind?"

"Actually, it all seems quite reasonable to me," said Dedrick, handing the compupad to his captain. The Humans were enjoying this. Ixbeth could taste their amusement.

Takamura scanned the text briefly and passed the device along to Yorell. "It's been worded specifically to avoid getting us in trouble with the Galactic Great Council and either of our planetary Councils. Well done, Mister Dedrick."

"Thank you, sir, but the brothers deserve most of the credit."

Frowning, Yorell pored over the document. "It contains no mention of the mission or the *Marco Polo*. It does stipulate a time frame, however, and it makes Arfan and me personally responsible for delivering the eleven helpers safely to Kula'as." She raised her head to stare with narrowed eyes at the Human officer. "Commander, did you tell them we were here?"

"They knew even before we arrived that the *Marco Polo* had Reyota aboard. All we did was supply your names for the final draft of the contract."

D'Ull made an impatient sound. "This whole discussion is a waste of time. A document drafted by Humans and recorded on a Human-made device is unenforceable outside of Earth space, since Earth is not part of the Great Council."

"Be that as it may, the brotherhood wanted me to tell you that this is the deal-breaker. If we want their help, you both have to sign the contract." Dedrick gave them a helpless shrug.

"It doesn't have to be stored on a Human-made device," the captain added. "We can export the finished product to any technology you wish."

D'Ull's expression darkened. "Outrageous! Dictating terms to us? Who do these scholars think they're dealing with?"

"With all due respect, Councilor, it sounds to me as though they know exactly who they're dealing with," said Gorse quietly.

The Reyota were cornered, and Yorell, at least, knew it. "Sign it, Arfan," she instructed him with a sigh. "Let's just finalize this and get them all on board so we can proceed with the mission."

Chapter Twelve

Once the Kularian passengers and their belongings had been satisfactorily tucked into guest quarters aboard the *Marco Polo*, Commander Dedrick piloted the short-hopper to Dimmla. As directed by Ixbeth, he set the craft down in a clearing on the edge of the former Kularian community. Yorell handed out translation devices to the landing party. Then they all jogged cross-country to the site of the Thryggian crash, half a kilopace away.

Even from the ground, it was hard to miss. Ixbeth winced when she saw the damage.

The Mitradean who had escorted their shuttle had advised them of what had happened. The Thryggian vessel had plowed a wide furrow across two meadows and bowled over a stand of trees before bouncing up and diving nose first into the middle of a *lalava* bean field ripe for harvesting. Fortunately, the only casualty on the ground had been the crop, but to the Dimmlesi that was bad enough. An unnatural metal object had dropped from the sky, disrupting the harmony of their lives and disfiguring the beauty of their garden world. Now this obscene chunk of technology was stuck in the ground, tipped at ten degrees and with strange appendages hanging off it at odd angles, and the only way to remove it was to bring in more technology and tear up the field even further. This was unacceptable to the Dimmlesi. To prevent the Mitrades from trying it anyway, the Prefect Major had posted guards to watch over the affected area.

The Dimmlesi were tall and physically powerful, much more imposing than the holograph stored in the Central Archives' forbidden files had seemed to suggest. Ixbeth already knew what to expect, having been born on this planet. For the rest of the landing party, however, it was going to be a first contact situation.

She had done all she could to prepare them. Nonetheless, nervous murmurs followed her as she stepped closer to address one of the guards. Already towering over her, he reacted to her approach by spreading his arms wide and puffing out his plumage in a territorial display.

Murmurs became gasps. She sensed a hand reaching toward her, ready to pull her to safety. She waved it away and stood her ground. She was not a stranger on this world. She refused to behave like one.

Ixbeth spoke to the guard in his own language, informing him, "I am Kularian, born on Dimmla, and we are here to rid this field of its abomination."

Hearing this, the Dimmlesi relaxed his feathers and dipped his head, peering closely at each alien face in turn. There were three Humans in the group this time. Besides Commander Dedrick, Takamura had sent Deneuve along in case the Thryggians needed medical attention; and Gorse and Lieutenant Tsieng, the ship's Chief Engineering Specialist, were there to assess the condition of the downed craft and devise a means of salvaging it. Yorell had insisted on being included as well, claiming it was to ensure that the translators and earpieces were functioning properly. Ixbeth had sampled her aura and knew better — the Prime Docent just wanted to see a Suhore in the flesh.

"And what race is this?" the guard demanded, tipping his head at the three in uniform.

"We're Humans," Dedrick replied. He squared his shoulders and threw out his chest. A second later Tsieng and Deneuve followed suit.

Before the guard could react to what Ixbeth hoped was an unconscious imitation of his warning stance, the Prefect Major arrived. The Dimmlesi were cross-country runners, like the Kularians. This one came galloping toward them from the direction of Turvanen, the closest thing the Dimmlesi had to a city. He was wearing a cape Ixbeth recognized. It had been fashioned from a piece of cloth woven by her brother.

The Prefect halted in front of the guard, turned to face the landing party, and announced, "Welcome, visitors! The Mitrades have told me of your purpose and I am happy to see you. When can you leave?"

Ixbeth understood what he meant. The Dimmlesi tended to omit from their conversation information that was already known by both parties. She just hoped the rest of the group were managing to keep up.

"First we must examine and assess the situation. What is the condition of the Thryggian crew? Are they still inside the ship?" she asked.

The Prefect Major deferred to a second guard, who replied, "Still inside, maybe alive, maybe not. A Mitradean tried to open the hatch but failed. No one has tried again."

"The crew probably locked themselves in, scared for their lives," Dedrick said, breaking into the discussion. "I can't say I wouldn't have done the same under the circumstances."

The first guard made a huffing sound, expressing approval. This admission of fear apparently canceled out the Humans' earlier challenge.

"If the Thryggians were injured in the crash, they might be too weak by now to reopen the hatch themselves," Deneuve pointed out. "We have to find a way to get them out of there."

But Ixbeth had been monitoring the Prefect Major's aura and knew what their top priority had to be. "First, we need to move the ship from the middle of this field to a different location."

"We have anti-grav packs aboard the shuttle," Tsieng suggested. "They're for onloading freight. Using all of them at once, we might be able to lift that thing straight up into the air. Then we could simply push it to where it has to go."

"More damage to the ground?" demanded the Prefect Major.

"If this works, there'll be a few more footprints in the soil, but that's all," the engineer assured him.

All three Dimmlesi were huffing now.

"Sounds like a plan," said Dedrick. "Let's do it."

———— «» ————

The Thryggian craft supported by eighteen anti-grav columns might once have had landing gear attached. It was difficult to discern where bracing could have been anchored on an outer hull that appeared to be little more than a patchwork of metal bits. Or maybe those strange appendages were meant to serve as legs on the ground, in which case the access hatch would be facing downward. Not what he would consider a practical arrangement for a ship this small, Dedrick mused, but it was an alien vessel, after all, and who knew how any alien's mind operated?

What had the Dimmlesi been thinking, for example, as they stood idly by, watching three Humans and two Kularians struggle to control the path of the Thryggian ship, which had been lifted half a meter above the ground by the anti-grav packs but retained every gram of its mass? (Predictably, the Reyot had stood aside as well, "giving herself preferential treatment" as one of the brothers had put it. She reminded Dedrick of an old Earth joke: "I love work. I could watch it for hours.")

Unassisted, the landing party had somehow managed to steer the huge metal egg back to the clearing where the short-hopper sat parked, and then bring it to a halt without so much as knocking a leaf off any of the nearby trees. Perhaps the Dimmlesi emotional repertoire didn't include gratitude, but surely this feat deserved some recognition from the two guards who had followed them back to the landing site? Instead, the guards had just huffed a couple of times and wandered off, making this officially the strangest first contact situation Dedrick had ever been part of.

Once the Thryggian vessel was in place, Tsieng stabilized it by dialing down the anti-gravs, letting part of its weight settle onto the grass. Then he and Gorse Pirrit took turns trying to open the hatch. After struggling with it without success, they turned their attention instead to inspecting the outside of the ship. Dedrick watched them walk around it, shaking their heads, occasionally placing a hand on the hull or pointing things out to each other.

"Well, gentlemen?" he asked when it appeared they were done.

"This is one very alien ship design," Tsieng declared. "There's no sign of external thrusters, and the outer hull is such an asymmetrical patchwork that it's hard to see where there might be ports concealing them. We know the Thryggians flew through space to get here, so this craft has to contain some sort of propulsion system. That's all I can say about its workings without getting inside for a look. As for the exterior…" He blew out a breath. "This egg crashed hard, Commander, and hull integrity has been visibly compromised. Without first making extensive repairs, I wouldn't advise even attempting to fly it."

Deneuve came over to join the discussion. "We need to evacuate the crew immediately. I just attempted to contact them on all frequencies. If there's anyone still alive in there, they aren't responding to a commcall."

"Let me try something," said Gorse. He reached into the sack at his waist, pulled out the headnet, and put it on. Then he returned to the Thryggian craft and carefully placed his palms against the hatch door, holding them there for a moment.

"There is life inside. I'm sensing one aura, but it's faint," he called over his shoulder to the others.

Struck by a thought, Dedrick called back to him, "Can you use psi power to unlock the hatch?"

Gorse returned hurriedly to the group, shaking his head. He glanced around before replying in a lowered voice, "I know it can be done. It requires a level of mastery that I don't possess but the brotherhood might. If we were able to bring one of them down here without the Reyota finding out why, then maybe—"

"Leave Yorell to me," Ixbeth cut in. "I know how to keep her busy and happy for at least the next few hours." With a smile, she explained, "The Prefect Major is wearing his cloak. That means it's market day in Turvanen. The favor we just did them has barter value, and I've been craving some Dimmlesi food."

⸻ «» ⸻

The Thryggian craft was too large to fit inside the short-hopper — it would have to be towed. Under the pretext of needing additional gear, Dedrick had flown back to the *Marco*

Polo for an urgent private conversation with its captain and the senior brother. Twenty minutes later, the shuttle left the landing deck, carrying some hastily gathered hardware in the cargo compartment and a purple-robed passenger in the copilot's seat.

The flight back to Dimmla was quiet. The brother spoke only to inform Dedrick that he should be addressed as Noris, and that he had been studying the ancient writings for a very long time, longer in fact than anyone else in the group of fifteen had even been alive.

Noris projected an intimidating presence. It drew attention and discouraged it at the same time. It halted conversations and froze people in place. From the access hatch of the short-hopper, Dedrick watched three beings drop everything and silently study Noris's progress as he crossed the clearing in long, rapid strides.

He halted an arm's length from the Thryggian craft. For a moment the Kularian scholar gazed at the downed ship. Then he placed one hand in the center of the hatch door and the other immediately beside it, lowered his head, and went still. Every other being in the clearing remained statue-like as well. No one moved a muscle or uttered a syllable for a good two minutes as he worked.

At last, they heard the hiss of a seal breaking. Noris removed his hands and stepped away. There was death inside that ship. Dedrick could practically see the stinking cloud that escaped from the hatch as the door sank inward and slid aside.

"We have a survivor!" bawled Deneuve. "Let's get him out of there!" And as though a vid had been unpaused, everyone leaped into action.

Everyone except Noris. He stood back, his gaze fixed on Gorse Pirrit. Gorse stopped and stiffened, as though he'd been physically struck. He lifted his head and returned the look. Then he broke eye contact and dived into the Thryggian vessel to help the others.

—— «» ——

Laden with sacks of produce, Ixbeth and Yorell returned to the landing site in time to see the end of a gurney disappear into the cargo compartment of the short-hopper.

Deneuve had been overseeing the transfer process. She glanced up at their approach and said grimly, "Two dead, one barely alive. Their cockpit is a mess. You'd better climb into the shuttle. We're returning to the *Marco Polo* right away."

Yorell pulled up short when she caught sight of Noris, already occupying one of the front seats. Dedrick saw this but decided to disregard it. There were too many other things vying for his attention at that moment.

Once everyone was aboard and the towing matrix was solidly engaged, he wasted no time lifting off. In short order, they were back on the Earth ship.

A trauma team was waiting on the landing deck to offload the Thryggian patient, and a suited-up decon crew stood ready to process the cockpit of the Thryggian vessel after the two space-frozen corpses had been removed from it. These would be sent immediately to the safelab to be vacuum-sealed and stored in a refrigerated vault. Later, they would be left on one of the planets in the Thryggian system. At least, that was the plan.

"Commander?"

Dedrick pivoted, searching for the owner of that anxious voice, and found Able Spacer Alex Topsias standing near the landing deck door, wringing her hands. The youngest uniformed Human aboard the *Marco Polo*, Topsias was the closest in age to Lania. She had therefore been assigned to keep the commander's cousin entertained and out of trouble when Lania had first arrived aboard ship. A year later, the crew member still drew that duty on occasion, albeit informally.

"Sir, I'm so sorry. I just—"

"What is it, Alex?"

"It's Lania, sir. I think she's gone into hiding again."

"You *think*, Able Spacer?" Dedrick's raised voice brought Ixbeth and Deneuve over to investigate.

"Well, she left her wristcomm in her quarters and— It was a mistake to leave her alone, I know that now, but Ensign Petersen was very definite and Chief Eames needed all hands and it was just for an hour—"

"Whoa!" Dedrick interrupted. "Slow down, Topsias. Once more, from the beginning."

Alex took a tremulous breath. With tears in her voice, she explained, "We were together in your quarters when Lieutenant Hammersmith buzzed me from the bridge to tell me the chief was looking for me. When I asked if he knew why, he said that you had just lifted off from the planet with the Thryggian ship in tow and one crash survivor on board, and Ensign Petersen wanted all details to suit up and prepare the landing deck for decon."

Dedrick's heart began spiraling slowly downward. Unfortunately, this was starting to make sense.

"Lania went very quiet then," Alex continued. "I asked her if she was all right. She told me she was tired. She went into her sleeping module to take a nap and I went to report for decon duty. After an hour I got permission to go check on her. But by then she was gone. All I found was her wristcomm lying on the bed. I've looked everywhere for her, Commander, I swear! I even got Engineering to run a life signs sweep, but it didn't pick her up. You — you don't think she's—"

"She's asleep, Alex," Ixbeth assured her. "The healing sleep is one of her talents. It slows down every part of the body, bringing it almost to a halt. When she wakes up, she'll be fine."

No, Dedrick thought bleakly, she wouldn't. It was one thing to salvage a crashed Thryggian ship to use on their mission. It was quite another to bring its Thryggian passenger home with them just one year after fighting a pitched battle to keep this traumatized girl out of Thryggian hands. He was her guardian, charged with protecting her. Instead, she had every right to feel that he'd betrayed her.

"*Que je suis idiote!*" Deneuve said with audible disgust. "She was finally opening up to us. Now we've driven her right back into her shell."

"This is all my fault, Commander. I should have realized something was wrong," Alex blubbered.

"Relax, Topsias," Dedrick told her. "No one is blaming you. You were on duty. You were given orders by a superior and you followed them."

"We have to find Lania," Deneuve decided. "And Ixbeth must try to reach her. She needs to understand that she's still safe, still among family."

"First things first, Doctor," said Dedrick. "You have a critically injured patient who can't be entrusted to anyone else's care. And I have a few places to check that Topsias might not have thought of."

———— «» ————

Half an hour later, while Dedrick and Ixbeth were still searching the ship, Takamura and the rest of the mission team received an urgent summons from Deneuve in Med Services. They arrived almost as a group. Gorse was followed closely by Noris, who took up a position just inside the entrance to the Trauma room. Odysseus scuttled in as well, stopping at the foot of the bed, then rearing up on his back legs and extending his eyestalks to give himself a better view.

"The Thryggian is barely conscious," Deneuve advised them, "and he's fading quickly. If we're going to get any information out of him, it will have to be now."

This was not the first time any of them had seen a Thryggian. It would, however, be the first time they had watched one die. Healthy, a Thryggian was physically unimposing but deceptively strong. About the same height as a Mitradean, he would have had a naturally blue-gray complexion, a large hairless head with bulging eyes, a rounded belly, and stumpy arms and legs. Near death, this Thryggian made a pitiful, child-sized lump under the blanket. His head on the pillow was the color of parchment, and his eyes were sunk deep in their sockets. His scalp was etched with troughs made by blood vessels collapsing beneath his skin. His beak-like mouth opened and closed as he worked to pull air into his damaged lung.

When the team had gathered to stand over him, the patient opened his eyes.

"Where am I?" he gasped.

"You're aboard the Earth star cruiser *Marco Polo*," Deneuve replied, "in orbit around Dimmla."

"An Earth ship ... in Dimmlesi space?" His gaze moved with growing alarm from face to face around his bed. "Human

... Kularian ... Mitradean ... Reyot ... working together against us? We are betrayed..." he moaned, turning his head weakly from side to side, "...betrayed..."

"Your race is the one that betrayed everyone else," D'Ull declared.

"No," said the Thryggian, his voice sinking to a whisper as he continued, "They promised amnesty ... but there was no forgiveness. All were punished ... and it never ends... Make diseases, they ordered us... Make them sick. Make them die... Keep their numbers small so they won't attack..."

"Who gave this order?" Takamura demanded. "Who were they afraid of?"

"They are here." And with that, the Thryggian closed his eyes and expelled a final, raspy breath.

«»

"Nothing has changed," Yorell informed them stiffly.

The team had come together in the strategy room, without Noris and Odysseus this time, and minus Deneuve, who was dealing with a situation in Med Services; and Captain Takamura was leaving no doubt in anyone's mind as to who was really in charge of this mission.

"You're mistaken, Yorell. Everything has changed," said Takamura. "Commander, since you are here, I trust that you have located your cousin?"

"Yes, sir. We found her in a corner of the arboretum, curled up unconscious behind a tree. She's been taken to Med Services."

"A fatally injured Thryggian comes aboard and this child is frightened enough by his mere presence to put herself into a coma. By now it should be blindingly clear what a huge mistake it would be to send Lania Dedrick into Thryggian space," the captain continued. "The damaged craft is still undergoing decontamination, but Tsieng and Pirrit tell me that there's a good chance it will never fly again. And we just heard a deathbed confession that casts doubt on the motives and integrity of every alien race represented on this ship. All of which leaves me extremely curious to know: Do you have a backup plan, Yorell? Or should we simply scrub the rest of this mission right now?"

Yorell and D'Ull exchanged a sour look.

"We do have alternatives, Captain," Yorell told him. "Our preference would be to send just two beings down to retrieve the Kularian ship — Ixbeth plus one other, a strong sender amplified by the headnet. She can focus and direct the energy—"

"No, she can't. Not by herself," Gorse interrupted.

"What are you talking about?" D'Ull snapped. "She's already done it once before."

"But not by herself," he repeated.

"Of course, we are aware that Tal helped her through their telepathic bond," said Yorell patiently. "And he can do it again."

"You're wrong," Gorse insisted. "Ixbeth and Tal didn't focus and direct all that energy. They couldn't. The brotherhood did."

"And you know this how, exactly?" said D'Ull.

Gorse leaned forward and stared directly into his eyes. "Because skills weaken when they are neglected for thousands of years. That is how long it's been since the treaty was signed, forbidding the Kularian race to use their psi powers to drive technology. And until last year, that is how long ago the last psi-driven ship was flown. No matter how strong Ixbeth's talent might have been, even combined with her brother's it wasn't powerful enough to do what you needed it to do. So, the brotherhood reached through the litter-twin bond and added their strength to hers, making it possible for her to create the pocket universe around the Thryggian system."

D'Ull's gaze acquired a dagger-like edge. "You're saying that without the brotherhood's cooperation, anything we attempt involving a psi-driven ship is bound to fail."

"Without their willing cooperation, yes."

"Including this mission," he persisted.

"Especially this mission," Gorse supplied cheerfully.

Even a Human could see the storm gathering in Yorell's eyes. "And we're expected to believe everything they've told you to repeat to us?" she said.

His brightness undimmed, Gorse replied, "No, quite the opposite. They're expecting you to go ahead and try to do this on your own. All docents being students as well, they are sure that it will be a valuable learning experience for you."

The room went quiet. Tension hung in the air like a dense fog.

Finally, D'Ull broke the silence. "All right, then," he said, spitting out the words and looking as though they had left a foul taste in his mouth. "No doubt the brotherhood have another condition to impose, now that we've conceded how indispensable they are?"

"Not a condition," Gorse assured him. "It's a proposed plan that is certain to succeed. Ixbeth stays aboard the *Marco Polo* with Lania, working the Kularian shields. The brotherhood create the space gate and then go down by themselves to retrieve the psi-driven ship."

Takamura's eyebrows arched momentarily. Then he let out an audible breath and said, "I don't think we have a choice in the matter, Yorell. Not if we want to keep that device out of the hands of the Thryggians."

"And what if we want to keep it out of the hands of the Kularians?" D'Ull returned.

"I guess that depends on which race you consider to be the greater threat," Dedrick pointed out. "My bet would be that it's the Thryggians."

"I agree," said Takamura. D'Ull opened his mouth to object, then met his mother's stern look and apparently thought better of it. "If the crashed ship can't be repaired, a pilot will have to transport them to the surface in one of our short-hoppers," the captain continued, "and then, of course, follow the Kularian vessel back out of Thryggian space."

"I can do it, Captain," said Dedrick.

Takamura shook his head. "I want to hear whether the metal egg is spaceworthy before assigning that task, Mister Dedrick. In any case, I believe you can make a more valuable contribution to this mission by remaining aboard the *Marco Polo*. That is where Lania will need you to be."

———— «» ————

Lania had found her focus and pulled herself deep inside, safe from danger. But she would never be safe from the fear.

She knew that now. For her, freedom was an illusion, and normal family life was an unattainable fantasy, just as Abner had said.

He'd been cruel, but he'd been truthful. There could be no happy endings for people like them. They were the products of an alien laboratory. Their Humanity was a deception. Their lives were a desperate fabrication, to disguise the fact that they were living in cages. Lania could run, but she could never escape. She could imagine the happiness of others but never win it for herself, because happiness withered inside a cage, and a cage was her reality.

Her life aboard the *Marco Polo* had been a year-long dream. Now a Thryggian had invaded it, turning it into a nightmare. And if she couldn't bear to stay asleep and she didn't dare wake up, what was left for her?

Why so afraid, little one?

Something was touching her thoughts, like a hand gently stroking her hair.

Is it death that terrifies you? Or is it those who have died?

She didn't recognize this voice. Where was it coming from?

I am a friend, it whispered. *I am of the same race as your defender. She cannot be constantly with you, but I can. I can help you conquer your fear. I can make you strong. But you have to wish it. Will you let me in?*

Chapter Thirteen

"Commander, I don't know how she knew that the survivor had died, let alone that there were three of them in total, but Lania just opened her eyes and insisted on seeing the corpses of the Thryggians from the crashed ship." Deneuve's voice over the comm sounded worried and excited at the same time.

She was right to be concerned, he thought. "You didn't show them to her, did you?"

"Of course not. Not without your consent, and certainly not without you and Ixbeth being present to provide support. Lania is very determined, though, and she won't be kept waiting for long. Is the meeting almost over?"

"I think so. We'll be there as soon as we can."

Six pairs of curious eyes watched Dedrick walk through the door of the strategy room and return to his seat at the conference table.

Looking directly at Ixbeth, he said, "Lania's awake. Somehow she knew we had three Thryggian bodies in cold storage. Now she's demanding to view them."

Ixbeth frowned. "And nobody told her about them?"

"According to Doctor Deneuve, who hasn't left her side since the medical team brought her to the Trauma room, no one else even came near her bed. So either Lania had an out-of-body experience while she was unconscious, or—"

"Well, Captain," Yorell broke in loudly, "perhaps the child isn't as fragile as you thought."

"Perhaps," he conceded. "But I prefer to make decisions based on facts, not speculation. Odysseus is ready to pilot us to the exact coordinates occupied by the Great Council's observer ship during the execution of the sentence on the

Thryggians. He tells me that we'll be passing through five space gates and arriving at our destination in approximately twelve days. That should give us sufficient time to iron out the details of our mission once we've received Mister Tsieng's report on the Thryggian craft. Until then, this meeting is adjourned."

Dedrick waited for Ixbeth to get to her feet. Then he leaned in and said softly, "We're needed in Med Services."

She followed him into the corridor and onto the nearest tube car. As the door closed in front of them, Dedrick turned to her and said urgently, "Please, tell me you didn't—"

"I couldn't, Commander. Kularians are not telepathic, except with a twin or with a mate. I can project emotion into her, but that's all."

He keyed in Medical Services as their destination. "And the Reyota?" he asked as the tube car lurched into sideways motion.

"Telepathy is like a language for them. They can only read the minds of other telepaths. I don't know much about this out-of-body experience that you refer to, but maybe—"

"No," he said flatly. "Someone put that information directly into her unconscious mind. If it wasn't the Kularian helpers and it wasn't the Reyota, then it had to be a member of the brotherhood. Whoever it was has crossed a line and needs to know it. Lania is a child, effectively *my* child, and I will protect her by any means necessary," he concluded, putting emphasis on the last three words.

Ixbeth drew herself up to her full height. "I'll make sure your message is delivered, Commander, I promise."

They rode the rest of the way in silence. After an uncomfortable few minutes, the door slid open again, depositing them in a corridor just outside the Trauma unit, where Lania and Deneuve stood face to face, deep in conversation.

"Are you absolutely certain about this, *chérie*?" They were in mid-argument — Deneuve's voice and expression were both strained. Guessing that the doctor had been stalling until he could arrive, Dedrick hurried over to join them, leaving Ixbeth to trail behind.

The youngster recomposed her expression, her lips forming a hyphen of determination. "Yes, absolutely. I can't conquer my fear by running away from it."

"That's very brave of you, but these alien corpses are not pleasant to look at," Deneuve pointed out. "They were terribly injured in the crash, and they died slowly."

"I still want to see all three of them, one at a time."

"All three?" Dedrick repeated. "Why?"

"Because repetition wears away the sharp edges on our emotions. It takes a lot more than three times to get rid of them completely, but three bodies are all we've got, so three times will have to do." She rhymed this off rapidly, as though reciting a memorized speech.

Someone had put these words into her mouth, most likely the same someone who'd broken into her unconscious mind. Her vulnerable, fifteen-year-old mind. The short hair on the back of Dedrick's neck came to attention.

"Where are you getting this from, Lania?" he demanded.

Her features contracted. "I'm not supposed to talk about it."

"Oh, really? And who gave you *that* instruction?"

"I'm not supposed to talk about him either."

Him?

Feeling Deneuve's steadying hand on his arm, Dedrick dragged in a deep breath and forced his voice to remain calm. "Why not?"

"He said you would be angry, and I need to deal with one fear at a time."

And he was right on both counts, Dedrick conceded. Nonetheless...

"What really makes me angry is not getting answers to my questions, Lania. I'm your guardian and I have a right to know who's been talking to you. Or in this case, thinking to you."

She pursed her lips briefly. "I don't know his name. I just know that he's helping me to be strong and not afraid."

"I thought *we* were doing that," Deneuve remarked softly.

"You are, Doctor," Lania replied. "You're doing all you can to support and comfort me, and I'm grateful for it. But support and comfort aren't as good as a cure. Can I please view the first dead Thryggian now?"

More of *his* words. Dedrick clenched his jaw. Deneuve threw him a resigned look, then turned and led Lania in the direction of the safelab.

Before Ixbeth could follow them, he stepped around in front of her, blocking her path. Startled turquoise eyes glanced up and met his gaze.

"A moment, Doctor Minegar?" he growled. Confident that he had her full attention, he continued in a low, intense voice, "You made me a promise earlier and I expect you to honor it. It's obvious to me that one of the brotherhood is inside Lania's mind. I don't care how benign his intentions may be — he's putting himself between me and a child that I'm sworn to defend. You're a defender too, so I know you understand what dangerous ground he is treading, even if he doesn't. Find out who this brain rapist is and tell him he's to get out of her head at once and stay out of it, or I'll see to it that the entire brotherhood pays for what he's done. Am I making myself clear?"

"Very clear, Commander," she replied evenly. "I'll begin making inquiries immediately." With that, she turned and stepped awkwardly back to the tube car.

"Where is Ixbeth?" Deneuve asked when Dedrick caught up to her and Lania.

His stomach cartwheeled when he saw the expression on the youngster's face. It was detached, disinterested — the way people looked when they were watching a vid or idly observing the activities of strangers. That was what they were to her as long as the Kularian intruder was inside her mind — kind, well-meaning strangers.

"Ixbeth had somewhere else to be."

Deneuve shot him a disapproving look. "Somewhere more important than here?"

There was no safe way to answer that question, so he ignored it, asking instead, "Shall we see whether Lania's new friend got it right, Doctor?"

———— «◊» ————

Tal!

Ixbeth? What's the matter?

You have to talk to the brotherhood. It's important.

I can't interrupt them. They're meditating right now.

Three of them are, perhaps. The fourth is in telepathic contact with Lania Dedrick and her guardian knows it. He's her defender, and he's furious.

Telepathic? You're sure it's not just a projection of courage?

He's thinking words to her, Tal, and she is repeating them to others. "Repetition wears away the sharp edges on our emotions." Does that sound familiar?

Yes. I once quoted it to you.

Humans are extremely protective of their offspring. The brother who is helping Lania needs to understand that Commander Dedrick sees this contact as an attack, a violation of her mind. If it continues, it will turn him against the brotherhood. If that happens, he may influence the captain to believe that they are a greater threat than the Thryggians. The brothers are in danger. You need to warn them.

Perhaps. Perhaps they already know.

What do you mean?

There was no answer.

—— «» ——

Deneuve had been understating when she'd described the appearance of the Thryggian corpses as "not pleasant to look at". Dedrick had already seen them close up, while removing the survivor from the crashed vessel, and that was quite enough for him, thank you. This time his thoughts were focused on Lania, on how she would react to the sight of their mangled and distorted faces, their broken, twisted limbs. Or just to the fact that these shrink-wrapped remains in the safelab's cold storage vault had once been living, breathing Thryggians.

He knew Lania was no stranger to death. She and Abner had had to burn and bury numerous plague victims on MF-307. And the brain rapist was right about one thing: repeated exposure to something did dull one's emotional response to it. But Lania was confronting more than death today. Today she was getting her first actual look at the race whose name alone had been used against her like a weapon for so many years. Today she was coming face to face with the bogeyman.

And, to his shame, part of Dedrick was hoping that it would make her collapse in tears and bury her face in his shoulder.

It didn't. Lania scanned the body on the pull-out shelf with impersonal eyes for a long moment before remarking, "It isn't as big as I thought it would be. Do they get smaller after they die?"

"No, this is a full-sized, fully-grown male Thryggian," Deneuve replied, pointedly adding, "the one who succumbed to his injuries in our Trauma room."

Lania tilted her head. "They're not scary at all when they're dead, are they? They're kind of fragile, even. I'll bet I could take this one apart without much effort."

Deneuve shuddered visibly. Dedrick felt the same mortal chill but managed to keep it inside.

"Not if he were healthy, you couldn't," he said. "Why would you even think about that, Lania? Is your new friend suggesting that you find a living Thryggian and pick a fight? Because, as your guardian, I can tell you with certainty that that is not going to happen."

She frowned. "Of course not. I still have two bodies to look at."

———— «》 ————

Gorse was not in his quarters or at his workbench in Engineering, and the Thryggian ship on the landing deck was still hours away from being ready for his inspection. Ixbeth followed a hunch and went to seek him out in the mess hall. He was there — she sensed his aura the moment she stepped inside the room. Glancing around, she found him sitting at an empty table, trying a serving of the cook's daily special. Today it was pasta and vegetables in a cheese-flavored sauce. Of course. It was a Fourthday, and Fourthday and Eighthday were meatless meal days aboard the *Marco Polo*.

Gorse glanced up at her approach and gestured to the seat across from him, inviting her to sit.

"How is it?" she asked as she lowered herself onto the bench.

"Passable. The flavor isn't unpleasant, and the vegetables are crunchy." He took another forkful and swallowed it thoughtfully. "But now I'm tasting anxiety," he remarked, setting his fork down on his plate. "Is there a problem, Docent?"

"Tal has cut me off again."

"We've been through this before. He doesn't want to be overheard by the Reyota."

"That's not it," she fretted, with an effort preventing her fingerclaws from extending. "We were having a telepathic conversation about one of the brothers and Tal just— There's a Human expression: he hung up on me. Then, when I went to his quarters to speak with him in person, he refused to see me. None of the others were available either. In fact, it appears you're the only other Kularian on this ship who'll have anything to do with me right now. So, you will have to carry my message to the brotherhood." She leaned closer and dropped her voice almost to a whisper. "I know that you and the senior brother sometimes think to each other. You aren't litter twins and you aren't mates. That means that one or both of you must have acquired the talent of bonding at will from studying the *Dr'rava Kula'as*. Don't bother denying it. Commander Dedrick has already figured out that the being who has been thinking to his cousin is a member of the brotherhood, and he is extremely angry about it. He demands that this connection with her be permanently severed."

"If she has accepted the brother's contact and is thinking back to him, then they are bonded, and bonding is for life. As the litter twin of a scholar, you should already know this, Ixbeth."

Shaking off Gorse's words, she tightened her voice, willing him to understand. "Listen to me. This is serious. Humans are limited to five senses, all physical. When I lived among them, my empathic talent was considered to be an intrusion on their emotional privacy. They tolerated it, but only because they knew I couldn't control it. A telepathic contact is different. It's not viewed by Humans as involuntary. To them, it's a deliberate invasion of their minds.

"The commander has made it clear to me that he considers this bonding with his cousin to be a criminal act, and he is prepared to do whatever is necessary to put an end to it. I am well acquainted with this Human, Gorse. He is a defender, and he does not make idle threats. Lania Dedrick needs to be unbonded immediately."

Frustration. "As I've just finished telling you, that's impossible."

Ixbeth got to her feet, placed her hands on the table, and leaned across it. "For you, perhaps," she said softly, "but not for a master of the mental discipline. If psi energy can break an unseen lock on the other side of a door, if it can reach through two minds and remotely operate a heavy ship from light years away, then dissolving an unwanted bond should be an easy task. And I'm guessing that that is something *you* should already know. Am I correct?"

Surprise, followed by resignation. "Sit down, Ixbeth, please." He waited for her to resume her seat, then told her, "You know I can't answer that question."

"You don't have to. I've seen what you can do, Gorse, and so have Yorell and D'Ull. Did you ever wonder why Avo'or called on a Reyot scholar to uncover the ancient ship that made possible the fulfillment of the prophecy? I've been thinking about that. It has also crossed my mind more than once lately that she wouldn't be much of a prime docent if she didn't have her own copy of the forbidden book to go with the forbidden files in the Central Archives."

He frowned. "Are you suggesting that the Prime Docent is actually a student of the *Dr'rava Kula'as*?"

"Not a student, exactly. I very much doubt whether she is doing it to improve her own mental discipline. What I suspect is that she has been attempting to decode the book in order to learn what a trained Kularian mind is actually capable of. Last year I dreamed that I was at an *ohe'elu* ceremony with my litter twin, and he said something in this dream that has only recently begun making sense to me: 'What we have are selfish neighbors.' Kula'as and Reyi'it occupy neighboring orbits. I think Councilor Enne is trying to determine how much of a threat Kularians pose to the security of her home world."

His expression hardened. "And if word reached the Reyota that one of the brotherhood had bonded with a child against the wishes of her defender..."

"...it would provide justification for whatever D'Ull is planning to do to them — and to the rest of us — once the mission is concluded. *Now* do you understand why it's in everyone's best interests to give the commander what he wants, as quickly as possible?"

Gorse digested this for a moment, then replied, "I don't have the authority to dictate to the brotherhood, but I'll do my best to convey the urgency of your request."

"I know you will," she assured him, and turned away from the table.

Just inside the mess hall door, she saw Dallia coming toward her with a smile on her face. "Ixbeth! The brotherhood wanted me to thank you for bringing them the fruit and melons from Dimmla—"

This was too much.

"I didn't do it for them, Mother," Ixbeth informed her coldly, then swept past her without another word.

———— «» ————

Summoned to the strategy room, Dedrick arrived to find Takamura already in conversation with Watch Commander Leslie Eberhart.

She glanced up as he walked through the door. Immediately, she tensed and turned away, directing her gaze to the polished surface of the conference table. Her blond hair was pulled away from her face and fastened at the crown of her head with the mother of pearl clip he'd given her a couple of years earlier for her birthday. For a moment his heart swelled with hope. She was wearing his gift, so she couldn't be *that* angry. Then he saw her expression — an impassive mask with eyes like smoky blue stones — and realized that yes, she could.

Dedrick sighed inwardly, wishing he'd never taken her into his confidence about the reason for his trip to Riviera Hub. That had apparently been his second strike. His first, the one that had chilled the air between them until he could practically see his breath, had been not letting her know that he had changed his mind about helping her brother Sam. But at least she hadn't frozen him out completely, the way she was doing now.

Once upon a time, they'd been lovers. Now? Let her in or keep her out — either way he was wrong, it seemed. This relationship business was tricky.

"Have a seat, Commander Dedrick," said Takamura, indicating the chair directly facing Eberhart's.

As Gael lowered himself onto it, Leslie finally acknowledged him with a brief, icy stare. It triggered an equally cold response in the pit of his stomach.

"I've called you both here because we need to agree on a cover story to tell the crew," the captain explained. "They can't be allowed to know the true nature of our mission. With all the secretive aliens we have aboard, there is already a great deal of speculation circulating that we may need to quash. Commanders, I am open to your suggestions."

Takamura leaned back in his chair, his gaze swinging expectantly between the faces of his two senior officers. He was far too intelligent not to have noticed that they weren't getting along. The captain was a patient man, Dedrick knew, but he had no tolerance for divisiveness. This conflict was recent. If it persisted, he would take action to end it, and his decision might not be to their liking.

Eberhart was the first to speak. "Our original story — that we were taking Doctor Minegar home for a reunion with her family — was simple and convincing, and from what I've gathered, most of the crew still believe it. There will always be a few skeptics in the crowd. Nothing we can do about that. So, I would recommend that we ignore the doubters and build on the credibility of the existing story using undeniable facts."

"Build on it how, Commander?" said Takamura.

"Fact: no one was expecting the kind of severe weather that the landing party encountered on Altera, including Doctor Minegar, and we know from our biofiles that she lived there for five years. Obviously, something cataclysmic is happening to this planet. It makes perfect sense that you would evacuate the remaining population.

"Fact: we already know that Human emotions give Kularian empaths terrible headaches. Doctor Minegar used to take refuge from them by sequestering herself in her quarters. Why wouldn't these fifteen new passengers do the same?"

"I see where you're going with this." And Dedrick continued, picking up where she'd left off, "Fact: our arrival at Ixbeth's birth world coincided with a Dimmlesi crisis. Since we had the wherewithal to help, how could we in good conscience withhold our assistance? Fact: the crashed ship and the bodies of its crew need to be returned to Thrygg. That is where we're now headed. It leaves out half the story, but it provides a plausible explanation for everything we'll have done before we go back to Kula'as."

"It also paints us in a very favorable light," Takamura remarked. "I'm sure Earth High Council and Fleet Control cannot object to anything that might earn Humanity a bit of good will from the aliens we encounter on this voyage. Nonetheless, I am not entirely comfortable about lying to the crew in a formal announcement, even if it does contain a grain of truth. There must be some unofficial way to disseminate the necessary information."

"There is, sir," Dedrick told him. "Leslie and I can arrange to have a discussion within earshot of some of the crew. We drop a few factual details, then let the rumor mill do its work. Word will spread quickly throughout the ship. Later, when we return to Earth space, you can decide whether and how to set the record straight."

"Very well," said Takamura with evident satisfaction. "Commander Eberhart, Commander Dedrick, you know what you must do next. And I need to be on the bridge. Good luck to you both." With that, the captain got up and left.

"Commander Eberhart," said Dedrick stiffly, "I believe that's our cue. Shall we go to the mess hall for a hot drink and a chat?"

"Is that an order, sir? You do outrank me by seniority."

He drew in and let out a breath. "Does it have to be an order?"

Her chin rose, her expression issuing a challenge. "I'm afraid so, sir."

"Then it's an order," he said, trying and failing to ignore the sinking sensation in his stomach. Regardless of her personal inclinations, Leslie could always be counted on to do what was required of her. So could Dedrick. But something told him that neither one of them was going to enjoy this cup of java.

———— ‹›» ————

Lania flopped down onto her bed and stared upward, into the dark. She'd purposely left the lights off inside her sleeping module. Being surrounded by blackness made it easier for her to picture her friend in her mind's eye, to pretend that he was in the room with her, not just inside her head.

She'd asked him to show her what he looked like, but he'd refused. So, she'd imagined a blank canvas and mentally drawn a face he might wear. When he laughed at it, she erased it and tried again. And again. Finally she produced an image that he approved of. This was the visage that she now projected into the darkness of her bedroom, an adult's face with round, ruddy cheeks and blue eyes sparkling with mischief, under a wild mop of curly brown hair.

Drovanu? she thought to him, using the word that he'd told her meant "my friend" in his own language.

I am here, Lania. You are well?

I am. I did what you told me. I looked at all three of them and pretended they were burned bodies pulled out of a pyre on Dedrick's Planet. I remembered how those bodies looked as though they'd never been alive, and I remembered how I felt inside when I saw them. And when I looked at the Thryggians, I made myself feel the same way. And it worked. I wasn't afraid.

Excellent! Now you have a weapon to use the next time fear tries to take you over.

And you're going to help me then too, right?

I've already helped you as much as I can. Now you need to help yourself. Anytime you are afraid, remember how you felt as you gazed upon the three dead bodies. Command that feeling to fill you up. It will free your mind from the fear, allowing you to do whatever you must in that moment.

But you said you would always be with me. You promised!

If you truly need my help, just imagine my face and think to me, and I will answer. But freedom means living your own life, making your own choices, taking your own risks, and solving your own problems as best you can. You have sacrificed a lot to win your freedom. Never give it away to anyone. Especially not to one like me.

Chapter Fourteen

After filling their cups with java, Dedrick glanced around the mess hall, searching for a likely group of eavesdroppers. He found a cluster of crew members chatting over their dinner at a table against the far bulkhead and nudged Eberhart in that direction. "Let's sit down over there," he said, pointing with his chin.

"Whatever you say, sir."

"Leslie," he warned her quietly, "this has to seem like a natural conversation or no one will believe a word of it."

She arched her eyebrows and gave him a feline smile. "Watch me and learn, *sir*."

With that, she turned and led the way to an empty table across the aisle from the one occupied by the designated rumor-spreaders. As she settled herself onto the bench, she declared abruptly, "I still say we should space them."

Dedrick nearly spilled their drinks. "Wh— what?"

He stole a sideways glance. All talk had ceased at the other table, where nearly a dozen diners had suddenly become extremely interested in the contents of their plates.

All right, then. She'd grabbed them an audience. Not the way he would have done it, but effective nonetheless. Now for the show.

With deliberate haste, he set their cups on the table, then stepped over the bench and sank onto it, facing Eberhart. "Keep your voice down, Commander," he scolded her in an undertone. "We have our orders."

"Come on. It's not as though we'd be killing anyone. Those Thryggians died when their ship crashed on Dimmla," she said, her voice just loud enough to carry to the other side of the aisle. "I can understand the captain wanting to make a humanitarian gesture, and I respect him for that. But for all we know, the Thryggians might just consider those three corpses to be garbage and get rid of them the same way. Whether we space them or the Thryggians space them, what's the difference?"

"The difference is that it will be the Thryggians doing it to their own. As you say, we don't know what their funeral rites are or how they treat their dead. But even if we did know, that does *not* give us the right to dispose of them however it suits us, not if there's a way to bring them home to their families where they belong!"

Eberhart stared at him, an unreadable expression playing across her features, and Dedrick suddenly realized two things: first, that he meant every word of his impassioned speech; and second, that he had been talking about more than Thryggian corpses.

"So, we're traveling all that way and risking the wrath of the Great Council just to make a pile of scrap metal and three dead aliens disappear? Seems like a waste of effort to me," she remarked softly.

Eberhart wasn't talking about the Thryggians either. Dedrick wasn't sure how it had happened, but suddenly they were having a very private conversation in a public place.

As an unaccustomed heat rose in his cheeks, he muttered, "I'm the only family she has, Leslie. She needs me. At least, I thought she did."

His java was cold but he drank it anyway, in large swallows.

Eberhart laid a hand on his forearm and continued *sotto voce*, "Oh, she does. Almost as much as you need her. It's okay to admit it, Gael. I understand."

He turned puzzled eyes to her face. "Then why did you—?"

"—disapprove of your reason for taking leave? Because I happen to think that throwing away your career should be a last resort, not the first thing you do when you're trying to help someone you care about." Lowering her voice even further, she added, "And because I need you too. It's bad enough that I may never sit in the same room as my brother again. I won't lose you the same way."

Dedrick risked a sidelong glance at the eavesdroppers' table. Crew members were excitedly chattering amongst themselves. Soon every unit on the ship would be buzzing about the Thryggian bodies being returned home for proper funerals, and about Dedrick's fierce defense of the captain's decision. And perhaps also about the fact that the two watch commanders had just spent long moments in whispered conversation, staring meaningfully into each other's eyes.

"I believe we're done here, sir," said Eberhart quietly, getting to her feet and moving toward the door.

Out in the corridor, he reminded her, "We never got around to mentioning the fifteen Kularians."

"I don't think it matters. We've thrown the grapevine into overdrive. At some point, someone will remember that you talked about taking the aliens home, and two plus two will become twenty-two. In the meanwhile," she said, pausing to give him an uncertain smile, "I'm not on duty for another three hours. If you'd like to spend them with me, there's a vid we haven't watched yet in my inbox and I've still got some cookies in my quarters. The ones Sam sent me for Christmas, filled with real strawberry jam."

He leaned backward, feigning shock. "Cookies? The ones you said I couldn't taste until hell froze over? You're willing to *share* them with me?"

"You can have one," she told him primly, "as a peace offering. I've been a little hard on you lately, so it seems only fair."

A *little* hard?

"Fair would be two cookies," he decided.

"A cookie and a video. Take it or leave it, Gael."

He took it.

For the next three hours they sat companionably together on her blue and white striped sofa, eating and talking while a lavish historical drama — her favorite genre — unfolded on Eberhart's light screen. Now Dedrick was thoroughly confused. Did this "first date" mean they were about to resume their romantic relationship? Or was it her way of letting him know it was over? He had no idea. But the snacks were tasty, and the conversation enjoyable, so perhaps there was reason to hope.

When the video was over, he returned to his suite, carrying a cookie as a treat for Lania and remembering Eberhart's parting words: "She's fifteen years old. She'll reach for your hand one second and push you away the next. You can't always give her what she wants. No parent can. Just keep giving her what she needs, and everything will turn out okay."

He sighed inwardly. What Lania needed was to forget her fears, and therein lay the problem. Not *that* she needed to forget, but *what* she needed to forget. Her fears weren't the lingering residue of a single traumatic incident. They had been instilled and relentlessly reinforced by Abner, day after day for the first twelve years of her life. Lania would have to forget almost everything that had made her who and what she was. Amnesia could be induced, but then she would become a mystery to herself, constantly feeling incomplete and driven to search for answers. Eventually she would find them, and the truth would reignite her fears, putting her right back at square one.

Lania's sleeping module was dark. Dedrick stepped quietly across the living area and placed the cookie on his desk. Then he leaned through the door of his cousin's room to check on her.

Lying on her back in bed, she turned her head and looked at him. "I'm sorry," she said in a small, whispery voice.

Dedrick's heart constricted. "For what, Lania?"

"For making you angry."

He closed his eyes briefly, then went to sit on the edge of her mattress. "I've never been angry with you."

She sat up, frowning. He half-expected her to pull away from him and was relieved when she didn't. "You *were* angry," she persisted. "I could feel it."

"Not at you. I get angry at anyone who might want to hurt you, or who tries to take advantage of you. Sometimes people pretend to be your friend so they can get close enough to take something away from you. It's my job as your guardian to keep you safe from beings like that."

"But he wasn't pretending, Gael. He helped me. I looked at those Thryggians and I wasn't afraid."

"I saw."

"And after that you were so angry you wouldn't even talk to me."

"That's because I wasn't sure who would be answering, you or him, and I didn't really want to find out."

She paused to digest this. "You avoided me because *you* were afraid?"

"Everyone's afraid at some point, Lania. What matters is how you handle that fear."

"He's gone away. He promised not to leave, but then he told me he couldn't help me anymore. Do you suppose maybe *he's* afraid?"

Dedrick smiled inwardly. *If he knows what's good for him, he is.*

―――― ‹›› ――――

"It looks like one of the plants in Doctor Tam's nursery." Lania peered into the thirty-centimeter-tall transparent cube sitting on Gorse's workbench in Engineering. Inside sat a fleshy brown bulb with things like tentacles radiating from a tuft of hair at its crown. They lay gray and inert on the bottom of the cube, each one long enough to touch one of the sides of the container.

It looked like a plant, but it wasn't. It was some kind of machine, like the control console in Abner's ship but immeasurably more powerful. Even out in the corridor, she had felt the raw energy sleeping inside that box. It had raced along her skin, made her nerves tingle — and drawn her irresistibly through the door and directly over to the table to investigate.

Gorse hadn't seemed surprised to see her.

"Where did this come from?" she asked him.

"No one knows for sure," he told her. "It's very old." A pause, then, "But that wasn't really your question, was it?" He turned and met her curious gaze. "The brotherhood brought it aboard. They're keeping it in a very deep sleep for now, but it's going to help us complete the mission." He studied her face for a moment more. "Ixbeth says that you have a special sense, that you're able to detect potential energy. Is that how you knew it was here?"

Lania frowned. "I don't know what potential energy means."

"She told me that you talk about machines as though they're alive, and for you, somehow, they are. A year ago, you 'woke up' a small ship and convinced it to protect you. You built yourself a computer that shares your feelings and won't work for anyone else. And when we were on Altera earlier, you sensed an emotion from the technology in the Archives."

"Yes. It was sad because it knew it was being abandoned."

"You have a rare and special gift, Lania. The rest of us make a clear distinction between the organic and the inorganic, but to you it's all the same."

"Yorell says I'm dangerous."

"Yorell is too busy enforcing the terms of the treaty to appreciate how unique you are. You're an evolved Kularian. You're a sample of what we might have become if we hadn't been forced to give up our psi-powered technology all those thousands of years ago. If your parents hadn't escaped when they did, the Thryggians would have created you in their laboratory. Your genome would have given them a blueprint from which to make many more like you. That's the prospect that truly terrifies the Reyota, and it's why the brotherhood had to come on this mission."

"To stop the Thryggians?"

"Among others."

——— «◊» ———

"According to Odysseus, we are approximately two standard days from the coordinates of the observation ship one year ago. Are we going to be ready?"

The mission team sat around the table in Takamura's strategy room, radiating a variety of emotions. Ixbeth tasted their auras. When she sampled D'Ull's, its darkness made her shiver inside. Her first impression of him had been correct. This being was capable of great cruelty, without a shred of remorse afterward. She hoped the same couldn't be said of the brotherhood, although she had lately begun to have her doubts.

"Mister Pirrit, what's the final word on that Thryggian vessel we salvaged?"

"It's dead weight, Captain," Gorse replied. "Its propulsion system is still a mystery. I could make it run on psi power, but since your intention is to load it with Thryggian corpses and crash it on one of the planets in their home system..."

"Quite right," Takamura agreed. "There's no point in leaving behind a piece of the very technology we're here to prevent them from using. So, our short-hopper will have to tow the wreck through the space gate and then cut it loose in low orbit before delivering the brotherhood to wherever the Kularian ship has been hidden."

"I insist on accompanying the brotherhood on this mission," said D'Ull.

Alarm. Yorell was staring fixedly at her son — telepathically denying him permission, Ixbeth guessed.

"The brotherhood won't allow it," Gorse told them.

"The brotherhood don't have a choice in the matter. The plan they forced on us dictated the placement of Docent Minegar and Lania Dedrick," D'Ull pointed out. "It said nothing about Yorell or me. Since this mission was our idea, I think it's only fitting that Yorell remain aboard ship to supervise while I go down to the planet to oversee that part of the operation."

Regret. "I'm afraid *I* can't allow it, Councilor," said Takamura. "The moment you boarded this ship, my crew and I became responsible for ensuring that you arrived safely back on Kula'as. This mission entails a sufficient amount of risk that I cannot guarantee your safety if you leave the *Marco Polo*. And while the loss of the brotherhood in Thryggian space would be unfortunate, your loss would be far too difficult to explain without blowing the cover off this entire venture."

Frustration. D'Ull glared around the table but was finally forced to concede. "Fine, then," he snapped. "They go down there alone. But they'd better come out again, with that heavy ship."

Tasting satisfaction, Ixbeth glanced at Gorse and saw a smile tweak the corners of his mouth. In that instant, she understood what the brotherhood must be planning to do, and why D'Ull was so worried about supervision.

The Kularian vessel was more than a getaway vehicle — it was also a devastating weapon. And it was never a good idea to place a weapon in the hands of someone you planned to attack, especially when your intended victims had already made it clear they didn't trust you.

"Do we know where in their system the Thryggians have concealed the ship?" Dedrick asked, pulling Ixbeth's thoughts back to the moment.

Yorell placed a datacube in the middle of the table. As she removed her hand, a holographic image sprang from the top of the cube. "The Thryggian star system," she said. "Thrygg is the fourth of five planets, all roughly the same size and in elliptical orbit around a small yellow star. The third and fourth planets are both capable of supporting air-breathing life, but Thrygg is the only one in the system that does not alternate night and day."

"So, one side is constantly in daylight and the other is always dark? If I wanted to hide something large, that's where I would put it." Dedrick jabbed with a forefinger that momentarily puckered the image. "Close by but completely out of sight."

"That isn't where it is," said Gorse. "Don't ask me how I know. I just do."

A flash of anger. Dedrick scowled across the table at him. "The same way that Lania knew about those Thryggian corpses in Med Services?" When Gorse did not answer, Dedrick went on, "Captain, why don't we just invite Noris to these meetings, since he seems to be present anyway?"

"Is this true, Mister Pirrit?" Takamura asked.

After a beat, he replied, "The brotherhood keeps records, some dating back to the Great War. When the terms of the treaty became known but before it was signed, the Kularian War Master arranged with an ally to safeguard one of the heavy ships from being destroyed. Its location was recorded for future reference, and that information has been passed down from senior brother to senior brother ever since. Noris knows where it is."

"And?" Yorell prompted impatiently.

Another pause. "And he'll reveal the place of concealment to the shuttle pilot once the mission has begun. Meanwhile, he recommends that the Thryggian craft be dropped onto the planet farthest from the star. The Thryggians will investigate, and that should distract them long enough to permit the heavy ship to be retrieved."

Silence fell over the room like a smothering blanket. Ixbeth glanced around the table. A faint, mirthless smile had taken up residence on the captain's face. Dedrick's frown looked permanently etched on his. The Reyota had been stunned speechless. They were all just realizing what Ixbeth had suspected and Gorse had evidently known for a while: the moment the brotherhood had boarded the *Marco Polo*, and perhaps even earlier than that, this mission to Thrygg had been theirs to control.

"Well," remarked Takamura, "it appears we've been given our plan."

"More like our orders," grumbled D'Ull. "Do you still believe the Thryggians are the greater threat, Commander?"

"To us, yes. To the Kularians? Maybe," Dedrick replied. "It depends on how much explosive the Thryggians have used to booby trap that ship. Because if I were them and I'd decided not to give it back to its owners, that is exactly what I would do. Perhaps Noris should think twice about going down there, Mister Pirrit."

"I'm sure he'll take it under advisement, Commander."

――― «◊» ―――

Ixbeth caught up to Gorse as he was stepping into the tube car opposite the entrance to the strategy room. Her head was crowded with angry questions, all jostling and clamoring to be expressed. The only one that actually made it to her mouth was a single word. "When?" she demanded.

He turned and stared at her in puzzlement. "When what?"

"When did the brotherhood decide to set things in motion? Was it when the Thryggian ship showed up in Dimmlesi space?"

He tugged her inside the tube car and let the door close before answering. "You want to know whether Noris instructed your brother to contact you," he said evenly, reaching across to key in their destination. His self-control was infuriating.

"At this point, I'm willing to believe that it wasn't Tal at all," she fumed. "Noris might have been the one who contacted me. You said it yourself, he's been inside my head before. For all I know, he may still be there."

"No. I can assure you that no one has bonded with you without your consent, and no one ever will."

"How comforting. Now answer my question, Gorse. When did the brotherhood begin implementing their plan? Did they cause that Thryggian ship to enter Dimmlesi space?"

"Actually," he said after a moment's hesitation, "*you* did."

"That's impossible!"

"Shortly after you concluded your testimony at the Tribunal last year, Thryggian scout ships were dispatched to search for your birth world. Think about it, Ixbeth — all that pure Kularian genetic material in one place. Finding and harvesting it would save the Thryggians years of experimentation. And until you announced yourself to the tribunes, no one even knew it existed."

Her thoughts were racing. "And the new quest Tal told me about, the one to locate other pure-blooded Kularian communities? It was a lie, wasn't it?"

Sympathy, repressed. "The ship we recently salvaged wasn't the first to come sniffing around the Dimmlesi system, but it *was* the first to bypass Dimmla and come directly to Altera. By then, the brotherhood had already realized what the Thryggians were up to and had devised a plan to move the Kularian population off Dimmla without causing panic. No one has lied to you, Ixbeth. The quest your people are now on is real, and so was Tal's telepathic call for help."

No one had lied to her? Perhaps. But no one had told her the truth, either, and that was the part that hurt.

She stared at Gorse, her gorge, sense hairs, and suspicion all rising. Letting out a low growl, she demanded, "How do you know all this? Did Noris take you into his confidence? Are you part of the inner circle now?"

At that moment, the tube car door opened onto a corridor in the community sector where Dallia stood waiting. Ixbeth stayed where she was, tasting sadness and refusing to let it affect her as the two females gazed into each other's eyes.

"You're still angry," said Dallia, breaking the silence.

"Yes."

"Why?"

Ixbeth hardened her voice. "Perhaps it has something to do with the fact that I'm being treated like a stranger by members of my own community, including my family. I've been away from home for two years. If you've decided that means I'm no longer one of you, I guess I shouldn't be surprised. No more than *you* should be at how that makes me feel."

She reached for the keypad.

"Wait!" Dallia cried, putting out a hand to stop the door from closing. "Come to our quarters in one hour and we'll answer as many of your questions as we can."

"No," Ixbeth decided. "I'm tired of half-truths and omissions. I'll get my own answers. And here's a word of warning, Mother. You can trust him if you wish, but Noris isn't just a name — it's also the Kularian word for danger."

Resignation. Dallia let her hand drop. Regret mixed with anger, planting a sour taste at the back of Ixbeth's throat as the door closed between them.

"Do you know why members of the brotherhood wear purple robes?"

Ixbeth started at the sound of Gorse's voice behind her. He'd muted his feelings so well that she'd forgotten he was there.

"It's because they're more than scholars," he continued. "They're defenders as well, doing whatever they must to protect and preserve our ancient knowledge. They've worked very hard for thousands of years to keep it alive and intact, and every Kularian, whether pure-blooded or hybrid, honors them for that. It's something you might want to remember the next time you have words with your mother."

Ixbeth watched in silence as the car door slid open again and he stepped past her into the corridor.

Chapter Fifteen

One hour later, Ixbeth stepped through the door of her quarters and found Dallia sitting on the edge of the bed.

"How did you—? Of course," she said, scalp muscles tightening as she remembered the senior brother's knack for breaking locks. "Noris."

Dallia tilted her head in confirmation. "We need to talk. Since you refuse to come to us, I've come to you."

And probably not alone, Ixbeth thought darkly. She could feel her tail stiffening beneath her blue robe, her fingerclaws trying to extend. "So I see," she replied. "So, talk."

"You've changed, Ixbeth. Your year among the Humans—"

"—was extremely enlightening. What do you want from me, Mother?"

"I want you to tell me what makes you feel that we are treating you like a stranger. When was the first time you felt this way? Was it at the Archives?"

Involuntarily, Ixbeth replayed her memories of that meeting, starting with the landing on the commons. "It began the moment I stepped off the shuttle, into that cold, harsh weather. The Altera I remember was warm and welcoming."

"I know. We'd made it that way, with technology. The planet reverted to its natural state when we shut down the climate controls. It was our own decision, in case you're wondering. Besides saving energy, it gave the impression that Altera was abandoned. We were hoping to discourage any further alien intrusion and earn ourselves a reprieve from the Mitrades. Unfortunately, it didn't work."

"How lucky for you that Tal and I were bonded, then, and you could call for help."

"And you came for us, like a gift from Avo'or. We were —
and still are — very grateful."

It was taking all of Ixbeth's self-control to keep her
fingerclaws retracted, leaving none to filter the bitterness out
of her voice. "Grateful? To Avo'or, maybe, but not to me. Ever
since you boarded this ship, you've kept yourselves closed
up in guest quarters with your auras so muted I couldn't
even sense your presence. I can understand your wanting
to separate yourselves from the *pritvanu* Humans, but from
me? In all the time since we left Altera, I've had no face-to-
face contact with any of you — not with my old docents,
not even with my family. My *family*! Anytime I've tried to
visit, I've been sent away on some pretext or other. You only
came out of hiding and spoke to me because I'd brought
some Dimmlesi fruit on board and the brotherhood assumed
it was an offering and sent you to thank me on their behalf."

Dallia gazed at her for a moment. "Please sit down,
Ixbeth."

Feeling contrary, she almost refused. But her mother's
aura was now a dizzying mixture of tastes, making Ixbeth
curious enough to reach for a chair.

"Do you remember telling Tal that you wouldn't be
coming home after the Tribunal because you had found a
mission?" Dallia said. Ixbeth nodded. "Well, we found a
mission as well, on Altera. A very important one."

"More important than spending time or just
communicating with your daughter whom you hadn't seen
in two years?"

"Ixbeth, you've chosen the blue of a scholar, but I'm still
a defender, and a defender has to set priorities. When there's
a mission, the mission comes first."

"Commander Dedrick is a defender too, and he has made
it clear that protecting his family comes first, even before the
mission."

"Yes, but that is the Human way, not ours. On Dimmla,
you were confused about your identity. It appears you still
are. If you want answers, then it's time for you to choose.
What are you, Ixbeth? Are you Kularian, or are you something
else?"

Ixbeth reared back, stung by the sudden cruelty of this question. "No!"

Surprise. "No?"

"No, Mother. I reject your premise that I can be only one thing at a time. The most basic tenet of our education rejects it as well. We are all docents *and* we are all students. I didn't choose to be Kularian — I *am* Kularian. I am also the sum total of everything I have learned from every being I've met and everywhere I've been, and that includes Altera and Kula'as *and* this Earth ship that surrounds us. The Humans have taught me a great deal, about the importance of belonging, and about the value of reaching out and making connections with other beings of all races. These are fundamental truths that I now strive to teach others, and no one should question where or how I learned them.

"On Kula'as, no one will. All the hybrids who have chosen to return to the ancestral home world are bringing with them everything *they've* learned from living among other races. Some of it contradicts traditional Kularian ways. So be it. That doesn't make them — or me — any less Kularian than you are, Mother. If you value our relationship, you won't even suggest it."

Satisfaction. To Ixbeth's confusion, Dallia's aura instantly brightened. "I do, daughter. I'll admit, some of us were uncertain, but it appears Docent Ribara was right about you. You have learned Avo'or's lesson, well enough to teach it."

"Avo'or's lesson?"

"The reason we were sent into concealment centuries ago. The reason only eleven of us will be returning to Kula'as. And the reason you were chosen over your brother to undertake the Quest. I'm tasting strong curiosity. Does that mean you are ready to listen to those reasons?"

Ixbeth leaned closer. "Why was I chosen, Mother?"

"You carry the Reyot gene. We didn't understand this until Noris explained it to us, after you had left Dimmla. Very long ago, the Kularians and the Reyota were a single race. What caused it to divide into two peoples is apparently lost in the shadows of time. We do know that Kularians are, in general, a practical people. We are makers and doers. We create with our hands. The Reyota create with their minds. They are inventors, dreamers, and gatherers of knowledge. The Reyota throw their thoughts. We throw our emotions, but we can also share thoughts with our mates and our twins. And the two races are physically identical to each other. That is because, in spite of our differences, we continue to share a genome.

"In every generation, some Reyot kits are birthed who need to be constantly moving, making and doing. They carry the Kularian gene. And in that same generation, some Kularian kits are birthed who have unskilled hands and an unquenchable thirst for knowledge."

"Like me," Ixbeth murmured.

"Like you. They carry the Reyot gene. The brotherhood added the summoning by the Oracle to their records. If our community is typical of all of them, then Noris believes that every Kularian chosen to go on the Quest just completed is probably carrying this Reyot gene."

"Did he tell you why the Oracle chose this way?"

"He doesn't know, but he does have a theory."

"Avo'or's lesson?"

Dallia smiled. "Yes. He believes the Kularian and Reyot peoples are being prepared by Avo'or for a momentous future event: the reunification of our two races."

Ixbeth nearly forgot to breathe. If Noris was right, "momentous" would be an understatement. Still...

"What about the prophecy? It was the whole purpose of the Quest. Weren't we scattered throughout the galaxy so the weight of our evidence would bring the Tribunal to a decisive end and ensure ten generations of peace? Wasn't *that* Avo'or's intention?"

Gentle reproof. "Ixbeth! As you said yourself so eloquently just a few minutes ago, why does it have to be just one thing at a time?"

———— «◊» ————

"We have arrived," the metal box announced.

Takamura came to attention in the captain's chair. "You're certain, Odysseus?"

"There can be no mistake," the pilot confirmed. "These are the coordinates that were occupied by the Galactic Tribunal's observation ship one standard year ago."

"And we're facing the pocket universe containing the Thryggian system?"

"Possibly."

It was the best they were going to get from the Mitradean. With luck, one of the other aliens aboard could offer something more specific.

"Mister Hammersmith, contact Commander Dedrick and tell him he needs to assemble the mission team for a last-minute briefing."

"Aye, sir."

Twenty minutes later, Takamura was occupying a seat at the head of the conference table in the strategy room, with Dedrick and Deneuve on his right-hand side and the two Reyota to his left. At the foot of the table sat Noris, flanked by Pirrit and Ixbeth. The senior brother emanated a powerful presence. Like Yorell, he was a force of nature, difficult to contain, even harder to control. Takamura kept his expression neutral and reminded himself whose ship they were on. At the right moment he would remind the others as well.

"The technology used by a Kularian craft to fold or seal space leaves a resonance signature behind," Noris was explaining. "Once the psi-driven part of your vessel knows what to look for, the margins of the pocket universe should be easy enough to detect. None of your people need to be placed at risk, Captain. Gorse Pirrit can pilot the shuttle transporting us through the space gate."

Takamura gave his head an emphatic shake. "I disagree. It's because this is a dangerous mission that the pilot must be a Human. If anything goes wrong down there, I want someone at the controls who can react reflexively without having to think about the technology. I have an experienced officer already picked out, one who has logged many hours on our short-hopper, knows precisely what it's capable of, and will be the credible witness that *we* need, even if you don't."

"Is it Commander Dedrick?" Noris asked.

"No. The commander will be supporting Ixbeth and Lania as they maintain the Kularian shields aboard the *Marco Polo*. Mister Pirrit and Lieutenant Tsieng will be supervising that end of the mission." Takamura paused, half-expecting an objection from one or both ends of the table. When none came, he continued, "Doctor Deneuve, you will stand by in Medical Services in case anyone needs your attention. Yorell and Arfan, you will be on the bridge with me, observing.

"Watch Commander Eberhart will meet the brotherhood on the landing deck, ready to transport them to whatever location they specify. She will wait, providing covering fire if needed, until they are inside the heavy ship. They will then activate the ship and follow her back through the space gate, hopefully without having to destroy too many Thryggian vessels in the process. Finally, the heavy ship will seal the gate behind it, leaving the Thryggians trapped in their pocket universe. That is the mission we agreed upon, and it is the one we'll carry out," he concluded sternly. "Are there any questions?"

"Captain," sputtered D'Ull, "once again I must protest—"

"No, Councilor, you mustn't. As you yourself pointed out back on Kula'as, this is a dangerous mission, and I won't risk any more lives, Human or otherwise, than is absolutely necessary. There will be five aboard that shuttle, the brotherhood and the pilot, and that's all. I'm told it will take another half-hour for the landing deck crew to prepare the Thryggian ship for its scuttle run. Commander Eberhart has been thoroughly briefed, and countdown will begin on her signal. Now, unless there are any final questions…?"

Takamura glanced around the table, seeing determined expressions on the two Human faces. Meanwhile, Yorell and Arfan sat glaring at each other, most likely embroiled in a telepathic argument. When the captain's gaze reached Noris, the senior brother met it — and smiled.

Takamura quashed the impulse to smile back. Breaking eye contact, he declared, "I believe we're done here."

Deneuve raised her chin, turned to face him, and said, in a tone of voice that he hadn't heard since the last time he'd interrupted his mother while she was speaking, "Captain, may I have a moment, please?"

He waited for the strategy room to empty out before replying, "Certainly, Doctor. You have a question?"

"I do. What was that just now between you and the senior brother? Noris smiled at you, and I sensed ... collusion? Are we helping the brotherhood to put one over on the Reyota?"

He rearranged his features into an expression of mild shock. "No, of course not. If you've been sensing subterfuge from our alien guests, then there may well be some sort of scheme afoot. However, I have not been made privy to it, nor do I wish to be. With all the interplanetary politics involved here, our situation is precarious enough. All I can do is walk the straightest line possible and keep my fingers crossed that reason and sanity will prevail. I recommend you do the same. Now, if there's nothing else you wish to discuss...?"

She stared into his face for the space of two heartbeats, then said, "No, Captain. Nothing else."

«»

The viewscreen on the bridge showed the short-hopper with the Thryggian egg-ship in tow emerging from the landing deck, coming alongside the *Marco Polo,* then angling away and gliding to a halt five kilometers off her port bow. For an endless moment, the three ships hung in the vastness of apparently empty space.

"Keep us steady, Odysseus," said Takamura, adding over his shoulder to the officer at the tactical console, "And keep them on our screen, Mister Harding."

"Aye, sir," the Human and the metal box replied in unison.

"Commander Eberhart, report."

"The commander is unable to respond, Captain," came a deep, familiar voice. "For her own protection, it was necessary to render her unconscious."

Instantly, another voice exploded through the comm. "Noris, if you've harmed her in any way—!"

"Relax, Commander Dedrick. Your shipmate is quite safe. We'll wake her when the space gate is fully formed. Now, Captain, I recommend you turn off all visual monitoring devices and shield your eyes."

Yorell had been standing near the tube car door. She stepped over to the captain's chair and said with some urgency, "You need to do as he says. I've seen a Kularian heavy ship in action. If that shuttle is creating a space gate, it's going to be brighter than a star in about one minute."

On the viewscreen, the short-hopper was emanating a glow. The vessel appeared to soften and swell as it rapidly became more radiant. Within seconds it was both fascinating and difficult to watch.

"Mister Harding," the captain ordered, "shut down all external vid feeds and opaque the viewports."

"Aye, sir."

"Commander Dedrick, are we ready to switch to psi power?"

———— «» ————

In Engineering, Dedrick stood beside a long metal work table, mentally crossing his fingers. Ixbeth and Lania sat at either end of it, their eyes closed, their expressions taut, their hands spread flat on the tabletop. Lania was wearing the headnet, and Tal's mind was reportedly joined with Ixbeth's, boosting her strength as well.

For shields, this was all the psi energy they would need, according to Gorse Pirrit. Dedrick hoped he was right.

Pirrit had been walking a circle around the table, staring intently back and forth from one face to the other. Doing whatever Kularians did to assure themselves that two brains were connected and on the same wavelength. Finally, he met the commander's inquiring gaze and gave him a single nod.

"Pirrit says we're ready, Captain," Dedrick told him.

"Shutting down all systems except for comms and emergency life support," announced Harding's voice.

A moment later the only light in the workroom was the red gleam of the exit sign over the door to the corridor.

"Now we join with the shield builder," Gorse said softly.

As Dedrick's eyes adjusted to the rosy dimness, he was able to discern the other male crouching beside Ixbeth's chair. "Maximize your senses," he heard him murmur to her. "Find its resonance pattern and harmonize it with your own. Are you one?"

"We are one," she sighed after a pause.

"Good. Surround the ship with psi energy, just as we practiced."

Almost immediately the air around the table changed. It became charged, almost effervescent. Inhaling it made Dedrick's nose tingle. Its touch on his skin bristled the hair on his arms and at the back of his neck. It pulled a glow from the tabletop, pale yellow at first but growing steadily brighter until he was forced to squint to keep Lania in his sight. Meanwhile, she sat motionless, a helmeted figure silhouetted by a powerful light that appeared to be both emanating from her and consuming her. Gael gritted his teeth. This had felt wrong to him from the beginning. Right now, it was taking all of his self-control not to yank the headnet off Lania, pull her out of that chair, and carry her out of the room.

"Is it done?" Gorse asked at last.

"Yes," Ixbeth replied slowly. "It is a radiant wall … all around the ship."

Gorse straightened up and came to stand beside Dedrick. "You can tell the captain that the *Marco Polo* has Kularian shields, and they're at full strength."

"For how long?" He knew the Kularian could sense his anger, so there was no point in trying to conceal it. "Until Lania has no more energy to give?"

"That's not how this works. Psi energy isn't stored and used up — it's constantly generated, and harnessed as needed."

"Generators run on fuel," Dedrick pointed out.

"Very true, and Lania's fuel is all around her. It's the air she breathes, the food she eats, the water she drinks. Didn't your scientists once try to measure the energy flowing from her brain, and fail?"

Gorse was right. Lania had burned out their biogalvanometer not once, but twice.

"Ixbeth wasn't exaggerating when she told me how fiercely you defend your family, Commander. It's a quality we Kularians admire greatly. So you can rest assured, Lania is not being harmed. Her talent is powerful, and it will stay that way for as long as she lives, whether or not she is wearing a headnet. Together, she and Ixbeth are more than capable of keeping every being aboard this ship safe from a Thryggian attack."

Chapter Sixteen

"Eberhart reporting in, Captain."

Takamura snapped erect in his chair. "What's your condition, Commander?"

"I'm all right, sir. Whatever they did that put me to sleep, it doesn't appear to have left any residual effects. The space gate is open and we're about to go through it. No sign of Thryggians yet. I'll keep you apprised. Eberhart out."

"Reinstate external video feeds and clear all viewports, Mister Harding," the captain called over his shoulder. "We'll need to keep a weather eye out."

"A whether what, sir?"

"Never mind, just do it."

"Aye, sir."

Takamura punched up a direct comm line to Engineering. "Mister Pirrit," he said in his sternest voice, "I'll want to talk to you later about the modifications that you apparently made to the short-hopper."

"You mean the shuttle? You didn't authorize any, Captain," Gorse reminded him. "You didn't have to. We agreed they weren't necessary, so I never suggested them to you."

Takamura scowled at his comm unit. "*We*, Mister Pirrit? Am I correct in assuming that you are referring to yourself and the brotherhood?"

After a moment of silence, the Kularian replied, "Yes. As it happened, they were able to bring the necessary technology with them."

Feeling eyes boring into the side of his head, Takamura turned and met Yorell's narrowing gaze.

"I knew it was a mistake to let them go down there by themselves," D'Ull fumed.

〈〉

"The egg is away, Captain. It lit up like a fireball as soon as it hit atmosphere. Proceeding as planned. Eberhart out." There was a click, then silence.

Hearing this, Gael glanced up at the wallcomm speaker and blew out a long breath. He and Gorse Pirrit now stood together, leaning their backs against the bulkhead beside the exit door.

"Your captain made the right decision, you know," Gorse said conversationally, "sending the other pilot instead of you. You wouldn't have been focused. Your body would have been on the shuttle, but your mind would have been here. It works better this way."

"Yeah."

That might have been the official reason to keep Dedrick aboard ship, but he knew it wasn't the only one. Takamura was aware of the bad blood between the commander and Noris and was smart enough not to put them together in close quarters.

Gael crossed his arms over his chest and turned his attention once more to Lania. She was fifteen now, almost an adult by the Relocation Authority's cold, numerical definition but still in many ways a child. In other words, as Leslie had already pointed out to him, she was a typical Human teenager — challenging, at times infuriating, and even more in need of a defender now that she'd had a taste of normal family life, the very thing the Relocation Authority was threatening to take away from her.

Like any adolescent, Lania yearned to test herself, to push the boundaries of her freedom. She was certain to be a different person at the end of this adventure — bolder, more confident of her abilities — and Dedrick was looking forward to watching her grow. But he also needed to keep her safe. She was a family secret now, just like the information on Dennis Forrand's datawafer.

Concealing her would be a challenge. Even if Novak managed to wipe all mention of her from the databases, there was no way to wipe her from the memories of all the people who knew she existed. The Relocation Authority was sure to come after her in any case, and the *Marco Polo* was the first place they would look. However, his chance meeting with Ross Posey earlier had planted an idea in his mind, one that he was liking better with each passing minute.

———— «◊» ————

Minutes crept by, then hours. Three ... four... The *Marco Polo* was on high alert, and the tension on the bridge was palpable. Takamura didn't want to imagine what might be happening right now inside that pocket of space, but he had no choice. He was responsible for the safety of more than two hundred living beings, and if a fleet of Thryggian ships began pouring through the open Gate, he would be in a battle for all their lives.

"Captain, we're coming out, and we're not alone." Eberhart's voice burst through the comm, taut as a bowstring.

Takamura slid to the edge of his chair. "How many Thryggian vessels?" he demanded.

"At least a dozen and they're not egg-shaped. They're bigger and faster than— What the—? Captain, the heavy ship has turned around. I think it's— *Damn!* That's a big gun!"

"Eberhart, report! What's happening?"

"The brotherhood are firing on Thrygg, sir. They're ignoring the fighters and targeting the planet instead. I'm too far away to tell what they're aiming at, if anything."

"Are you still being pursued?"

"No, sir. The Thryggians have broken off their pursuit and are engaging the heavy ship."

Takamura became aware of movement behind him. A second later D'Ull was standing beside the captain's chair, glaring furiously at him. "They're attacking the Thryggian home world?" he exclaimed. "That was never part of the mission."

"My officer returning safely *was*," Takamura informed him, not deigning to make eye contact. "They've found and activated the heavy ship. Now they're using it to draw the Thryggians away from the shuttle so Eberhart can escape. After that—"

"Go through the space gate, Human!" Noris's voice sounded strained, as though he were holding back the Thryggians by sheer brute strength. "Go now!"

"Do as he says, Commander." Twisting in his seat, Takamura added, "Keep the Gate on our monitors, Mister Harding. Watch for the short-hopper, and prepare to fire on anything that follows her through."

The tactical officer looked confused. "With respect, Captain, our weapons are offline."

"For the moment," Takamura responded grimly. "Mister Pirrit, have you been listening?"

"I have, Captain," came the reply. "We can expand the shield to encompass the shuttle after it comes through the space gate. Instruct Commander Eberhart to approach the landing deck entrance at speed. She will need to be right beside the ship when she stops, no more than twenty of your meters from it."

Takamura turned toward his communications officer. "Pass it along, Mister Hammersmith."

"Aye, Captain."

It would be a tricky maneuver, pulling up short that close to the landing deck doors. Fortunately, this pilot was one of his best.

"Now, what about weapons?" Takamura continued.

"The shield *is* your best weapon, Captain. You have no need of any other," Gorse replied.

That sounded disturbingly similar to something Lania's neurotic computer had once told her.

"If you don't mind, Mister Pirrit, I would like a second opinion."

"Captain, this is Tsieng in Engineering. From what I've seen, the Kularian shield is designed to serve as defensive armament. It absorbs directed energy, then sends it back to its source. Any ship that fires on us — or misses the short-hopper and hits our shield instead — will automatically draw return fire of equal or superior strength."

"Just like what happened the last time, Captain," Dedrick added. "Lania's AI delayed returning fire, then released it in powerful energy pulses that knocked out all the pirate vessels around our ship at once."

With effort, Takamura stifled his impatience. He had always been a man of action, and sitting on his hands when others were in peril went against his grain. However, he could not in all conscience jeopardize the lives of over two hundred passengers and crew for the sake of one individual. Especially not after having preached repeatedly and insistently to the Reyota about his obligation to minimize their risk and get everyone back home safely.

Sighing inwardly, the captain said, "Thank you, gentlemen. It appears we will just have to wait for now."

"And what about the heavy ship?" D'Ull reminded him.

"What about it, Councilor?"

"What happens when it comes through that space gate? We have to destroy it. If you can't fire on it—"

"What I can't and won't do," Takamura said, rising slowly to his feet, "is betray four beings who have just put themselves in harm's way to save one of my officers. It would be dishonorable to attack them while they are in the midst of escaping from the very same danger that threatens her."

"It is pointless to argue about this," Yorell informed them both. "The brotherhood have no intention of coming back through that space gate. They'll seal it behind the shuttle and make another, taking the heavy ship to a part of the galaxy where no one will find it, or them, again."

"How can you be certain of that, Mother?" demanded D'Ull.

"Because the same thing happened the last time you were about to destroy one of their ships without warning," she replied. "There were thirteen Kularians aboard it then, as I recall, including Ixbeth. Face it, Arfan, the brotherhood have no reason to trust either of us. Why else would they have insisted on a written contract, signed and witnessed, regarding the disposition of their helpers?"

"So, the mission was in vain?" D'Ull persisted.

"I wouldn't call it a total failure," she told him. "It hasn't gone as planned, but we will have accomplished our main objective, which was to remove the ship from Thryggian space before the Thryggians could activate it."

"And now it's in the hands of the brotherhood," D'Ull grumbled, "which means we haven't succeeded at all."

"I agree with Yorell," said Takamura as he settled back onto his seat. "Assuming that the brotherhood survive the battle raging inside that pocket of space and the heavy ship remains operational, they will have the means to isolate themselves from the rest of the galaxy, in effect creating their own sanctuary. They've let you off the hook, Councilor. All that's left to do is transport their household staff back to Kula'as and your obligation to them will be fulfilled. If I were in your place, I would not be displeased with this outcome."

Yorell considered him for a moment. "No, Captain," she said softly, "I imagine you would not."

Five minutes later, the short-hopper emerged through the gate, speeding on a collision course toward the flank of the *Marco Polo*. No other vessels of any description came through. All that followed the shuttle was a message from the brotherhood:

"We have ended the Thryggian threat and are removing the heavy ship from Thryggian space, as agreed," said Noris's voice. "Any space gates we make will be immediately sealed behind us. Remember your promise to take care of our helpers. Thank you for your hospitality, Captain, and goodbye."

Chapter Seventeen

The Kularian shields were collapsed and the short-hopper taken safely aboard as soon as the space gate was confirmed to be sealed shut. After some routine diagnostics, all normal systems were reactivated, returning control of the *Marco Polo* to her various consoles, and prompting exhalations of relief from the officers and crew working at them.

The mission debriefing had been delayed by two hours so that Doctor Deneuve could put Ixbeth, Lania, and Commander Eberhart through a battery of neurological tests. Deneuve especially needed to satisfy herself that the shuttle pilot had suffered no lasting effects from being "rendered unconscious for her own protection" by the brotherhood. She found none and was forced to pronounce Eberhart unscathed and fit for duty. Sitting in the adjacent cubicle in Med Services, Ixbeth had tasted Deneuve's reluctance to speak these words.

It was understandable. Head trauma — or anything else that caused a loss of consciousness — was a serious problem for Humans, so much so that not only their healers worried about it. As if to prove Ixbeth's point, a wave of relief rolled through the strategy room as Eberhart entered, smiling, and took a seat across the table from her.

When all the available mission team members were present, Takamura began the debriefing by remarking to Eberhart, "You're looking well, Commander."

"Thank you, sir. Doctor Deneuve has checked me out and I feel fine."

"It has been confirmed that no modifications of any kind were made to the short-hopper. And yet, the Kularians aboard that vessel were able to create a space gate. Did you notice anything that might explain how they managed it?"

Sampling the auras of the various beings around the conference table, Ixbeth tasted curiosity from the captain, impatience from the Reyota, and anxiety from Commander Dedrick, whose thoughts were no doubt of Lania, still under observation in Med Services. Ixbeth also tasted the bitterness of frustration, an emotion emanating primarily from Councilor D'Ull. Gorse Pirrit must have tasted it too. It was making him smile.

"I didn't actually see them make the Gate, sir. I don't know how relevant this is, but they did bring something odd aboard the shuttle, something that they were secretive about and that they handled with great care. It piqued my interest, so at the first opportunity, I stole a look at it. The object appeared to be a plastiplex cube containing…" She struggled visibly to find the right words. "It reminded me of an octopus standing on its head. I'm pretty sure it was alive. Some of the tentacles were moving. Then I felt a touch on the back of my neck and I blinked. And when I opened my eyes, the cube was gone and there was a space gate in front of the short-hopper."

Nascent anger. "They smuggled an animal aboard my ship?" said Takamura, his voice ominously soft.

Resignation. "Not just an animal, Captain," Pirrit explained. "What the commander saw was the power core of a psi-driven heavy cruiser."

"And it's a living creature?"

"Living but not sentient, and with a gluttonous appetite for energy, as I warned you earlier. This being was waking up from hibernation and it was hungry. If Commander Eberhart hadn't been put into a deep sleep, her life force would have been noticed by the creature and quickly consumed."

Ixbeth's own dawning horror was an acrid taste at the back of her throat. "Was there one of these power cores in the ship we used a year ago to imprison the Thryggians?"

Regret. A hesitation. "Yes. That is why the brotherhood had to help you and Tal."

It had been a struggle to control that vessel. Orrin Phail had sensed something evil living within it and had begged them to bury the "psi monster" in pieces once their task had been completed. Now Ixbeth understood why.

"So, not just an animal," Takamura summed up. "A very dangerous alien creature. And where is it now, Mister Pirrit?"

"Nowhere aboard this ship, Captain, I promise you," Gorse replied. "The brotherhood have taken it with them, and they are fully capable of controlling it, so there's nothing for anyone to worry about."

Sudden alarm. Yorell was staring at Pirrit with widened eyes. As well she should, Ixbeth reflected. There was a power core sleeping inside the heavy ship the thirteen "doubly chosen ones" had concealed on Kula'as and, with the departure of the brotherhood, quite possibly no one with the power to control it if it should wake up.

———— «» ————

"She'll be all right, Gael. She's just tired," Deneuve assured him.

Tired? Lania was exhausted. Dedrick had rushed back to Med Services as soon as the debriefing was over. Now he stood just inside the door of the Prevention and Rehab ward, carefully watching the rhythmic rise and fall of his cousin's chest as she lay on the bed, sound asleep. He was only partly comforted by Deneuve's words. She hadn't been there to witness Lania's panic at being unable to break off the mental contact with Ixbeth when it came time to collapse the Kularian shields. She hadn't seen Lania's legs wobble and fold under her when the youngster tried to get up from the chair she'd been sitting in for more than five standard hours.

Just thinking about it made him angry all over again. Lania's mental powers might be strong, but strength without training, without the stamina that built up through repeated practice, didn't count for much. Ixbeth was trained. Lania was not.

A year earlier, the *Marco Polo*'s alienized shields had apparently drawn power from the ship as well as from her mind. This time Lania was the sole energy source, and Pirrit's modifications had enhanced the technology, making it even hungrier than it had been before. He should have known better. They all should have known better. And they weren't going to make this mistake again, not if Gael Dedrick had anything to say about it.

———— «» ————

There had definitely been a different flavor to the energy Lania was sending her. A mixture of Kularian and something else, just like the AI Lania had built for herself. Just like the hybrid shields that had helped the *Marco Polo* defeat the Thryggian pirates a year earlier. Ixbeth considered this as she left the debriefing meeting and called up a tube car to carry her to her quarters.

There had been no need for Kularian shielding this time, and it wasn't because they'd been lucky. The brotherhood had wanted to ensure that they were the only ones aboard the heavy ship when it lifted off, because they knew — had always known, in fact — that they would not be bringing it back through the space gate. So, they'd devised a plan that would keep everyone else busy aboard the Earth vessel, claiming it was to minimize the number of lives being put at risk, and, for his own reasons, Captain Takamura had gone along with it.

The Reyota were evidently not the only ones who practiced deception, she thought darkly. Unbidden, the final words of the dying Thryggian in Med Services echoed in her mind: *We are betrayed.*

When the tube car door slid open on the guest quarters deck, Ixbeth stepped out into the corridor and paused, debating with herself. Then she turned and trotted in the direction of her parents' stateroom. She still had questions. Now that the brotherhood was no longer a hovering presence aboard ship, she might finally get some answers.

Dallia had been sitting at her work table, organizing her next herb garden. She looked up from her packets of seeds and cuttings as Ixbeth entered.

"Hello, Mother."

"I'm tasting curiosity and determination. And some skepticism. Thanks for the warning. Or are you just too tired to bother muting your emotions right now?"

"A little of both. You said you would answer all my questions in good time. Is this a good time?"

Dallia smiled and turned in her chair. "Ask."

"If having pure-blooded Kularians on our home world is bound to create conflict, then why are the eleven of you returning to Kula'as? Is a civil war part of Avo'or's grand plan?"

"No, it isn't. But Kula'as is where we need to be in order to carry out our mission. Sit down and I'll explain." When Ixbeth had settled onto the other chair in the room, she continued, "Last year, the brotherhood told us they were very close to a breakthrough. A moontide later, they made it."

"They've finished decoding the *Dr'rava Kula'as*?"

"Not all of it yet, but enough for them to realize what it really is, and what we used to be, and what they were becoming. For the safety of all Kularians, this knowledge — and the brotherhood — must remain hidden for now. At the same time, the *Dr'rava Kula'as* itself must be preserved as an important part of our heritage, and it needs to be made available for future generations of Kularians to study. It is forbidden by order of the Great Council for anyone to own a copy of the *Dr'rava Kula'as*. So, the brothers devised a way to return the book to our ancestral home world in a form the Council would never detect.

"They divided the text into ten parts. Do I need to say more, daughter?"

Ixbeth's ears twitched as the significance of her mother's words broke over her. Now she understood why Krodus, Tal, and the other scholars had isolated themselves in their quarters. They hadn't been excluding her. They'd been focusing on engraving their respective sections of the *Dr'rava Kula'as* into their memories.

Satisfaction. Dallia resumed speaking. "These ten pure-blooded Kularians are the teachings of Avo'or, given life, and I am their defender, for the rest of *my* life. When we return to Kula'as, they will incorporate Avo'or's wisdom into everything they do, spreading it across the planet right under the noses of the Reyota and the Great Council. And then, slowly but surely, Kula'as will rise again."

"Is Gorse Pirrit aware of this?"

"Of course. He was a student of the book on his birth world. Noris sensed his talents and made contact with him shortly after we boarded this ship." Dallia tilted her head.

"You didn't know?"

"He never told me."

"He will. He'll tell you that and much more, I'm certain. But not until you are ready to listen."

Chapter Eighteen

Odysseus's little wedge-shaped craft was right where they had left it, in high orbit above Kula'as. The *Marco Polo* had been gone for four and a half intervals — a little under two Kularian moontides, or about fifty Earth days. Sensing what Commander Dedrick's response would be if they so much as suggested that Lania assist them, Ixbeth and Gorse remotely activated the psi-driven technology aboard the Mitradean ship themselves. They then brought it onto the landing deck of the Earth vessel, where Gorse immediately set to work reversing the modifications he'd made to its control systems.

Meanwhile, the Human scientists on the planet had been alerted to wrap up their studies, and the eleven Kularian "helpers" had busied themselves preparing to be shuttled down to the surface. Ixbeth joined them in what had earlier been the brotherhood's stateroom. Everything was packed and ready to go, filling enough sacks and parcels to cover most of the floor and reach nearly to the ceiling. Their departure from Altera had been an emergency evacuation, forcing them to leave behind anything they couldn't personally carry onto the short-hopper. Now they would be repeating the exercise, bearing their few material possessions in their arms or slung over their shoulders, and holding their most precious cargo inside their heads. Emotions were muted. Nonetheless, the air fairly crackled with anticipation as ten scholars and one defender waited for a ship's officer to call them down to the landing deck.

"There are unoccupied dwellings waiting to be claimed in Capital City, and teaching positions still to be filled in the Archives," Ixbeth assured them. "You won't be able to begin working right away. Your credentials will first have to be registered with the Council of Docents. But with Prime Docent Enne endorsing your applications, I don't think there will be any problems placing you where you need to be."

"You're certain she will support us?" said Docent Ribara. "After all, the brotherhood did mislead her regarding our background and qualifications."

Ixbeth smiled. "Discovering that should make her even more determined to monitor your activities. And what better way to keep you all together and in view than by ensuring that you're working directly beneath her as docents at the Kularian Archives?"

Amusement. Eyebrows rose and heads bobbed up and down. Ixbeth heard a deep chuckling and identified its source as Docent Quibbo. He'd always had a keen appreciation for irony.

"Attention, please," announced a voice over the comm. "Would our Kularian guests please make their way to the landing deck, where the shuttle is ready for boarding."

Twelve Kularians rapidly divided up the baggage and transported it out the door.

A gathering of Humans and the two Reyota stood waiting for them around the short-hopper. Yorell scanned the group of refugees and frowned, and Ixbeth tasted the tang of dawning suspicion at the back of her throat.

So did Dallia. She leaned closer and murmured, "Don't worry about us, daughter. Avo'or will provide, as he's done in the past." She disencumbered Ixbeth of the bags she'd been carrying, placing them on the deck beside her own portion of the load. "Go talk to her. Distract her mind."

"Docent Minegar," purred Yorell as Ixbeth approached. "Does this mean you will be accompanying your family down to the surface?"

"I was just assisting with their belongings, Prime Docent. I still have to pack my own, and there will be plenty of time for a family reunion once everyone is settled in."

"I see. And have you gathered enough information for your scholarly textbook about the Humans? Or do you plan to remain aboard the *Marco Polo* a while longer?"

Ixbeth sought and found Captain Takamura's interested gaze. Her response was for him. "I'm sure the captain is anxious to refuel and return to Earth space. I won't detain him beyond the time that it will take for Gorse to restore the Mitradean ship — which will also require additional fuel, by the way."

"Of course. Thank you for reminding me. And afterward, you will be resuming your Human Studies post at the Kularian Archives?" Yorell persisted.

There was nothing benign about this question. It tightened Ixbeth's scalp, raising her sense hairs.

"Actually, I was hoping to be able to turn that discipline over to someone better qualified."

Yorell's eyes widened. "There's a Kularian better qualified than yourself to teach Human Studies?"

"Not a Kularian. The docent I have in mind is a Human — Doctor Deneuve."

Hearing her name mentioned, Deneuve drew nearer to join the conversation. "You want me to teach at the Archives? Ixbeth, I'm honored!"

"That would be highly irregular," Yorell pointed out sternly. "The Council of Docents—"

"—will come around if you endorse the appointment. This Human healer not only has extensive and accurate knowledge about the Human body, she is revered by her own people. She could be our greatest teacher, bringing students here from all over this arm of the galaxy."

Disbelief. "You really think that other races would be interested in knowing more about Humans?" D'Ull demanded scornfully.

"Not at first," said Yorell, her aura lightening as she visibly warmed to the idea. "For the first while, a Human docent would be nothing more than a novelty. But then word would spread."

"Excuse me, Docents," Takamura broke in, "but you may be getting ahead of yourselves here. Relocating a Human to a world in alien space is no simple matter. First you must make the offer to Doctor Deneuve and she has to accept it. Then begins the lengthy process of cutting through all the bureaucratic red tape generated by both our governments. Consider how long it took and how many obstacles had to be surmounted just to make possible this one visit by the *Marco Polo* to Kula'as."

"Quite true, Captain," Yorell agreed. "I would need to consult with the Council of Docents before the offer could be officially made. But I promise I will present Ixbeth's proposal in a very positive light."

Of course she would. Years might pass before the Kularian economy was well enough established to operate independently. Until then, travelers to Kula'as meant profits for Reyi'it. And for a Reyot-dominated Council, profit was the best distraction of all.

———— «〉» ————

Gorse dropped his hands to his sides and slid out from under the control console of the Mitradean vessel. Sitting on the edge of the forward hatch, he growled, "You're staring at me. What do you need, Docent?"

Tasting bemusement rather than anger, Ixbeth stepped out of the shadows. "I brought you some *caranth*," she told him, holding out a lidded cup from the mess hall. "The ship's cook brewed it from the last few *bokhara* leaves. How is the work progressing?"

"More smoothly when I'm not being interrupted. And I'm discovering how much easier it is to convert conventional technology to psi-powered than it is to change it back. Odysseus told me that Mitradean ships are subject to random inspections, so I can't leave any tool marks or other signs to indicate that this one has been tampered with." He accepted the cup and took a long swallow.

"I've had a talk with my mother."

"I'm glad that you're back on speaking terms. Defenders shouldn't quarrel among themselves."

"You were right about me. I wasn't seeing the brotherhood for what it was."

"And now?"

"Now I understand things much better."

"That's good."

"Commander Eberhart is standing by to transport the four of us — you, me, and the Reyota — down to the surface whenever you're done."

He watched her for a moment. "You're wishing you could stay aboard and go exploring with the Humans."

"Yes, and so are you. But we're defenders, with important work to do on Kula'as. Defenders have to set priorities," she told him primly.

"True. However, Avo'or teaches us that defenders can be other things as well. For example, once I've converted your *trada* to run on conventional fuel, you're going to need someone to teach you how to drive it."

"Yes, I will. At your earliest convenience, Mister Pirrit." And with that, smiling inwardly, Ixbeth turned and trotted away. The sweetness at the back of her throat told her that he was smiling as well.

《 》

"Well, Captain, this has been an adventure. Of all the Humans I've met so far, I believe you are my favorite."

The short-hopper was ready to take Ixbeth, Gorse and the Reyota down to the surface. As the others gathered on the landing deck, Yorell and Takamura stood alone in the corridor just outside the door. He bowed from the shoulders in acknowledgement of the compliment, then added with a smile in his voice, "Because you enjoy a challenge, Yorell?"

"Because you care, about your people and about the future. It's an attitude we both share. Education not only broadens the mind, it opens it. As Prime Docent, I have learned far more than I will ever be able to teach.

"Our two races have something in common, Captain. We have long been misunderstood. The Reyota have taken some questionable actions in the past, it's true, but only out of a strong desire to establish a lasting peace in the galaxy. Now that we have succeeded, we are considered by the other races to be selfish and overbearing, and not to be trusted. Even sadder, your race is mistrusted for reasons that have never been made clear to you, over things that have never been under your control. I'm certain your Earth High Council would appreciate an opportunity to remedy that."

"Are you suggesting a formal diplomatic agreement between our planetary governments, Councilor?"

"No. The Great Council would never sanction such a relationship, even if the Reyot High Council voted unanimously in favor of it. This would have to be completely unofficial and off the record, like our knowledge of the continuing existence of that Kularian heavy ship, and of Lania Dedrick's dangerously strong mental powers. We already have an alliance of sorts, Captain, built upon secrets. For now, that will have to suffice.

"Having worked with you and seen for myself that everything Ixbeth said about Humans is true, I would have no qualms about calling on you again for discreet assistance should the need arise. In return, I am prepared to represent Humanity to the Great Council in a way that will help dispel their negative preconceptions about you. This would definitely facilitate the addition of your Doctor Deneuve to the teaching staff at the Kularian Archives, should she decide to accept Ixbeth's offer. It could also potentially lead to an invitation to Earth to join the Council as a protectorate of Reyi'it. I would be doing this all on my own initiative, of course, and out of the goodness of my heart. For obvious reasons, our ... arrangement must remain confidential."

With difficulty, Takamura managed to keep his expression neutral. "That is a very generous offer, Councilor. I will convey it to my superiors at the first opportunity and report this initial visit as a diplomatic success."

Once more a force of nature, she bestowed a regal nod on him and swept through the doorway, her dark blue robe billowing behind her. Takamura waited for her wake to settle before stepping across the threshold to join Dedrick, Lania, Tsieng, and Deneuve in saying goodbye to their last four guests.

——— «» ———

"You need to be careful," said the metal box.

The *Marco Polo* had left orbit and was on her way back to Earth space. Takamura shifted in the captain's chair, more than ready to be relieved at the end of a completely uneventful watch. As Commander Dedrick stepped off the tube car and came to join him, Takamura responded, "Careful about what, Odysseus?"

"Reyota trust no one, fear everyone. They say what others wish to hear, then do as they always intended. That is how Mitrades became slaves. How Thryggians became weapons after the war was over. How the Great Council became servants of Reyi'it."

Takamura leaned forward. "The Thryggian who died in our Trauma room said they had been betrayed, that someone had ordered the Thryggians to make a sickness to prevent someone else from attacking. Who was he talking about, Odysseus?"

"I just told you," said the metal box, a note of impatience creeping into its manufactured voice. "The Reyota want Earth to want to join the Great Council, for protection. It is a trap. They promise protection, then they take away freedom. They say it is to create peace. That is what others wish to hear, so no one opposes them. Then it is too late. Humans need to be careful."

"Captain?" Dedrick ventured, frowning. "The sickness you just mentioned — is that the Angel of Death plague? Was that a preemptive strike with a biological weapon?"

"It would appear so, Commander. Developed and delivered at the behest of the Reyota, according to Odysseus, to drive us into a trap — and from what I've seen of them so far, I think he may be right."

"But Humanity wasn't the only race targeted. Alien worlds and colonies were hit as well."

"Collateral damage, I suspect," said Takamura, his expression hardening. "Or perhaps a fortuitous side benefit for those who ordered the strike. The galactic treaty, after all, is quite oppressive. Remember what I said earlier about plague dogs. What better way to head off rebellion than by demoralizing the general population?"

Dedrick was visibly struggling to maintain his composure. "With respect, sir, knowing what we know about the Thryggians, how can we be certain they weren't acting alone? You said yourself that they're sociopathic. The one that died in Med Services could easily have been lying to us, and this sort of experiment would have been right up their alley."

Interesting. Takamura gave his second in command a narrow look, then stepped away from the captain's chair. To the officer sitting at the communications console behind him he said, "The commander and I will be in my office if you need us."

Dedrick followed him into the room just off the bridge. Takamura waited for the door to sigh closed behind them before speaking. "I know you weren't playing devil's advocate for the fun of it out there. What were you trying to avoid saying, Commander?"

Dedrick hesitated, clearly choosing his words. "We both know what the truth is, and how important it is for atrocities to be brought to light, but in this case I would strongly advise against it. Humanity is already considered to be dangerous by the Galactic Great Council. Maybe they're right. But we're not yet ready to hold our own against all the other races in an interstellar war, and that's where I can see this ending up if the Great Council finds out that we suspect what they've done. To protect themselves, they'll have to attack us."

"Agreed. That is why I've decided to assign you to draft a voyage report that we can present to Fleet Control and the Earth High Council, one that will contain all the indisputable facts, while omitting or obfuscating any details that might prompt them to contact the aliens' government with a complaint. It will have to be carefully worded, and you mustn't discuss it with anyone but me."

"Understood, Captain."

"It is especially important that this report not include any derogatory statements about the Reyota. If Odysseus is correct and the Great Council really is their 'servant', we will need to tread lightly around them, at least until we have a clear picture of what their agenda is."

"They have an agenda, the Mitrades have an agenda, the brotherhood definitely had an agenda… It seems as though everyone has an agenda except us," Dedrick mused aloud.

Takamura's lips quirked briefly. "That's not entirely true, Commander. As *de facto* ambassadors, we're out here to break down walls between Humanity and the other races. That's our agenda. When we left Earth space, our only alien friend was Ixbeth Minegar. Now the Dimmlesi and the Mitrades are in our debt, the Kularian brotherhood owe us their freedom, the Reyot Prime Docent has offered to grease the diplomatic wheels for us with the Great Council, and, last but not least, we played an important role in saving the galaxy. I would call this an extremely successful voyage. And it isn't over yet. Come with me."

Raising a curious eyebrow, Dedrick followed him back onto the bridge.

Takamura crossed to the navigation console where the Mitradean sprawled over the controls. "Odysseus," he said, "when we reach the edge of Earth space, you're going to have a choice to make."

The metal box emitted an interrogative buzz.

"You are welcome to stay aboard the *Marco Polo* and claim sanctuary among us Humans, if that is what you wish."

"What I wish…" The Mitradean paused, deciding. "What I wish is to bring all Mitrades with me. This can be done?"

"How many beings are we talking about, Odysseus?" Dedrick inquired. "Thousands?"

The segmented shell darkened. "Once, we were millions. Then our home world was destroyed by the Suhore. We became thousands. We fought a war, lost many more of our kind. Now we are only hundreds, enslaved by the treaty. All must be working. We are allowed to spawn only to replace those who die."

"Your thoughts, Commander?"

"It's not a genocide, exactly," said Dedrick, "but it may as well be. I would say the Mitrades fit our definition of an endangered species, sir."

"I would agree. Our first scheduled stop inside Earth space should be Daisy Hub."

"Yes, sir, it is. We'll be docking there to resupply and to pick up our messages."

"Good. Give Odysseus the coordinates of Daisy Hub so he can put the information out on the Mitradean telepathic news network. I'll alert the station manager to expect an influx of alien immigrants." Addressing the pilot, he added, "And then Earth's government will help you choose a new home world, Odysseus, where your people can live, and thrive, and finally be free."

The Mitradean's carapace erupted in blossoms of blue and green that swirled and scalloped all the way to his tail. "Thank you, Captain Takamura," said the metal box.

"And when Fleet Control finds out about this?" murmured Dedrick.

"I plan to tell them the truth: on Earth's behalf, I decided to grant refugee status to a race of sentient, intelligent beings who are on the verge of extinction after being denied the most basic need of any living creature — a home. Any organization that can find fault with that is not one that Humans should be interested in being part of."

PART IV

THE BEST LAID PLANS OF BARRY NOVAK

Earth space 2400 — 2401 C.E.

Juno Vargas (b. 2358 — d. unknown) came to prominence as the Chief Adjudicator for New Chicago, a post she held from 2397 until 2403 C.E. Little is known of her early life. However, in the year leading up to the Battle of Daisy Hub, she was instrumental in initiating the decentralization of power on Earth, thus opening the door for a bloodless takeover by the Reformation Movement. Afterward, working with its leader Barry Novak, she is credited with brokering Earth's first formal alliance with an alien world (Stragon), a step that later led to our recognition by the Galactic Great Council. She was a registered passenger on the arrow class vessel *Liberty*, captained by Gael Dedrick, when it vanished while en route to a meeting with the Great Council in 2417 C.E.

— *Sic Transit Terra, An Unauthorized Planetary History* *(2673 C.E.)*

Chapter Nineteen

"Welcome back to Earth space, *Marco Polo*! Due to a glitch with one of our field generators, we must request that you take all weapons offline at a distance of ten kilometers from the station. Your supplies have arrived and are waiting for you on Deck M. We will begin transferring cargo into your holds as soon as your ship has passed a routine customs inspection. Please dock at module 5 and prepare to be boarded."

"Well! That was friendly," Eberhart remarked to no one in particular.

"Commander, Daisy Hub is transmitting our saved messages," called the communications officer from her console. "There are a lot of them, five commbursts so far."

"Are any of them for Commander Dedrick?"

After a pause, she responded, "Just one that I can see, marked 'personal'."

"Move it onto a datawafer. I'll give it to him myself at shift's end. And forward anything marked 'urgent' or 'immediate action' to the captain right away."

"Aye, ma'am."

Dedrick was sitting at his desk when Eberhart entered his quarters, three hours later. "This arrived for you from Earth," she told him, handing over the wafer. Then she looked around and added, "Where is Lania?"

"As soon as we docked, she ran out the door, all excited. She's probably peppering the customs inspectors with questions right now about what it's like to live aboard a space station. Sometimes I envy her."

"Oh?"

"She's seeing so many things for the first time. Makes me wonder—" Shaking off the rest of that thought, he plugged the wafer into the slot in his desktop and brought Novak's "routine communication" up on the screen.

Leslie waited politely on the other side of his desk while he read the text in silence. When he'd finished and glanced up at her, she prompted him, "Well?"

"It's just the usual. Weather's fine. Food is plentiful." He paused. "Aliens are unpopular."

She made an impatient sound. "That's nice, but it's hardly 'eyes only'. What's the actual message?"

For a moment, Dedrick debated with himself. Let her in or don't let her in — which one would he end up regretting?

Eventually, he replied, "It's encrypted."

"Then decrypt it. I'll wait."

"Leslie, I — I have to do this in private. Trust me, if you're here, you'll have no choice but to report me."

She pressed her lips together. "Fine. But you will tell me what your old family friend says. Right?"

"I'll tell you as much as I can without jeopardizing your career."

"Dammit, Gael!" Eberhart launched both her hands into the air in exasperation. Then, leaning in with stormy eyes, she said in a low, intense voice, "Stop trying to be such a hero. I'm not some kid you need to protect, and there are more important things to me than my career. The Fleet is my job. The *Marco Polo* is my workplace. There will be other jobs and other workplaces, but family is precious. That's why you stand by your loved ones. You fight for them. I know you feel that way about Lania. You've already risked your commission for her. Why is it so hard for you to accept that I can feel the same way about you?"

Stunned, he stammered, "Leslie, I'm just—"

"Shut up, mister, I'm not finished. You are the stubbornest, most infuriating man I've ever met, next to my father. Every time I try to help you, you push me away. I've been watching you learn how to be a family for that girl, all by yourself, and I know it hasn't been easy. Well, I'm giving you one, ready-made. I'm adopting you both into *my* family. Like it or not, you're Eberharts now. And there are dozens more of us. We're everywhere. You don't have to do this alone anymore."

"But—"

"Don't argue with me, Gael Dedrick! And stop trying to protect my career! Do you think for one standard second that I would stay behind if you messed up and got yourself discharged from the Fleet? Honestly, if I didn't love you so damn much, I would have killed you several times by now."

Her cheeks unnaturally flushed, she charged around the side of his desk and stood over him. Her fists were clenched, and for a moment he thought she was going to slug him. Instead, she bent down, cradled his face in both her hands, and planted a kiss on his lips that tasted like honey, stopped time in its tracks, and warmed him all the way to his toes.

At last she pulled away, breathing hard. "There!" she declared. "Have I made my position clear, Commander?"

His brain was alphabet soup. All he could do was nod his head.

"Good!" She took an unsteady step backward. "Let me know when you've decrypted that message." And she turned and walked out the door.

Almost a minute passed before Dedrick trusted his legs to carry him from his chair to the sleeping area where he'd concealed the playback device. The last time he'd felt this weak and disoriented, he'd been seven years old and had needed help to disembark after four go-rounds on a level five thrill park ride. That was what his relationship with Leslie had been like over the years — fast-moving, heart-pumping, and utterly unpredictable. So, was it pleasure or panic that had struck him dumb and set the room spinning? He wasn't sure. Maybe that was for the best.

Still feeling a little light-headed, he pulled the piece of rogue technology out of its hiding place and slipped the datawafer into the slot in its side. A moment later he was able to read the text Novak had sent him:

The problem has been dealt with. Not cleanly, I'm afraid. No details, just a word of advice. Stand fast. You have total deniability. The other matter is under investigation. More later.

He was still processing the meaning of these words when a voice erupted from his deskcomm. "Commander Dedrick, please report to the captain's strategy room immediately."

Hastily pocketing the datawafer and shoving the playback device into its cubbyhole in the bulkhead, he responded, "On my way."

Officers' quarters were located at the north end of the community sector, seconds away by tube car from the command sector of the ship. As Dedrick came through the strategy room door, he found Captain Takamura sitting at the head of the conference table, looking official. Deneuve was in a chair to his left, looking weary. And two Security officers stood at ease behind the captain, one to either side of him, simply looking.

Deneuve threw Dedrick a sympathetic glance, then returned her gaze to the tabletop.

"Commander, please take a seat," Takamura began. "I have been going through the messages recently forwarded to us by Daisy Hub. Imagine my surprise at finding among them an order from Fleet Control to place you under arrest."

Stunned, Dedrick sank onto the chair opposite Deneuve. He knew he'd heard correctly when the guards immediately moved to stand at attention behind him. "I'm under arrest?" he echoed. "On what charge, sir?"

"There are three, all related to data tampering. I'm sure you understand how serious this is. Five intervals ago a virus was introduced into Earth's population database. By the time Data Management became aware of it, it had migrated into the Fleet Control database as well, corrupting so many files that both entire systems had to be purged and then restored from backups."

Gael's jaw dropped. *This* was Novak's solution? "What?" he sputtered. "Why would I want to—?"

"That was my reaction as well, Commander, until I read further and learned that after the databases were restored, all mention of your cousin Lania had disappeared. Apparently, the backups had already been tampered with at the time the virus was activated. Earth High Council is treating both events as part of the same crime."

The taste of bile was rising at the back of Dedrick's throat. Not cleanly? That was putting it mildly!

"Captain, I assure you, this was not my doing."

"Oh, I believe you. Everyone on this ship has an ironclad alibi for the time the virus was activated. However, you are from a powerful family on Earth, one that still has influential friends, and you took a leave of absence shortly before we left Earth space. Fleet Control did some digging and discovered that you met twice on Riviera Hub with a man named Mark Reznick, of Reznick and Ohr, an off-Earth accounting firm."

Dedrick recognized the name. And the cover story.

Total deniability. Okay, Novak, here goes.

"Reznick was my uncle's financial advisor, and mine as well after Uncle Dennis died and left me a portion of his wealth."

"So this meeting was not a coincidence?"

"No. It was pre-arranged. That's the reason I chose Riviera Hub for my R and R. It's the closest resort to the Terran star system. Captain, I don't see how—"

"Is it possible you might have remarked to him, in passing perhaps, how convenient it would be if all the records regarding your cousin were simply to vanish?"

"I'd be lying if I said I hadn't thought about it, sir, but no, I didn't mention anything like that to him. I'll tell you what I did talk about, though, loudly and bitterly. It was the fact that two men I'd never heard of got my cousin Abner toxed on his birthday and then took him to Thrygg so he could become a plague dog. My Uncle Dennis had determined enemies. The whole time he was in power, they kept trying to bring him down. This was the scandal that finally did it, destroying my family in the bargain. And right after I begin investigating the two men who instigated it, I find myself accused of capital crimes? Now *that's* what I would call convenient, Captain."

"Under normal circumstances, I would have to agree," Takamura told him. "However, things are not normal right now, or simple. A process was set in motion while we were in alien space, and that process will have to run its course. Charges have been laid by both Earth's High Council and

Fleet Control. There will be a combined hearing to determine whether a full tribunal should be convened. That is where you and Doctor Deneuve will get a chance to explain your side of things."

"Doctor Deneuve is being charged as well?"

"Yes, as an accessory. Her report to Earth regarding Lania was submitted shortly before you went on leave. The virus could have lain dormant in that file for some period of time before it attacked the databases. A forensic computer analyst has been dispatched from Space Installation Security to identify any irregularities in our InfoComm system. This individual should be arriving within the next few days. In the meanwhile, I regret that I must impose restrictions on both of you."

Dedrick pulled himself to attention in his chair. "Understood, sir."

Deneuve just breathed a disgusted syllable.

In the end, the "restrictions" amounted to little more than being constantly shadowed by Security as they went about their customary routine, and being forbidden to speak privately with each other, in person or via the ship's intranet. Takamura clearly believed they were both innocent. Nonetheless, it galled Dedrick that Deneuve — whose reputation he had taken such pains to protect — had been dragged into what should have been a battle between himself and the Relocation Authority. He was going to have a few choice words for Barry Novak the next time they met.

Chapter Twenty

"So, what's going on with the *Marco Polo*?"

Station manager Drew Townsend leaned back in his chair and gazed across his desk at the grinning face of Ruby 'Mom' McNeil, his second in command, who had just plopped herself down in front of him, looking ready to burst.

"The plot thickens, Chief."

"Oh?"

"It looks as though these folks are in a spot of trouble. There's some sort of expert coming out from Earth to inspect their ship's intranet."

"Well, they did just spend eight-and-a-bit intervals in alien space," he reasoned. "Maybe Data Management wants to confirm that they didn't bring any bugs back with them."

"That's not it," cut in Lydia Garfield, Daisy Hub's communications specialist. "O'Malley found a virus in our most recent bundle of updates, and it's home grown. I was going to wait until the *Marco Polo* left before bringing it to your attention, but since it appears they'll be with us for a while..." She sat down at her station on the other side of C Deck and busied herself with her keyboard for several seconds. Then she swiveled her chair and informed him, "I've sent O'Malley's report to your InfoComm unit. The virus was a seeker, a search-and-destroy subroutine. He picked it apart to find out what, exactly, it was looking for."

"And?"

"It was a name. Lania Dedrick. Whoever created this virus wanted to wipe someone from the database."

Townsend felt a sudden chill, remembering how thoroughly his murdered friend Bruni Patel had been erased from Earth's records just a couple of years earlier. Reburying the thought, he asked, "And who is Lania Dedrick?"

Lydia smiled. "That's where it gets interesting. She was found on a plague dead world in Sector Two, along with evidence indicating that she may be the cousin of Gael Dedrick, one of the officers on the *Marco Polo*. He was granted temporary guardianship until it could be determined whether they were, in fact, genetically related, at which time the Relocation Authority was supposed to decide where she belonged. However, the ship's SMS took her own sweet time about reporting her findings to Earth. Bottom line is, Lania's been living aboard ship with him for the past standard year, without the official blessing of the Relocation Authority."

"They can't be happy about that," he observed.

"Oh, they're ticked, all right," she continued cheerfully, "and they're making him pay dearly for it. Would you believe Gael Dedrick is the one who's been charged with planting that virus? Anyway, O'Malley searched our onboard database and compiled everything we've got on the Dedrick family. It's in the file I just sent you. You should have a look at it. It's better than Teri's soap opera."

Frowning, Drew pulled the information up onto his screen and began reading. His brain lurched when he came to the names of Gael Dedrick's mother and aunt: Regina and Emma Dedrick, respectively.

Townsend's mother had had two aunts named Emma and Regina. He'd only ever heard her talk about them once, during an argument with his father shortly after Drew had lost his Eligibility. She couldn't contact her aunts, she kept saying. She'd struck a deal. She'd made a promise. She didn't dare break it or the whole family would suffer.

Being only twelve years old back then, Drew hadn't fully understood what was happening. Now, remembering those words — and the tears in his mother's voice as she'd spoken them — was enough to send a shiver down his spine.

He read further. Emma and Regina had been sisters. Their maiden name had been Forrand. Their only brother, Dennis Forrand, was the late Supreme Adjudicator for Americas.

Townsend tried to continue reading but couldn't. His attention had been snagged by that paragraph, and his mind refused to move beyond it. He'd been outraged earlier to learn how his younger self had been manipulated. This was so much worse. And yet, somehow, he knew that he shouldn't be surprised.

If this information was correct, then Olivia's powerful mentor, the man for whose purposes Drew's entire life had been shaped, was her and Drew's grandfather. And Gael Dedrick, who was in all probability being railroaded for not playing by the Relocation Authority's rules, was their cousin.

A cousin he'd never met, from a family that Drew felt no part of, at a time when he was already up to his eyebrows in dangerous secrets and needed to keep a low profile. Wonderful.

Townsend cursed silently. Then he came to a decision, the only one he *could* make and still stand to look at himself in the mirror each morning. "Lydia, contact the captain of the *Marco Polo*. Tell him we need to talk right away."

———— ‹›› ————

They met in the caf, over cups of Fritz Jensen's famous sludge. At this hour they had the room to themselves. Townsend watched the captain take a sip and struggle visibly not to make a face. He wasn't surprised. Jensen was Cordon Bleu-trained, but definitely java-impaired — to the extent, in fact, that it had become a point of pride on the station to be able to say that Daisy Hub's chef made the worst java anyone had ever tasted.

"Your message was marked 'urgent', Mister Townsend," said Takamura. "Was there some irregularity regarding our customs inspection?"

"No, quite the opposite. But it appears that you have a problem, since we've been instructed by the Space Installation Authority to detain you until another ship arrives. We believe we know what — or rather, who — the problem is, and we also believe we can help you, if you will let us."

The captain sat even straighter in his chair. "I see," he said quietly. "And what sort of help are you offering us, exactly?"

"Technical and logistical assistance, sir. There's a great deal of expertise aboard this station, and I'm placing it at your disposal. Let us know what you need, and it will be provided, no questions asked and no debt incurred."

Takamura frowned. "It's a generous offer, Mister Townsend, and it's much appreciated. Still, I can't help wondering…"

"…why it's being made? Let's just say that anyone who isn't a friend of the Relocation Authority is a good friend of ours."

———— «» ————

Five standard days later, the pilot of a sprint class cruiser of Earth design announced himself to Daisy Hub and demanded docking instructions.

Townsend and Takamura were conferring at Drew's desk in AdComm when the call came in. Hearing Lydia exclaim, "Keep your shirt on!" brought them instantly to their feet. Four strides later they were looking over her shoulder at the screen of the communications console.

"Is this the one we've been expecting?" Takamura asked.

"Oh, yeah," muttered Lydia. "I'm getting choice attitude from this guy. Like a bear with a toothache. He's going to love what I tell him to do next."

"All right, Captain," Drew told him. "Go back to the *Marco Polo* and make sure your officers know what to say. Ms. Garfield will stall the government agent until everything is ready at both ends."

Takamura bowed, first to Lydia, then to Townsend, before heading toward the tube car door.

———— «» ————

The simplest cons were the best ones. Drew had never liked Tommy Novotny, *aka* Rex Regum, but the leader of the Warrior Kings had taught him a lot during those six hellish years on the street. Keep it uncomplicated and let the mark do the work, Tommy would say. Make sure there's a grain of truth to your story. And if you need a script to keep things straight, you're just asking for trouble.

Apparently, the captain of the *Marco Polo* was also acquainted with these principles. On boarding the ship,

O'Malley had been handed a copy of the fraudulent report Takamura was planning to file with Earth's High Council. Having a blueprint to follow as he doctored the ship's intranet had made the hacker's job a great deal easier, but there was a problem: He was still tweaking the officers' personal logs, a task he would need at least another three hours to finish, and the sprint cruiser would be docking in two.

Lydia knew what to do. The moment Takamura left AdComm, she informed the incoming pilot that he would have to take his weapons offline or risk being blown up by a malfunctioning shield generator. She then promptly "lost" the hub-to-ship commlink. For about an hour, she pretended not to be able to hear the pilot as he cursed Daisy Hub from one end to the other, pausing only to make snide remarks regarding the probable ancestry and evident incompetence of its crew.

At last, Orvy Hagman, the Hub's Head of Security, buzzed through to let AdComm know that O'Malley was back aboard the station and all was in readiness. The commlink was then miraculously restored. And the pilot, evidently worn out from his ranting, complied with Lydia's instructions and came in on final approach.

When the government ship was securely docked, it was show time. Townsend gave a thumbs-up sign to Lydia and took a tube car to A Deck to welcome their newest arrival.

The man who walked through Portal 1 was tall and brawny, with his hair cut so short that his head might as well have been clean-shaven. Looking at Townsend the way a bored cat might size up a mouse, he stepped forward and extended a hand for shaking. "Mister Townsend? I've been looking forward to meeting you. I'm Forensic Analysis Specialist Grant Sullivan, formerly of Earth, currently assigned to Space Installation Security."

Drew's stomach went into free fall. He'd dealt with men like this in the past, men on both sides of the law who held grudges and settled scores. And the most vindictive and unrelenting among them, by far, had been the ones who carried badges and used their authority like a cudgel. Sullivan's pleasant façade was just that — an act. Once he had finished running diagnostics on the *Marco Polo*'s intranet, he would continue his hunt on Daisy Hub, as payback for being inconvenienced earlier. He probably had a pocketful of signed warrants with him, some of them with fields left blank so the particulars could be filled in later.

First things first, however. The con had to play out. So, ignoring his still-shrilling mental alarms, Townsend shook the offered hand while pinning on his most affable smile. "Welcome aboard, Specialist Sullivan. How long do you expect to be staying?"

"Hard to say. It depends on what I find here."

"Let me know if you require a billet, and I'll have my assistant manager prepare guest quarters for you. We do have amenities aboard the station, so if you'd like to have a meal or take advantage of our Shared Programmable Activities room...?"

"Thank you, that's very hospitable. However, you know what's involved in running an investigation, Mister Townsend, and I'd like to wrap this one up as soon as possible. If you don't mind, I'm going to head directly to the *Marco Polo*. Portal 5, I believe?"

Still smiling, Townsend took a step backward and waved him in the right direction. As soon as Sullivan was out of sight, Drew summoned a tube car, buzzing AdComm while he waited for it to arrive. Lydia responded a moment before the door slid open.

"You saw?" he demanded, glancing up at one of the surveillance cams installed on A Deck.

"I saw and I heard. Is there a problem?"

"You might say that. Call a meeting of all the senior staff, to begin in fifteen minutes. Tell them it's about security. Ours."

———— «» ————

"His name is Grant Sullivan, or so he claims, and he's with Space Installation Security."

"Or so he claims," O'Malley piped up. "Want me to look into him, boss?"

Townsend surveyed the dozen sober faces surrounding his desk in AdComm and replied, "No. He's a data bloodhound, and the last thing we want to do right now is create a trail for him to sniff out. We worked hard to set up the con aboard the *Marco Polo*. I think we should just stay low and let that scenario run. Once it's wrapped and Captain Takamura and his crew are on their way, there's a distinct possibility that Forensic Analyst Sullivan will decide to turn his magnifying glass on us. If he does, we'll need to make damn certain he can't find anything to put on a warrant."

"So it's a full station lockdown, Chief?" Ruby asked.

"Just like we've been practicing," he told her, "only this isn't a drill. When Sullivan sends in his report on Daisy Hub, I want the only noteworthy thing in it to be that diabolical piece of alien technology on the landing deck. Otherwise, we've got to be as boring as a plaincoated wall. O'Malley, when are you expecting our next update bundle to arrive from Data Management?"

"Not for another five days. With luck, Sullivan will be gone by then."

Right. Townsend exhaled audibly and reminded him, "We don't have that kind of luck."

Chapter Twenty-One

Forensic Analysis Specialist Grant Sullivan clearly knew his way around an InfoComm system. He also knew his way around a star cruiser and considered no part of it to be immune from scrutiny. Sullivan camped out in one of the guest staterooms and took three full days to conduct a thorough inspection of the *Marco Polo*'s intranet. He sifted through its databases, performed diagnostics on every work station, and searched each crew member's logs and messages, both incoming and outgoing, for anything that might be the slightest bit irregular. On the fourth day, Sullivan commandeered the captain's strategy room and began calling in ship's officers and crew one at a time for what he referred to as "fact-finding interviews".

Meanwhile, Dedrick's stress levels were rising. Novak's encrypted message kept playing on a loop inside his mind. *Stand fast. You have total deniability.* Of course, he did. Neither he nor Deneuve had done anything even remotely criminal in this case. But Novak had evidently been assuming that the investigation itself would be impartial and aboveboard. From what Gael had seen and heard of this government man so far, that was not by any means a certainty.

Dedrick had watched Sullivan board the ship, noting a smug confidence in the way he surveyed his surroundings, a predatory stealth to his movements. The longer Gael spent observing, the tighter the knot in his midsection grew, and the firmer his conviction became that Sullivan had an agenda. He'd no doubt been told what to look for aboard the *Marco Polo*, and he wouldn't rest — or let anyone else rest — until he found it. If the interviews yielded nothing useful, he might decide to search crew quarters. And there was a piece of rogue technology in Dedrick's suite that, if revealed, could be damning.

"Where is she, Commander?"

Yanked back to the present, Dedrick turned and met Sullivan's hard gray stare. He took a second to match it with a stony look of his own. "I'm sorry. I wasn't paying attention. What was your question?"

The government man chuckled. "You don't like me, do you?"

"I wasn't aware that being liked was part of your assignment."

"Fortunately for me, it's not. I just have to get the job done. That means I need to speak with Lania Dedrick. No one is admitting to having seen her lately. You're her legal guardian, so you must know where she is."

They had all practiced answering this question, as Sullivan had to have figured out by now. Gael wiped all expression from his face and replied evenly, "Actually, I'm not, and I don't. My guardianship was conditional on Lania's being genetically proven to be my relative. We got a ruling on that from Prime Docent Yorell Enne during our stay on Kula'as. The Prime Docent assured us that the Great Council considers Lania to be Kularian."

"That's impossible. Lania Dedrick is the daughter of Abner Dedrick, an Earth-born Human—"

"—and of a humanoid female of unknown origin, the product of a Thryggian laboratory experiment. Apparently, those were the genes Lania inherited, not Abner's. The Thryggians were replicating the Kularian genome at the time. That makes Lania an alien. I've done a bit of research. By order of Earth's High Council, any aliens who cross peacefully into Earth space are automatically granted diplomatic immunity."

"You denied the Thryggians ownership of her by maintaining the girl was Human. Now you deny the High Council control over her by insisting she's an alien. Very clever. But you can't have it both ways, Commander."

Dedrick had practiced this response as well. "I'm not trying to. We earlier assumed that she was Human because of her physical resemblance to her father. However, the Prime Docent has now confirmed Lania's status based on genetic evidence, which takes precedence over outward appearance. As you must have seen while going through the ship's records, we have already sent copies of Enne's ruling to both the Earth High Council and the Relocation Authority. If you still feel the need to talk to Lania as part of this investigation, I'm afraid you'll first have to get permission from the Galactic Great Council. If the past is any indication, that should only take about a standard year."

"Well played, Commander. Or should I say, well rehearsed? However, I'm not here to debate the girl's status with you. I'm investigating a case of data tampering, and well before the *Marco Polo* traveled to Kula'as, you had a powerful motive for erasing Lania's name from the official Earth records."

"I'm not contesting what my feelings were, Sullivan, only the erroneous conclusions that have been drawn by linking them to someone else's actions. Yes, I had motivation. But I'm a trained Fleet officer, operating within a strict set of rules. As a Ranger, so are you. Before you can build a solid case, you also need to prove means and opportunity, neither one of which I had before, during, or after the commission of the crime you are investigating."

"And what about Doctor Deneuve?"

"What about her?"

"She delayed submitting her report on Lania Dedrick for nearly eight Earth months. In fact, it took a direct order from her superior at Earth Medical Services to move her to action. When I questioned her about that, she told me she was, and I quote, 'buying the commander some time'. Time to do what, exactly? To find someone who could plant a virus for you in Earth's databases?"

Stand fast. You have total deniability.

"Listen," he said earnestly, "Deneuve and I both knew what would happen as soon as that report was filed, and you know it too. Some monolithic government agency would have swooped in and taken control of that traumatized girl who was quite possibly my last living relative, a cousin I never even knew I had until the census scanner picked her up on MF-307. Deneuve delayed sending in her report so I could spend as much time as possible with Lania before I lost her again. Is that so difficult for you to believe?"

Apparently, it was. Sullivan's expression grew even harder. "What I believe is irrelevant, Commander. I was sent here to dig up the facts."

"Well, here's what I believe. It's not just facts you're after, it's dirt. You found nothing incriminating on the ship's intranet, so now you're coming after us individually, hoping to hear something that you can spin into a semblance of a case. You're wasting your time, Sullivan. More to the point, you're wasting mine. Go bark up some other tree." Getting to his feet, Gael turned and spoke to the Security guard who had accompanied him and now stood just inside the door. "We're done here."

"I wouldn't bet on that," Sullivan called after him as Dedrick stalked out of the room.

———— «» ————

"Captain Takamura's on the comm, Drew," Lydia called from across the deck.

Townsend walked over to her console and saw the captain of the *Marco Polo* on the screen.

"Mister Sullivan has completed his forensic examination and left the ship, and we are finally cleared to continue our voyage," said Takamura. "Before we depart, I want to thank you for your help. Know that if you or Daisy Hub should ever require our assistance, you have only to contact us."

"That's good to hear, Captain. We're glad we could be of service. A safe journey to you."

Takamura took a step back from the screen at his end and gave them a respectful bow. Townsend returned the gesture, then signaled to Lydia to close the commlink.

"Is everything ready aboard the Hub?" he asked her.

"Ready as it'll ever be."

Right on cue, the tube car door to the right of Drew's desk hummed open and Hagman emerged, one large hand firmly clamped on the shoulder of an obviously irritated Grant Sullivan.

"I found this intruder wandering around the station," Hagman announced. "Figured you would want to talk to him."

Shrugging himself free, Sullivan squared his shoulders inside his jacket and growled, "I need a word with you in private, Townsend. That's private, as in alone."

"Uh-oh," said Lydia, blanking her screen and rising to her feet.

This was getting to be a habit.

"All right, give us the room," Townsend ordered.

When the tube car door had closed, leaving only Sullivan and Townsend on C Deck, Drew stared a question at the other man.

Sullivan's demeanor shifted into neutral. "Do they know who they're really working for?" he asked.

"Of course, they do," Drew told him without hesitation. "They're working for me."

"And do they know who *you're* working for?"

"They should. I've been sending regular reports to the Space Installation Authority for well over a standard year now. Is there a point to this line of inquiry, Sullivan?"

The government man gave him a speculative look. "All right," he said slowly, "since that's the way you're playing it... I just wanted to congratulate you on a job well done. Giving the Relocation Authority its own reason for deleting Lania Dedrick from the population database — that was brilliant. And I tip my hat to whoever altered the ship's records. The splicing was perfect."

As the truth dawned on Drew, he was momentarily at a loss for words. Finally he blurted, "Dammit, Sullivan, you could have let me know who'd sent you as soon as you arrived. It would have saved us all a lot of trouble."

"It would also have invalidated the results. We had a situation to resolve, the *Marco Polo* was already docked here, and the higher-ups decided it was a perfect opportunity to assess the operational status of the Daisy Hub cell. My report will be flattering. You can expect more assignments to come."

"Identified as such, I would hope."

"Perhaps. Yours is the most autonomous cell in the organization, so it will depend on the circumstances. Oh, and I also have a personal message for you: Your sister sends her best regards, and she wants you to know that in spite of the way things have appeared over the years, she never stopped watching your back."

——— «◊» ———

"So that's it?" said Lydia. "We weren't the target after all?"

"Not this time. He told me we could expect future visits, though, so we mustn't let ourselves get too comfortable." As the words left his lips, he realized how ridiculous they sounded. Comfort was an alien concept to the crew of Daisy Hub. Dealing with Rangers and Nandrians had turned life aboard the station into an ongoing thrill park ride. And now the EIS was officially part of the mix, making things even more of an adventure.

Drew and Lydia watched in silence as the dot representing Sullivan's ship slid off the side of her screen.

"By the way, on Captain Takamura's instructions, O'Malley transferred over some data from the *Marco Polo*'s logs before he doctored them. I've sent the file to your desk unit. It's—" She broke out in a mischievous grin. "You won't believe what's coming our way."

"He did mention something to me about expecting alien visitors to show up, but we didn't have time to discuss the details. Is that what he sent us?"

"Oh, yeah!" she confirmed.

Curious now, Drew went to his desk and pulled up the file. As he scanned it, his jaw and belly dropped in unison. What the hell had Takamura been thinking?

Large, clawless, telepathic lobsters. Hundreds of them. Escaped slaves from alien space, promised a home world and given Daisy Hub's coordinates as the final stop on some sort of galactic underground railroad. Wasn't *that* just what the Hub needed right now — another way to start an interstellar war!

Townsend groaned aloud. Beyond his wall of filing cabinets, he could hear Lydia chortling to herself. Wearily, he blanked his screen and leaned backward in his chair.

At least some things were starting to make sense to him: the message from Barry Novak, warning him about Olivia's political ambitions and reminding him of what he owed to Rex Regum; the fact that this information had been carried by a man assigned to guard Townsend from "anyone who might want to harm him"; the certainty Drew had had for some time now that there was at least one crew member aboard the Hub taking orders directly from a higher-up at the EIS; and now a greeting from his sister, mentioning her promise made years ago to protect him no matter what and claiming to have kept it.

Really, Olivia? Six years in a criminal street gang and five more in detention were your idea of protection?

He gave his head a quick shake. None of that mattered. There was evidently a power struggle going on back on Earth. Townsend was being courted separately by Novak and Olivia, each evidently expecting him to throw his support behind one of them. They couldn't possibly know — and he wasn't about to tell them — that his loyalty had already been pledged. When everything hit the fan, Drew would be backing House Daisy Hub, period.

———— «» ————

"You wanted to see me, Captain?" Dedrick stepped into the strategy room, leaving his Security detail outside the door.

Takamura was seated at the head of the conference table, with Doctor Deneuve occupying the chair to his left. He gestured to Dedrick to take the one directly across from her and waited until he was in it before telling them, "I prevailed upon Forensic Analyst Sullivan to give me a preview of the report he intends to file with Space Installation Security."

The captain didn't look pleased. Dedrick's midsection tightened in anticipation of the bad news.

"Bottom line, sir, are we cleared?" asked Deneuve.

"*You* are. He's found nothing to indicate that Doctor Deneuve was involved in any way with the planting of the virus, and he will be recommending that all charges against her be dropped. However, he is planning to request that the charges against Commander Dedrick remain on the books, and that his hearing be stayed until further evidence can be brought to light."

"Brought to light? Manufactured is more like it," Deneuve fumed, her expression darkening. "I sensed he had an agenda from the moment he boarded the ship."

"Unfortunately, Commander, once his report is filed, you will need that hearing in order to be exonerated," said Takamura. "Even though I will exercise my discretionary power to end all shipboard restrictions on your freedom, you are still considered to be a suspect under investigation and may not leave the *Marco Polo* or communicate with anyone outside the ship until your status has been determined."

"Can we stop him before he submits the report?" Deneuve asked.

"Stop him? He's already on his way to Earth, Doctor. Unless you're suggesting that I contact one of our sister ships to overtake him. And then what? Do you honestly believe that anything we say will change Forensic Analyst Sullivan's mind?"

She looked ready to explode. "This is a travesty! Captain, there must be something we can do. Some recourse. Maybe an appeals procedure?"

"Once the panel has ruled at the hearing, the commander can appeal, but not before. By postponing the hearing, Sullivan has blocked that course of action."

Dedrick thought for a moment. "Sir, if Sullivan recommends and requests in his report, who decides?"

"Normally, for data tampering, it would be the Earth High Council. However, because you're a career officer and Fleet Control has also laid charges against you, it will have to be a joint decision. As long as it's unanimous, they can choose to ignore Sullivan's recommendation and either clear your name or proceed with the hearing, based on already gathered evidence," Takamura explained, adding after a beat, "evidence that is clearly circumstantial and unsubstantiated. Otherwise, an investigator would not have been sent out to uncover more. Commander, you're not contemplating using your family's influence, are you?"

"No, sir, I'm just thinking out loud. Bastards like Sullivan are hard-wired to be mean and obnoxious, and they can't help showing it. Space Installation Security must have realized what kind of man they were sending out here. If I'm correct about this being an attempt to stop me from investigating what happened to my cousin Abner, then Sullivan wasn't picked for this assignment by accident."

"The entire situation could be a setup, Captain," Deneuve pointed out. "Surely there's something Fleet Control can do, even if our hands are tied."

"I suspect they're already flexing their muscles," Takamura replied. "When a charge of data tampering has been laid, it is standard procedure for the accused to be taken into custody immediately and confined by Security. There was a Ranger detachment sharing orbit with Daisy Hub. They could easily have removed you from the ship and transported you directly to Earth for detention awaiting your hearing. And yet, here you still are, where Lania needs you to be. Since Fleet Control appears to be working quite effectively on your behalf, I think we should be patient and avoid doing anything that might interfere with their further efforts."

As Dedrick stood watching Takamura and Deneuve walk out the door, one thing became crystal clear in his mind: Lania would not be safe as long as she remained on a Fleet ship, within reach of Earth's various government authorities. He would have to find a way to move her somewhere else as soon as possible.

Chapter Twenty-Two

Cursing, Barry Novak flipped open the cover of a concealed keyboard in his desktop and rattled out an urgent message to the operative currently on his way back to Earth. Then he leaped off his chair, stormed out of his office, seethed in the elevator all the way down to the Warrior Kings' parking level, and drove to the mansion that had once belonged to Dennis Forrand and was now the property of Juno Vargas, Chief Adjudicator for New Chicago.

Sweeping past her startled housekeeper, he made directly for the stairs leading to the clean room in her basement. The door was closed. It swung rather than slid. He gave it a hard shove and strode into the room.

Two women were sitting having tea, one on the midnight blue loveseat facing the door and the other on a lighter blue padded armchair. They froze in place for a moment. Then, with deliberate movements, Juno put her cup back on its saucer and deposited them both on the glass-topped, wrought iron coffee table in front of her. "Good afternoon, Barry," she said coolly. "To what do I owe this invasion of my privacy?"

"You co-opted one of my field agents, Grant Sullivan. I want to know why."

"Sullivan? I learned that he was going to Daisy Hub and I gave him a message to take to my brother," she replied.

"You did more than that. You superseded my instructions to him."

The second woman, as plain and sturdy as Juno was elegant and shiny, got to her feet. "I'll give you two the room."

"No, stay, Angeli," Juno commanded her, keeping her frosty gaze fixed on Novak's face. "I may need a witness."

Angeli cast a longing glance in the direction of the door, then settled back onto her chair.

"What instructions did I allegedly supersede, exactly?" Juno inquired.

He stepped around the furniture and stood over her, expecting a show of defiance but eliciting only a puzzled frown.

"Sullivan was supposed to clear both parties involved, regardless of what he found," he informed her.

"What are you talking about? Found where?"

"You know where — aboard the *Marco Polo*."

She mouthed the name, struggling visibly to place it. "That's one of our star cruisers. Isn't Forrand's nephew—?"

"Drop the act, Juno. I was trying to help Gael Dedrick with a problem, but things went a little sideways on me. I ordered a power failure and got a computer virus instead. Now Dedrick has been charged with a capital crime that he never committed. I sent Sullivan out there to make sure the charges wouldn't stick. If he hadn't thought to update me right after leaving Daisy Hub, I wouldn't have found out about his report to Space Installation Security until after he'd filed it. Then Dedrick would have gone into detention to wait for an exoneration hearing that would probably never come. Dammit, Juno, we promised Forrand that we would protect his family, not screw it over!"

Her back went rigid. "I swear to you, Barry, I would never have done such a thing. All I gave Sullivan was a message to deliver on Daisy Hub."

"Well, you're the only other person who could have changed his orders. He told me the new instructions came with a valid verification code, and those codes are known only by you and me."

"And by me."

They both turned and stared at the woman who had calmly resumed drinking her tea.

"Angeli?" Juno ventured, her voice rising in disbelief.

Novak's anger had begun to subside. Now it was building again, straining his self-control. "You share our operational codes with her?"

"I tell her what she needs to know in order to do her job. And you're one to talk," she pointed out tartly. "You and Randy Chin share information all the time."

"Information," he snapped. "Not confidential codes. You tell her what she needs to know? So you're admitting you set out to sabotage Sullivan's assignment?"

"Absolutely not," Juno replied. Still sitting, she elevated her chin and impaled him with a cool gray stare. "However, I'm certain Angeli had an excellent and compelling reason for what she did."

They remained that way for a long moment — eyes locked, bodies taut — as an ominous silence settled over the room. Then Angeli carefully replaced her teacup on the table, cleared her throat, and explained:

"A friend of mine is a low-level bureaucrat at Fleet Control. I supplement his credit balance and he keeps me informed about their intranet activity. A couple of years ago, Abner Dedrick's voice log was recovered from his sprint craft on MF-307, a plague-dead colony world. In it, he gave a detailed account of how he'd ended up on Thrygg back in 2384, mentioning Paul Travanti and Ian McCormack by name."

"Those were two of our earliest shell identities," said Juno, "the first ones that Forrand personally designed for Earth Intelligence. They were signed out for a mission and then he ordered them wiped from the database, about two years before he died."

Novak remembered hearing about that mission. It had predated his appointment to the post of Chief Operations Officer, so he hadn't been privy to any of the details. All anyone knew was that it was classified above top secret and that all the pertinent records had subsequently been expunged.

Angeli continued, "I waited to see whether the discovery of the voice log would generate any follow-up activity. Aside from a handful of InfoComm inquiries that quickly dead-ended, there was nothing. Then, a short while ago, Fleet Control received a request from a Commander Gael Dedrick aboard the *Marco Polo*. The message was directed to specific high-ranked officers. It mentioned Dennis Forrand's name and asked each one of them to dig deeper and find out who and where Paul Travanti and Ian McCormack might be."

"He had a suspicion and was pulling every string he could reach," Juno remarked.

"And your friend intercepted these communications?" said Novak.

"Yes, and replied apologetically on behalf of each officer that there was simply no information to be had. It was the truth, and that should have been the end of it, but—"

"—but he's part Forrand and wouldn't give up," Novak concluded. "That explains why he came to me."

Juno shot him a troubled look. "He asked *you* to find McCormack and Travanti? What are you planning to tell him?"

"I don't know," he replied. "I was still considering that when Sullivan's end-of-mission message crossed my desk unit. I was forced to drop everything and go into disaster prevention mode, thanks to your friend here."

"Barry, you can't reveal that the EIS had anything to do with what happened to Abner."

"Give me some credit, Juno. I wouldn't jeopardize the entire organization just because two operatives stole a couple of shell identities and went rogue."

"Mmm," said Angeli, her features contracting into a pained expression.

Novak's jaw muscles instantly tightened.

He'd always believed the official explanation — that Forrand had "killed off" Travanti and McCormack because they'd been compromised by the activities of a pair of rogue agents and couldn't be used for legitimate EIS operations anymore. But what if that story had been fabricated as a cover-up? What if someone had ordered those operatives to step into those shells and take Abner Dedrick out of the picture?

The look on Angeli's face gave him his answer.

"They weren't rogues, were they?" he grated. "They were on a mission for someone in the EIS. Who was it, Angeli?"

She stiffened in her chair. "I promised never to talk about it."

"Look around you," he commanded her. "You're in a clean room, sharing total privacy with the two people Forrand trusted most in all the world. Nothing you say will shock us, and nothing will be repeated once we leave. Who ordered the hit on Abner Dedrick?"

"It wasn't a hit. That was the problem. It was supposed to be a disappearance, and it boomeranged."

"Angeli?" Juno's tone of voice left no room for argument or delay.

When the other woman spoke, the words came out in a rush. "Dennis Forrand gave the order. He had to protect the EIS."

Novak had lied about not being shocked. "From Abner Dedrick? What kind of threat could that kid possibly—?"

"Forrand had made the mistake of trying to recruit Abner into the organization. He thought it would straighten him out by giving him a purpose in life. Instead, Abner turned around and tried to blackmail him, threatening to reveal to the Earth High Council what he'd learned about the EIS. If this had been someone outside the family, Forrand would have simply had him eliminated. It would have been quick and clean. But he couldn't bring himself to terminate a blood relative, even by proxy. Instead, he instructed two agents to take Abner somewhere far enough away that he couldn't return to Earth. He left the details up to them to give himself deniability. They're the ones who chose Thrygg."

"And to prevent Gael Dedrick from learning who was really to blame for destroying the Dedrick family," said Novak, "you decided to hang him up in limbo, under arrest and unable to communicate with anyone outside his ship. How long were you planning to leave him like that, Angeli?"

She shrank a little. "I don't know. I just knew I had to do *something*. Listen, you promised to protect Forrand's family. I took a slightly different oath. I promised Forrand I would protect his reputation while he was alive and his memory once he'd passed. That's all I was trying to do. I'm sorry if I derailed your operation."

If she derailed it?

When she finally met his stern gaze, the misery in her eyes was enough to melt Novak's anger. Good intentions, he thought wearily. Everyone had them these days. No one was evil except the Thryggians, and for all anyone knew, they might have had their own, alien good intentions to justify derailing the evolution of Humanity. And creating and unleashing the plague. There was probably some excellent, compelling reason for that, too.

The other loveseat was looking very comfortable. But he couldn't stay here, not even if Juno asked him to, not even briefly. He had promises to keep.

«»

By the time Novak had parked his PV and ridden the elevator back up to his office, he was almost as furious as he'd been when he left it. Juno Vargas found it easy to forgive Angeli's trespasses. All Novak could think about at that moment was what her interference had nearly cost him.

It had taken years of patient grooming and maneuvering to plant Sullivan in Space Installation Security. Almost as long, in fact, as the twenty-four Earth years that it had taken Forrand and Vargas to put Drew Townsend in the station manager's chair on Daisy Hub. If Sullivan had filed his final report with SIS and its recommendations had been accepted, the quickest way to clear Gael Dedrick's name would have been by discrediting the report. That would have meant discrediting the investigator who had written it. Grant Sullivan would have been fired or reassigned, and all the time and effort Novak had invested in him would have been for nothing.

The alternative would have been to manufacture and plant exculpatory evidence, a project that would have tied up the EIS's resources for an unconscionably long time. In the end, questions would have been raised about Sullivan's competence and/or impartiality, since he'd failed to notice the evidence that would clear Dedrick's name. Again, Sullivan would have been bounced from SIS, wasting years of careful planning.

And what about Gael Dedrick, the nephew Forrand had been most proud of, the one with not only a passion for space exploration but a gift for it as well? Novak's final instructions from Dennis Forrand regarding the promising young Fleet officer had been quite specific. There was an admiralty in Gael's future, and nothing could be allowed to jeopardize his career or deprive him of his Eligibility. That was why it was so important that he have deniability in the current situation.

It was a lesson Novak had learned on the streets when he was still Tommy Novotny: ignorance wasn't bliss, but it usually guaranteed a pass on a lie detector scan. Deniability was why Forrand had kept his family unaware of his risky pet project, the Earth Intelligence Service. Deniability should have ensured that Gael Dedrick would be cleared of all charges. Thanks to Angeli's meddling, however, deniability hadn't been enough.

Juno was close to launching her Reformation, Novak could tell. Angeli had begun intruding more boldly into the operations side of the organization. He needed to put a stop to this. He had agents in the field, some of them deep undercover, and nothing could be allowed to endanger them or compromise their missions.

Hmm. There was an entire wardrobe of shell identities in the EIS closet, some of which hadn't been used in a while. Maybe it was time to take a page from Dennis Forrand's playbook and make Angeli disappear.

"That's a very intriguing smile you're wearing, Barry. Care to share with the class?"

Novak glanced up to find Nayo Naguchi, *aka* Randall Chin, watching him from the doorway of his office.

"Or would you rather I went away? Either one is a valid response."

"Is there something I can do for you, Nayo?"

"I heard that you stormed out of the building earlier, and just now I watched you storm back in. It seems to me that there might be something you need *me* to do for *you*."

"I have a problem."

Naguchi crossed to the visitor's chair and dropped onto it. "And you're smiling. Do I want to know why?"

"No."

"Fair enough. So what's your problem?"

"Forrand's nephew is trying to investigate us. He doesn't realize that's what he's doing. He thinks he's just getting to the bottom of what happened to his cousin Abner sixteen Earth years ago. If it were anyone else, my path and my conscience would both be clear. But I made Forrand a promise before he died, and I owe him too much to even think of breaking it."

"This nephew is Gael Dedrick, correct?" Novak nodded. "I gather he's asking questions. Are they the right ones?"

Novak leaned back thoughtfully in his chair, recalling the interrogation he had earlier conducted of the Stragori agent, Nestor Quan. "Because asking the wrong questions will change the complexion of the situation, leaving it open to interpretation," he mused aloud from memory.

"Can you answer his questions factually without revealing the truth?"

Novak grinned. "Nayo, you're brilliant."

"I just plagiarized Nestor Quan. Brilliant is not the word I would use. However, I do appreciate the sentiment. If you need me for anything further, I'll be in my lab." And with that, Naguchi got to his feet and headed for the door.

Novak flipped open his concealed keyboard, activated the encryption module, and drafted his next private message to Gael Dedrick:

The Dedrick family has already been avenged. Travanti and McCormack were acting on their own when they took your cousin to Thrygg. They were terminated by Dennis Forrand shortly before his death in 2387 C.E. All records containing these names were deleted from the database to protect Forrand's reputation while he was alive, and to keep his memory unsullied once he'd passed.

Chapter Twenty-Three

Dedrick reported to the captain in his strategy room as ordered and found Deneuve there as well, looking mildly pleased.

"I have an update regarding your case, Commander," said Takamura. "It isn't all good news, but there is some."

Dedrick sank slowly onto a chair. "What's the good news, sir?"

"Mister Sullivan apparently had a change of heart before he filed his report. Either that or someone at Fleet Control has brought pressure to bear. In any case, your preliminary hearing has been scheduled and we are currently on course for Earth."

"You get to clear your name, Gael," said Deneuve. "Finally, common sense prevails!"

"Our ETA is in just under two intervals," Takamura supplied.

"And the bad news?"

"When we arrive, Earth Medical Services will be taking temporary custody of Lania. Earth High Council wants them to corroborate Doctor Deneuve's findings before they will accept Yorell Enne's ruling."

Dedrick's stomach tipped over into a barrel roll. So, all his efforts to keep Lania out of the High Council's hands had been for nothing. Play by the rules or throw them away — it didn't seem to matter. He and Lania were caught in a web. The more they struggled, the more entangled they became, and the more inevitable the result appeared to be.

"Appeared" being the operative word.

"No," he decided.

"They won't hurt her, Gael," Deneuve assured him. "They'll take the same samples as I did and put them through the same tests, and they'll get the same results as I did, leading them to the same conclusion."

"And once they've confirmed that she's genetically an alien, what then?" he demanded. "They won't let her stay with me, and she's too young to be on her own. So either Earth Medical Services will lock her up in one of its laboratories, or Earth Council will contact the Galactic Great Council to arrange for her deportation. And when the Great Council finds out about her — you heard Yorell — Lania will be killed."

Deneuve and Takamura shared a worried look.

"I'm afraid we have no choice in the matter, Commander. We have our orders."

"There's always a choice, Captain. Sometimes it's not obvious, but it's there," Dedrick declared.

"I'll need to know what you're planning, Mister Dedrick. Don't forget, we're already co-complicit in several illegal activities. One more should not make a difference."

"It's better if you don't know, sir. Not yet, anyway."

———— «‹›» ————

Dedrick arrived at Leslie Eberhart's door with gift in hand, fingers crossed, and heart in mouth. She was the linchpin in his escape plan. If she refused to help, he would be dead in space. If she'd meant what she said earlier, she couldn't possibly deny him now. But she had also told him that she wouldn't stand by and watch him throw away his career. That was what this last desperate attempt amounted to — getting Lania to safety at the expense of everything he'd been working toward for the past twenty-one Earth years — and the knowledge that Leslie could scuttle it with a single word was enough to make beads of sweat pop out on his forehead.

He'd purposely waited for her to come off bridge duty. By now she should be back in her quarters, out of uniform, relaxing with some music or watching a video. Putting herself in the right frame of mind to do him a very important favor. Dedrick had to focus on keeping his hand steady as he pressed the button to announce his presence outside her door. An endless moment later, it slid aside, allowing him to enter.

Leslie's suite was the mirror image of his own, but done up in soothing blues and greens instead of pensive golds. Standing in her living area, he saw her sitting with her legs up on the sofa, watching him expectantly. She was barefoot and wrapped in a fuzzy white robe, he noted, and there was a paused image on her light screen. A battle scene. He recognized it from a flat-screen video they had once watched together about ancient Earth warriors. It was fiction, of course. He remembered what he'd said the first time he'd seen it. "No one with any sense would go to war wearing nothing but a helmet and a skirt."

"And sandals," she added, smiling as she got to her feet. "Don't forget the sandals."

He held out the square container he'd been carrying. "I bring you an offering."

Her eyes widened when she opened it. "Dried fruit? Wherever did you get this?"

"From Ixbeth. She brought it back from the market on Dimmla, so I can't guarantee that we're going to like the taste of it, but—"

Leslie had already popped a piece into her mouth. "Mmm!" She helped herself to another. "If the jam-filled cookies hadn't come from my brother, I'd say this leaves them in the dust."

"Speaking of your brother..." Suddenly aware of how high his shoulders had risen, Dedrick consciously relaxed them.

Leslie stopped chewing and tilted her head, frowning. "What about Sam? You're not here to break some bad news, are you?"

"No! Nothing like that. I just— I need you to do me a favor."

"*You* need a favor? Well, that's a switch."

"I'm under house arrest and need you to send a message for me, to Earth."

"I see." She sat back down on the sofa. "Won't it arouse suspicion, my contacting one of your powerful friends?"

"No, because the transmission will be addressed to Sam Eberhart."

Her face lit up with understanding. "Aha! I gather it will be something appropriately personal and chatty, concealing an encrypted text? Which reminds me — you never did tell me what that other one said."

"It was a warning that my old friend had tried and failed, and that I was on my own."

"And that explains why you've been charged with data tampering. Some friend! All right, I'll help you on one condition, Gael. You have to let me in on your plan. All of it. If I know the details, I can't accidentally give anything away."

Dedrick hesitated. He'd wanted her to have deniability, but he couldn't argue with her logic.

"Agreed," he said with a sigh, and bit into the piece of dried fruit that she had left in the box for him. It was sweet and tart at the same time.

———— «» ————

The *Marco Polo* was three standard days away from Earth.

Dedrick let Lania sleep while he packed up their belongings. He'd already changed into civilian clothing. His uniforms, and anything else Fleet Control had provided, would be left behind. The Dedricks weren't thieves. When he was done and two of their three cases were standing near the door of their quarters, he entered Lania's module and sat down on the edge of her bed.

Her eyes opened. "Is it time to leave?" she murmured.

"Almost. Pick something to wear from your suitcase and get dressed."

Minutes later, they were making their way along empty corridors to the landing deck. Outside the door, Dedrick paused to check his chronometer. The officer on duty in the control room overlooking the shuttle apron would be going off shift in less than twenty standard seconds. When her relief arrived, attention would be distracted from what was happening on the deck. That was when he and Lania would sneak aboard the short-hopper he'd had refueled several hours earlier.

Mentally crossing his fingers, he led the way through the door. He threw a quick glance in the direction of the control booth, then did a double take. The little room was empty. That wasn't right.

"I'm sorry, Commander, but I cannot let you do it."

Dedrick whipped around and saw Takamura and Eberhart standing beside the hatch of the getaway shuttle. His heart dropped. Then he realized that they were alone. Security was nowhere in sight.

"Captain, you know how important this is."

"Indeed. That is why I've approved Commander Eberhart's request for emergency leave. She and Lania will take the shuttle and rendezvous with the ship that her brother has arranged for, while you return to Earth and clear yourself of all charges."

All by itself, Gael's head began turning from side to side.

"No. Once Fleet Control finds out what you've done, both your careers will be over. I refuse to be responsible for that."

Takamura scowled. "And I won't let my second in command throw away his entire future with a single act of misguided heroism." He drew himself up to his full height and continued, "I've been in the captain's chair for over twenty standard years. This isn't my first scrape with the big hats at Fleet HQ and, trust me, it won't be my last. Commander Eberhart was well aware of the consequences she could be facing as well when she came to me with this plan, but she made an extremely convincing case for it."

"We're both going into this with our eyes wide open, Gael," Leslie assured him. "You're not dragging us into anything. We've chosen to do it."

Dedrick drew a calming breath before trying again.

"Look, I appreciate that you want to help me keep Lania safe, and I'm grateful for the offer. But why ruin three careers if two can be spared? Regardless of who carries out the plan, I'll be taking the heat for it. Earth's authorities are going to know that I'm the one hiding her from them."

"No doubt," said Takamura. "But you'll take the heat much better if you can't tell them where to find her. And isn't that the real point of this exercise, Commander?"

He was right. Before Dedrick could acknowledge the fact, however, a determined young voice piped up, "When is it *my* turn to choose?"

Startled, all three adults turned to look at the teenaged girl patiently standing at the end of a row of suitcases. Eberhart walked over, placed an arm around Lania's shoulders, and said to the others, "You know, since she's a person and not a piece of luggage, I think she *should* have some input into this discussion."

An unwelcome warmth rose in Dedrick's cheeks. He'd been so busy protecting his cousin from the coming danger that it had never even occurred to him to ask her what she thought or how she felt about it, and that was wrong. Despite what he had told the Kularians earlier, Lania was not a child. She was just two years younger than he had been when he'd entered the Fleet Academy.

"Commander, since you're her guardian, you have the final say on this," Takamura pointed out.

"All right," said Dedrick, "but whatever she chooses, it needs to be an informed decision. She needs to know what all her options are, and what the consequences will be in each case."

Lania considered for a moment, her expression sober. "If I go to Kula'as, what will happen?"

"Regardless of how you get there, if you're found and recognized anywhere in alien space you'll be caught and killed, by order of the Great Council," Dedrick told her. "Yorell Enne was very clear about that."

"And if I run away from Earth but stay in Earth space?"

Eberhart summed up flatly: "You'll either spend the rest of your life in hiding or you'll be a fugitive, constantly looking over your shoulder, until you're caught. When that happens, Commander Dedrick will face charges again, this time for something he actually did, and you'll be taken to Earth for testing, found to be an alien, and probably deported to Kula'as."

"So the result for me will be the same, only it will be worse for Gael. And if I go to Earth now and let them test me?"

Takamura replied, "The scientists at Earth Medical Services will confirm and certify that you are not Human."

"And then?"

"We don't know," Eberhart said. "That's the problem. They might deport you, but they might let you stay in Earth space. It's a risk Commander Dedrick was not willing to take. That's how he ended up in this fix in the first place."

He shot her a warning look. She returned it with *You know I'm right!* attached.

"And what happens to Gael if I go to Earth?" Lania persisted.

"Then he will have his hearing and will be able to clear his name," said Takamura.

"And this is my choice to make?"

Before Dedrick or Takamura could respond, Eberhart declared, "Your choice."

"Then I choose to take my own risk by going to Earth." And without another word, Lania picked up her suitcase and headed for the door to the corridor, leaving the three adults to stare at one another in wondering silence.

———— «» ————

A Security shuttle was already docked at the Fleet transfer point orbiting Earth when the *Marco Polo* arrived. Dedrick and Lania were quickly and quietly ushered onto it by a detail of blue-uniformed officers, then flown to a holding facility adjacent to Fleet Control Headquarters for processing. Not a word was spoken directly to either of them during the entire journey.

At the facility, Dedrick and Lania were separated. He watched her walk calmly toward an exit, flanked by two female Security guards. He hoped that she would turn at some point and give him a reassuring smile, but she didn't. His heart clenched, forcing a lump into his throat. This wasn't his cousin — it was the girl who had gazed indifferently at three mangled Thryggian corpses and had then looked at him with alien eyes not so long ago aboard the ship.

As soon as she was out the door, a pair of armed guards took Dedrick brusquely in hand. They marched him into a small room, verified his identity using Fleet Control records, then escorted him to one of a row of circular cells to await his hearing. Dedrick surveyed his new accommodations and realized how fortunate he'd been. If someone hadn't interceded on his behalf, persuading the Earth High Council to let him remain aboard the *Marco Polo*, this was where he might have spent the past few Earth weeks.

The cell was shaped like a large bird cage, with a round concrete floor surrounded by a double-layered plastiplex wall. Each circular layer had a door and a small pass-through at waist level. The door openings were lined up to allow him inside. Then the outer layer rotated, offsetting the doors and trapping him there.

Dedrick sank onto the edge of his cot and wondered how long it was humanly possible to go without using the hygiene facilities. The stainless steel toilet and basin should have been politely concealed. Instead, they sat out in the open, in full view of anyone who happened to walk by. The toilet in particular set his teeth on edge. Privacy was a privilege he would have to earn, it seemed, by being cleared of wrongdoing. Until then, his every action would be monitored by securecams and scrutinized by strangers. But it could have been worse, he reminded himself. The cells to either side of his could have been occupied, forcing him to observe the personal habits of his neighbors as well.

"Hey! How long until the hearing?" he called out.

The guard on duty glanced up, looking as though he'd just been rudely awakened from a very pleasant dream. "It'll take as long as it takes, Commander," he rumbled. "They're having trouble finding qualified people who are willing to sit on the panel. Imagine that."

Dedrick could guess the reason. Dennis Forrand might be dead and buried, but his influence lived on. Barry Novak was proof of that. Nobody with political ambitions would risk having to return an unfavorable decision against the last surviving member of the Supreme Adjudicator's family.

"And what about Lania?"

"Lania?"

"Lania. The girl I came here with. When will—?" The guard gave a huge yawn. "Never mind," Gael sighed.

"It's two a.m. in this time zone, Commander. You'd better get some sleep."

Sure. Like *that* was going to happen.

———— «» ————

"She's waiting for you, boss. In your office."

Barry Novak halted in mid-stride and stared at his second in command. Novak had stepped out of the elevator in the Warrior Kings' headquarters and found DeWitt waiting for him, looking like a little kid bursting to share a secret.

"She? She who?" Novak demanded.

"Boss lady. Juno Vargas. She got here about ten minutes ago. Says she has intel for your ears only and won't leave until she delivers it."

This was a switch. Usually they discussed Earth Intelligence business in her clean room. If the Chief Adjudicator was willing to risk being seen entering the Zone, the information she carried had to be a matter of extreme urgency. His mind bubbling with questions, Novak quickened his pace.

She was sitting on one of the guest chairs. As he swung the door wide and came through it, she turned toward him and said, "We have to talk."

No tea. No polite rituals.

"Here?"

"It's as good a place as any in this building," she told him briskly. "I've been doing some digging."

"And?"

"Angeli has definitely overstepped her bounds. She's set off a whole chain of problems."

"Tell me something I don't already know," he grumbled, dropping into the armchair behind his desk.

"All right. Sullivan's orders weren't the only ones that she interfered with. I just learned that she has contacts at Data Management, and that one of them, supposedly on a hunch, decided to inspect the main power supply a little over fourteen weeks ago. He found and replaced a faulty component, thus heading off what very shortly would have been a catastrophic surge corrupting all of the databases. A few days later, the system was infected with a virus that accomplished the same thing. Interesting timing, wouldn't you say?"

Novak leaned back thoughtfully. So, Angeli was responsible for the slip-up in that operation? He'd actually suspected as much. She probably numbered a hacker — not a terribly good one — among her acquaintances as well. In any case... "Shouldn't we be having this conversation in a clean room?"

Cool gray eyes met and captured his gaze. "Only inside a jamming field."

"You believe she's planted listening devices in your basement?"

"At this point, I wouldn't put it past her. And I think she's doing more than just protecting Forrand's memory, Barry."

"Oh?"

"I — have reason to suspect that she sees herself as my protector as well."

"Having a protector could be a good thing for someone in your position," he pointed out.

"Not if she's on a mission to eliminate anyone who might try to topple me from that position."

That got his attention. Novak straightened in his chair. "Such as?"

"Gael Dedrick. Abner knew about the EIS and tried to blackmail Forrand. We know how that ended up, and I'm pretty sure Angeli had a hand in it. Now Gael Dedrick's hearing has stalled because only two of the three chairs on the panel have been filled. One is the Supreme Adjudicator from Indo-Asia. The second is a high-ranking officer from Fleet Control. The third is supposed to be a civilian adjudicator with no connection to the accused. For some strange reason, no one can be found who fits that description and is available to serve."

"Do you think she has something to do with that?"

"I think it's possible. Forrand called her a loose cannon and used her as an *agent provocateur*. It's a role she fills very effectively. I also happen to know that Gael recently received something from Dennis Forrand's estate. A late bequest. The fact that it was delivered so long after his death to a spacer, someone who would take it far away from Earth — that has to be significant."

"I guess the question is, does Angeli know about it?"

"I can't say for certain what she knows or doesn't know right now. But I came here to tell you this: I've offered to fill the third chair at Gael Dedrick's hearing. If I'm accepted, since I know for a fact that he's innocent of all charges, I will do my damnedest to get him exonerated."

"And if your suspicions about Angeli are correct, and she sees you getting in the way of her efforts?"

"Loose cannons are volatile and have trouble following orders. That's what makes them dangerous, and it's why I want you to keep an eye on her, if you're not already doing so."

He feigned shock. "Spy on our own people? Why, Juno, that would be—"

"Prudent. Barry, you're the only one I trust to handle this. If she tries anything, I want you to stop her. Do it however works best, with prejudice if necessary, but without exposing the EIS. We still have Forrand's work to carry out, and it must remain secret."

Vargas was as close to rattled as Novak had ever seen her. Smiling inwardly, he told her, "You can depend on me, Madame Chief Adjudicator. In exchange for this service, however, I have a request to make."

"Of course, you do," she said. "Does it involve Nestor Quan, whom you still haven't terminated despite my explicit instruction to do so?"

"It does."

"Why am I not surprised?" A beat, then, "All right, Barry, what is it you want from me?"

"I want you to give him a fair hearing, just as you're trying to guarantee for Gael Dedrick."

She was silent for a moment, her gaze wandering to something over his right shoulder. He imagined she was weighing the cost of a deal with the devil. Novak was weighing something too. He wasn't sure he had it in him to refuse to protect her if she decided to turn him down.

Finally, she looked directly into his face and said, "Agreed. I'll hear him out. But I won't promise anything more than that."

"You don't have to," he assured her.

Chapter Twenty-Four

The Justice Building next to Fleet Control Headquarters in Congoville had been constructed sometime between the second pandemic of 2172 and the third pandemic of 2232, a period when Earth was facing a worldwide lumber shortage. So, the new High Council had declared a moratorium on the felling of trees and had initiated a global reforestation project. The use of wood for any purpose was restricted.

That didn't stop the wealthy and powerful from installing oak or maple flooring, or putting custom-made wooden cabinetry in every room of their homes, nor did anyone expect it to. Wealth and power were as much a perception as they were a fact. Similarly, the fledgling government needed to present its various branches as being entitled and authoritative. That explained the interior of the tribunal chamber in which Gael Dedrick's hearing was about to take place.

The chamber was spacious, with walls, floor, and ceiling all finished using the same locally grown wood. This particular variety had been chosen for its darkness and density, and for an exquisitely fine grain that seemed to flow from one polished board to the next. The effect was both somber and sobering, precisely the gravitas needed when judgment was being pronounced on one's past and the course of one's future was being determined.

In case that wasn't intimidating enough, the three adjudicators would be ensconced behind a massive, ornately carved wooden desk with gold-leaf trim delineating every edge. The message to the accused was clear: this was an immovable object, and by extension, so the panel would be as well.

"All rise!"

Standing beside his Fleet-appointed advocate at a table that appeared flimsy by comparison, Gael Dedrick stared at the desk directly in front of him. His stomach churned as the black-robed hearing adjudicators filed in through a door at the front of the chamber and took their places on the dais.

"All be seated!"

He lowered himself onto his chair. There was only one way to conquer a fear, Lania had said. Gael raised his eyes to the grim faces of the three beings who currently held his life in their hands. One of them looked very familiar. He frowned, struggling to place her. Then he recalled where they had met, and quickly dropped his gaze.

She was Dennis Forrand's protégée, Juno Vargas. She had attended the reading of Forrand's will in 2387. And she and Gael Dedrick had definitely not hit it off that day. Apparently, inheriting his home and its furnishings hadn't been enough for her. She'd scowled and crossed her arms over her chest when she'd heard how much of his liquid wealth Forrand had left to his spacer nephew. That had been more than thirteen Earth years ago. He couldn't help wondering what her presence signified today. Did Gael have a friend on the panel? Or was she there to make sure his case went to a full tribunal?

His mouth suddenly dry, Dedrick turned in his seat and scanned the gallery behind him. He'd expected the room to be packed with reporters. After all, despite his name, he was a Forrand. As Abner had amply demonstrated, anything a Forrand did was newsworthy, especially if it was scandalous. A Forrand accused of a capital crime should have generated a whirlwind of media attention.

Except that this Forrand was a career Fleet officer, and the Fleet protected its own. Fleet Control had evidently moved quickly, laying its own charges in order to have some control over the proceedings, then ensuring that the hearing would take place in a restricted area, closed off to the general public and especially to the tabs. Not even the crew of the *Marco Polo* were permitted to attend in person. Instead, they had been ordered to remain aboard ship, watching a delayed video feed on a selected number of viewscreens.

As a result, the gallery was nearly empty. Dedrick saw Eberhart and Takamura sitting together beside a red-haired man with deep-set eyes, an aquiline nose, and a smile that was the twin of Leslie's. This had to be Sam Eberhart. Across the aisle from them, Lania sat between Deneuve and a man Dedrick didn't recognize. The three of them appeared to be chatting quite comfortably. It had taken long intervals for Lania to feel that relaxed around strangers. It was because of Gael's own patience and determination that she was now able to make friends so easily. He knew he should be proud. And yet, seeing her like this, at this moment and in this room, planted a nameless unease at the back of his mind.

Forcing his attention away from Lania, Dedrick noticed a plain-looking woman on a chair near the door. She wore her brown hair in a knot at the crown of her head, and she was glancing around with mild interest, as though she'd wandered in off the street and decided to stay out of curiosity.

Gael had no time to wonder about her. His advocate, a man of average build and with forgettable features, gave him a hard nudge in the ribs and hissed, "It's starting."

"Would the accused please stand," said a deep male voice from the dais, speaking in unaccented Anglo.

As he got to his feet, Dedrick glanced up. The Fleet admiral was leaning forward on his elbows, staring down sternly at him. *Stand fast. You have total deniability.* Gael squared his shoulders and held the admiral's gaze.

"Watch Commander Gael Arthur Dedrick, you have been charged with the following: data tampering; counseling or inciting others to commit data tampering; and conspiracy to commit data tampering. Do you understand the nature of these charges that I have just read to you?"

"I do, sir."

"Data tampering is a capital offence, whether or not you personally committed the crime. If we find sufficient cause to hold you over for a full tribunal on any of these charges and the resulting verdict is 'guilty', the sentence will be death. There can be no other. Do you understand that?"

Dedrick swallowed hard. "I do, sir."

"For the record, this is a hearing, not a tribunal," the admiral continued. "Guilt or innocence will not be determined here. We will be ruling on the strength of the evidence to make a case, and whether it would serve the public interest to take that case further. We on the panel have already reviewed the evidence against you. Now you will have the opportunity to hear that same evidence and give us your side of the story before we make our decision. Your advocate is not here to speak for you, to provide additional evidence, or to call witnesses to rebut the existing evidence. He is here to advise you as you speak for yourself. Is *that* understood?"

Dedrick felt as though he was drowning in words, but he managed to reply, "Yes, sir."

"Then be seated, Commander. Advocate Roth, you may begin."

The prosecuting advocate was a civilian, a tall woman with dark hair, sharp features and a throaty voice. As she got to her feet and went to stand behind one of the two podiums in the room, she threw Dedrick a look that made Eberhart's frostiest glare seem hospitable by comparison. It took all of his resolve not to turn his eyes away from it.

Without preamble, Roth began, "My first piece of evidence is the report filed with Earth Medical Services two days ago. Would Doctor Randall Chin please step forward."

The man who had been sitting with Deneuve and Lania stood up and walked to the second podium, where he was met and sworn in by a uniformed official with a compupad. As he watched this, Dedrick's thoughts were racing. First Noris had gotten inside her head, and now a government scientist had befriended her. What had he told her? What had he promised? Beset by a sudden wave of restlessness, Gael had to fight the urge to grab Lania and make a run for the door.

"You are the physician and scientist who performed genetic testing on Miss Lania Dedrick at the laboratories of Earth Medical Services in New Chicago, Americas. Is that correct?" Roth was saying.

"It is."

"Please tell the accused what conclusions you were able to draw as a result."

"Lania Dedrick's DNA does not match the scientific definition of Humanity as established by the well-known geneticist Doctor Nayo Naguchi in Earth year 2382."

"Since I'm sure Commander Dedrick is not familiar with that definition, please elaborate, Doctor Chin."

"It's based on a series of comparative analyses with non-Human genomes. Naguchi was able to identify those genes that were uniquely Human. He discounted the ones that determined our physical appearance, since we know of at least one alien race that is outwardly identical to ourselves. What remained was a handful of genetically transmittable characteristics pertaining to the internal workings of the body. By Naguchi's definition, any being in possession of these particular genes can be designated Human."

"And by examining the genome of Lania Dedrick, you were able to determine that she does not have these genes and is therefore to be classified as alien by the Earth Relocation Authority?"

"That's correct."

"Could any Human geneticist perform the same examination and come to the same conclusion as you did?"

"Any competent geneticist who'd been following Naguchi's work should be aware of his definition of Humanity, so I would imagine the answer is yes."

"I see. The reason for your examination was to corroborate a ruling by an alien authority, specifically the Prime Docent of the Galactic Central Archives. We have no way to establish what her credentials are as a geneticist, or what sort of criteria or measuring tools she used. All that reached the Earth High Council was her final determination that Lania is alien. They could have rejected it out of hand. Instead, they gave it enough credence to call for a second — Human — opinion. Yours, Doctor Chin. Would you *imagine* for us please what might have prompted them to make that choice?"

"Why they chose me, you mean? Or why they took her seriously?"

"Both."

"I believe they took the Prime Docent's assessment seriously because it had already been corroborated by Doctor Sylvie Deneuve, a brilliant Human physician and researcher of considerable reputation, currently the Supervisor of Medical Services aboard the Fleet star cruiser *Marco Polo*. As for the High Council's choosing me to corroborate Doctor Deneuve's corroboration — prior to Nayo Naguchi's unfortunate death, I was the second most respected geneticist on the planet. Were he alive, he would be standing here in my place."

"You're correct in stating the impressive credentials of Doctor Deneuve, who is well known and highly regarded in the Human medical community. However, two related facts stand out in this case. First, she and Commander Dedrick had served aboard the same ship for a number of years and knew each other quite well. And second, Doctor Deneuve has already admitted to purposely delaying the submission of her report on Lania Dedrick to Earth, as a favor to him. That is why a second opinion was needed — the objectivity of the first one could not be trusted.

"Please remember that you are under oath, Doctor Chin, and give some thought to your next answer. Was there any enticement or pressure, subtle or otherwise, placed upon you to agree with either the Prime Docent's ruling or Doctor Deneuve's corroboration of it?"

"Not at all. I was instructed by the Earth High Council to perform the examination and arrive at an objective and scientific conclusion."

"As long as it was timely and definitive, correct?"

He dipped his head slightly in reply.

Roth gave him a mirthless smile. "Thank you, Doctor. You've been most helpful."

The admiral turned his attention to the accused. "Commander Dedrick, do you have anything to say?"

His advocate leaned closer and murmured, "If she can demonstrate that you've used your family's influence in the past and that you had a strong motive for removing Lania from the database, then she can connect those dots and make you look guilty enough to warrant a tribunal. That's her strategy. Don't challenge the testimony. Only explain your side of things if it conflicts with the spin she puts on the evidence."

And therein lay the problem, Gael reflected, because Roth was right. Dedrick *had* used his family's influence. It didn't matter that he'd spent most of his life trying to forget that he was part of the Forrand family tree. The first time he'd invoked Dennis Forrand's name in a request for help to the Fleet admiralty, he'd broken a solemn promise to himself never to follow in his uncle's footsteps. The first time he'd asked Barry Novak for a favor, a string of dominos had begun to fall, culminating in this moment.

Stand fast. You have deniability. And Lania needs you.

Dedrick got to his feet and replied, "No, sir. Not at this time."

There was more evidence, most of it gathered by Grant Sullivan and easily explained away when Takamura and Eberhart were called to testify. The forensic analyst was absent, Gael noted. It was just as well. Sullivan had a knack for getting under people's skin, and Dedrick would have a difficult time maintaining his composure if they had to be in the same room together for more than a couple of minutes.

Finally, Roth zeroed in on his visit to Riviera Hub.

"On August 18 and 19, Earth year 2400, you met with a man who identified himself as Mark Reznick of Reznick and Ohr, the financial management company that for many years has represented the business and personal interests of the Forrand family. The Forrand pharmaceuticals empire and the firm of Reznick and Ohr are both well known to the judicial branch of Earth's High Council. Many of their dealings have been described as questionable. What's more important, however, is the fact that they have directly and indirectly benefited the Dedrick family. In a word, Commander, you are connected. Your uncle looked after you when he was alive, showed you which strings to pull to get things done. Now that he's gone, you're still pulling them. A word in the right ear and any problem you have will be taken care of. Isn't that right?"

He wanted to smack the knowing smirk right off her face, but he knew what the result of *that* would be. And, as Leslie's voice at the back of his mind kept repeating, Lania needed him.

While waiting in his bird cage with its completely exposed hygiene facilities, Gael had realized for the first time that there was a strong possibility of things coming out at this hearing. Not family secrets, just personal things he would much rather have kept to himself. Having to bare his butt for an audience each time he relieved himself in the toilet had embarrassed and annoyed him. The prospect of being forced to bare his soul the same way in a tribunal chamber had angered him. But this woman's smugness angered him even more. She wanted to connect some dots? He would give her a few of his own choosing.

Dedrick unclenched his jaw and deliberately relaxed his shoulders before asking in as steady a voice as he could manage, "Is that a rhetorical question, Ms. Roth?"

"It is, if my assumption about you is correct."

"Actually, you've made several assumptions about me, and none of them are correct," he pointed out. "So maybe I'd better respond." With that, he stood up and walked to the second podium.

"Do you swear that what you are about to say will be the whole truth and only the truth?"

Mentally crossing his fingers, Dedrick replied, "Yes."

"You say I've made unwarranted assumptions about you, Commander. This is your opportunity to set the record straight." Roth invited him with a wave of her hand. "Tell me what I got wrong."

"All right. Let's begin with the meeting on Riviera Hub," he said, "which you've portrayed as me pulling one of Forrand's strings. When Dennis Forrand died, I inherited part of his wealth. That was thirteen or fourteen Earth years ago, and it was his choice, not mine. From then until last year when I decided to take R and R, I hadn't touched a credit of it. I'd been out in space, serving the Fleet while my inheritance sat in a special account Forrand's executor had set up with Reznick and Ohr. Nine standard years is a long time to let an investment sit. While on leave, I consulted with someone about my options. We talked, he gave me some ideas, and I've been thinking about them. That's it. That's all there is to tell about that meeting."

"Really! And you never once mentioned Lania Dedrick to the man you met with on Riviera Hub?"

"I didn't say that. Becoming the guardian of a teenaged cousin I never knew I had was a huge change in my life, and a lot of responsibility. I wanted to provide for her future. So, of *course* I mentioned Lania to him. Why wouldn't I?"

"Witnesses said you became visibly agitated during the meeting. Didn't you also share with him the fact that you had previously asked the Relocation Authority to postpone classifying her, and that you were extremely unhappy with the answer they gave you?"

"No, I didn't tell him that. It's true that I was upset when they turned me down flat. I made my feelings known to a number of people, including most of the officers aboard my ship and at least a couple of bureaucrats at the Relocation Authority. However, by the time I took my R and R, I was far more frustrated by the non-answers I was getting regarding what had happened to my cousin Abner. If someone overheard me raising my voice, that's what I was venting about — constantly running into dead ends and stone walls while trying to uncover the truth."

"It still sounds to me as though, being a Forrand, you felt entitled to receive preferential treatment from Earth's government, Commander."

Leveling a steady gaze at her, he replied, "In fact, Ms. Roth, what I felt entitled to was the same right as any other Human to complain about the inflexibility of the Relocation Authority. If I had a credit for every time someone griped about the Authority, I'd be able to buy the *Marco Polo* and sail her to the edge of Earth space."

Someone on the panel chuckled briefly, then abruptly stopped.

"As for your suggestion that Reznick and Ohr and the Forrand family may have been involved in shady dealings, I can't comment on that because I've never been close enough to either one to find out about their business. It's ironic that you would call me connected. If anything, I'm *dis*connected.

"My earliest memory is of my mother warning me never to ask for a favor or accept a gift from Uncle Dennis. I grew up with that warning constantly in my ears, and I never disobeyed her instructions. And if you'd known my mother, you wouldn't have disobeyed her either. As the record shows, I entered the Fleet Academy at the age of seventeen, mainly with the intention of distancing myself from the Forrand family."

With a predatory gleam in her eyes, Roth cut in, "Because it was corrupt?"

"Because it was dysfunctional," he snapped back at her. "I was fortunate enough to be assigned off-world immediately upon graduation, and during my career aboard the *Marco Polo*, I kept to a minimum all contact with my family on Earth. Now I have none."

"No family on Earth, or no contact with them?"

"Both."

Dedrick risked a glance at the gallery. Leslie's mouth was an 'O' of comprehension, and her eyes were shining. So were Deneuve's.

"Actually, Commander, that's not quite true. About four Earth years ago you interceded on behalf of a man named Sam Eberhart, pulling strings to prevent him from losing his Eligibility. So you do wield some of the Forrand influence, despite your protestations."

"Actually, Ms. Roth, *that's* not quite true. I contacted a man I'd renewed acquaintances with at the reading of my uncle's will. He was an old family friend, and I asked him to meet Commander Eberhart's brother at the airfield and help him out. Sam had just been ripped away from his family by the Relocation Authority, and I realized that he would need an ally on Earth, someone to stand by him and protect him from anyone who might try to take advantage of Sam's emotional state. That's it. That's all I asked for. Look me in the eye and tell me you wouldn't do the same thing."

"You're making my point for me, Commander. You don't *have* to ask for more. You just have to use a vague expression like 'help him out', knowing that anyone who had dealings with your late uncle will feel obligated to go above and beyond to keep his favorite nephew happy, even if it means bending the rules, breaking the rules, or twisting an arm or two. And by anyone's definition, that means you have influence. How else do you explain the exception that was made for Sam Eberhart?"

"I don't know," he bristled. "Maybe someone at the Relocation Authority grew a heart."

"You're not helping yourself, Commander Dedrick," warned the admiral.

Juno Vargas leaned forward now and said, "Ms. Roth, it seems to me that this line of questioning would be more appropriate for a tribunal than for a hearing. Meanwhile, I have several questions for the accused that are relevant to our purpose here."

Roth dipped her head in acknowledgment and stepped out from behind the podium.

"Commander, do you need a moment?" said Vargas.

He steeled himself and looked her in the face. "Not necessary, Madame Adjudicator."

"Good. Then please answer these questions with a simple yes or no. Have you at any time or by any means asked, suggested, or expressed the wish that someone hack into a computer database for any reason?"

Finally! "No."

"Have you at any time or by any means been approached by someone offering to hack into a computer database for any reason?"

"No."

"Have you at any time or by any means witnessed another person talking about hacking into a computer database for any reason and either expressed approval or withheld disapproval of the subject matter?"

"No."

"And if Ms. Roth could produce witnesses willing to testify to the contrary?"

"They would be lying through their teeth," he told her, hardening his voice. "There can be no witnesses, because I've never done any of those things."

"Is it possible that someone who knew your uncle and felt they owed him a favor might have become aware of your situation and decided to repay the debt by solving your problem without your knowledge?"

Reluctantly, Dedrick replied, "I suppose."

"Yes or no, Commander, for the record," said the admiral.

"Yes, it's possible."

"Do you have any idea who that someone might be?" Vargas continued.

He shrugged helplessly. "No. A lot of people knew Dennis Forrand. A lot of people probably owed him favors when he died. However, as I said earlier, I made a point of distancing myself from the family when I was younger, and I've been out in space since 2384. I'm sorry, Madame Adjudicator."

"As am I, Commander."

That wasn't what her eyes were saying. He braced himself for the next question: Did he know anyone with the skills to hack into a computer database? Of course, he did — Barry Novak. And that O'Malley fellow on Daisy Hub.

"I'm done," said Juno Vargas.

Gael's thoughts stumbled. What had just happened?

Advocate Roth stepped behind the other podium. "Admiral, Mister Supreme Adjudicator, do you have any further questions for the accused?"

The members of the panel traded looks back and forth for a moment. Finally, the admiral replied, "No further questions, Ms. Roth. The accused may be seated."

A sudden release of tension pulled much of the strength out of Dedrick's legs. He barely managed to reach his chair without tripping. As he dropped onto it, his advocate congratulated him quietly, "You did well. But it's not over yet. Roth gets the final word. She'll present her theory of the case, and we have to sit calmly and listen to it. Then the panel may or may not retire to deliberate before announcing their decision."

Gael said nothing. He was arriving at a decision of his own.

"Esteemed adjudicators, should you decide to hold the accused over for a full tribunal, it is my intention to show that Commander Dedrick had the means, motive and opportunity to commit the crimes of which he is accused.

"First, I will show that although Commander Dedrick may not personally possess the skills to create a computer virus or hack into a computer database and plant one, he is well acquainted with — and easily able to reach — individuals who can.

"Second, I will show that despite his claims of ignorance and his physical distance from Earth, Commander Dedrick has always been well aware of his late uncle's *modus operandi*. The accused has demonstrated by his own actions over the years that he knows which strings to pull and where to apply pressure in order to accomplish his own ends. This gives him the means.

"Third, I will show that Commander Dedrick had a powerful motive to keep Lania Dedrick out of the hands of Earth's government agencies. It was so powerful, in fact, that after being denied a postponement by the Relocation Authority, he resorted to exerting his own and his family's influence to get all mentions of Lania Dedrick wiped from Earth's databases. We know that aboard the *Marco Polo*, he used his personal connection with Doctor Deneuve to buy himself more time. On Riviera Hub, he could have taken advantage of the meeting with the man who identified himself as Mark Reznick to get a message to a contact on Earth. And while the *Marco Polo* was visiting Kula'as, he could have talked the Prime Docent of the Central Archives into verifying that Lania wasn't Human. That's motive and opportunity."

"You intend to discredit the Prime Docent by suggesting that she was an accomplice, Ms. Roth?" the Supreme Adjudicator observed. "You'll be treading dangerous ground."

"I'm merely pointing out that getting Lania Dedrick classified as alien was another way to accomplish the commander's goal, sir."

"Advocate Roth, have you completed your presentation?" Juno Vargas asked. Her tone of voice left no doubt as to what the correct answer had to be.

Roth hesitated for a moment, then replied, "I have, Madame Adjudicator."

Vargas turned to address the other two members of the panel. "Then I'm ready to rule, gentlemen."

"As am I," said the admiral. "Supreme Adjudicator?"

"Yes," came the response.

"The accused will stand to hear the panel's ruling," declared the admiral. Dedrick and his advocate got obediently to their feet.

"Be advised," murmured the advocate. "When they rule this quickly, it means their minds were already made up, and nothing you've said has changed them."

"So are they for me, or against me?" Gael murmured back.

"Hard to say. There were three separate charges. Any one of them could stick."

A throat was loudly cleared, drawing their attention to the three stony faces on the dais.

"If you're done, Advocate?" said the admiral.

The man's cheeks flushed. "Yes, sir. I'm sorry, sir."

"Mm-hmm. Regarding the charge of data tampering, this panel finds insufficient supporting evidence to recommend going to tribunal."

Dedrick felt painful knots forming across his shoulders and had to resist the urge to shrug them loose. He stood as straight as possible and focused his gaze on the admiral's face.

"One down," muttered his advocate unnecessarily.

"Regarding the charge of counseling or inciting others to commit the crime of data tampering, this panel finds insufficient supporting evidence to recommend going to tribunal."

They knew he'd perjured himself by omission. They just didn't feel it was in anyone's best interests to prove it. At least, that was what Dedrick was hoping.

Stand fast.

Silence filled the tribunal chamber, seeming to drive out all the air. Dedrick worked to fill his lungs. He longed to steal a glance at the gallery but was powerless to turn his eyes away from the dais.

"Two down," whispered his advocate.

"Regarding the charge of conspiracy to commit the crime of data tampering…" The admiral gave him a long look.

Of course, they knew. But Fleet Control were as guilty as anyone else of pandering to those in positions of power. Fleet Control had bent over backward for the Forrands in the past, as Gael Dedrick well knew, and they'd "flexed their muscles" to spare him the indignities that anyone else accused of his crimes would have suffered. Sending this case to a full tribunal would bring everything out into the open.

Dedrick felt a lump rise to sit stubbornly at the back of his throat.

At last, the admiral continued, "This panel finds insufficient evidence of the criminal intent that would justify a recommendation to go to tribunal. Therefore, we are ruling in favor of Watch Commander Dedrick and ordering that all charges against him be dropped. However, we feel the need to warn the watch commander that he must exercise extreme caution in future when interacting with anyone who might have known the late Dennis Forrand, in order to avoid misunderstandings regarding the watch commander's intentions."

Dedrick exhaled, only that moment aware that he'd been holding his breath. "Yes, sir. Thank you, sir."

Juno Vargas was staring fixedly across the room. Dedrick turned to follow her gaze, just in time to see the plain-faced woman hurry out the door. For a moment Gael let himself speculate. Then he dragged his thoughts back to the present. There had already been more than enough drama in his life for one day. It was time someone else took a turn.

After shaking the departing advocate's hand, Dedrick stepped forward to greet the spectators rushing toward him from the gallery. To his joy and relief, Lania was the first to launch herself into his waiting arms.

———— «» ————

They were back aboard the *Marco Polo*. This had been a very stressful day for all concerned. Leslie Eberhart had opted to spend the rest of it with her brother before he had to return to New Chicago. Pending the final decision of the Earth High Council regarding Lania's status, she had been handed over to Takamura, who had returned her into her cousin's care the moment Gael had boarded the ship. She was currently sound asleep in the Dedricks' quarters. The captain was on the bridge. The subordinate officers and crew were going quietly about their duties as ordered, respecting the watch commander's need for privacy.

The post-hearing paperwork had taken an hour to complete. Once the final signature had been recorded, officially releasing him from custody, Gael's stomach had spoken up, reminding him that he hadn't eaten since breakfast. Now he sat in the ship's mess, making his way through a bowl of warmed-over chili, while Deneuve sipped java across the table from him and critiqued the cook's latest attempt to create the perfect blueberry scone.

Neither of them wanted to talk about what was really on their minds.

For Deneuve, it was the fact that they were still docked in Earth orbit with fingers crossed, and with a couple of different ways remaining for things to blow up in their faces before Fleet Control gave the *Marco Polo* leave to depart.

Lania's classification as an alien still had to be entered in Earth's central database. After that, the Earth High Council would declare her to be either *grata* or *non grata*; and if they deemed her *non grata* — an unlikely occurrence but still a possibility — their next step would be to contact the Great Council to arrange her deportation.

The charges against Gael Dedrick were similarly not officially dropped until the panel's ruling was entered in both the central and the Fleet Control databases, as well as on his service record. Could hearing adjudicators change their minds after the fact? Deneuve wasn't sure she wanted to know. She certainly didn't want to jinx the process by asking that question aloud. So, she concentrated instead on the sweetness and quantity of the blueberries in the pastry she was eating.

Dedrick was just as glad to be discussing the relative merits of jalapeño and chili peppers for spicing up a casserole. It left part of his mind free to consider the final details of a plan that he had been putting together for some time now.

Thanks to Barry Novak and the real Mark Reznick, there was still a sprint cruiser, fully fueled, waiting for him on a private airfield just outside of Ares. If worse came to worst, he could remove Lania from the *Marco Polo* before anyone arrived to take her back into custody, and there wasn't a soul aboard ship who would try to stop him. And if the High Council decided she was *grata* after all and let her stay where she was...?

Dennis Forrand had left him a moderately large inheritance. Under Reznick and Ohr's expert management the credit balance in Dedrick's special account had more than doubled since 2387. It was now sufficiently large to purchase a medium-sized ship in good repair. A working vessel, Gate-enabled, perhaps an arrow class hauler. Gael could apply for an independent ship owner's license, resign his Fleet commission, and go into business for himself, in that order, taking Lania and the Forrand family's secrets with him. And Leslie Eberhart, if her feelings for him hadn't changed. Between contract jobs, they could explore some of the uncharted regions of Earth space.

Assembling a crew wouldn't be a problem. Ross Posey would probably jump at the chance to sign on, and together they would find other spacers whose dreams the Relocation Authority had stolen, and give them their chance for an adventure as well.

That was how Lania would see it — as a grand adventure. And after all the years Gael Dedrick had spent in uniform, pulling shifts and implementing someone else's agenda, he was looking forward to seeing it that way as well.

PART V

THE TRIBULATIONS OF DREW TOWNSEND
Daisy Hub 2401 C.E.

The Nandrians (home world: Nandor) were the second race of aliens to make contact with Humanity, but they rapidly became our first real trading partners. Reptilian in appearance, Nandrians are merchants and explorers, but they are first and foremost warriors, with a highly ceremonial society that values honor above all else. They are quick to anger if they sense any sort of slur and this intensifies if they have been ingesting citric acid. They also tend to speak in riddles, making conversing with them extremely challenging.

Nandrians were among the combatants at the Battle of Daisy Hub in 2402 C.E. The Nandrians also supported Earth's petition for recognition by the Galactic Great Council in 2417, and the Nandrian delegation to the Council helped to draft the Reunification Agreement of 2420.

The Nandrian planetary sport, *tekl'hananni*, is actually formalized combat, to the death. Due to the aliens' sheer size and strength, Humans are actively discouraged from attempting to participate in it. Nonetheless, several have tried, with mixed results. (*See* **Leon Goldman**, **Vince Trager**.)

— *Sic Transit Terra, An Unauthorized Planetary History (2673 C.E.)*

Chapter Twenty-Five

Drew Townsend had just returned to AdComm from a loud and angry discussion with the captain of a departing Earth ship, and he saw no point in keeping his frustration to himself. "Lydia," he announced while striding from the tube car to his desk, "inform the crew that we need to give priority to figuring out that damned field generator before the next crisis descends upon us."

She spun in her chair, wearing a pained expression. It stopped him in his tracks.

"Don't tell me," he begged her.

"I'm sorry, Drew. The *tekl'hananni* scoreboard just went up. House Trokerk took on House Drellith, and Drellith cleaned their clocks. They're ahead by more than twenty points."

Ouch! The final score in *tekl'hananni* was a body count. Each "point" was a warrior killed in action. This was how the Nandrians, embroiled in a millennia-long civil war, got around the Great Council's requirement that each member race have a peaceful home world. They'd turned their planetary conflict into a sport played in space, complete with rules and officials. And, thanks to a previous station manager, there were also regular post-match victory parties held on Daisy Hub.

Townsend exhaled noisily and sat down behind his desk. "How many ships can we expect?"

"Drellith had three light cruisers in the last encounter. One is too badly damaged to go anywhere under its own power. The other two have evacuated its surviving crew and will be here in approximately forty-three hours. They've had heavy casualties, but there are still about thirty-five warriors on their feet, in total." After a pause, she appeared, sober-faced, at the end of his improvised wall of filing cabinets. "That means more than half of their three original crews are dead or seriously injured. And they're ahead on points."

Meaning that Trokerk's losses had been even worse.

"Okay. Send them a friendly reminder about the House rules. And find out the status of the *Krronn* and the *Nannssi*." The Chief Officers of those two Trokerk vessels were personal friends of the Hub's crew. With luck, neither ship had been involved in this match.

"Will do," she told him.

As silence fell over AdComm, Townsend closed his eyes and pressed himself more deeply into his chair. The fun and games just never seemed to stop.

——— «» ———

Thirty hours to go.

"Drew? Gouryas and Singh are on their way up here." Ruby's voice floated across the deck and over top of his filing cabinets. "They said to tell you that they have good news and bad news."

A moment later, the tube car door to the right of his desk hummed open and the two engineers stepped out. They were a study in opposites, Singh wearing a perpetual smirk and Gouryas's swarthy face etched with a near-constant scowl. Good news and bad news personified.

"Gentlemen?" he said, inviting them with a gesture to sit. He waited until both their gazes were level with his own before continuing, "I understand you have something to report."

Singh was the first to speak. "I've made a breakthrough with the paintbrush, and I think we now have a way to reverse the soft spots on the bulkheads resulting from the Midnight Muralist's work."

This was the good news.

Drew nodded approvingly, then added after a beat, "But...?"

Gouryas's frown had deepened perceptibly. "In the process of finding it, he's managed to ruin almost every spare wall panel in the parts locker, leaving us short if there's an emergency," he declared. "And I can't think of a single reason to give for ordering more that won't put us under scrutiny by the Space Installation Authority."

"And that's the bad news?"

"That's just half of it. Tell him," Gouryas commanded, looking daggers at his partner.

The smirk wilted slightly. "You remember what happened when we went to Zulu to investigate their field generator?"

"As I recall, and the Rangers may never let us forget," said Townsend, "the molecular paintbrush turned their landing deck and several other enclosed spaces a lovely shade of purple." Gripped by a sudden suspicion, he added, "What's the color this time?"

Hesitantly, Singh replied, "A deep red."

"You can't simply overpaint it using a different setting on the same device?"

"I tried that," said Singh. "It collapses the molecular latticework of the metal."

"It does what?"

"Fatigues it," the other man explained. "Makes it so brittle you can break it apart with your fingers. The air pressure we maintain inside the Hub would be beyond its tolerances."

Intrigued, Drew leaned forward on his elbows on the desk. "Resulting in explosive decompression?"

"Theoretically, yes. The effect would be the same as if a bomb had detonated right beside the hull."

"Congratulations, Mister Singh," said Townsend. "I mean that sincerely. You've turned the paintbrush into a short range defensive weapon. Now, if the two of you can just get a handle on the field generator, you might be able to extend and widen that range, giving us enough firepower to take out a ship or two if the Hub should come under attack."

"Like monkeys with typewriters," Gouryas remarked sadly, "using them to bash in the heads of other monkeys."

Drew remembered that earlier conversation. It had taken place on L Deck shortly after his arrival on Daisy Hub. He'd postulated back then that the Nandrians might have given the Humans on the Hub a puzzling piece of technology in order to see what they would do with it. It was beginning to look as though he'd been right.

"Like it or not, Mister Gouryas, it's the kind of monkey we are. The Nandrians are warriors and, given cause, so are we. We know that *tekl'hananni* is a war game, and that every Nandrian ship is equipped with one of these field generators. So, maybe the test of worthiness we're undergoing is to see how long it takes us to recognize a weapon for what it is."

"And to assemble it." Ruby had been listening so quietly that Drew had forgotten she was there. Now, wearing a purposeful expression, she rounded the end of his wall of filing cabinets and settled herself onto one of the guest chairs. "I've been sifting my mind for all the places on Daisy Hub where the Nandrians might have left us a clue, and something occurred to me. The generator arrived in pieces, and we've been logically assuming that they were all delivered at the same time, to the same address. What if that assumption is only half right?"

"You're talking about our missing part being on the Zoo," Townsend remarked.

She tilted her head and arched a knowing brow. "Unless a third party that we're not aware of received a package from the Nandrians at the same time as we did."

As three pairs of eyes came to rest expectantly on his face, Drew blew out a breath and leaned back into his seat. That the answer might lie on the Rangers' platform wasn't a brand new idea for him. It had actually been meandering across his mental landscape for a while now, raising red flags everywhere it went. If Ruby was right — and he strongly suspected that she was — then a visit to Zulu was definitely in order. However...

"It can't be a stealth mission," he finally told them. "Rodrigues is sharp, nothing like Bonelli. He knows about the first con we ran and he'll be watching for another. Hoping for it, I'm guessing. It will give him the excuse he needs to establish a permanent Ranger presence on Daisy Hub. Since that is the last thing we want, I'm going to be upfront with him and get official clearance for you to board the Zoo. But not for a treasure hunt. 'I'll know it when I see it' won't fly with Rodrigues. He's career Security, and he's familiar with search warrants. Unless you already have an idea of what you're looking for and can tell him what it is, he won't even open his landing deck doors for you."

"Then we're done before we start," Gouryas complained. "The emitter resembles an overgrown crystal. The generator is a plain black metal cube. The paintbrush could be mistaken for a wall ornament. The missing component might be as small as a wristcomm or as large as one of your filing cabinets."

"Maybe there's something else we can do over there," said Singh. He threw Gouryas a defiant glance, then straightened in his seat and continued, "Somewhere on each generator there must be the equivalent of a settings display, or a readout of some sort. We've lost the ability to see what the original settings were on our field generator, but no one's been tinkering with the one on the Zoo. If we can find and record that display, then we'll know where to look for it on our own generator. And if we can duplicate those settings, we may be able to return our sensor field to the way it was before."

"Putting the genie back in the bottle," said Drew.

"And making the invisibility field useless," Gouryas pointed out. "We talked about this, Dev. It's a big step backward. We'll be effectively returning to square one."

"Not true," retorted Singh. "The next time we approached the problem, we'd have all the lessons learned from the mistakes that were made the first time around, plus the ability to press reset and start over."

"I agree," Townsend declared, repeating it more loudly to cut through their bickering. Once he had their full attention, he continued, "Mister Singh, conditional on Rodrigues's going along with it, I'm green-lighting your proposal as a short-term measure. If you're successful, it will buy us all some breathing time. Go and gather whatever you require for the mission. Pick a technician to accompany you in case two hands aren't enough. Then sit tight and wait for further instructions. Ruby, you're on standby to fly them to Zulu and back on *Devil Bug*. And don't let them dawdle. I'll need you all here and at your stations before the Nandrians arrive."

"You got it, Chief."

———— «» ————

House Drellith was no stranger to Daisy Hub. Drellith and Trokerk had been switching back and forth between first and second place on the *tekl'hananni* scoreboard for the past half-year. So, Drew was spared from having to recite a first contact speech — a small mercy. There would still be two ships full of warriors arriving simultaneously and two Chief Officers to be welcomed onto the station in accordance with Nandrian ritual. Two crews of large, evolved carnosaurs with venomous bites, fresh from battle and quick to respond with violence to any perceived insult. And if the past was any indication, they would probably lumber through the docking portals with the smell of citric acid already on their breath.

"I'm not getting paid enough," Drew muttered as he perused the speeches Gavin Holchuk had written for him.

"Who among us is?" Sitting opposite him at the small round table in the caf, Holchuk grinned and took a swig from the mug of java that Fritz Jensen had just placed in front of him. "Cheer up, boss man. When you've finished describing your latest exploit, you'll be a hero as well as a *Hak'kor*."

"A hero who used guile and deception to pull the wool over a government agent's eyes. I thought the Nandrians abhorred dishonorable conduct."

Holchuk shrugged. "If Trokerk were coming, that would be an issue. With Drellith, it's not."

"Wait a minute. We've had at least four visits from House Drellith. Now you're telling me they're dishonorable?"

"Not really. At least, not in the sense that we should be locking up our valuables before they arrive. All I'm saying is that Drellith isn't as averse as Trokerk is to using sneaky tactics to win a match. They never actually cross the line and cheat. That would get their entire First Shield slaughtered and the rest absorbed by the other Houses. But Nagor tells me that several of their victories have been questionable, sparking lively debates among the referees."

"Sneaky tactics," Drew repeated, not liking the sound of those words. "Is that how they won their latest battle against Trokerk?"

"I guess we'll find out when they get toxed and start bragging about it. Will you be joining the party this time?"

"That depends. Will I have to threaten to call in the Rangers again to restore order?"

Before Holchuk could respond, Townsend's wristcomm buzzed.

"Drew," said Lydia's voice, "*Devil Bug* is on its way back, ETA in about three hours. No problem there. But I've got Zulu on the comm screen. You need to come up to AdComm right away."

"My cue," he said to Holchuk, getting to his feet.

The Chief Cargo Inspector raised his mug in a farewell salute as Townsend headed for the corridor.

Drew took the tube car to C Deck and strode directly to Lydia's station.

On the communications console's light screen, Captain Rodrigues was visibly struggling to keep a straight face. "Are you expecting company, Townsend?"

"Yes, two shiploads of Nandrians in about twenty-four hours. Why?"

"I've been tracking an approaching small craft, the size of a short-hopper. It's definitely alien. We've made voice and visual contact with the pilot. He calls himself Odysseus. Says he's ready to claim his new home."

"Paul, I have no idea what—"

"He also says that a Human ship's captain gave him Daisy Hub's coordinates and assured him that he would be welcome there."

Lydia's lips were pressed tightly together, holding back laughter. Abruptly, Drew understood.

"Does this Odysseus look like a large, clawless lobster?" he asked wearily.

Rodrigues was now grinning from ear to ear. "More like an overgrown prawn, actually, with a bullhorn voice. I've cleared him to enter the system. Good luck welcoming Odysseus home." Chuckling, the Ranger captain broke off the commlink.

"Terrific," Drew muttered. "Just what we need right now. Lydia, you'd better warn him about the—"

"I'm on it. Direct him to the landing deck?"

"Sure, why not. Tell Hagman to meet him there and bring him down to Med Services. That's where I'll be for the next few minutes, giving the Doc a heads-up."

It appeared this was going to be another interesting day.

———— «» ————

Twenty hours until the Nandrians were due to arrive.

There was a reason Drew Townsend hated having to wait around for things to happen. It gave him time to think. Right now his mind was crowded with disturbing possibilities, and with memories that tumbled and spun. They spawned questions that he wasn't sure he wanted answered.

He and Olivia were almost certainly related by blood to Dennis Forrand, the late Supreme Adjudicator for Americas. By now, Olivia had to be aware of this as well. Had she known it when she'd sought out Forrand to be her mentor all those years ago? Had Forrand known it when he'd accepted her as his protégée while at the same time leaving her twelve-year-old brother to the not-so-tender mercies of a street gang? Had Olivia been aware of what was happening to Drew, as she'd claimed in her message? And if so, why hadn't she done something about it? Or even just gotten word to him?

What kind of man would he be now if Olivia had kept her promise to protect him?

He guessed he would never know.

"It's no use hiding, Mister Townsend."

Dragged back to the moment, Drew looked up from the mug of java he'd been gazing into and found Doctor Ktumba standing across the table from him.

"Hiding? I'm not hiding," he replied, and spread his arms to indicate the rest of the caf. "I'm in plain sight in an empty room."

"Mm-hmm. Sitting hunched over, with your back to the door. Maybe that's not hiding by *your* definition, but— Never mind. I've completed my examination of our newest arrival. I don't know how you plan to explain this in your next report to the Space Installation Authority, but I've brought you a printout of mine."

As he reached for the sheet of paper she was handing him, Townsend did a double take. A pair of eyes were perched on the edge of the table beside her. They were perfectly round, with deep orange irises, and with lids that moved sideways. They blinked lazily at him twice before he was able to find his voice. "Is this—?"

"Ja-va?" boomed a voice that seemed to come from under the table. Drew couldn't help noticing that one of the eyes was now staring at his mug.

"Yes, it is," he replied.

"Ja-va means wel-come," declared the voice.

The Doc inhaled sharply. "Wait! Don't let him—"

Too late. Something that looked like the end of a narrow black tube had whipped over the edge of the table and plunged itself into the mug. In two heartbeats all the liquid was gone.

"Ja-va!" the voice caroled. "Ja-va-ha-*ha*!" The alien reared up, startling Drew to his feet as well. The eyes were on stalks. As they extended, raising the alien's height to about the level of Townsend's waist, he caught a glimpse of something metallic jammed under the edge of the creature's segmented carapace, and a kaleidoscopic display of bright colors dancing around on top of it.

"Mister Townsend, meet Odysseus," said the Doc. "That was his third cup, by the way."

Wonderful. The overgrown prawn was now over-caffeinated as well. His shell appeared to be doing everything but shoot off fireworks. Odysseus dropped down onto all eight of his legs and began scuttling rapidly around the caf, singing in a baritone voice, "Java-java-java-java!"

"He's toxed," Townsend declared. "Isn't there a sedative or something you can give him?"

"I can't calculate a safe dose without knowing more about his physiology. At least he's not a danger to anyone. We'll just have to keep him confined somewhere and wait until the caffeine is out of his system."

"That's easy to say, Doctor, but first we'll have to catch him."

A humming sound drew their attention to the front of the caf. Three crew members were strolling through the door, deep in conversation.

Together, Townsend and the Doc yelled, "Close the—!"

Too late again. Odysseus had already raced into the corridor. As he scuttled away, they could hear his singsong voice echoing off the bulkheads: "Java-java-java-hee-hee-*heeee!*"

One of the crewmen came over. "What the devil was *that?*"

Townsend and the Doc shared a look.

"It's an alien," Drew replied. "A java junkie. If he comes back here, seal the door and call AdComm, in that order. Stop and hold him if you can. But whatever you do, don't let him near the urn behind the counter."

Townsend's wristcomm buzzed. "What?!" he snapped at it.

Silence. After a moment, Lydia's tentative voice replied, "I just thought you'd want to know that Singh and Beale are back and they're ready to give you a report."

He took a calming breath. "Sorry, Lydia. I just— Never mind, I'll fill you in later. Where are they? On L Deck?"

"Or they can meet you up here if you'd prefer."

"L Deck is fine. Tell them I'm on my way."

——— «» ———

Gouryas and Beale stood together, poring over a printout that occupied most of a work table. They barely glanced up as Townsend stepped off the tube car and crossed the deck toward them. Meanwhile, Singh was pacing back and forth behind them, shaking his head and looking caught between tears and laughter. Drew's first thought on seeing him was that the mission must have been either a spectacular success or a colossal failure.

"You're not going to believe this," Singh told him.

"Try me."

"When the field generator was installed on Zulu, their main console was retrofitted with a dedicated control panel. They've had full command of their sensor field for the past two and a half standard years, but until now nobody realized it, because all the engineering talent was on Daisy Hub and none of the Rangers were curious enough—"

"—or brave enough," Beale opined, her voice dripping disdain.

"—or something," Singh continued, "to play with the alien technology. Those lazy bastards simply set everything on automatic and then forgot about it. Literally."

"Meanwhile, we've been wracking our brains this whole time, trying to figure out how it works and getting ourselves deeper and deeper in trouble," Gouryas cut in. He was a portrait of disgust. "And the most infuriating part of it is that we could have spared ourselves all that grief if either we'd asked them for help or they'd thought to offer it."

"Neither of which was going to happen as long as Bonelli was in charge of the Zoo," Singh pointed out. "Let's be honest. After what happened to Lydia when she and O'Malley went over there to set up their SPA room, would any of us have trusted an offer of assistance from a Ranger?"

Gouryas swatted the question aside. "What I don't understand is why the Nandrians would have provided a control panel for only one of the field generators. It makes no sense!"

Drew swallowed the answer that rose to his lips. To someone who had been both a convict and a cop, this situation made perfect sense. The generators had been ordered installed by Earth's High Council. As far as Earth was concerned, Daisy Hub was an orbiting detention center and the Rangers were its guards. And it was the guards who got to control the prison boundaries, not the inmates.

Evidently, the Nandrians didn't share Earth's point of view, or the paintbrush and operating manual would never have found their way into the hands of the Hub's crew. The aliens had also been dropping hints that the Humans and Nandrians would soon have to face a common enemy. Getting the field generator under control might be part of Daisy Hub's test of worthiness, but it seemed clear to Townsend that it was also an important step in preparing for the coming conflict. That meant time was of the essence.

"Did the Rangers give you the information you went there for?" he asked.

"They gave us something better," Singh replied, indicating with a flourish the diagrams on the work table. "On Captain Rodrigues's orders, they gave us a copy of the schematics for their control panel, along with a wiring map, so that we could build and install one of our own."

Townsend glanced over Beale's shoulder and saw mazes of crisscrossing lines, sprinkled with alien symbols. She shuffled the pages, showing him one incomprehensible diagram after another. "Okay," he said, trying to sound more intelligent than he felt at that moment. "This is for the control panel. What about the settings for the sensor field?"

Singh and Beale exchanged a long look. A mental coin toss? If so, Beale was the loser. She broke eye contact and replied, "It's on automatic, and Rodrigues wouldn't let us switch it over to manual to bring the settings up on their display. He's so spooked by the problems we've been having with our generator that he won't even let anyone touch the controls on theirs. So, it appears that we're going to have to build the control panel and figure things out from there. Fortunately, we have plenty of engineering expertise on the Hub."

"That's nice, but there's a problem," Drew said.

"Just one?" growled Gouryas. "I can see half a dozen."

Drew pressed on. "This control panel is made up of alien materials. How are you going to reproduce it using Earth-made parts?"

Beale broke out in a grin. "One of the Rangers slipped me this as we were leaving," she said, reaching under the table and coming up with a fistful of colored wires. "Apparently, the Nandrians left a second panel behind, in pieces, just in case something needed to be replaced."

"So Ruby was right. The missing clue was on Zulu all along," Townsend remarked, and Singh nodded agreement.

"Anyway, these spare parts had been sitting in a locker, gathering dust, and the Ranger — whose name is Jacques — very kindly put them all into a couple of carry-cases and transferred them onto *Devil Bug* for me."

Drew shot her a dubious look. "And he did this out of the goodness of his heart?"

"Not exactly. We hit it off." She turned her back on Townsend, leered over her shoulder at him, and batted her eyelashes extra hard.

He turned accusing eyes on Singh. "You let her flirt over there, knowing what had happened to Lydia?"

The engineer stared defiantly back at him. "My mother didn't raise a fool, Mister Townsend, and neither did Vera's," he replied. "I didn't 'let her flirt', as you put it. I instructed her to get one of the Rangers on our side in case we needed a favor in order to complete our mission successfully. And that's what she did. It was a calculated risk, but I knew she could handle herself. Besides, you'd said more than once that Rodrigues was a different kind of leader, more like us than Bonelli was, and that implied that the Zoo itself would be a safer place than before."

Drew wanted to be stern with them, but he couldn't. They'd done exactly what he would have done — stretched their luck and gotten away with it — and the expressions on their faces showed that they knew it. "All right," he said, letting out an exaggerated sigh. "Now, put this control panel together and let's see how successful the mission was."

———— «» ————

Seventeen hours to go.

Remembering how easily the Überrats, Yoko and Akiko, were able to hide out in the between-decks of the station, Townsend had consulted with Gouryas to find out whether Odysseus could do the same. Fortunately, the dimensions of his shell made it impossible for him to slip through the hatches covering the maintenance passageways. Unfortunately, he was clever as well as sentient, and tall enough to reach the keypad of a tube car.

In the past three hours, there had been Odysseus sightings all over the station, but no one had been able to corner or catch the little alien, even when they knew where to wait for him. He barreled through doorways like a miniature armored tank, knocking Humans aside with ease. Several crew members had required medical attention after trying to stop him in the corridor, including Security Chief Orvy Hagman.

Clearly, the "overgrown prawn" was a lot stronger than he looked, and he didn't appear to be slowing down at all. So, Drew decided to put his best — in fact, his only — Stragori warrior on the assignment.

Swiveling his seat, he called across AdComm, "Lydia, where's Karlov right now?"

A moment later her face appeared atop his bank of filing cabinets, reminding him unsettlingly of Odysseus's eyes perched on the tabletop in the caf.

"He's on Tannis Walker's maintenance detail this shift," she told him. "They're cleaning and inspecting our solid waste processing system. Another hour or two and they'll be done."

He exhaled noisily, wondering how best to classify the current situation. Could one alien running all over the station be called an infestation? How much of an emergency did they actually have?

Picking up on his disappointment, Lydia added, "I can get him here right away, but he's probably standing up to his hips in—"

"Never mind. Tell him to report to me as soon as he's presentable."

Two hours later, Max Karlov stepped off the tube car and approached Townsend's desk, not bothering to conceal his amusement.

"Last year you were frantically hunting down rats. Now it's some sort of alien bug? It sounds as though Daisy Hub needs an exterminator," he remarked, pulling a chair over and sitting on it.

"First of all, Odysseus is not a bug. At least, I don't think he is. Regardless, you mustn't kill him. It's not his fault that his race gets toxed on caffeine. We just need him captured and confined until the effects wear off."

"Odysseus? That's an Earth name, isn't it?"

"He had contact with Humans before coming here, and that's the name they gave him. I've just finished reading their file on him. He's a Mitradean."

Karlov sat up straighter in his seat. "Mitradean," he echoed, a note of respect creeping into his voice. "Now I understand why your people haven't been able to catch him."

"You're familiar with this race?"

"Oh, yes. The Mitrades have a perfect sense of direction. One look at a schematic and they know exactly where to hide and which spots to avoid. And they're fast, even when they're not revved up on caffeine. You're lucky there's only one of them aboard the station. They do telepathic data transfers. Put them close enough together and what one knows, they all know."

Townsend leaned forward on his elbows. "The Nandrians will be here in fifteen hours. Can you catch him before they arrive?"

"I doubt it. But I wouldn't worry too much. If these Nandrians are like all the others we've met, it's a safe bet they won't be able to catch him either."

Chapter Twenty-Six

Eleven hours to go.

Every section had reported in, and every work detail was on schedule. This was to be expected. In the standard year since the invisibility field had activated, Daisy Hub had hosted about a dozen Nandrian victory parties. Each time, the docking modules at the north end of the Hub had had to be separated and reconnected, twice. By now, Townsend's crew had the routine down pat.

Soaring Hawk's team was working with Gouryas and Singh to make sure the operation would proceed without a hiccup. Soaring Hawk himself was attending to the spotter shuttle, *Devil Bug,* tuning its propulsion systems to optimum. Will DeVries, the crewman who would be alone on A Deck working the controls, had been practicing with the sim program Lydia had created earlier.

It was encouraging to hear that *some*thing was going according to plan. In the past four hours, there had been no news from Karlov regarding the Odysseus hunt. Just considering the possibility that the little alien could come scuttling out of a tube car booming, "Java-java-java!" in the middle of the Nandrian welcoming ceremony was enough to give Drew a permanent facial tic.

He had been awake at this point for more than twenty standard hours and was having trouble remembering the words of his speech. Townsend hated having to leave AdComm while the Mitradean problem remained unsolved, but common sense (and Ruby and Lydia) demanded that he go to his quarters to get some sleep. Reluctantly, he complied.

Just as he was about to step through the door of his suite, he heard a faint but unmistakable voice coming toward him along the corridor.

"Java! I love java! Hoo-hoo!"

Drew straddled the threshold to keep the door from closing, then bellowed in his most authoritative voice, "Odysseus! Get in here! Now!"

To his amazement, Odysseus obeyed. Maybe the caffeine was finally wearing off. Regardless, it was best not to take chances. As soon as the little alien was inside the room with him, Townsend sealed the door shut.

"Odysseus," he said firmly, "we have to talk."

The Mitradean's carapace was a muddy brown color. He reared up on his four hind legs, rocking back and forth on his tail. His eyes were rolling and swaying as well. They looked as though they were operating on separate circuits.

Cautiously, Drew asked him, "How do you feel?"

"Strange." This uncertain voice was coming from the metal box stuffed under the edge of his shell. "I have never felt like this before. I don't like it. Everything is moving."

"Listen to me. In a little while, two ships will be arriving. I need you to remain here until they leave."

"Why is everything moving?"

"Odysseus? Odysseus! Close your eyes and pay attention! You have to stay here until the Nandrians are gone."

A screeching noise erupted from the box, piercing Townsend's skull like an arrow.

"Nandrians? Here? I must hide!" wailed the voice.

With a hand clapped to his temple, Drew exclaimed, "Yes! That's what I've been saying."

"Why are they here? Earth space is safe for Mitrades. The Takamura Human *promised* me—!" The segmented carapace had darkened almost to black. The alien's front legs were gyrating wildly.

"Calm down!" Townsend ordered. "You *are* safe here. The Nandrians are visiting for a short time only."

"They will see my ship. They will tell the Great Council! I will be hunted and cast out!"

Odysseus was already a refugee. Under the circumstances, Drew didn't see how being shunned could make things worse for him. However...

"Let me worry about concealing your ship. You just need to rest for now and let your body recover from the ja— from the caffeine you've ingested. And if you feel the need to throw up...? Please! Do it in there," he added, turning and pointing to the hygiene closet.

Thud.

Drew spun around, startled. The alien was lying on his back on the deck, his eyestalks completely retracted, his eight legs sticking up in the air. Townsend's heart nearly stopped. Then he heard a soft, clicking sound that couldn't possibly be coming from the little metal box, and he was able to breathe again.

He opened a channel to AdComm and instructed Ruby to call off the search. She laughed when he told her where the Mitradean was and what he was doing, but Drew was too tired to care. As soon as he'd signed off, he flung himself onto his bed and was very soon unconscious himself.

— «» —

"Hey, Chief! It's morning, and this is your wake-up call."

Ruby's obscenely cheerful voice interrupted the first pleasant dream Drew could remember having since his arrival on Daisy Hub. "Okay, I'm up," he grumped. "What time is it?"

"The Nandrians are a couple of hours away. I figured you'd want to have some breakfast and go over your speeches once or twice before they got here. Is Odysseus still snoring?"

He checked. "Yep. Still out cold."

"Do you want a guard posted at your door in case he tries to leave?"

"I don't think it will be necessary. Odysseus won't be a problem. His ship, however, is another matter. I want you to seal off the landing deck. It's to be off-limits to everyone for as long as the Nandrians are with us. Dock *Devil Bug* at one of the modules on A Deck once the top of the Hub is reconnected. And spread the word to the crew that no one is to mention we have a Mitradean aboard. Odysseus is terrified the Nandrians will hand him over to the Great Council. We can't let them find out that he's here."

"So he's a fugitive as well as a refugee? Interesting. Consider it done, Chief."

———— «·» ————

Two hours later, Townsend was standing on A Deck, flanked by Ruby McNeil and Gavin Holchuk, waiting for six reptilian warriors to emerge from two of the docking portals. Yoko the Überrat sat in her cage at his feet, still refusing to let him hold her during the welcoming ceremony.

"I'll bet your clone wouldn't be so picky," he'd muttered as she'd slithered out of his arms yet again. Maybe Holchuk was right and Yoko did know something about him that the rest of the crew didn't. Maybe it was a damned good thing she couldn't talk.

He heard the familiar hiss of a docking portal unsealing and a door sliding aside.

Just one?

Drew shot Holchuk a puzzled look as three hulking Nandrians stepped slowly through the opening and halted a respectful distance away. They were wearing red sashes over their uniforms, fastened at the shoulder with ornate pins. And they were stone cold sober.

"There's something wrong, boss man," Holchuk murmured. "Look at his sleeve markings. That's not the Chief Officer. It's not even the Second Officer."

Dread trickled icily down Drew's back. All his instincts were screaming at him to make up an excuse and send the Nandrians back to their ship. But this was a fiercely ceremonial warrior race, House Drellith especially so, and he had no intention of inviting disembowelment for failing to stick to tradition and follow the script. Drawing in a huge breath, he began to speak.

"Greetings, honored guests from House Drellith, and welcome to House Daisy Hub. Daisy Hub has a glorious history dating back to—"

"Forgive us, *Hak'kor*. We mean no offence, but we must break with ritual," said the leading Nandrian.

Oka-ay, this was different, not to mention possibly dangerous. Unfortunately, remaining silent was not an option for the *Hak'kor*. He had to reply. Mentally crossing his fingers for luck, Townsend pointed out in a tone of voice he hoped wouldn't be taken as an insult, "You have already broken with ritual by standing in the place of your Chief Officer. Please honor me by explaining the reason for this."

"I am Sillurv ban Etkuram, Sixth Shield of House Drellith and Third Officer of the *Seppsal*. Our recent victory in *tekl'hananni* was costly. All officers superior to me in rank were killed, along with many of our warriors. We believe it would be inappropriate to celebrate such a loss as a victory. Instead, we beg to be allowed aboard your station to honor those who have fallen, in accordance with a Human custom we have heard about."

Townsend sidled closer to Holchuk and murmured, "Is there a script for this?"

"No, he's winging it. However, they are dressed for a funeral and looking pretty mournful, in a King Kong, T-Rex kind of way. He's the one who first broke protocol, so I think you can safely play it by ear as well."

All right, then. Returning his attention to Sillurv, Drew said, "Are you talking about a memorial service?"

The Nandrian didn't answer, just tilted his head, first one way and then the other.

"Maybe he's asking for a wake," Ruby suggested.

But Sillurv didn't seem to recognize that word either. "We have heard it is called 'a toast'," he said. "One drink in honor of the dead."

"Careful, boss man," Holchuk warned quietly. "They've come a long way for just one drink apiece."

Drew was already ahead of him — his internal con detector had red-lined the moment Sillurv had begun speaking. Now the needle was off the scale. However, this wasn't a situation in which he could simply out the Nandrian and send him and his crew packing. The mark would have to play along.

After looking directly into one of the securecams installed around A Deck, Drew pinned on his most hospitable smile and told Sillurv son of Etkur, "Yes, a toast to your fallen comrades would be a most appropriate way for you to honor them. Let us complete the introductions, so that I may properly invite you and your warriors onto the station."

———— «» ————

The crew of Daisy Hub had spent the past year preparing to defend it — and themselves — for several hours without conventional weapons in the event of an attack. The reason for this: the Space Installation Authority, in its wisdom, had decided not to arm the station. Instead, they'd put all the ordnance on Platform Zulu, some four hours away. Assuming the Rangers scrambled immediately once a distress call had been received, that was how long it would take for help to arrive. It was much too long for Townsend's liking.

Therefore, in consultation with Hagman and Karlov, he had devised a security protocol that included regular situation drills, to ensure that everyone would know where to go and what to do if the Hub were boarded. They'd practiced every scenario, including this one. Lydia's close monitoring of the securecams on A Deck was part of the plan, and Drew's deliberate eye contact with one of them was a prearranged signal. In the time that it would take for the introductions to be made, Lydia should have issued an all-crew alert via wristcomm and then programmed the tube car system for express travel between A and D Decks only.

If the Nandrians were sincere about sharing a peaceful toast and then leaving, they wouldn't notice anything amiss. On the other hand, if this was just a ploy to gain access to the Hub, well, that was what Orvy Hagman and his expanded Security team were for.

So it was that when Sillurv and his thirty-six warriors stepped out of the tube cars on D Deck, they were met by an "honor guard" and respectfully escorted directly to the Daisy Hub caf.

Warned ahead of time, Jensen had already prepared glasses of lemonade and placed them on trays around the room. Sillurv picked up his drink, then turned to Drew and said, "Would the *Hak'kor* and his second and third honor us by participating in our toast?"

Toast the fallen of House Drellith? Now Townsend understood why the Nandrian officer had brought his ships so far out of their way for just one drink. Drellith and Trokerk were sworn and deadly enemies, as the ferocity of their battles had amply demonstrated, and House Daisy Hub was one ritual away from sealing an alliance with Trokerk. Word of this had to have made it back to the Nandrian home world. What better way to derail the alliance and embarrass House Trokerk than by revealing Daisy Hub's *Hak'kor* to be dishonorable? And what better way to accomplish *that* than by tricking him into appearing sympathetic toward House Drellith? Sillurv probably had a recording device concealed in the pin of his sash.

It was a clever plan, with just one flaw: the mark was a con artist himself.

Drew smiled at Sillurv — a genuine smile this time — and responded, "You honor me with your invitation. However, Drellith was not the only House to suffer great losses in this battle. The dead of both sides fought valiantly, would you not agree?"

Sillurv replied guardedly, "I would, *Hak'kor.*"

"And having fought well, surely they all deserve to be honored with a toast."

Sillurv's complexion darkened. "Are you asking us to honor our foe, *Hak'kor?*" he demanded.

It was what a Human would do, but evidently not a Nandrian. Townsend took a mental step backward and said evenly, "No. That would be inappropriate for a House participating in *tekl'hananni*. However, Daisy Hub is a neutral House, enemy of none and welcoming to all. After you have toasted the fallen of House Drellith, we would consider it a privilege to honor the sacrifices made by your worthy opponent."

Silence rolled across the room like a carpet unfurling. Sillurv's massive body was rigid. Townsend held his breath, hoping he'd read the Nandrian correctly. Then a glint of recognition came into the large yellow eyes.

"We beg that you wait to honor Trokerk until after our ships have departed," he said. Drew smiled graciously and nodded his *Hak'kor*ly assent. On Sillurv's signal, each of his warriors reached for a glass of lemonade.

"We are not here to celebrate a victory," he announced. "We are here to remember the strength and courage of forty-one officers and crewmates who fought well and died well at our sides. The names of these warriors will be inscribed on the heroes' wall of House Drellith on Nandor. They will not be forgotten. We drink to seal that oath. May we be cut into pieces and fed to a wild *lorssh* if we ever break it." He raised his glass and proclaimed, "To honor!"

"To honor!" bellowed the others, raising their glasses as well, then rapidly emptying them.

The Nandrians wasted no time returning to their ships. Following an abridged leave-taking ceremony, Sillurv and his acting second disappeared through the docking portal. As Lydia monitored from AdComm, Deck A was separated from the rest of the Hub, and the *Seppsal* and her sister ship were sent on their way. Meanwhile, the *Hak'kor* and his third stood behind Lydia's chair, breathing matching sighs of relief as the blips representing the two light cruisers slid off the side of her screen and DeVries commenced the reconnection process.

"It was a lovely toast, you know," she remarked over her shoulder. "Quite stirring. Up until he got to the *lorssh* part, anyway. I found that a little…"

"…Nandrian," Holchuk supplied. "It was very Nandrian. Nagor would have said the same thing."

Lydia kept her attention on her bank of light screens. "Speaking of Nagor," she said, "you'll be happy to know that the *Krronn* and the *Nannssi* were not involved in the latest match against Drellith."

"Good! Their Chief Officers are probably already planning an unpleasant surprise for House Drellith in the next round." Holchuk threw Townsend a conspiratorial grin. "I can't wait to write your speech describing how you turned Sillurv's own guile against him. That was well played, boss man."

"I have my moments," Townsend conceded. "Meanwhile, there's an overgrown prawn in my quarters, detoxing from three cups of Jensen's java. Lydia, once A Deck is locked down, I need you to contact the *Marco Polo* and ask them as persuasively as you can to swing by and pick up their Mitradean friend. If his race is looking for a new home world, Takamura's ship is better equipped to find one for them than we are. And he certainly owes us that much after giving out our address all over alien space."

"I'll let them know," she replied absently.

"Holchuk, I want you and Karlov to babysit Odysseus until his ride gets here."

"You want us to sit on him?"

"If you have to. Just keep him safe and out of trouble. And away from caffeine."

"You got it, boss man." With that, Holchuk turned and headed toward one of the tube car doors, leaving Drew and Lydia alone on C Deck.

Still sounding distracted, she asked, "So, was the Zulu mission successful?"

"More or less. With luck, we'll soon have a working control panel for our Nandrian field generator. Once we're able to make it do what we want, when we want, then I think we'll be ready to contact the resistance on Earth and offer them our expertise."

"Uh-huh. Right."

The cynical edge on her voice snapped him to attention. "Is there something you want to say to me, Lydia?"

She swiveled her seat and gave him a reproachful stare. "Come on, Drew, I'm not one of your marks, so don't play dumb with me. We've had the resistance on board from the moment you arrived."

He went cold all over, hearing Grant Sullivan's voice once again in his mind: *Do they know who you're really working for?*

Townsend wanted to kick himself. He knew that there were securecams all over the Hub, constantly recording. He'd personally authorized the rewiring necessary to transmit all the feeds in real time to Lydia's station on AdComm as part of the Hub's new security protocol. But he had assumed — obviously incorrectly — that when the station manager demanded privacy he would get it, no questions asked and no further instructions necessary. It was a mistake he wouldn't be repeating any time soon. Still, the damage was done.

Rapidly recalling the rest of his conversation with Sullivan, Drew was relieved to note that neither of them had actually mentioned the EIS aloud. Better yet, the omission had apparently led Lydia to make an incorrect assumption of her own.

He took it as a gift.

"Okay, just for argument's sake, let's say you're right, and I came here with the express intention of recruiting everyone into the resistance. Hypothetically, what would you do with that information?"

Her gaze softened. "Nothing."

"Nothing at all? Or nothing *now*?"

He watched her face, expecting a tell, but her expression remained neutral. When a faint smile did appear, it was distant and unrevealing.

"Nothing, period. I'm your eyes and ears, remember? Your secrets are safe with me."

"Reconnection complete," came DeVries's voice from her console. "All seals and latches read green. You have control, AdComm."

Returning her chair to its normal position, Lydia scanned her panel and pressed a button on her console. "AdComm has control," she confirmed. Then she pressed a second button, and a message window came up on one of her screens: *File Deleted*.

"Was that—?"

"Video feed from A Deck. The departure ritual. I only keep what's interesting. Or potentially useful. You never know when you're going to need a visual record as proof that something happened. Or as leverage to get something done."

With a shiver that was equal parts dread and anticipation, Townsend bent and murmured into her ear, "You recorded the Nandrians in the caf earlier. Did you keep that file?"

Still facing frontward, she replied, "When Drellith is aboard, always."

"Thank you, Ms. Garfield." Unwilling to risk saying more, he straightened up and strolled to his desk. Lydia's definition of a defensive arsenal was clearly much broader than the one he'd been working with. For now, she appeared to be on his side. In the future? Who could say?

Damn! He'd really wanted to be able to trust her.

———— «» ————

Manager of Station Operations was a pretty title, but as far as Earth Intelligence was concerned, that was all it was. Sullivan's brief visit had been an unpleasant reminder to Townsend that he was considered by the higher-ups to be an agent on assignment, heading up a cell but only nominally in command of it. Soon, he would begin receiving orders, and the EIS would expect him to put his people to work carrying them out.

There was just one problem. Well, two problems. First, no one on Earth knew the truth about what had been going on aboard Daisy Hub, and Townsend didn't dare enlighten them for fear of starting an interstellar war. Consequently, he'd been purposely vague, even misleading, on all his status reports to the Space Installation Authority, as well as in the encrypted messages they contained for Earth Intelligence. And second, no one aboard the Hub knew the truth about why he'd been sent there, and he'd been putting off telling them for fear of sparking a mutiny.

Safeguarding the truth was supposed to be his mission for the EIS, but not being able to share it with anyone was proving to be more stressful than he'd anticipated. Drew could practically feel his blood pressure rise with each new secret that got dumped into his lap.

His gut wasn't happy with him either. The dinner he'd eaten an hour earlier was sitting in his stomach like a stone. Like an ember, actually, burning his chest from the inside out. Taking a final swallow of the antacid the Doc had just given him, Townsend came to a decision. Confession might not be good for his soul right now, but he suspected it would do wonders for his digestive tract.

He boarded a tube car and rode it up to AdComm.

On C Deck, as expected, he found Ruby McNeil standing watch alone at her main console.

"I am sick to death of keeping secrets," he announced to her back.

She turned and gave him a sympathetic smile. "I know. So am I." She went to the comm panel and toggled a switch, then pulled something out of her jacket pocket. Drew recognized the object immediately. It was a black tube, ringed with ridges along half its length — an EIS encryption device, keyed to an agent's DNA, useless to anyone else.

Townsend's jaw dropped open. He reminded himself to close it. Then he remembered the securecams. "That's an interesting-looking gadget," he remarked, adopting a casually interested tone of voice. "Where did you find it?"

"Don't worry, Chief, we're not being recorded," she assured him, grinning. "I've 'accidentally' paused the feed from this deck. And I was given this 'gadget' by the same people who gave you yours."

"How do you know that I've got one?" he demanded.

"Steve Bonelli told me you were one of us when I picked you and Teri up from the Zoo. Remember how I went to check on the number of barrels in the cargo hold? That was so he and I could have a quick meeting."

Staring into her face, Drew sank slowly onto the nearest chair. "I don't believe this," he declared. "Why didn't you say something earlier?"

In an instant, mischievous grandma evaporated, leaving Ruby looking every day of her seventy-five years old. "Lots of reasons," she said, pulling up a second chair and lowering herself onto it. "Most of them don't matter. Bear with me now, because there's a preamble to the one that does.

"I was the very first operative to be assigned to Daisy Hub. The EIS didn't formally exist yet. Forrand was just starting to put his organization together, so I didn't actually have a mission. However, when the Hub went online in 2368, he saw all kinds of useful possibilities for it. He decided to position himself so that he could take advantage of them when the time was right.

"In the meanwhile, he needed someone to come out here and 'stake his claim', so to speak. Someone he could trust to manage things at this end once he was ready to move. We were old friends who thought very much alike, so he offered me the job, and I accepted. I've been on this station for thirty Earth years now, watching people come and go, and noticing who stayed. They were the keepers."

"The keepers?" he echoed, frowning.

"The ones you hang onto, because their combined skills and strengths are exactly what you're going to need once everything else is in place and you're ready to set your grand plan in motion. Over the years, I've assisted six different station managers. Two of them might have been keepers, but they didn't stay. Naguchi had unfinished business on Earth and left when his contract ran out. Khaloub's tenure was cut short when he was killed. Then you arrived."

"And your brain began itching." She nodded once in confirmation. "From trying to decide whether I'd be a keeper?"

"Actually, I was trying to figure out which came first. Was it Karim's death? Or was it your EIS assignment to the Hub?"

"It's a good question," he told her, wiping all expression from his face. "Wish I had the answer."

She leaned forward, her gaze acquiring a laser-like intensity. "I've been sitting out here watching pieces come together for a very long time. If Karim was taken out to make room for you, it means the plan was finally ready to launch, and you were Forrand's handpicked mission leader. I don't need to know the details. Just tell me, am I right about this?"

"You're not wrong," he told her after a beat. Then, to distract her from pursuing the subject any further, he pointed at the encrypter still in her hand and asked, "How many of those are aboard the station?"

Ruby slid the device out of sight, pursing her lips thoughtfully. "Hard to say. Three or four, maybe, including yours. It's a safe bet that anyone put in command of Zulu will have one as well."

"Lydia?"

"It's possible, but not likely. Knowing a lot about what's going on is just part of her job description. I can tell you with certainty, however, that she is completely onside with the idea of a resistance movement, and I think you'll find all the others are, as well."

"And what about you?"

"Absolutely. One thing that you've demonstrated clearly in the short time that you've been here is that you care about the people on this station, just as much as Naguchi and Khaloub did and a lot more than the EIS or any government organization ever will. No one aboard the Hub wants to be a pawn or a patsy, ordered around by some faceless entity on Earth. As I recently found out, you're not crazy about the idea either. Lydia showed me the vidclip of you and Sullivan saying goodbye on A Deck. The expression on your face as you watched him walk through the portal was eloquent, to say the least.

"So, I figured the time was finally right to let you know that you're not alone. We've already broken away from Earth, and I'm guessing that it won't be long before we cut ties with the EIS as well. Regardless of what happens from now on, rest assured that you'll have the crew of Daisy Hub backing you up."

For a moment, he hesitated, silently correcting her statement. Not all the Hub's residents trusted him fully yet, and there were a couple he still had doubts about as well. Nonetheless, it was gratifying to hear a message of support right now.

"Thanks, Ruby. That's good to know."

"My pleasure. Do we have a plan?"

Good question. It appeared that House Daisy Hub was about to spawn an actual resistance movement, independent of anything on Earth. That made two charges of treason that he would probably have to answer for down the road. And the Hub would soon be filling up with alien refugees. Fleeing from what, Townsend had no idea, but he suspected that he would soon be finding out.

Otherwise, had anything changed? Not really, he decided.

"A plan?" he said with a sigh. "Sure, as much as we ever did. First, we're going to finalize our alliance with Trokerk. Then, we're going to protect the secrets that have been entrusted to us and go about our business one day at a time, while keeping our eyes open for the trouble that we know is going to find us. And when it does, we're going to impress the bejeezus out of all concerned by coming through it in one piece. How's that for a plan?"

Her cheeks dimpled and, just like that, the mischievous grandma was back.

"Works for me, Chief."

It worked for him as well, and for the first time since his arrival on Daisy Hub, he was able to understand why.

Dennis Forrand hadn't just been meddling in his life — he'd been preparing him. Everything that Drew had experienced — the six years in the street gang, the five in detention, and the thirteen that he had spent with New Chicago Security, dealing with the dregs of Humanity — had been, like *tekl'hananni*, a test of his personal worthiness. Ruby had guessed right: Townsend was Forrand's handpicked leader, toughened and trained to meet whatever challenges lay ahead.

And that was exactly what he intended to do.

About the Author

Born and raised in Toronto, Arlene F. Marks began writing stories at the age of 6 and can't seem to stop. Although she's been published in multiple genres, her first love has always been speculative fiction. Her work has appeared in *H. P. Lovecraft's Magazine of Horror*, *Onder Magazine*, and *Daily Science Fiction*. Her science fantasy novel, *The Accidental God*, was nominated for the 2015 Stephen Leacock Medal for Humour. Arlene lives with her husband on Nottawasaga Bay but spends an inordinate amount of time in the Sic Transit Terra universe.